HALO

HALO

ALEXANDRA ADORNETTO

FEIWEL AND FRIENDS
NEW YORK

To frau hale, for teaching me about
the things that really matter

A Feiwel and Friends Book
An Imprint of Macmillan

HALO. Copyright © 2010 by Alexandra Adornetto. All rights reserved.
Printed in August 2010 in the United States of America by R. R. Donnelley
& Sons Company, Harrisonburg, Pennsylvania. For information, address
Feiwel and Friends, 175 Fifth Avenue, New York, N.Y. 10010.

Adornetto, Alexandra.
Halo / Alexandra Adornetto. — 1st ed.
p. cm.
Summary: When three angels are sent from heaven to protect the town
of Venus Cove against the gathering forces of darkness, their mission is
threatened as the youngest angel, Bethany, enrolls in high school and falls
in love with another student.
ISBN: 978-0-312-65626-3
[1. Angels—Fiction.   2. Interpersonal relations—Fiction.   3. High
schools—Fiction.   4. Schools—Fiction.   5. Good and evil—
Fiction.]   I. Title.
PZ7.A26182Hal 2010
[Fic]—dc22
2010015464

Book design by Rich Deas and Tim Hall
Feather image is from iStockphoto

Feiwel and Friends logo designed by Filomena Tuosto

First Edition: 2010

10 9 8 7 6 5 4 3 2 1

www.feiwelandfriends.com

O, speak again, bright angel, for thou art
As glorious to this night, being o'er my head,
As is a winged messenger of heaven
Unto the white-upturned wond'ring eyes
Of mortals that fall back to gaze on him.
— William Shakespeare, *Romeo and Juliet*

Baby, I can see your halo
You know you're my saving grace
— Beyoncé, "Halo"

{ Contents }

{ 1 }

Descent

OUR arrival didn't exactly go as planned. I remember it was almost dawn when we landed because the streetlights were still on. We had hoped our descent would go unnoticed, which it mainly did, save for a thirteen-year-old boy doing a paper round.

He was on his bicycle with the newspapers rolled like batons in plastic wrap. It was misty and the boy was wearing a hooded jacket. He seemed to be playing a mental game with himself to estimate where exactly he could get each paper to land. The newspapers hit the driveways and verandas with a thud, and the boy smiled smugly whenever he estimated right. A Jack Russell terrier barking from behind a gate caused him to glance up and alerted him to our arrival.

He looked up just in time to see a column of white light receding into the clouds, leaving three wraithlike strangers in the middle of the road. Despite our human form, something about us startled him—perhaps it was our skin, which was as luminous as the moon or our loose white traveling garments, which were in tatters from the turbulent descent. Perhaps it was the way we looked at our limbs, as though we had no idea what to do with them, or the water vapor still clinging to our hair. Whatever the reason, the boy lost his balance, swerved his bike, and crashed into the gutter. He scrambled to his feet and stood transfixed for several seconds, caught between alarm and curiosity. In unison we reached out our hands to him in what we hoped was a gesture of reassurance. But we forgot to smile. By the time we remembered how, it was too late. As we contorted our mouths in an attempt to get it right, the boy turned on his heel and fled. Having a physical body was still foreign to us—there were so many different parts that needed to run concurrently, like a complex machine. The muscles in my face and body were stiff, my legs were trembling like a child's taking his first steps, and my eyes hadn't yet adjusted to the muted earth light. Having come from a place of dazzling light, shadows were foreign to us.

Gabriel approached the bicycle with its front wheel still spinning and righted it. He propped it against the closest fence knowing that the boy would return later to collect it.

I imagined the boy bursting through the front door of his home and relating the story to his stunned parents. His mother would push the hair back from his forehead to check his temperature. His father, bleary-eyed, would comment on the mind's ability to play tricks on you when it has time to wander.

We found Byron Street and walked along its uneven sidewalk, scanning for Number 15. Already, our senses were being assaulted from all directions. The colors of the world were so vivid and so varied. We had come from a pure white world to a street that looked like an artist's palette. Apart from color everything had its own different texture and shape. The wind brushed against my fingertips, and it felt so alive I wondered if I could reach out and catch it. I opened my mouth and tasted the crisp, sharp air. I could smell gasoline and burning toast mingled with pine and the sharp scent of the ocean. The worst part was the noise. The wind seemed to howl, and the sound of the sea beating against the rocks roared through my head like a stampede. I could hear everything that was happening in the street, the sound of a car ignition, a slamming screen door, a child crying, an old porch swing creaking in the wind.

"You'll learn how to block it out," said Gabriel. The sound of his voice startled me. Back home, we communicated without language. Gabriel's human voice, I discovered, was low and hypnotic.

"How long will it take?" I winced as the shrill cry of a seagull sounded overhead. I heard my own voice, which was as melodic as a flute.

"Not long," Gabriel answered. "It's easier if you don't fight it."

Byron Street rose and peaked in the middle and there, at its highest point, stood our new home. Ivy was immediately charmed.

"Oh, look." She clapped her hands in delight. "It even has a name." The house had been named after the street and BYRON was displayed in an elegant script on a copper plaque. We would later discover that the adjoining streets were named after other English Romantic poets: Keats Grove, Coleridge

Street, Blake Avenue. Byron was to be both our home and our sanctuary while we were earthbound. It was a double-fronted, ivy-clad sandstone house set well back from the street behind a wrought-iron fence and double gates. It had a gracious Georgian façade and a gravel path leading to its flaking front door. The front yard was dominated by a stately elm, wrapped in a tangled mess of ivy. Along the side fence grew a profusion of hydrangeas, their pastel heads quivering in the morning frost. I liked the house—it looked like it had been built to weather any adversity.

"Bethany, hand me the key," said Gabriel. Looking after the key to the house was the only job I had been entrusted with. I felt around the deep pockets of my dress.

"It's here somewhere," I assured him.

"Please tell me you haven't lost it already."

"We did fall out of the sky, you know," I said indignantly. "It's easy for things to go missing."

Ivy laughed suddenly. "You're wearing it around your neck."

I breathed a sigh of relief as I slipped off the chain and handed it to Gabriel. As we stepped into the hallway we saw that no expense had been spared in preparing the house for our arrival. The Divine Agents who'd preceded us had been meticulous in their attention to detail.

Everything about the house suggested light. The ceilings were lofty, the rooms airy. Off the central hallway were a music room to the left and a living room to the right. Farther along, a study opened onto a paved courtyard. The rear of the house was an extension that had been modernized and was made up of an expansive marble-and-stainless-steel kitchen that spilled into a large den with Persian rugs and plump sofas. Folding doors opened onto an extensive redwood deck. Upstairs were all the bedrooms and the main bathroom with its marble vanities and sunken bath. As we walked through the house, its timber floors creaked as if in welcome. A light shower began, and the rain falling on the slate roof sounded like fingers playing a melody on a piano.

THOSE first weeks were spent hibernating and getting our bearings. We took stock, waited patiently as we adjusted to having a physical form, and immersed ourselves in the rituals of daily life. There was so much to learn and it certainly wasn't easy. At first we would take a step and be surprised to find solid ground beneath us. We knew that everything on earth was made up of matter knitted together in a complex molecular code to form different substances: air, rock, wood, animals. But it was very different experiencing it. Physical barriers surrounded us. We had to navigate our way around these barriers and try to avoid the accompanying feeling of claustrophobia. Every time I picked up an object, I stopped to marvel at its function. Human life was so complicated; there were devices to boil water, wall sockets that channeled electrical currents, and all manner of utensils in the kitchen and bathroom designed to save time and increase comfort. Everything had a different texture, a different smell—it was like a circus for the senses. I could tell that Ivy and Gabriel wanted to block it all out and return to blissful silence, but I relished every moment even if it was overwhelming.

Some evenings we were visited by a faceless, white-robed

mentor, who simply appeared sitting in an armchair in the living room. His identity was never disclosed, though we knew he acted as a messenger between the angels on earth and the powers above. A briefing usually followed during which we were able to discuss the challenges of incarnation and have our questions answered.

"The landlord has asked for documents regarding our previous residence," Ivy said, during our first meeting.

"We apologize for the oversight. Consider it taken care of," replied the mentor. His whole face was shrouded from view, but when he spoke small clouds of white fog appeared from beneath his hood.

"How much time is expected to pass before we understand our bodies entirely?" Gabriel wanted to know.

"That depends," said the mentor. "It should not take longer than a few weeks, unless you resist the change."

"How are the other emissaries coping?" Ivy asked with concern.

"Some are adjusting to human life, like yourselves, and others have been thrown straight into battle," replied the mentor. "There are some corners of the earth riddled with Agents of Darkness."

"Why does toothpaste give me a headache?" I asked. My brother and sister flashed me stern looks, but the mentor was unfazed.

"It contains a number of strong chemical ingredients designed to kill bacteria," he said. "Give yourself a week, the headaches should pass."

After the consultations were over Gabriel and Ivy always

lingered for a private discussion and I was left hovering out-side the door, trying to catch snippets of the converation I couldn't be part of.

The first big challenge was taking care of our bodies. They were fragile. They needed nourishment as well as protection from the elements—mine more so than my siblings because I was young; it was my first visit and I hadn't had time to develop any resistance. Gabriel had been a warrior since the dawn of time, and Ivy was blessed with healing powers. I, on the other hand, was much more vulnerable. The first few times I ventured out on a walk, I returned shivering before realizing I was inadequately clothed. Gabriel and Ivy didn't feel the cold. But their bodies still needed maintenance. We wondered why we felt faint by midday, then realized our bodies needed regular meals. The preparation of food was a tedious task, and in the end, our brother Gabriel graciously offered to take charge of it. There was an extensive collection of cook-books in the well-stocked library, and he took to poring over these in the evenings.

We kept human contact to a minimum. We shopped after hours in the adjoining larger town of Kingston and didn't answer the door or the phone if it happened to ring. We took long walks at times when humans were occupied behind closed doors. Occasionally we went into the town and sat together at sidewalk cafés to observe passersby, trying to look absorbed in one another's company to ward off attention. The only person we introduced ourselves to was Father Mel, who was the priest at Saint Mark's, a small bluestone chapel down by the water.

"Good heavens," he said when he saw us. "So you've finally come."

We liked Father Mel because he didn't ask any questions or make any demands of us; he simply joined us in prayer. We hoped that in time our subtle influence in the town might result in people reconnecting with their spirituality. We didn't expect them to be observant and go to church every Sunday, but we wanted to restore their faith and teach them to believe in miracles. Even if they stopped by the church on their way to do the grocery shopping and lit a candle, we would be happy.

Venus Cove was a sleepy beachside town, the sort of place where nothing ever changed. We enjoyed the quiet and took to walking along the shore, usually at dinnertime when the beach was mostly deserted. One night we walked as far as the pier to look at the boats moored there. They were so brightly painted they looked like they belonged in a postcard. We reached the end of the pier before noticing the lone boy sitting there. He couldn't have been more than eighteen, but it was possible to see in him the man he would someday become. He was wearing cargo shorts that came to his knees and a loose white T-shirt with the sleeves cut off. His muscular legs hung over the edge of the pier. He was fishing and had a burlap bag full of bait and assorted reels beside him. We stopped dead when we saw him and would have turned away immediately, but he had already seen us.

"Hi," he said with an open smile. "Nice night for a walk." My brother and sister only nodded in response and didn't move. I decided it was too impolite not to respond and stepped forward.

"Yes, it is," I said. I suppose this was the first sign of my weakness—my human curiosity drew me forward. We were supposed to interact with humans but never befriend them or welcome them into our lives. Already, I was disregarding the rules of our mission. I knew I should fall silent, walk away, but instead I gestured toward the boy's fishing reels. "Have you had any luck?"

"I come out here to relax," he said, tipping up the bucket so I could see it was empty. "If I happen to catch anything, I throw it back in."

I took another step forward for a closer look. The boy's light brown hair was the color of walnuts. It flopped over his brow and had a lustrous sheen in the fading light. His pale eyes were almond shaped and a striking turquoise blue in color. But it was his smile that was utterly mesmerizing. So that was how it was done, I thought: effortlessly, instinctively, and so utterly human. As I watched, I felt drawn to him, almost by some magnetic force. Ignoring Ivy's warning glance, I took another step forward.

"Want to try?" he offered, sensing my curiosity and holding out the fishing rod.

While I struggled to think of an appropriate response, Gabriel answered for me.

"Come away now, Bethany. We have to get home."

I noticed how formal Gabriel's speech pattern was compared with the boy's. Gabriel's words sounded rehearsed, as though he were performing a scene from a play. He probably felt like he was. He sounded like a character in one of the old Hollywood movies I'd watched as part of our research.

"Maybe next time," the boy said, picking up on Gabriel's tension. I noticed how his eyes crinkled slightly at the corners when he smiled. Something in his expression made me think he was poking fun at us. I moved away reluctantly.

"That was so rude," I said to my brother as soon as we were out of earshot. I surprised myself with those words. Since when did angels worry about coming across as slightly stand-offish? Since when had I mistaken Gabriel's distant manner for rudeness? He had been created that way, he wasn't at one with humankind—he didn't understand their ways. And yet, I was berating him for lacking human traits.

"We have to be careful, Bethany," he explained as if speaking to an errant child.

"Gabriel is right," Ivy added, ever our brother's ally. "We're not ready for human contact yet."

"I think I am," I said.

I turned back for a final look at the boy. He was still watching us and still smiling.

Flesh

WHEN I woke in the morning, sunlight was streaming through the tall windows and spilling across the bare pine boards of my room. In the beams of light, dust motes swirled in a frenzied dance. I could smell the briny sea air; recognize the sounds of gulls squawking and the yeasty waves crashing over the rocks. I could see the familiar objects around the room that had become mine. Whoever had been responsible for decorating my bedroom had done so with some idea of its future occupant. It had a girlish charm with its white furniture, iron canopy bed, and rosebud wallpaper. The white dressing table had a floral stencil on its drawers, and there was a rattan rocking chair in one corner. A dainty desk with turned legs stood against a wall beside the bed.

I stretched and felt the crumpled sheets against my skin; their texture still a novelty. Where we came from, there were no textures, no objects. We needed nothing physical to sustain us and so there was nothing. Heaven was not easy to describe. Some humans might catch a glimpse of it on occasion, buried somewhere in the recesses of their unconscious, and wonder briefly what it all meant. Try to imagine an expanse of white, an invisible city, with nothing material to be seen but still the most beautiful sight you could imagine. A sky like liquid gold and rose quartz, a feeling of buoyancy, of weightlessness, seemingly empty but more majestic than the grandest palace on earth. That was the best I could do when trying to describe something as ineffable as my former home. I was not too impressed with human language; it seemed absurdly limited. There was so much that couldn't be put into words. That was one of the saddest things about people—their most important thoughts and feelings often went unspoken and barely understood.

One of the most frustrating words in the human language, as far as I could tell, was *love*. So much meaning attached to this one little word. People bandied it about freely, using it to describe their attachments to possessions, pets, vacation destinations, and favorite foods. In the same breath they then applied this word to the person they considered most important in their lives. Wasn't that insulting? Shouldn't there be some other term to describe deeper emotion? Humans were so preoccupied with love. They were all desperate to form an attachment to one person they could refer to as their "other half." It seemed from my reading of literature that being in love meant becoming the beloved's entire world. The rest of the universe paled into insignificance compared to the lovers. When they were separated, each fell into a melancholy state, and only when they were reunited did their hearts start beating again. Only when they were together could they really see the colors of the world. When they were apart, that color leached away, leaving everything a hazy gray. I lay in bed, wondering about the intensity of this emotion that was so irrational and so irrefutably human. What if a person's face was so sacred to you it was permanently inscribed in your memory? What if their smell and touch were dearer to you than life itself? Of course, I knew nothing about human love, but the idea had always been intriguing to me. Celestial beings never pretended to understand the intensity of human relationships; but I found it amazing how humans could allow another person to take over their hearts and minds. It was ironic how love could awaken them to the wonders of the universe, while at the same time confine their attention to one another.

The sounds of my brother and sister moving around in the kitchen downstairs broke into my reverie and drew me out of bed. What did my ruminations matter anyway when human love was barred to angels?

I wrapped a cashmere throw around me to keep warm and padded barefoot down the stairs. In the kitchen I was met by the inviting smell of toast and coffee. I was pleased to find myself adjusting to human life—a few weeks ago such smells might have brought on a headache or a wave of nausea. But now I was starting to enjoy the experience. I curled my toes, enjoying the feel of the smooth timber boards underfoot. I didn't even care when, still only half awake, I clumsily stubbed my toe on the refrigerator. The shooting pain only served to remind me that I was real and that I could feel.

"Good *afternoon*, Bethany," said my brother jokingly as he handed me a steaming mug of tea. I held it a fraction too long before putting it down, and it scalded my fingers. Gabriel noticed me flinch, and I saw a frown crinkle his forehead. I was reminded that unlike my two siblings I was not immune to pain.

My physical form had the same vulnerabilities as a human body did, although I was able to self-heal minor injuries like cuts and broken bones. It had been one of Gabriel's concerns about my being chosen for this in the first place. I knew he saw me as vulnerable and thought the whole mission might prove too dangerous for me. I had been chosen because I was more in tune with the human condition than other angels—I watched over humans, empathized with them, and tried to understand them. I had faith in them and cried tears for them. Perhaps it was because I was young—I had been created only seventeen mortal years ago, which equated to infancy in celestial years. Gabriel and Ivy had been around for centuries; they had fought battles and witnessed human atrocities beyond my imagination. They'd had all of time to acquire strength and power to protect them on earth. They'd both visited earth on a number of missions so they'd had time to adjust to it and were aware of its perils and pitfalls. But I was an angel in the purest, most vulnerable form. I was naïve and trusting, young and fragile. I could feel pain because years of wisdom and experience did not protect me from it. It was for this reason that Gabriel wished I had not been chosen, and it was for this reason that I had.

But the final decision hadn't been up to him; it was up to someone else, someone so supreme even Gabriel didn't dare argue. He had to resign himself to the fact that there must be a divine reason behind my selection, which was beyond even his understanding.

I sipped tentatively at my tea and smiled at my brother. His expression cleared, and he picked up a box of cereal and scrutinized its label.

"What'll it be—toast or something called Honey Wheat Flakes?"

"Not the flakes," I said, wrinkling my nose at the cereal.

Ivy was seated at the table idly buttering a piece of toast. My sister was still trying to develop a taste for food, and I watched her cut her toast into neat little squares, shuffle the pieces around her plate and put them back together like a jigsaw puzzle. I went to sit next to her, inhaling the heady scent of freesia that always seemed to pervade the air around her.

"You look a little pale," she observed with her usual calm, lifting away a strand of white-blond hair that had fallen over her rain gray eyes. Ivy had become the self-appointed mother hen of our little family.

"It's nothing," I replied casually and hesitated before adding, "just a bad dream." I saw them both stiffen slightly and exchange concerned glances.

"I wouldn't call that *nothing*," Ivy said. "You know we aren't meant to dream." Gabriel returned from his position by the window to study my face more closely. He lifted my chin with the tip of his finger. I noticed his frown had returned, shadowing the grave beauty of his face.

"Be careful, Bethany," he counseled in his now-familiar older brother tone. "Try not to become attached to physical experiences. Exciting as it may seem, remember we are only visitors here. All of this is temporary and sooner or later we will have to return. . . ." Seeing my forlorn look made him stop short. When he continued, it was in a lighter voice. "Well, there's plenty of time before that happens so we can discuss it later."

It was strange visiting earth with Ivy and Gabriel. They attracted so much attention wherever we went. In his physical form, Gabriel might well have been a classical sculpture come to life. His body was perfectly proportioned and each muscle looked as if it had been sculpted out of the purest marble. His shoulder-length hair was the color of sand and he often wore it pulled back in a loose ponytail. His brow was strong and his nose arrow straight. Today he was wearing faded blue jeans worn through at the knees and a crumpled linen shirt, both of which gave him a disheveled beauty. Gabriel was an archangel and a member of the Holy Seven. Although his clique ranked only second in the divine hierarchy, they were exclusive and had the most interaction with human beings. In fact, they were created to liaise between the Lord and mortals. But at heart Gabriel was a warrior—his celestial name meant "Hero of God"—and it was he who had watched Sodom and Gomorrah burn.

Ivy, on the other hand, was one of the wisest and oldest of our kind, although she didn't look a day over twenty. She was a seraphim, the order of angels closest to the Lord. In the Kingdom, seraphim had six wings to mark the six days of creation. A gold snake was tattooed on Ivy's wrist as a mark of her rank. It was said that in battle the seraphim would come forward to spit fire on the earth, but she was one of the gentlest creatures I'd ever met. In her physical form, Ivy looked like a Renaissance Madonna with her swanlike neck and pale oval face. Like Gabriel, she had piercing rain gray eyes. This morning she wore a white flowing dress and gold sandals.

I, on the other hand, was nothing special, just a plain, old transition angel—bottom of the rung. I didn't mind; it meant I was able to interact with the human spirits that entered the Kingdom. In my physical form, I looked ethereal like my family, except my eyes were as brown as river stones and my chestnut brown hair fell in loose waves down my back. I'd thought that once I was recruited for an earth posting I'd be able to choose my own physical form, but it didn't work that way. I was created small, fine boned, and not especially tall, with a heart-shaped face, pixielike ears, and skin that was milky pale. Whenever I caught a glimpse of my reflection in the mirror, I saw an eagerness that was missing from the faces of my siblings. Even when I tried, I could never look as removed as Gabe and Ivy. Their expressions of grave composure rarely altered, regardless of the drama unfolding around them. My face always wore a look of restless curiosity no matter how hard I tried to look worldly.

Ivy crossed to the sink holding her plate, as always moving as though she were dancing rather than walking. Both my brother and sister moved with an unstudied grace that I was incapable of imitating. More than once I'd been accused of *stomping* through the house as well as being heavy-handed.

When she'd disposed of her half-eaten toast, Ivy stretched out on the window seat, the newspaper open in front of her.

"What's news?" I asked.

In reply she held up the front page for me to see. I read the headlines—bombings, natural disasters, and economic collapse. I felt immediately defeated.

"Is it any wonder that people don't feel safe," Ivy said with a sigh. "They have no faith in one another."

"If that's true then what can we possibly do for them?" I asked hesitantly.

"Let's not expect too much too soon," said Gabriel. "They say change takes time."

"Besides, it's not for us to try and save the world," Ivy said. "We must focus on our little portion of it."

"You mean this town?"

"Of course." My sister nodded. "This town was listed as a target of the Dark Forces. It's strange the places they choose."

"I imagine they're starting small and working their way up," said Gabriel in disgust. "If they can conquer a town, they can conquer a city, then a state, then a country."

"How do we know how much damage they've already done?" I asked.

"That will become clear in time," said Gabriel. "But so help us, we will put an end to their destructive work. We won't fail in our mission, and before we depart, this place will once again be in the hands of the Lord."

"In the meantime, let's just try and blend in," Ivy said, perhaps in an effort to lighten the mood. I almost laughed aloud and was tempted to suggest she look in a mirror. She might be as old as time, but sometimes Ivy could sound quite naïve. Even I knew that *blending in* was going to be a challenge.

Anyone could see that we were different—and not in an art student's dyed-hair-and-kooky-stockings kind of way. We were *really* different—out-of-this-world different. I guess that wasn't unusual given who we were . . . or rather, what we were. There were several things that made us conspicuous. For starters, human beings were flawed and we weren't. If you saw one of us in a crowd, the first thing you'd notice was our skin. It was so translucent you might be persuaded into believing that it contained actual particles of light. This became even more evident after dark when any exposed skin emitted a faint glow as if from some inner energy source. Also, we never left footprints, even when we were walking on something impressionable like grass or sand. And you'd never catch any one of us in a tank top—we always wore high-backed tops to cover up a minor cosmetic problem.

As we began to assimilate into the life of the town, the locals couldn't help but wonder what we were doing in a sleepy backwater like Venus Cove. Sometimes they thought we were tourists on an extended stay; other times we'd be mistaken for celebrities, and they'd ask us about TV shows we'd never even heard of. No one guessed that we were working; that we had been recruited to assist a world on the brink of destruction. You only had to open a newspaper or flick on a television to see why we'd been sent: murder, kidnapping, terrorist attacks, war, assaults on the elderly . . . the ugly list went on and on. There were so many souls in peril that the Agents of Darkness were seizing the opportunity to gather. Gabriel, Ivy, and I had been sent here to offset their influence. Other Agents of Light had been sent to various locations across the globe, and eventually we would be summoned to evaluate our findings. I knew the situation was dire, but I was certain that we couldn't fail. In fact, I thought it would be easy—our presence would be the divine solution. I was about find out just how wrong I was.

We were fortunate to have ended up at Venus Cove. It was a breathtaking place of striking contrasts. Parts of the coastline were windswept and rugged, and from our house we could see the looming cliffs overlooking the dark, rolling ocean and hear the wind howling through the trees. But a little farther inland, there were pastoral scenes of undulating hills with grazing cows and pretty windmills.

Most of the houses in Venus Cove were modest weatherboard cottages but, closer to the coast, was a series of tree-lined streets with larger, more impressive homes. Our house, Byron, was one of these. Gabriel wasn't overly thrilled with our accommodations—the cleric in him found it excessive, and he would no doubt have felt more at ease in something less luxurious, but Ivy and I loved it. And if the powers that be didn't see any harm in us enjoying our time on earth, why shouldn't we? I suspected the house might not help achieve our goal of blending in, but I kept quiet. I didn't want to complain when I already felt too much like a liability on this mission.

Venus Cove had a population of around three thousand, although this doubled during the summer break when the town transformed into a teeming resort. Regardless of the time of year, the locals were open and friendly. I liked the atmosphere of the place: There were no people in business suits charging off to high-powered jobs; no one was in a hurry. The people didn't seem to care if they had dinner at the swankiest restaurant in town or at the beachside snack bar. They were just too laid back to worry about things like that.

"Do you agree, Bethany?" The rich timbre of Gabriel's voice recalled me to the present. I tried to remember the threads of the conversation but drew a complete blank.

"Sorry," I said, "I was miles away. What were you saying?"

"I was just setting out some ground rules. Everything will be different as of today."

Gabriel was frowning again, mildly annoyed by my inattention. The two of us were starting at the Bryce Hamilton School that morning, me as a student and Gabriel as the new music teacher. It had been decided that a school would be a useful place to begin our work of countering the emissaries of darkness, given it was full of young people whose values were still evolving. Ivy was too unearthly to be herded off to high school, so it was agreed that she would mentor us and ensure our safety, or rather, *my* safety, as Gabriel could look after himself.

"The important thing is not to lose sight of why we're here," Ivy said. "Our mission is clear: to perform good deeds, acts of charity and kindness; to lead by example. We don't want any miracles just yet, not until we can predict how they would be received. At the same time we want to observe and learn as much as we can about people. Human culture is so complex and different from anything else in the universe."

I suspected these ground rules were mostly for my benefit. Gabriel never had difficulty handling himself in any kind of situation.

"This is going to be fun," I said, perhaps a little too enthusiastically.

"It's not about fun," retorted Gabriel. "Haven't you heard anything we've said?"

"Essentially we are trying to drive away the evil influences and restore people's faith in each other," said Ivy in a conciliatory tone. "Don't worry about Bethany, Gabe—she'll be fine."

"In short, we are here to bless the community," my brother continued. "But we mustn't appear too conspicuous. Our first priority is to remain undetected. Bethany, please try not to say anything that will . . . *unsettle* the students."

It was my turn to be offended.

"Like what?" I demanded. "I'm not that scary."

"You know what Gabriel means," said Ivy. "All he's suggesting is that you think before you speak. No personal talk about home, no 'God reckons' . . . or 'God told me' . . . they might think you're *on* something."

"Fine," I said huffily. "But I hope I'm at least allowed to fly around the corridors during lunch hour."

Gabriel threw me a disapproving look. I waited for him to get my joke, but his eyes remained serious. I sighed. Much as I loved him, Gabriel could be totally lacking in any sense of humor.

"Don't worry, I'll behave. I promise."

"Self-control is of the utmost importance," Ivy said.

I sighed again. I knew I was the only one who had to worry about self-control. Ivy and Gabriel had enough experience of this kind for it to be second nature—they knew the rules back to front. It wasn't fair. They also had steadier personalities than I did. They might as well have been called the Ice King and Queen. Nothing fazed them, nothing troubled them, and most important, nothing upset them. They were like well-rehearsed actors whose lines came to them without effort. It was different for me; I'd struggled from the outset. For some reason, becoming human had really thrown me. I wasn't prepared for the intensity of it. It was like going from blissful emptiness to experiencing a roller coaster of sensations all at once. Sometimes the sensations crossed over and shifted like sand so the end result was total confusion. I knew I was supposed to detach myself from all things emotional, but I hadn't worked out how. I marveled at how ordinary humans managed to live with such turmoil bubbling below the surface all the time—it was draining. I tried to hide my difficulties from Gabriel; I didn't want to prove him right or have him thinking less of me because of my struggles. If my siblings ever experienced anything similar, they were expert at suppressing it.

Ivy suggested she go and lay out my uniform and find a clean shirt and pants for Gabe. As a member of the teaching staff, Gabriel was required to wear a shirt and tie, and the idea wasn't exactly appealing to him. He usually wore loose jeans and open-neck sweaters. Anything tight made us feel too constricted. Clothes in general gave us a strange feeling of being trapped, so I sympathized with Gabriel as he came back downstairs squirming in the crisp white shirt that hugged his well-built chest and tugging at the tie until he'd sufficiently loosened the knot.

Clothing wasn't the only difference; we'd also had to learn to perform grooming rituals like showering, brushing our teeth, and combing our hair. We never had to think about such things in the Kingdom, where existence was maintenance free. Life as a physical entity meant so much more to remember.

"Are you sure there's a dress code for teachers?" Gabriel asked.

"I think so," Ivy replied, "but even if I'm wrong, do you really want to be taking a chance on the first day?"

"What was wrong with what I had on?" he grumbled, rolling up his shirtsleeves in an attempt to liberate his arms. "It was comfortable, at least."

Ivy clicked her tongue at him and turned to check that I'd put on my uniform correctly.

I had to admit that it was fairly stylish as far as uniforms went. The dress was a flattering pale blue with a pleated front and a white Peter Pan collar. With it we were required to wear knee-high cotton socks, brown buckle-up shoes, and a navy blazer with the school crest emblazoned in gold on the breast pocket. Ivy had bought me pale blue and white ribbons, which she now weaved deftly into my braids.

"There," she said with a satisfied smile. "From celestial ambassador to local school girl."

I wished she hadn't used the word *ambassador*—it was unnerving. It carried so much weight, so many expectations. And not the sort of expectations humans had of their children to clean their rooms, babysit their siblings, or complete their homework. These were the kind of expectations that had to be met, and if they weren't . . . well, I didn't know what would happen. My knees felt as if they might buckle underneath me at any minute.

"I'm not so sure about this, Gabe," I said, even as I realized how erratic I must sound. "What if I'm not ready?"

"That choice is not ours," Gabriel replied with unfailing composure. "We have only one purpose: to fulfil our duties to the Creator."

"I want to do that, but this is *high school*. It's one thing observing life from the sidelines, but we're going to be thrown right in the thick of it."

"That's the point," Gabriel said. "We can't be expected to make a difference from the sidelines."

"But what if something goes wrong?"

"I'll be there to make it right."

"It's just that the earth seems like such a dangerous place for angels."

"That's why I'm here."

The dangers I imagined weren't merely physical. These we'd be well equipped to handle. What worried me was the seduction of all things human. I doubted myself, and I knew that could lead to losing sight of my higher purpose. After all, it had happened before with dire consequences—we'd all heard the dreadful legends of fallen angels, seduced by the indulgences of man, and we all knew what had become of them.

Ivy and Gabriel observed the world around them with a trained eye, aware of the pitfalls, but for a novice like me the danger was enormous.

Venus Cove

THE Bryce Hamilton School was located on the outskirts of town, set high on the peak of an undulating slope. No matter where you were in the building, you looked out to see a view: either vineyards and verdant hills with the odd grazing cow, or the rugged cliffs of the Shipwreck Coast, so named for the many vessels that had sunk in its treacherous waters over the last century. The school, a limestone mansion complete with arched windows, sweeping lawns, and a bell tower, was one of the town's original buildings. It had once served as a convent before it was converted to a school in the sixties.

A flight of stone steps led to the double doors of the main entrance, which was shadowed by a vine-covered archway. Attached to the main building was a small stone chapel; the occasional service was still held there, we were told, but mostly it served as a place for students in need of refuge. A high stone wall surrounded the grounds, and spiked iron gates stood open to allow cars access to the gravel driveway.

Despite its archaic exterior, Bryce Hamilton had a reputation for moving with the times, and was favored by progressive parents who wanted to avoid subjecting their children to any kind of repression. Most of the students had a long-standing association with the school through parents and grandparents who were former pupils.

Ivy, Gabriel, and I stood outside the gates watching the students arrive. I concentrated on trying to settle the butterflies that were doing callisthenics in my stomach. The sensation was uncomfortable and yet strangely exhilarating. I was still getting used to the way emotions could affect the human body. I took a deep breath. It was funny how being an angel didn't make me any more prepared for the first-day nerves of starting somewhere new. I didn't have to be human to know that first impressions could make all the difference between acceptance and ostracism. I'd listened in on the prayers of teenage girls and most of them centered on being accepted by the "popular" crowd and finding a boyfriend who played on the rugby team. I just hoped I would find a friend.

The students came in groups of three and four: the girls dressed just like me; the boys wearing gray trousers, white shirts, and blue-and-white-striped ties. Even in school uniform, it wasn't difficult to distinguish the particular social groups I'd observed in the Kingdom. The music posse was made up of boys with shoulder-length hair, untidy strands falling over their eyes. They carried instrument cases and had musical chords scrawled on their arms in black felt pen. There was a small minority of goths who had set themselves apart by the use of heavy eye makeup and spiky hairdos, and I wondered how they got away with it. Surely it must contravene school regulations. Those who liked to think of themselves as artistic had accessorized the uniform with berets or hats and colorful scarves. Some girls traveled in packs, like a group of platinum blondes who crossed the road with their arms linked. The academic types were easily identified; they wore pristine uniforms with no alterations and carried the official school backpack. They tended to walk with a missionary zeal, heads down, eager to reach the sanctity of the library. A group of boys in untucked shirts, loose ties, and sneakers loitered under the shade of some palms, taking swigs from soda cans and chocolate milk cartons. They were in no hurry to move inside the school gates, instead taking turns at punching and leaping on one another. They tumbled to the ground laughing and groaning at the same time. I watched one boy throw an empty can at his friend's head. It bounced off and rattled on the sidewalk. The boy looked stunned for a moment before bursting into laughter.

We watched with growing consternation and still hadn't moved from our position outside the front gates. A boy sauntered past us and looked back with curiosity. He was wearing a baseball cap backward and his school pants hung so loosely on his hips that the label of his designer underwear was in full view.

"I must admit, I struggle with some of these latest fashion trends." Gabriel pursed his lips.

Ivy laughed. "This is the twenty-first century," she said. "Try not to look so critical."

"Isn't that what teachers do?"

"I suppose so, but don't expect to be popular." She looked

resolutely toward the entrance and stood a little straighter even though she already had perfect posture. It was easy for her to be confident; she wasn't the one facing the firing squad. Ivy squeezed Gabriel's shoulder and handed me a manila folder with my class schedule, a school map, and other notices she had collected for me earlier in the week. "Are you ready?" she asked.

"As ready as I'll ever be," I replied, trying to steel my nerves. I felt as if I were about to go into battle. "Let's do it."

Ivy stood at the gates waving like a proud but anxious mother seeing her children off on their first day of school.

"We'll be fine, Bethany," Gabriel promised. "Remember where we come from."

We had predicted that our arrival would make an impression, but we hadn't counted on people stopping to openly gawk at us, or stepping aside as though they were being visited by royalty. I avoided making eye contact with anyone and followed Gabriel to the administration office. Inside, the carpet was dark green and a cluster of upholstered chairs were arranged in a row. Through a glass partition we could see an office with an upright fan and shelves almost to the ceiling. A short, round woman with a pink cardigan and an inflated sense of self-importance bustled up to us. A phone rang on a desk nearby and she glared pointedly at an office assistant, indicating it was her job to answer it. Her expression softened a little when she got close enough to see our faces.

"Hello there," she said brightly, eyeing us up and down. "My name's Mrs. Jordan and I'm the registrar. You must be Bethany, and you"—her voice dropped a notch as she scanned Gabriel's flawless face in appreciation—"must be Mr. Church, our new music teacher."

She came out from behind the little glass wall and tucked the folder she was carrying under her arm to shake our hands enthusiastically. "Welcome to Bryce Hamilton! I've allocated Bethany a locker on the third floor; we can head up there now, and then I'll escort you, Mr. Church, to our staff room. Briefings are Tuesdays and Thursdays at eight-thirty sharp. I hope you enjoy your time here. You'll find it's a very lively place, never a dull moment!"

Gabriel and I exchanged glances, unsure now what to expect of our first day at school. Mrs. Jordan bustled us outside and past the basketball courts, where a group of sweaty boys were furiously pounding the asphalt, shooting hoops.

"There's a big game on this afternoon," Mrs. Jordan confided, winking over her shoulder. She squinted up at the gathering clouds and frowned. "I sure hope the rain holds off. Our boys will be so disappointed if we have to forfeit."

As she prattled on, I saw Gabriel glance up at the sky. Discreetly, he turned his hand so that it was palm up toward the heavens and closed his eyes. The engraved silver rings he wore glinted in the sunlight. Immediately, as if in response to his silent command, beams of sunlight burst through the clouds, washing the courts in gold.

"Well, would you look at that!" Mrs. Jordan exclaimed. "A change in the weather—you two must have brought us luck."

In the main wing the corridors were carpeted in a dark burgundy and oak doors with glass panels led to antiquated-looking classrooms. The ceilings were high and some of the old ornate light fixtures still remained. They were a stark contrast to the graffiti-covered lockers lining the corridor and the slightly nauseating smell of deodorant coupled with cleaning agents and the greasy odor of hamburgers coming from the cafeteria. Mrs. Jordan took us on a whirlwind tour, pointing out the main facilities (the quadrangle, multimedia department, science block, assembly hall, gymnasium, and tracks, playing fields, and the performing arts center). She was obviously pressed for time, because after showing me my locker, she blurted some vague directions to the nurse's office, told me not to hesitate should I have any questions, and took Gabriel by the elbow and whisked him away. He looked back at me apprehensively.

"Will you be okay?" he mouthed.

I gave him a wan smile by way of reply, hoping I looked more confident than I felt. I certainly didn't want Gabriel worrying about me when he had matters of his own to deal with. Just then a sonorous bell rang, reverberating through the building and signaling the beginning of the first class. I found myself suddenly standing alone in a corridor full of strangers. They pushed indifferently past me as they headed to various classrooms. For a moment I felt invisible, as if I had no business being there. I studied my schedule and realized that the jumble of numbers and letters may as well have been written in a foreign language for all the sense they made to me. V.CHES11—how on earth was I supposed to decipher that? I even considered ducking through the crowd and making my way back to Byron Street.

"Excuse me." I caught the attention of a girl with a tumble

of titian curls who was striding past. She stopped and surveyed me with interest. "I'm new," I explained helplessly, holding out my schedule. "Can you tell me what this means?"

"It means you have chemistry with Mr. Velt in room S-eleven," she said. "It's just down the hall. I'll take you if you like—we're in the same class."

"Thanks," I said with obvious relief.

"Do you have a spare after chem? If you do I can show you around."

"A what?" I asked, my confusion growing.

"A spare—as in a free period?" The girl gave me a funny look. "What did you call them at your old school?" Her face changed as she considered a more disturbing possibility. "Or didn't you have any?"

"No," I replied with a nervous laugh. "We didn't."

"That must've sucked. I'm Molly, by the way."

The girl was beautiful with glowing skin, rounded features, and bright eyes. Her rosiness reminded me of a girl in a painting I'd seen, a shepherdess in a bucolic setting.

"Bethany," I said with a smile. "It's nice to meet you."

Molly waited patiently at my locker while I rummaged through my bag for the relevant textbook, a spiral notebook, and a handful of pens. Part of me wanted to call Gabriel back and ask him to take me home. I could almost feel his strong arms encircling me, hiding me from everything, and steering me back to Byron. Gabriel had a way of making me feel safe, no matter what the circumstances were. But I didn't know how to find him in this vast school; he could have been behind any of the numberless doors in any one of the identical corridors; I had no idea how to find the music wing. I silently reproved myself for my dependence on Gabriel. I needed to survive here on a daily basis without his protection, and I was determined to show him that I could. Molly opened the classroom door and we walked in. Of course, we were late.

Mr. Velt was a short, bald man with a shiny forehead. He was wearing a sweater patterned with geometric shapes that looked like it had faded from overwashing. When Molly and I came in, he was in the middle of trying to explain a formula scrawled on the whiteboard to a bunch of students, whose vacant faces indicated they wished they were anywhere but in his classroom.

"Glad you could join us, Miss Harrison," he said to Molly, who slunk quickly to the back of the room. Having already checked the roll he seemed to know who I was.

"Late on your first day, Miss Church," he said, clicking his tongue and raising an eyebrow in reprimand. "Not exactly off to a good start. Hurry up and sit down."

Suddenly he remembered he had forgotten to introduce me. He stopped writing long enough to make a perfunctory introduction. "Everyone, this is Bethany Church. She's new to Bryce Hamilton, so please do your utmost to make her feel welcome."

Almost every pair of eyes in the room followed me as I took the last seat available. It was at the back next to Molly, and when Mr. Velt stopped talking and told us to work through the next set of questions, I was able to study her more closely. I saw now that she wore the top button of her school dress undone and large silver hoops in her ears. She had drawn an emery board from her pocket and was filing her nails under the desk, blatantly ignoring our teacher's instructions.

"Don't worry about Velt," she whispered, seeing my look of surprise. "He's a total stiff, bitter and twisted after his wife served the divorce papers. The only thing that gets him going these days is his new convertible, which he looks like a loser driving." She grinned, and I saw she had a broad smile and white teeth. She wore a lot of mascara but her skin had a natural glow. "Bethany, that's a pretty name," she went on. "Kinda old-fashioned though. But hey, I got stuck with Molly, like some character in a picture book."

I smiled awkwardly at her, not entirely sure how to answer someone so confident and forthright.

"I guess we're stuck with the names our parents chose for us," I said, knowing it was a lame attempt at making conversation. I figured I really shouldn't have been talking at all, seeing as we were in class and poor Mr. Velt needed all the help he could get. It also made me feel like a fraud, as angels didn't have parents. For a moment I felt like Molly would see right through my lie. But she didn't.

"So where are you from?" Molly wanted to know, blowing on the nails of one hand and shaking a bottle of fluorescent pink polish.

"We've been living overseas," I told her, wondering what her reaction might be if I told her I was from the Kingdom of Heaven. "Our parents are still there."

"Really?" Molly seemed impressed. "Whereabouts?"

I hesitated. "Different places. They move around a lot."

Molly seemed to accept this as if it were fairly common-place.

"What do they do?" she asked.

I fumbled for the answer in my head. I knew we'd discussed this but my mind went blank. It would be just like me to make a critical mistake within my first hour of being a student. Then I remembered.

"They're diplomats," I said. "We came with our older brother. He just started as a teacher here. Our parents will join us when they can." I tried to cram in as much information as I could to satisfy her curiosity and stem further questions. By nature, angels were bad liars. I hoped Molly hadn't seen through my story. Technically speaking, none of it was a lie.

"Cool," was all she said. "I've never been overseas but I've been to the city a few times. You'd better be prepared for a change of lifestyle at Venus Cove. It's usually pretty chill around here except things have been a bit weird lately."

"How do you mean?" I asked.

"Well, I've lived here my whole life; my grandparents even lived here and ran a local business. And in all that time, nothing really bad has ever happened; there's been the occasional factory fire and some boating accidents—but now . . ." Molly lowered her voice. "There's been robberies and freak accidents all over the place—there was a flu epidemic last year and six kids died from it."

"That's devastating," I said weakly, feeling a hollowness in the pit of my stomach. I was starting to get a sense of the extent of the damage done by the Agents of Darkness, and it wasn't looking good. "Is that all?"

"There was one other thing," Molly said. "But you'd want to be careful bringing it up at school—a lot of kids are still pretty torn up over it."

"Don't worry, I'll watch my mouth," I assured her.

"Well about six months ago, one of the senior boys, Henry Taylor, climbed up on the school roof to get a basketball that had landed up there. He wasn't screwing around or anything, he was just trying to get it down. No one saw how it happened, but he slipped and fell. He came down right in the middle of the courts—his friends saw the whole thing. They were never able to completely get rid of the bloodstain, so no one plays there anymore."

Before I could respond, Mr. Velt cleared his throat and looked daggers in our direction.

"Miss Harrison, I assume you are explaining to our new student the concept of covalent bonding."

"Um, not exactly, Mr. Velt," Molly replied. "I don't want to bore her to death on her first day."

I saw a vein throb on Mr. Velt's forehead and realized I should probably intervene. I channeled a calming energy toward him and watched with satisfaction as he started looking less harangued. His shoulders seem to relax, and his face lost its livid hue and returned to a more natural shade. He looked at Molly and gave a tolerant, almost paternal chuckle.

"Your sense of humor is unfailing, Miss Harrison."

Molly looked confused but was smart enough to refrain from further comment.

"My theory is he's having a midlife crisis," she whispered to me instead. Mr. Velt ignored us and busied himself setting up a projector slide. I groaned inwardly and tried to suppress a rising wave of panic. We angels were radiant enough in daylight. In the dark it was worse but concealable, but in the halogen light of an overhead projector, who knew what might happen. I decided it wasn't worth taking the risk. I asked for permission to go to the bathroom and then slipped out. I hung around just outside, waiting for Mr. Velt to finish his presentation and switch the lights back on. The slides clicked sharply into place, and through the glass panel on the classroom door I could see that they demonstrated a simplified description of the valence bond theory. I was glad I wouldn't have to study such basic things on a permanent basis.

"Are you lost?"

The voice came from behind, startling me. I spun around to see a boy lounging against the lockers opposite the classroom. Even though he looked more formal with his shirt buttoned, tie neatly knotted, and school blazer, there was no mistaking that face or the nut-colored hair flopping over vivid blue eyes. I hadn't expected to run into him again, but now the boy from the pier was standing right in front of me, wearing that same wry smile.

"I'm fine, thank you," I said, turning away quickly. If he had recognized me, he wasn't giving himself away. I hoped that turning my back on him, as rude as it seemed, might cut the conversation short. He had caught me unawares, and something about him made me unsure where to look or what to do with my hands. But he seemed in no hurry.

"You know, the more conventional way to learn is from inside the classroom," he continued.

I was forced to turn back then and acknowledge his presence. I tried to communicate my reluctance to engage in conversation with a cool look, but when I met his eyes, something entirely different happened. I had an instant, gut-wrenching physical reaction as if the world were falling from under me and I had to steady myself to stop from falling with it.

I must have looked like I was about to pass out because he involuntarily put out an arm to catch me. I noticed the fine cord of plaited leather he wore around his wrist, the only item out of keeping with his otherwise traditional appearance.

My memory of him hadn't done him justice. He had the striking good looks of an actor but without any trace of conceit. His mouth was curved into a half-smile, and his limpid eyes had a depth I hadn't noticed the first time. He was tall and slender, but underneath his uniform I could make out the shoulders of a swimmer. He was looking at me as though he wanted to help me but didn't quite know how, and as I stared back at him, I realized that his attractiveness had as much to do with his air of composure as his regular features and smooth skin. I wished I could come up with some witty retort to match his confidence, but I couldn't think of anything.

"Just feeling a little light-headed, that's all," I mumbled. He took a step closer, still looking concerned.

"Do you need to sit down?"

"No, I'm fine now." I shook my head decisively.

Reassured that I wasn't going to faint, he held out his hand and flashed me a dazzling smile.

"I didn't get a chance to introduce myself last time we met—I'm Xavier."

So he hadn't forgotten.

His hand was broad and warm. He held mine a fraction too long. I remembered what Gabriel had said about steering clear of risky human interaction. Warning bells sounded in my head as I frowned and pulled my hand away. It wouldn't exactly be the wisest move befriending this boy with his ridiculous good looks and hundred-watt smile. The flutter in my chest when I looked at him told me I was already in hot water. I was learning to read the signals given out by my body and knew that this boy was making me nervous. But there was a hint of another feeling, one that I couldn't identify. I backed away from him, toward the classroom door, where I could see the lights had just come on. I knew I was being rude, but I was too unsettled to care. Xavier didn't look offended, just bemused by my behavior.

"I'm Bethany," I managed to say, already halfway through the door.

"See you around, Bethany," he said.

My face felt beet red as I came back into the chem lab, and Mr. Velt threw me an accusatory look for having taken so long in the bathroom.

BY lunchtime I'd realized that Bryce Hamilton was a mine-field of projector slides and other traps designed to ferret out undercover angels like me. In gym class I had a mild panic attack when I realized I was expected to change in front of all the other girls. They peeled off their clothes without a second thought and tossed them into lockers or onto the floor. Molly got her bra straps tangled and asked for my help, which I gave nervously, hoping she wouldn't notice the unnaturally soft touch of my hands.

"Wow, you must moisturize like mad," she said.

"Every night," I replied lightly.

"So what do you think of the Bryce Hamilton crowd so far? Boys hot enough for you?"

"I wouldn't say *hot*," I said, puzzled. "Most of them seem to have a normal body temperature."

Molly stared at me. She looked like she was about to snicker, but my expression convinced her I wasn't trying to be funny. "Hot means good-looking," she said. "Have you seriously never heard that before? Where was your last school—Mars?"

I blushed as soon as I understood the meaning of her original question. "I haven't really met any boys yet," I said, shrugging. "I did run into someone called Xavier." Speaking his name aloud was strange. There was a cadence to it that made it sound special. I was glad the boy with the intense eyes and the floppy hair wasn't a Peter or Rob. I'd hoped to sound casual bringing him up, but his name exploded into the conversation like a firework.

"Which Xavier?" Molly quizzed, all ears now. "Is he blond? Xavier Laro's blond and plays on the lacrosse team. He's pretty hot. I wouldn't blame you for liking him, but I think he might already have a girlfriend. Or did they break up? I'm not sure; I could try and find out."

"This one had light brown hair," I interrupted her, "and blue eyes."

"Oh." Molly's expression changed. "That would be Xavier Woods. He's the school captain."

"Well, he seemed nice."

"I wouldn't go for him if I were you," she counseled. Her expression was all concern, but I got the feeling she expected me to take her advice no matter what. Maybe that was one of the rules in the world of teenage girls: "Friends are always right."

"I'm not really *going for* anyone, Molly," I said, but was unable to resist asking, "Why, what's wrong with him?" It didn't seem possible that the boy I'd met could be anything other than perfect.

"Oh, he's nice enough," Molly replied, "but let's just say he's got baggage."

"What does that mean?"

"Well, a whole heap of girls have been trying to get his attention for ages, but he's emotionally unavailable."

"You mean he's already got a girlfriend?"

"He did have. Her name was Emily. But no one's been able to comfort him since . . ." She trailed off.

"They broke up?" I prompted.

"No." Molly's voice dropped and she twisted her fingers uncomfortably. "She died in a house fire almost two years ago. Before it happened they were inseparable, people even talked about them getting married and everything. No one's been able to measure up to her. I don't think he's ever really gotten over it."

"How awful," I said. "He would have been only . . ."

"Sixteen," Molly finished. "He was pretty close with Henry Taylor as well—he spoke at the funeral. He was just getting over Emily when it happened. Everyone kinda expected him to break down, but he just shut off emotionally and kept going."

I didn't know what else to say. Looking at Xavier's face, you would never have guessed the pain he must have endured, although now I remembered there was a slightly guarded look about his eyes.

"He's all right now," Molly said. "He's still friends with everyone, still plays on the rugby team, and coaches the junior swimmers. It's not like he can't crack a smile, it's just that relationships are sort of off-limits. I don't think he wants to get involved again after the crappy luck he's had."

"I guess you can't blame him," I said.

Molly suddenly noticed that I was still in my uniform and her serious tone lifted. "Hurry up and get changed," she urged. "What are you, shy?"

"Just a bit." I smiled at her and disappeared into a shower cubicle.

My thoughts about Xavier Woods were cut off as soon as I saw the sports uniform I was expected to wear. I even contemplated crawling out the window to make my escape. It was completely unflattering; the shorts were too short, and the top rode up so much that I could hardly move without flashing my midriff. That was going to be a problem during games seeing as we angels didn't have a navel—just smooth white skin, freckle and indentation free. Luckily my wings (feathered but paper thin) folded flat across my back, so I didn't have to worry about them showing, but they were starting to cramp from lack of exercise. I couldn't wait until the predawn flight in the mountains that Gabriel had promised us soon.

I tugged the top down as far as I could and joined Molly, who was at the mirror applying a liberal coating of lip gloss. I wasn't sure why she needed lip gloss for gym class, but when she offered me the brush, I accepted, not wanting to appear ungracious. I wasn't exactly sure how to use the applicator but managed to apply a fairly uneven coating. I assumed it was something that took practice. Unlike the other girls, I hadn't been experimenting with my mom's cosmetics since I was five. I hadn't even known what my human face looked like until recently.

"Rub your lips together," said Molly. "Like this . . ."

I mimicked her and found that the motion smoothed out the gloss, making me look less clownlike.

"That's better," she said approvingly.

"Thanks."

"I guess you don't wear makeup very often."

I shook my head.

"Well, it's not like you need it. That color suits you though."

"It smells amazing."

"It's called Melon Sorbet." Molly looked pleased with herself, then became distracted by something and began sniffing the air.

"Can you smell that?" she asked.

I stiffened, gripped by a sudden rush of insecurity. Was it me? Was it possible that we smelled terrible to people on earth? Had Ivy sprayed my clothes with some sort of perfume that was socially unacceptable in Molly's world?

"It smells like . . . like rain or something," she said. I relaxed instantly. What she could smell was just the characteristic scent that all angels carried, and rain was a pretty good description on her part.

"Don't be a ditz, Molly," one of her friends said. Taylah, I thought her name was, recalling earlier rushed introductions. "It's not raining in here, duh."

Molly shrugged and tugged on my sleeve, leading me out of the locker room and into the gym where a blonde fifty-something woman with a sun-ravaged face and Lycra shorts was bouncing on the balls of her feet and shouting at us to drop and give her twenty.

"Don't you just hate gym teachers?" Molly said, rolling her eyes. "They're so . . . *up* all the time."

I didn't reply, but given the steely-faced look of the woman and my lack of athletic enthusiasm, we probably weren't going to get along very well.

Half an hour later we had run ten laps of the court, done fifty each of push-ups, sit-ups, squats, and lunges, and that was only the warm-up. I felt sorry for the other students who were staggering around with chests heaving and shirts damp with sweat. Angels didn't get tired; our energy was limitless and so didn't need to be conserved. We didn't perspire, either; we could run a marathon and not produce a single drop of sweat. Molly became suddenly aware of this.

"You're not even puffing!" she said accusingly. "Jeez, you must be really fit."

"Or use a really good deodorant," added Taylah, tipping the contents of her water bottle down her cleavage. It attracted the attention of a gaggle of boys nearby, who gaped at her. "It's getting hot in here!" she teased, parading past the boys with her now see-through shirt until the gym teacher noticed the spectacle and charged over to us like a raging bull.

The rest of the day passed uneventfully, except that I found myself scouring the corridors, hoping to catch another glimpse of the school captain, the boy called Xavier Woods. Given what I had learned about him from Molly, I was feeling flattered that he had paid me any attention at all.

I thought back to our meeting on the pier and remembered marveling at his eyes—such a brilliant, startling blue. They were the kind of eyes you couldn't look into for too long without going weak at the knees. I wondered now what might have happened had I accepted his invitation and sat down beside him. Would we have talked while I tried my hand at fishing? What would we have said?

I shook myself mentally. This wasn't why I had been sent to earth. I made myself promise that in the days that followed I wouldn't think about Xavier Woods at all. If I chanced to see him, I would ignore him. If he tried to speak to me, I would give token answers and move away. In short, I wouldn't allow him to have any effect on me.

Needless to say, I was to fail spectacularly.

Earthbound

WHEN the last bell sounded, I grabbed my books and literally made a run for it, eager to avoid the teeming halls. I'd been jostled, interrogated, and scrutinized enough for one day. Despite my efforts I hadn't managed to find a single quiet moment; during my breaks Molly had dragged me off to meet her friends, who all shot questions at me like rounds of machine-gun fire. Despite that, I'd made it to the end of the first day without serious mishap, and I was pleased with my achievement.

I loitered under the palms outside the school gates, waiting for Gabriel. I leaned back and rested my head against the tree's cool, jagged trunk. I was awed by the earth's varied vegetation. Palms, for one, struck me as such strange-looking creations. They reminded me of sentries with their lean, straight trunks and their exploding branches that looked just like the plumed helmets of palace guards. As I stood there, I watched the students tossing their bags into cars, peeling off their blazers, and looking visibly more relaxed. Some were heading off in the direction of the town to gather at local cafés or favorite haunts.

I didn't feel relaxed; I was suffering from information overload. My head buzzed as I tried to make sense of everything that had happened in the space of a few hours. Even the limitless energy we had been created with couldn't prevent the creeping feeling of exhaustion that was coming over me. I wanted nothing more than the comfort of home.

I spotted Gabriel making his way down the main steps, closely followed by a small gaggle of admirers, mostly girls. My brother might have been a celebrity for the attention he attracted. The girls lingered several yards behind him, trying hard not to appear conspicuous. Judging by his appearance, Gabe had managed to maintain his composure and poise throughout the day, but I could see from the hard set of his jaw and the slightly ruffled look of his hair that he was ready to go home. The girls stopped speaking mid-sentence when he glanced in their direction. I knew my brother and guessed that despite his apparent composure, he would never welcome such attention. He seemed embarrassed rather than flattered by it.

Gabriel was nearly at the gates when a shapely brunette stumbled in front of him in a poorly executed attempt at an accidental fall. In one smooth movement Gabe caught her in his arms just before she hit the ground. There were audible gasps of admiration from the watching students, and I saw some of the other girls bristle with jealousy at not having come up with the idea themselves. But there was little to warrant their envy: Gabriel merely steadied the girl, replaced the items that had fallen from her bag, wordlessly picked up his battered briefcase, and kept walking. He wasn't being unfriendly; he simply wouldn't have seen the need for any exchange of words. The girl stared wistfully after him and her friends crowded around, hoping some of the glamour of the moment might rub off on them.

"You poor thing, you have a fan club already," I said, patting his arm sympathetically as we began our walk home.

"I'm not the only one," Gabriel replied. "You didn't exactly escape attention either."

"Yes, but no one's really tried to talk to me." I didn't mention my encounter with Xavier Woods—something told me Gabriel wouldn't approve.

"Be grateful for small mercies," said Gabriel drily.

I related the day, point by point, to Ivy when we got home. Gabriel, who hadn't been thrilled by every little detail, remained silent. Ivy smothered a smile when I told the story of the swooning girls.

"Teenage girls can be quite lacking in subtlety," Ivy mused. "The boys, on the hand, are much harder to read. It's all very interesting, don't you think?"

"They all just seem lost to me," Gabe said. "I wonder if any of them really know what life is all about. I didn't realize we'd be starting from scratch. This is going to be harder than I thought." He fell silent, and we all were reminded of the epic task we had ahead of us.

"We always knew it was going to be hard," Ivy said softly.

"You know something I noticed," I said. "It seems like a lot has gone on in this town over the last few months. I heard some of the most awful stories."

"Like what?" Ivy asked.

"Two students have died from freak accidents recently," I

said. "And there have been outbreaks of sickness and fires and all sorts of strange things. People are starting to notice that something's wrong."

"Looks like we got here just in time," said Ivy.

"But how will we find whoever . . . or whatever is responsible?" I asked.

"There is no way to find them yet," said Gabriel. "It's our job to clean up the mess and wait until they show up again. Trust me; they won't go down without a fight."

We all fell silent as we thought about confronting such random destruction.

"So . . . I made a friend today!" I announced, in an attempt to lighten the gloom that was settling over us. It came out sounding as if it was a major achievement, and they both looked at me with their now-familiar mix of concern and disapproval.

"Is there something wrong with that?" I said defensively. "Aren't I allowed to have friends? I thought the whole idea was to blend in."

"Blending in is one thing; but do you realize that friends require time and energy?" said Gabriel. "They'll want to *bond*." He winced as if the thought was painful to him.

"As in physically meld together?" I was confused.

"I mean, they'll want to be emotionally close," my brother explained. "Human relationships can be unnaturally intimate— I'll never understand it."

"They can also be a distraction," Ivy somehow felt the need to add. "Not to mention the fact that friendship comes with expectations, so choose carefully."

"What kind of expectations?"

"Human friendships are based on trust. Friends share problems, exchange confidences and . . ." She petered out with a shake of her golden head and looked imploringly at Gabriel.

"What Ivy means is that anyone who becomes your friend will start to ask questions and expect answers," said Gabe. "They will want to become part of your life and that's dangerous."

"Well, thanks for the vote of confidence," I replied indignantly. "You know I'd never do anything that might jeopardize the mission. How stupid do you think I am?"

I was pleased to see them exchange guilty looks. I might have been younger and less experienced than they were, but it was no reason to treat me like an idiot.

"We don't think that," said Gabriel in a more conciliatory tone. "Of course we trust you; it's just that we want to avoid things getting complicated."

"They won't," I said. "But I still want to experience life as a teenager."

"We just have to be careful." Gabriel reached out to give my hand a squeeze. "We've been entrusted with a task that is much more important than our individual desires."

Put like that he had a point. Why was he so irritatingly wise? And why was it so impossible to stay mad at him?

I felt much more relaxed at home. In a short time we'd already made the place our own. We were manifesting a typically human trait—to personalize and identify with a space—and home felt like a sanctuary after the day we'd had.

Even Gabriel, although he would have been loath to admit it, was starting to enjoy living here. We were rarely bothered by the doorbell ringing (the house's imposing façade seemed to deter visitors), so once inside we were free to pursue our own interests.

Although I'd been eager to get home, I now found myself at a loss as to how I should be occupying my time. It was all right for Gabriel and Ivy. They were always absorbed in a book, playing the baby grand, or up to their elbows in flour in the kitchen. Without a hobby of my own, I was left to wander aimlessly around the house. I decided to focus on domestic chores for a while. I brought in a load of laundry and folded it before putting the kettle on. The house smelled a little musty from being shut up all day, so I opened some windows and cleared the clutter on the dining table. I picked sprigs of pungent pine from the yard and arranged them in a slender vase. I noticed there was some junk mail in the mailbox and made a mental note to purchase one of the No Junk Mail stickers I'd seen displayed on some of the other mailboxes in the street. I glanced at one of the leaflets before dropping them into the trash and saw that a new sports store had opened in town. It was called, rather unoriginally, I thought, SportsMart, and was advertising its opening sale.

It felt strange to be carrying out ordinary tasks when my whole existence was so far from ordinary. I wondered what other seventeen-year-old girls were doing at that moment—cleaning their bedrooms at the behest of frustrated parents, listening to their favorite bands on their iPods, sending each other text messages to make plans for the weekend, checking their e-mails when they should be studying?

We'd been given homework in at least three subjects and I'd written it down diligently in my school planner, unlike many of my fellow students who seemed happy to rely on memory. I told myself I should start it now in order to be prepared for the following day, but I knew that it would take hardly any time and was unlikely to pose any intellectual challenge. In short, it would be drop-dead easy. I'd know the answer to any question asked, so going through the motions of homework seemed like a tedious waste of time. Nevertheless, I hauled my school bag up to my room. My bedroom was the loft at the very top of the stairs, facing the sea. Even with the windows shut you could hear the sound of waves crashing over rocks. There was a narrow lacework balcony with a wicker chair and table that looked out over the sea where boats bobbed rhythmically on the water. I sat there for a while, highlighter in hand, my psychology textbook open in front of me on a page titled, "Galvanic Skin Response."

I desperately needed to keep my mind occupied, if for no other reason than to stop thinking about my encounters with Bryce Hamilton's school captain. Everything seemed to stay with me—his piercing eyes and his tie slightly askew. Molly's words kept echoing in my mind: *I wouldn't go for him if I were you. . . . He's got baggage.* But why was I so intrigued? As much as I wanted to shut him out of my mind, I couldn't seem to. I would make myself think of other things, but before long there he was again, his face floating across the page I was trying to read, the image of a smooth hand wearing a plaited leather wristband cutting across my thoughts. I wondered what Emily had been like; what it felt like to lose someone you loved.

I made a pretense of tidying my room before wandering down to the kitchen to offer Gabriel some help with dinner. He'd continued to surprise Ivy and me by throwing himself wholeheartedly into the task of cooking for us all. Part of his motivation was our well-being, but he also found the handling and preparation of food fascinating. Like music, it provided him with a creative outlet. When I walked in, he was standing at the white marble workbench, cleaning an assortment of mushrooms with a checked dish towel and occasionally frowning as he referred to a cookbook propped open on a metal stand. Soaking in a small bowl were what looked like pieces of black bark. Over his shoulder I read the title of the recipe: "Mushroom Risotto." It looked ambitious for a beginner, but then I reminded myself that this was the Archangel Gabriel. He excelled at everything without needing to practice.

"Hope you like mushrooms," he said, seeing the curiosity in my face.

"I guess we're about to find out," I replied, sitting down at the table. I liked watching Gabriel work and was always struck by the deftness and precision of his movements. Under his touch, ordinary things seemed transformed. The transition from angel to human had been much smoother for Gabe and Ivy; they seemed removed from the trivialities of life, but at the same time seemed to know exactly what they were doing. They were used to being able to sense each other in the Kingdom, a skill that had followed them on our mission. They found me much trickier to read and it worried them.

"Would you like some tea?" I asked, wanting to make some kind of contribution. "Where's Ivy?"

She walked in just at that moment, wearing linen pants and a tank top, her hair damp from the shower. Already there was something different about my sister. She had lost some of her dreaminess, and there was a purpose in her face I hadn't seen before. She seemed to have other things on her mind, because as soon as I'd poured the tea, she excused herself from our company. I'd also caught sight of her recently scribbling page upon page in a notebook.

"Is Ivy okay?" I asked Gabriel once she'd gone.

"She just wants to get things rolling," he said. I didn't know or ask exactly how Ivy planned to do this, but I was envious of her sense of purpose. When would I discover mine? When would I have the satisfaction of knowing I'd done something really worthwhile?

"Get things rolling how?"

"You know your sister's never short on ideas. She'll come up with something." Was Gabriel being deliberately mysterious? Did he realize how much in the dark I felt?

"What should I do?" I asked, hating the way I sounded so petulant.

"That will come to you," said my brother. "Give yourself some time."

"And in the meantime?"

"Didn't you say you wanted to experience being a teenager?"

He gave me an encouraging smile, and as always, my unease dissolved.

I peered into the bowl with the black strips floating in gritty liquid.

"Is this bark part of the recipe?"

"Those are porcini mushrooms—they need soaking before you can use them."

"Mmm . . . they look delicious," I lied.

"They're considered a delicacy. Don't worry, you'll love them."

I passed Gabriel his mug of tea and continued to entertain myself by watching him. I gasped when the sharp paring knife he was using slipped from his grasp, slicing open the top of his index finger. The sight of blood shocked me—a frightening reminder of how vulnerable our bodies were. Warm, crimson blood was so human and seeing it spill from my brother's hand seemed so unnatural. But Gabriel hadn't even flinched. He just brought his bleeding finger to his mouth and when he withdrew it any trace of injury had disappeared. He washed his hands with the soap from the dispenser on the sink and went back to his methodical slicing.

I picked up a piece of celery that was destined for the salad and chewed absently on it. Celery, I decided, must be more about texture than taste as it didn't really have much flavor, but it was certainly crunchy. Why anyone would eat it voluntarily was beyond me, apart from its nutritional value. Good nutrition meant a healthier body and a longer life. Humans were inordinately afraid of death, but I supposed we couldn't expect anything else from them given their lack of knowledge about what lay beyond. They would find out in due course that there was nothing to fear.

Gabriel's dinner turned out to be the usual success. Even Ivy, who took no real pleasure in food, was impressed.

"Another culinary triumph," she said after the first forkfull.

"Amazing flavors," I added. Food was just another wonder the earth had to offer. I couldn't help marveling at how every food could have such a different texture and flavor—bitter, sour, salty, creamy, tangy, sweet, spicy—sometimes more than one at the same time. Some of them I liked and some made me want to wash my mouth out—but everything was a unique experience.

Gabriel modestly dismissed our praise, and talk turned once again to the events of the day.

"Well, that's one day down. I think it went well, although I hadn't expected to find so many musical students."

"I think you'll find a lot of them developed an interest in music once they saw you." Ivy said with a smile.

"Well, at least it gives me something to work on," Gabe replied. "If they can find beauty in music, they can find beauty in one another and the world too."

"But aren't you bored in class?" I asked Gabe. "I mean, you already have access to all human knowledge."

"I expect he wasn't really concentrating on the content," Ivy said. "He would have been trying to pick up on other things." Sometimes my sister had an infuriating way of speaking in riddles she just expected everyone else to understand.

"Well, I was bored," I persisted. "Especially in chemistry. I've decided it really isn't *my thing*." Gabriel gave a low chuckle at my choice of words.

"Well, you'll just have to find out what is *your thing*. Try things out and see what you like best."

"I like literature," I said. "We started watching the film version of *Romeo and Juliet* today."

I didn't tell them this, but the love story fascinated me. The way the lovers fell so deeply and irrevocably in love after their first meeting sparked a burning curiosity in me about what human love might feel like.

"How are you finding that?" Ivy asked.

"It's very powerful, but the teacher got really mad when one of the boys said something about Lady Capulet."

"What did he say?"

"He called her a MILF, which must be offensive because Miss Castle called him a thug and sent him out of the room. Gabe, what is a MILF?"

Ivy smothered her smile behind a napkin while Gabriel did something I'd never seen before. He blushed and shifted uncomfortably in his chair.

"Some acronym for a teenage obscenity, I imagine," he mumbled.

"Yes, but do you know what it means?"

He paused, trying to find the right words.

"It's a term used by adolescent males to describe a woman who is both attractive and a mother." He cleared his throat and got up quickly to refill the water jug.

"I'm sure it must stand for something," I pressed.

"It does," Gabriel said. "Ivy, can you remember what it is?"

"I believe it stands for 'mother I'd like to . . . befriend,'" said my sister.

"Is that all?" I exclaimed. "What a fuss over nothing. I really think Miss Castle needs to *chill*."

{ 5 }

Small Miracles

WITH dinner over and the dishes washed, Gabriel took a book out onto the veranda even though the light was already fading, while Ivy continued to clean, wiping down surfaces that already looked immaculate. She was starting to come across as obsessive in her desire for cleanliness, but it might have just been her way of feeling closer to home. I looked around the room for something I could do. In the Kingdom time didn't exist and therefore didn't need to be filled. Finding things to do was very important on earth; it was what gave life purpose.

Gabriel must have sensed my unease because he seemed to change his mind about reading and poked his head back through the door.

"Why don't we all go for a walk and watch the sunset?" he suggested.

"Great idea." I felt my mood lift immediately. "You coming, Ivy?"

"Not until I go upstairs and get us something warmer to wear," she said. "It gets very cold in the evening."

I rolled my eyes at her display of caution. I was the only

one who got cold, and I'd already put my coat on. Ivy and Gabriel had trained their bodies to maintain normal temperature on previous visits, but I still had a long way to go.

"You're not even going to feel the cold," I objected.

"That's not the point. We may be seen not feeling the cold and draw attention."

"Ivy's right," said Gabe. "Best to play it safe." He disappeared upstairs, returning with two bulky jackets.

Our house was set high on the hill, so we had to meander our way down a series of sandy wooden steps before reaching the beach. The steps were so narrow that we had to walk single file. I couldn't help thinking how much more convenient it would be if we could just release our wings and swoop down to the sand below. I didn't articulate my thought to either Gabriel or Ivy, certain of the lecture that would follow if I did. I knew how dangerous flight was under the circumstances, a surefire way of blowing our cover. So we took mortal steps, all one hundred and seven of them, before reaching the shore.

I threw off my shoes to savor the feel of the silky grains beneath my feet. There was so much to notice on earth. Even the sand was complex, shifting in color and texture and quite iridescent in places where the sun hit it. Aside from the sand, I noticed that the beach held other small treasures: pearly shells, fragments of glass worn smooth by the motion of the water, the occasional half-buried sandal or an abandoned shovel, and tiny white crabs that scuttled in and out of little pea-size holes in the rock pools. Being so close to the ocean was thrilling for the senses—it seemed to roar like a living thing, filling my mind with noise that subsided and reared up again unexpectedly. The sound hurt my ears, and the sharp, salty air scratched my throat and nose. The wind whipping against my cheeks left them pink and stinging. But I was growing to love every minute of it—every part of being human brought with it some new sensation.

We walked along the shore, chased by the frothy waves of the tide coming in. Despite my recent resolve to exercise greater self-control, I couldn't resist the sudden impulse to splash Ivy with my foot. I watched to see whether she might be annoyed, but she only checked to see that Gabriel was far enough ahead not to notice before aiming a retaliatory kick in my direction. It sent an arc of water into the air, which scattered like jewels over my head. Our laughter drew Gabriel's attention, and he shook his head in wonder at our antics. Ivy winked at me and gestured in his direction. I knew what she had in mind and was more than happy to comply. Gabriel hardly noticed the extra weight when I jumped on his back and wrapped my arms around his neck. Supporting my weight with ease, he began running along the beach so fast the wind made a whistling noise in my ears. On his back I felt more like my old self again. I felt closer to Heaven and could almost believe I was flying.

Gabriel stopped abruptly and I let go of him, landing with a thud on the wet sand. He picked up some slimy strips of seaweed and lobbed them at Ivy, hitting her squarely in the face. She wrinkled her nose as the taste of the salty, bitter tendrils filled her mouth.

"Just you wait," she spluttered. "You're going to regret that!"

"I don't think so," Gabriel teased. "You'd have to catch me first."

At sunset there were still a few people on the main beach, catching the last weak rays of the day before the icy wind sprang up, just as Ivy had predicted, or quietly enjoying picnic dinners. A mother and child were packing up nearby. The child, who couldn't have been more than five or six, ran up to her mother tearfully. There was a swelling on her tiny plump arm, probably the result of an insect bite, which she had further inflamed by rubbing. The child cried even harder while her mother rummaged helplessly in her bag for some ointment. She brought out a tube of aloe gel but couldn't calm her wriggling daughter enough to actually apply it.

The mother looked grateful as Ivy bent to comfort the child. "That's a nasty bite," she crooned softly.

The sound of her voice soothed the girl instantly, and she stared up at Ivy as if she were someone she'd known all her life. Ivy opened the tube and dabbed some ointment on the inflamed skin. "This should help," she said. The child stared at her in awe, and I saw her eyes flicker to the space above her head, where her halo was. It was usually only visible to us. Was it possible that the little girl, with a child's heightened awareness, may have sensed Ivy's aura?

"Feel better?" Ivy asked.

"Much better," the girl agreed. "Did you use magic?"

Ivy laughed. "I have a magic touch."

"Thanks for your help," said the young mother, watching in confusion as the redness and swelling on her child's arm faded before her eyes until there was nothing but smooth, unblemished skin. "That's some gel."

"You're welcome," said Ivy. "Amazing what science can do these days."

Without lingering further, we moved on down the beach toward the township.

By the time we reached the main street, it was about nine o'clock, but there were still people around even though it was a weeknight. The town center was a quaint place, full of antique shops and cafés that served tea and iced cakes on mismatched china. The shops had all closed save for the one pub and the ice cream parlor. We had barely walked a few feet when I heard a high-pitched voice calling out, carried over the chords of the banjo-playing busker on the street corner.

"Beth! Over here."

At first I didn't even realize that the person was calling out to me. Nobody had ever called me Beth before. The name I was given in the Kingdom had never been modified; it was always Bethany. There was an intimacy about "Beth" that I liked. Ivy and Gabriel froze in unison. When I turned back, I saw Molly with a group of friends sitting on a bench outside the ice cream parlor. She was wearing a backless halter dress, which was completely inappropriate given the weather, and was perched on the lap of a boy with sun-bleached hair and tropical board shorts. His broad hands were stroking her bare back in long rhythmic strokes. Molly waved frantically and beckoned me over. I glanced uncertainly at Ivy and Gabriel. They didn't look happy. This was exactly the sort of interaction they wanted to avoid, and I saw Ivy stiffen at the commotion Molly was making. But both she and Gabriel knew that to blatantly ignore her would contravene laws of courtesy.

"Aren't you going to introduce us to your friend, Bethany?" Ivy asked.

She placed a hand on my shoulder and guided me across to where Molly and her friends were sitting. The surfer looked peeved when Molly extricated herself from his grasp but was soon distracted, gawking unashamedly at Ivy, his jaw slack, his eyes taking in the symmetry of her body. When Molly saw my siblings up close, her face took on exactly the same awed look I'd seen all day at school. I waited for her to say something but she didn't speak. Instead she opened and closed her mouth like a fish, before recovering her composure enough to give a wobbly smile.

"Molly, this is Ivy, my sister, and my brother, Gabriel," I said quickly.

Molly's eyes traveled from Gabriel's face to Ivy's, and she only just managed to stammer a hello before coyly averting her eyes. This was something of a surprise. I had watched her all day talking freely with the boys at school, luring and teasing them with her charm, then flitting away like an exotic butterfly.

Gabriel greeted Molly in the same manner as he greeted all new acquaintances—with impeccable politeness and an expression that was friendly but distancing.

"Pleased to meet you," he said with a slight bow that seemed absurdly formal given the surroundings. Ivy was warmer and flashed Molly a kind smile. The poor girl looked like she'd just been hit by a ton of bricks.

Raucous shouts coming from down the street put an end to the awkwardness. The disturbance was caused by a group of burly young men coming out of the pub, so inebriated they were either unaware of the noise they were making or simply didn't care. Two were now circling each other with fists clenched and faces contorted, and it was clear that a brawl was about to break out. Some people who'd been enjoying an evening coffee outside now retreated into the safety of the pub. Gabriel stepped forward so that Molly, Ivy, and I were positioned safely behind him. One of the men, unshaven and with an untidy mass of black hair, swung at the other. There was a crack as a fist connected with a jaw. The other man lunged, tackling his opponent to the ground, while the others in their circle cheered and spurred them on.

A look of repulsion flitted across Gabriel's usually impassive face. He strode purposefully away from us toward the center of the scuffle. The onlookers were confused, wondering what this third party was doing there. Gabriel took hold of the dark-haired man and pulled him easily to his feet, despite the man's weight. He hauled his companion, whose lip was already puffy and oozing blood, up from the ground and stood between them. One of them swung at Gabriel, but he intercepted the punch midair, his expression unchanged. Enraged by the interference, the two men joined forces and now directed their combined anger at Gabriel. They swung wildly at him, but every punch failed to find its mark. Yet, Gabriel had not moved. Eventually both men tired and slumped to the ground, their chests heaving from the effort.

"Go home," Gabriel said, his voice resonating like a crack of thunder. It was the first time he had spoken to them and the authority in his voice had a sobering effect. They lingered a moment or two, as if weighing up their decision, then staggered off, steadied by their friends and still swearing under their breaths.

"Wow, that was amazing," Molly gushed when Gabriel returned to us. "How did you do that? Are you like a karate expert or something?"

Gabriel shrugged off the attention. "I'm a pacifist," he said. "There's no honor in violence."

Molly struggled to come up with an adequate response.

"Well . . . do you wanna hang out with us?" she said eventually. "The mint-chocolate-chip ice cream here is to die for. Here, Beth, have a taste. . . ."

Before I could object, she leaned over and shoved her outstretched spoon into my mouth. Immediately something cold and slippery began dissolving on my tongue. It seemed to be shifting shape—transforming from velvety solid to liquid that trickled down my throat. The cold made my head ache and I swallowed as quickly as I could.

"It's great," I said truthfully.

"Told you," said Molly. "Here, let me get you some. . . ."

"I'm afraid we have to get home," Gabriel cut in, rather brusquely.

"Oh . . . right, sure," said Molly.

I felt for her as she tried to hide her disappointment.

"Maybe some other time," I suggested.

"Sure thing," she said more hopefully, turning back to her friends. "See you tomorrow, Beth. Hey, wait, I almost forgot. I got you something." She dug into her bag and pulled out a tube of the Melon Sorbet lip gloss I had tried at school. "You said you liked it, so I got you some."

"Thanks, Molly," I stammered. I had just received my first earthly gift and was touched by her thoughtfulness. "That's so sweet of you."

"No big deal. Hope you like it."

No comments were made about my new friendship with Molly on our way home, although I saw Ivy and Gabriel exchange meaningful looks a few times. I was too tired by then to try and decipher what they meant.

Getting ready for bed that night, I stared at myself in the bathroom mirror that stretched across an entire wall. It had taken some getting used to—being able to see what I looked like. In the Kingdom we could see others but never our own image. Sometimes you caught a glimpse of yourself reflected in someone's eyes, but even then it was a blur, like an artist's rudimentary sketch that still lacked color and detail.

Having human form meant the sketch was fleshed out. I could see every hair, every pore, with perfect clarity. Compared with the other girls at Venus Cove, I knew I must look strange. My skin was alabaster pale while they still sported tans from the summer. My eyes were wide and brown; my pupils hugely dilated. Molly and her friends looked as if they never tired of experimenting with their hair, but mine was simply parted in the middle and fell in natural chestnut waves.

I had a full, coral-colored mouth, which, I was later to learn, could give the impression that I was sulking.

I sighed, pulled my hair into a loose knot on top of my head, and put on flannel pajamas with a black-and-white print of dancing cows. Even with my limited experience of the world, I seriously doubted any other girl in Venus Cove would be caught wearing something so unglamorous. Ivy had bought them for me and so far they were the most comfortable item of clothing I owned. Gabe had received a similar pair except with sailboats on them, but I had yet to see him wear his.

I went up to my room, grateful for its simple elegance. I especially liked the narrow French doors that lead to the tiny balcony. I liked to open them a crack and then lie under the muslin canopy and listen to the sounds of the sea. It was peaceful there, with the briny smell of the ocean wafting in and the sound of Gabriel playing the piano downstairs. I always drifted to sleep listening either to the strains of Mozart or the low murmur of my siblings' voices.

In bed I stretched luxuriously, relishing the feel of crisp sheets. I was surprised to find how inviting the prospect of sleep was, seeing as we didn't need a lot of it. I knew it would be the early hours of the morning before Ivy and Gabriel went to bed. But I had found the day full of new and unfamiliar interaction draining. I yawned and curled up on my side, my head still swimming with thoughts and questions that my exhausted body chose to ignore.

As I drifted in and out of sleep, I imagined a stranger coming quietly into my room. I felt his weight as he sat on the edge of my bed in silence. I was sure he was watching me as I slept, but I didn't dare open my eyes because I knew he would prove to be a figment of my imagination and I wanted the illusion to continue a little longer. The boy lifted his hand to brush a wisp of hair out of my eyes and then leaned to kiss my forehead. His kiss was like being touched by butterfly wings. I felt no alarm; I knew I could trust this stranger with my life. I heard him get up to close the doors to the balcony before turning to leave.

"Good night, Bethany," the voice of Xavier Woods whispered. "Sweet dreams."

"Good night, Xavier," I said dreamily, but when I opened my eyes I found the room was empty. Then my eyelids were too heavy to keep open, and the dim lamplight and the sound of the sea faded away as a deep and peaceful sleep overcame me.

{ 6 }

French Class

SOMEONE was calling my name. Even though I tried to ignore it, the voice persisted and I was forced to surface from the warm, shadowy depths of sleep.

"Wake up, sleepyhead!"

I opened my eyes and saw morning light spilling into the room like warm liquid gold. I squinted, sat up, and rubbed the sleep from my eyes. Ivy was standing at the foot of my bed with a cup in her hand.

"Try this, it's awful but it wakes you up."

"What is it?"

"Coffee—a lot of humans think they can't function properly without it."

I sat up and sipped at the bitter, black brew, resisting the urge to spit it out. I wondered how people could actually pay money to drink it, but it didn't take long for the caffeine to hit my bloodstream, and I had to admit that I did feel more alert.

"What time is it?" I asked.

"Time you were up."

"Where's Gabe?"

"I think he's gone for a run. He was up at five this morning."

"What's wrong with him?" I groaned, pushing back my covers reluctantly and sounding like a bona fide teenager.

I shook out my hair and ran a comb through it before washing my face and traipsing downstairs to the kitchen. Gabriel, back from his run, was cooking breakfast. He had just showered and combed his wet hair back from his forehead, which gave him a leonine look. He wore only a towel wrapped around his hips, and his taut body gleamed in the morning sun. His wings were contracted and looked like nothing more than a rippling line between his shoulder blades. He was standing by the stove, holding a stainless steel spatula.

"Pancakes or waffles?" he asked. He didn't have to turn around to determine who had come into the room.

"I'm actually not very hungry," I said apologetically. "I think I'll skip breakfast and have something later."

"No one leaves this house on an empty stomach." He sounded implacable on the subject. "So what'll it be?"

"It's too early, Gabe! Don't make me, I'll be sick!" I sounded like a child trying to get out of eating my Brussels sprouts.

Gabriel looked offended. "Are you suggesting my cooking makes people sick?"

Oops. I tried to rectify my mistake. "Of course not. I just . . ."

My brother put his hands on my shoulders and looked at me intently. "Bethany," he said, "do you know what happens when the human body isn't fueled properly?"

I shook my head irritably, knowing he was about to present facts I wouldn't be able to argue with.

"It can't function. You won't be able to concentrate and you might even feel light-headed." He paused to allow the impact of his words to register. "I don't think you want to faint on your second day of school, do you?"

This had the effect he hoped it would. I slumped unceremoniously into a chair, visualizing myself keeling over from lack of nutrition and a host of concerned faces looking down at me. Maybe even the face of Xavier Woods, suddenly wanting nothing to do with me.

"I'll have the pancakes," I said glumly, and Gabriel turned back to the stove with a satisfied look.

Breakfast was interrupted by the sound of the doorbell, and I wondered who could be calling at such an unconventional hour. We had been careful to steer clear of the neighbors and thwart any offers of friendship. We must have appeared stand-offish compared to the locals.

Ivy and I looked at Gabriel expectantly. He was able to sense the thoughts of those around him, a useful talent in many circumstances. Ivy's celestial gift was her healing hands. My gift was yet to be determined—apparently it would surface when the time was right.

"Who is it?" Ivy mouthed.

"The woman from next door," Gabriel said. "Ignore her, and she might go away."

We sat very still and silent, but our neighbor was not the type to be easily dissuaded. Gabriel left the kitchen and returned wearing a pair of freshly laundered jeans. A few minutes later we were surprised to hear the click of the side gate, and next thing we knew she was at the window, waving at us enthusiastically. I was outraged by the intrusion, but my siblings maintained their composure.

Gabriel went to open the door and came back followed by a woman somewhere in her fifties with platinum blond hair and a bronzed face. She was wearing a lot of gold jewelry, bright lipstick, and a velour tracksuit. Tucked under her arm was a large paper bag. She looked dazed for a moment when she saw all three of us together. I couldn't blame her; it must have been an unnerving sight.

"Hello there," she said in a bright voice with a Southern drawl, leaning across the table to shake our hands. "I'd check out that doorbell if I were you—it doesn't seem to be workin'. I'm Dolores Henderson from next door."

Gabriel took care of the introductions, and Ivy, ever the perfect hostess, offered her a cup of tea or coffee and set a plate of muffins on the table. I saw Mrs. Henderson eyeing Gabriel in much the same way as the girls at school had.

"Oh, no, thank you," she said in response to the offer of food. "I'm watching my caloric intake. I just wanted to pop over and say hello now that you're all settled in." She set the paper bag down on the countertop. "Thought you might enjoy some homemade jam, I've popped in an apricot as well as a fig and strawberry—I wasn't sure what you'd like."

"That's very kind of you, Mrs. Henderson." Ivy was all politeness, but I could see Gabriel bristling with impatience.

"Oh, call me Dolly," she said. "You'll find we're all like that around here—very neighborly."

"That's good to hear," Ivy said.

I marveled at how she seemed to have a ready response for every circumstance. As for me, a few moments later, I'd already forgotten the woman's name.

"You're the new music teacher at Bryce Hamilton, aren't you?" persisted Mrs. Henderson. "I have a very musical niece who is keen to take up the violin. That's your instrument, isn't it?"

"One of them," Gabriel replied distantly.

"Gabriel plays several instruments," said Ivy, flashing him an exasperated look.

"Several! Oh my, how talented you must be," Mrs. Henderson exclaimed. "I hear you playin' most nights from my porch. Are you two girls musical as well? What a good brother you are to take care of your sisters with your parents away."

Ivy sighed, the news of our arrival and our personal story seemed to have become town gossip very quickly.

"Will your folks be joinin' you anytime soon?" Mrs. Henderson asked, looking around nosily, as if expecting a set of parents to jump out of the cupboards or drop from the ceiling.

"We hope to see them soon," Gabriel said, his eyes flicking to the clock.

Dolores waited expectantly for him to elaborate, and when he didn't, she pursued another line of questioning. "Do you know anyone in town yet?" It amused me to watch how the more she tried prying information out of him, the less forthcoming Gabriel became.

"We haven't had much time for socializing," said Ivy. "We've been quite busy."

"No time for socializing!" Mrs. Henderson cried. "Good-lookin' young things like you! We're gonna have to do somethin' about that. There are some very *hip* clubs in town; I'll have to introduce you to them."

"I look forward to it," said Gabriel tonelessly.

"Look, Mrs. Henderson . . . ," Ivy began, realizing that the conversation was not about to wind up any time soon.

"Dolly."

"Sorry, *Dolly*, but we are in a bit of a hurry to get to school."

"Of course you are. How silly of me to prattle on. Now, if you need anythin', don't hesitate to ask. You'll find we're a very tight little community here."

BECAUSE of Dolly's "pop in" I missed the first half of English, and Gabe found his class of seventh graders enter-taining themselves by throwing stationery at the ceiling fan. I had a free period next so I caught up with Molly at the lockers. She touched her cheek to mine by way of greeting and then gave me a rundown of last night's adventures on Facebook while I unpacked my books. Apparently a boy named Chris had signed off with more hugs and kisses than usual, and Molly was theorizing on whether or not it marked a new phase in their relationship. The Agents of Light had cleared our home of any "distracting" technologies, so I didn't know much about what Molly was talking about. But I managed to nod at regular intervals, and she seemed not to notice my ignorance.

"How can you tell what someone's really feeling online?" I asked.

"That's why we have emoticons, silly," Molly explained. "But you still don't want to read too much into things. Do you know what today's date is?" Molly, I was discovering, had a disconcerting habit of jumping from one topic to another without warning.

"It's March sixth," I said.

Molly pulled out a pink pocket diary and, with an excited squeal, crossed off the day with a feathery tipped pen.

"Only seventy-two days to go," she said, her face flushed with excitement.

"Until?" I asked.

She looked at me in disbelief.

"Until the prom, you loser! I've never looked forward to anything more in my life." Ordinarily I would have been offended by her use of the word *loser*, but it hadn't taken me long to realize that the girls around here used insults as a form of endearment.

"Isn't it a little early to be thinking about that?" I suggested. "It's more than two months away."

"Yeah, I know, but it's *the* social event of the year. People start planning for it early."

"Why?"

"Are you for real?" Molly's eyes widened. "It's a rite of passage, the one event you'll remember your whole life, apart from maybe your wedding. It's the whole shebang—limos, outfits, hot partners, dancing. It's our one night to act like princesses." It occurred to me that some of them already behaved like that on a daily basis, but I refrained from commenting.

"It sounds fun," I said. In reality, the whole thing sounded ridiculous, and I resolved on the spot to avoid it at all costs. I could just imagine how strongly Gabriel would disapprove of such an event, with its emphasis on vanity and all things shallow.

"Any idea who you want to go with?" Molly nudged me suggestively.

"Not yet," I dodged. "How about you?"

"Well," Molly lowered her voice. "Casey told Taylah that she overheard Josh Crosby telling Aaron Whiteman that Ryan Robertson is thinking of asking me!"

"Wow," I said, trying to pretend like I'd understood a word of what she'd said. "That sounds great."

"I know, right!" Molly squealed. "But don't tell anyone. I don't want to jinx it."

She grinned and circled a date in mid-May in my school planner, drawing a big red heart around it before I could stop her. She handed it back and tossed her own into the mess of her locker. There were books piled haphazardly, posters of famous bands taped to the inside walls, empty snack wrappers, a half-finished bottle of diet soda, and an assortment of lip glosses and tins of mints littering the bottom. In striking contrast, my books were arranged in a neat row, my blazer was pegged on the hook provided, and my color-coded class schedule was taped neatly inside my locker door. I didn't know how to be messy like a human; every instinct in me screamed for order. The proverb that "cleanliness is next to Godliness" couldn't have been more accurate.

I followed Molly to the cafeteria, where we frittered away time until she had to go to math and I to French. But first

I needed to detour back to my locker to collect my French books, which were big and cumbersome. I stacked them on top of my folder while I bent to retrieve my English-French dictionary, which was wedged at the back.

"Hey, stranger," said a voice behind me. I was startled and jumped up so fast that I hit my head on the roof of my locker. "Careful!" the voice said.

I spun around to find Xavier Woods standing there with the same half-smile on his face that I remembered from our first meeting. Today he was dressed in a sports uniform—dark blue track pants, white polo top, and a track jacket in the school colors slung over his shoulder. I rubbed the top of my head and stared at him, wondering why he was talking to me.

"Sorry I scared you," he said. "Are you okay?"

"I'm perfectly fine," I replied, surprised to find myself once again dazzled by his striking looks. His turquoise eyes were fixed on me, his eyebrows half raised. He was standing close enough this time for me to notice that his eyes were flecked with streaks of copper and silver. He ran a hand through the hair that flopped over his forehead, framing his face.

"You're new to Bryce Hamilton, aren't you? We didn't get much of a chance to talk yesterday."

I couldn't think of a single thing to say in response, so I nodded and focused on my shoes. Looking up was a huge mistake. Meeting his gaze caused the same intense physical reaction I'd had last time. I felt as if I were falling from a great height.

"I hear you've been living overseas," he continued, undeterred by my silence. "What's a well-traveled girl like you doing in a backwater town like Venus Cove?"

"I'm here with my brother and sister," I mumbled.

"Yeah, I've seen them around," he said. "Hard to miss, aren't they?" He hesitated a moment. "So are you."

I could feel myself starting to blush and I backed away from him. I felt so feverish that I was sure I must be radiating heat.

"I'm late for French," I said, snatching up the closest books I could find and half stumbling along the corridor.

"The language center's the other way," he called after me, but I didn't turn back.

When I did eventually find the right room, I was relieved that our teacher had also only just arrived. Mr. Collins, who didn't look or sound very French to me, was a tall, lanky man with a beard. He was wearing a tweed jacket and cravat.

It was a small classroom and almost full. I glanced around for the closest empty seat and stifled a gasp when I saw the person who was sitting right next to it. My heart somersaulted in my chest as I moved toward him. I took a breath and steadied my nerves. He was just a boy, after all.

Xavier Woods looked mildly amused as I took my seat beside him. I tried my best to ignore him and focused on opening my textbook to the page Mr. Collins had written on the blackboard.

"You're going to have some trouble learning French from that," I heard Xavier murmur in my ear. I realized with a flood of embarrassment that in my confusion I had picked up the wrong book. In front of me lay not my French grammar book but one on the French Revolution. I felt my cheeks flush scarlet for the second time in less than five minutes, and I leaned forward, attempting to conceal them with my hair.

"Miss Church," Mr. Collins called out, "would you please read aloud the first passage on page ninety-six titled: À la bibliothèque."

I froze. I couldn't believe I was going to have to announce to everyone that I had brought along the wrong books to the very first class. How incompetent would I seem? I opened my mouth to begin an apology just as Xavier slid his book inconspicuously across the desk toward me.

I gave him a grateful look and began to read the passage with ease, although I'd never read or spoken the language before. That was just the way it was with us—we only needed to start something before we excelled at it. By the time I was finished, Mr. Collins had come to stand beside our desk. My reading had been fluent—too fluent. I realized that I should have mispronounced a few words or at least stumbled once or twice, but it hadn't occurred to me to do so. Maybe part of me was trying to show off in front of Xavier Woods to make up for my previous clumsiness.

"You're as fluent as a native speaker, Miss Church. Have you lived in France?"

"No, sir."

"Visited perhaps?"

"Unfortunately, no."

I glanced across at Xavier, whose raised eyebrows indicated he was impressed.

"We must put it down to natural ability then. You might be happier in the advanced class," Mr. Collins suggested.

"No!" I said, not wanting to attract any more attention and wishing Mr. Collins would let the matter drop. I vowed to be less perfect next time. "I've still got plenty to learn," I assured him. "Pronunciation is my strong point, but grammatically I'm all over the place."

Mr. Collins seemed satisfied with that explanation. "Woods, continue from where Miss Church left off," he said, then looked down at Xavier and pursed his lips. "Where's your textbook, Woods?"

I quickly passed the book back to him, but Xavier made no move to accept it.

"Sorry, sir, I forgot my books today; had a late one last night. Thanks for sharing, Beth."

I wanted to protest but Xavier's warning look silenced me. Mr. Collins glared at him, scribbled something in his notebook and muttered all the way back to his desk.

"Not setting much of an example as school captain. See me after class."

The lesson over, I waited outside for Xavier to finish with Mr. Collins. I felt I at least owed him a thank-you for saving me from embarrassment.

When the door opened Xavier strolled out as casually as someone taking a walk on the beach. He looked at me and smiled, pleased that I had waited for him. I was supposed to be meeting Molly at morning break, but the thought floated into my head and straight out again. When he looked at me it was easy to forget to breathe.

"You're welcome and it was no big deal," he said before I could even open my mouth.

"How did you know what I was going to say?" I asked irritably. "What if I wanted to tell you off for getting yourself into trouble?"

He looked at me quizzically. "Are you angry?" he asked. There was that half-smirk again, playing around his lips, as if he was deciding whether the situation was amusing enough to warrant a full smile.

Two girls walked past and looked daggers at me. The taller one waggled her fingers at Xavier.

"Hey, Xavier," she said in a syrupy voice.

"Hi, Lana," he replied in a friendly but dispassionate tone.

It seemed obvious to me that he had no interest in talking to her, but Lana didn't seem to notice.

"How'd you do on the math test?" she persisted. "I thought it was *sooooooo* hard. I think I might need a tutor."

I couldn't help but notice the way Xavier looked at her—blankly, like someone might look at the screen of a computer. Lana was chatting away and arching her back so that Xavier could get the full effect of her curvaceous figure. Any other boy would have been unable to resist giving her body an appreciative appraisal, but Xavier's eyes didn't move from her face.

"I think I did okay," he said. "Marcus Mitchell does tutoring; you should ask him if you really think you need it." Lana's eyes narrowed in annoyance at having given so much and received so little.

"Thanks," she snapped before flouncing away.

Xavier didn't seem to notice that he had offended her, or if he did, he wasn't perturbed by it. He turned back to me with a very different expression. His face was serious as if he were trying to solve some sort of puzzle. I tried not to feel a rush of pleasure at this; he probably looked at lots of girls in the same way, and Lana was just an unlucky exception. I remembered what I'd been told about Emily and scolded myself for being so conceited as to think he was showing interest in me.

Before our conversation could resume, Molly spotted us with a look of surprise. She approached cautiously, looking a little worried that she might be interrupting something.

"Hi, Molly," Xavier said when it became apparent that she wasn't going to initiate conversation.

"Hi," she replied briskly and gave my sleeve a proprietary tug. When she spoke, it was in the wheedling voice of a small child. "Beth, come to the cafeteria with me—I'm practically dying of starvation! And after school on Friday I want you to come back to my place—we're all getting facials from Taylah's sister, who's a beautician. It's going to be awesome. She always brings lots of samples so we can do our own at home."

"That does sound awesome," said Xavier with a feigned enthusiasm that made me giggle. "What time should I come over?"

Molly ignored him.

"Will you come, Beth?"

"I have to ask Gabriel and let you know," I said. I saw a look of surprise cross Xavier's face. Was it the idea of a night spent having facials or my need to ask my sibling for permission that puzzled him?

"Ivy and Gabriel are welcome to come too," Molly said, her voice picking up.

"I'm not sure it would be their cup of tea." I saw Molly's face fall and added quickly, "But I'll ask anyway."

She beamed at me.

"Thanks. Hey, can I ask you something?" She glared at Xavier who was still standing there. "In private?"

He raised his hands in mock defeat and walked away. I resisted the urge to call him back. Molly's voice dropped to a low whisper. "Has Gabriel . . . um . . . said anything about me?"

Neither Gabriel nor Ivy had mentioned Molly since our encounter at the ice cream parlor, except to repeat their general warning about the danger of making friends. But I knew from her tone that she was captivated by Gabriel, and I didn't want to disappoint her. "Actually, yes," I said, hoping I sounded convincing. There was only one circumstance when lying was permitted: in order to avoid causing someone unnecessary pain. But even then it didn't come easily.

"Really?" Molly's face lit up.

"Of course," I said, thinking that, technically, I hadn't really lied. Gabriel *had* mentioned Molly, just not in the context she hoped for. "He said it was good to see I'd found such a nice friend."

"He said that? I can't believe he even noticed me. He's so gorgeous! Beth, sorry, I know he's your brother and all, but he is seriously hot."

In an elated mood Molly took my arm and pulled me in the direction of the cafeteria. Xavier was there, sitting with a table of athletes. This time when our eyes met, I held his gaze. As I looked at him, I felt my mind go completely blank and I couldn't think about anything except his smile—that perfect, endearing smile that made his eyes crinkle ever so slightly at the corners.

Partay

MOLLY hadn't failed to notice my interest in Xavier Woods and decided to offer some unsolicited advice. "I really don't think he's your type," she said, twirling her curls around her fingers as we stood in line at the cafeteria.

I was standing close to her in order to avoid being jostled by students eager to reach the counter. The two careworn teachers who were on duty tried to overlook the pandemonium around them. They kept sneaking looks at the clock and counting down the minutes before they could return to the sanctuary of the staff room.

I tried to ignore the elbows digging into me, as well as the sticky patches on the floor from spilled drinks, and listen to what Molly was saying.

"Who are you talking about?" I said.

She gave me a shrewd look that said she was unconvinced by my naïve act. "I admit Xavier is one of the hottest guys at school, but everyone knows he's trouble. The girls that try only end up brokenhearted. Don't say you weren't warned."

"He doesn't seem deliberately cruel," I said, overcome by

a desire to defend him even though I knew next to nothing about him.

"Look, Beth, falling for Xavier is only going to get you hurt. That's just the truth."

"What makes you such an expert on him?" I asked. "Was yours one of the hearts that got broken?"

I had asked the question in jest, but Molly's face was suddenly serious. "You could say that."

"I'm sorry. I had no idea. What happened?"

"Well, I liked him for ages and finally got sick of dropping hints, so I asked him out." She said it offhandedly as if it had happened a long time ago and no longer mattered.

"And?" I prompted.

"And nothing." She shrugged. "He turned me down. He was polite about it, told me he saw me as a friend. But it was still the single, most humiliating moment of my life."

I couldn't tell Molly that what she'd described didn't sound so bad. In fact, Xavier's conduct could have been seen as honest, even honorable. When Molly had talked about broken hearts she'd made him sound like some kind of villain. All he'd really done was decline an invitation in the best way he knew how. But I'd learned enough so far about female friendship to know that sympathy was the only acceptable response.

"It's not right," Molly continued accusingly. "He walks around looking gorgeous, being friendly to everyone, but won't let anyone get close to him."

"But does he mislead girls into thinking he wants more than friendship?" I asked.

"No," she admitted, "but it's still completely unfair. How

can anyone be too busy for a girlfriend? I know it sounds harsh, but he has to move on from Emily sometime. It's not like she's coming back. Anyway, enough about Mr. Perfect. I hope you can make it to my place on Friday—it'll take our minds off annoying boys."

"THE point of us being here isn't to socialize," said Gabriel when I asked permission to go to Molly's on Friday.

"But it would be rude of me not to go," I objected. "Besides, it's Friday night—no school the day after."

"Go if you wish, Bethany," said my brother with a sigh. "I would have thought there'd be more profitable ways to spend an evening, but it's not for me to prevent you."

"It's just this once," I said. "I won't be making a habit of it."

"I should hope not." ·

I didn't like the implication behind his words and the subtle suggestion that I was already losing focus. But I didn't let that ruin my mood—I wanted to experience all facets of human life. After all, it might give me a better understanding of our mission.

By seven o'clock I had showered and changed into a fitted green wool dress. I teamed the dress with ankle boots and dark tights and even put on some of the lip gloss Molly had given me. I was pleased with the result; I looked a little less like my usual pale self.

"There's no need to dress up, you're not going to a ball," Gabriel said when he saw me.

"A girl must always endeavor to look her best," Ivy said in my defense and gave me a wink. She might not have been pleased about my plans to spend time with Molly and her gang, but she wasn't the type to harbor a grudge. She knew when to let things go in order to keep the peace.

I kissed them both good-bye and headed out the front door. Gabriel had wanted to drive me over to Molly's in the black Jeep that we'd found parked in the garage, but Ivy had managed to talk him out of it, telling him there was plenty of daylight left and it was perfectly safe as Molly's house was only streets away. I accepted Gabriel's offer to pick me up, though, and agreed to call when I was ready to come home.

I felt a rush of pleasure walking to Molly's that night. Winter was drawing to a close, but the breeze ruffling my dress was still chilly. I breathed in the clean scent of the ocean coupled with the smell of crisp evergreens. I felt privileged to be there, walking on the earth, a breathing, sentient being. It was so much more exhilarating than observing life from another dimension. Looking down from Heaven on the teeming life below was like watching a show. Being on the actual stage might be more frightening, but it was also more thrilling.

My mood changed when I got to 8 Sycamore Grove. I looked up at the house, thinking I must have copied the number down wrong. The front door was wide-open and it seemed that every light inside was on. Music boomed from the front room and scantily dressed teenagers swaggered out onto the front porch. This couldn't be it. I checked the address that Molly herself had written on a slip of paper and saw that I hadn't made a mistake. Then I recognized some faces from school and a few people waved to me. I headed up the steps of the bungalow-style house and almost bumped into a boy retching over the side of the veranda.

I considered turning and going straight home, inventing a headache as an excuse for Ivy and Gabriel. I knew they would never have allowed me to come had they known what Molly's "girls" night really involved. But my curiosity prevailed, and I decided to go inside just long enough to say hello to Molly and offer my apologies before making a rapid exit.

There was a crush of bodies in the front hallway, which was pungent with smoke and cologne. The music was so loud people had to shout into each other's ears to be heard. The shaking floor and the lurching dancers made me feel like I was trapped in the middle of an earthquake. The driving beat was so loud it shattered against my eardrums, making me cringe. I could feel hot breath on my cheeks, smell beer and bile in the air. The whole scene was so painfully overwhelming I was almost knocked off balance. But this was human life, I thought to myself, and I was determined to experience it firsthand even if it did make me feel ready to collapse. So I took a deep breath and pushed on.

There were young people in every corner and recess, some smoking, some drinking, and others just draped over each other. I wound my way through the crowd and watched in fascination a group playing a game that I heard someone call Treasure Hunt. It involved girls standing in a row while boys aimed marshmallows at their cleavages from an easy distance. Once successful they had to retrieve the marshmallows using only their mouths. The girls laughed and squealed as the boys burrowed their heads into their chests.

I couldn't see Molly's parents anywhere. They must have gone away for the weekend. I wondered how they'd react to seeing their home in its current state of mayhem. In the back living room, couples lay entwined in drunken affection on the brown leather couches. I could see empty beer bottles strewn on the floor, and the snacks of corn chips and M&M's that Molly had put out in glass bowls had been ground into the carpet. I spotted the familiar face of Leah Green, one of the girls from Molly's group, and made my way over to her. She was standing by glass doors that opened onto a wide deck area and a pool.

"Beth! You made it!" she shouted over the music. "Great party!"

"Have you seen Molly?" I shouted back.

"In the hot tub."

I squirmed out of the grasp of an inebriated boy who was trying to drag me into the mêlée of dancers and dodged another who called me "bro" and tried to give me a bear hug. A girl pulled him off me apologetically. "Sorry about Stefan," she yelled. "He's wasted already."

I nodded and slipped outside, making a mental note to add the new words to the glossary I was compiling.

More empty bottles and cans littered the ground outside, and I had to pick my way carefully around them. Despite the cold, teenagers in bikinis and shorts lounged by the pool and crowded the hot tub. The lights threw an eerie blue glow over the frolicking bodies. Suddenly a naked boy streaked past me and dived into the pool. He emerged shivering but looking pleased with the loud cheers he drew from the others. I tried not to look as horrified as I felt.

I felt a flood of relief when I finally located Molly sandwiched between two boys in the hot tub. Seeing me, she hoisted herself out, stretching like a cat, and lingered long enough for the boys to admire her wet, toned body.

"Bethie, when did you get here?" she said in a singsong voice.

"Just now," I said. "Has there been a change of plans? What happened to the facials?"

"Oh, babe, we ditched that idea!" Molly said as if this detail was of minor importance. "My auntie's sick, so Mom and Dad are out of town for the weekend. Couldn't pass on an opportunity to *partay*!"

"I've just come in to say hello. I can't stay," I said. "My brother thinks we're testing out face masks."

"Well, he isn't here, is he?" Molly grinned mischievously. "And what Brother Gabriel doesn't know can't hurt him. Come on, just have one drink before you head off. I don't want you in trouble because of me."

In the kitchen we met up with Taylah, who was standing behind the kitchen counter mixing something in a blender. An impressive array of bottles were scattered around her. I read a few of the labels: Caribbean white rum, single malt scotch, whiskey, tequila, absinthe, Midori, bourbon, champagne. The names didn't mean much to me. Alcohol had been omitted from my training—a gap in my education.

"Can I get two Taylah Specials for Beth and me?" Molly asked, draping her arms around her friend and swaying her hips in time to the music.

"Comin' right up," said Taylah, filling two cocktail glasses almost to the brim with a greenish brew.

Molly shoved one of the drinks into my hand and took a big gulp of her own. We made our way into the living room. The music was blaring so loudly from two colossal speakers positioned in the corners of the room that even the floor was vibrating. I sniffed my drink cautiously.

"What's in this?" I asked Molly over the din.

"It's a cocktail," she said. "Cheers!"

I took a swig out of politeness and regretted it instantly. It was sickly sweet but at the same time burned my throat. Determined not to be labeled a buzzkill, I continued sipping at the mixture. Molly was enjoying herself and led me into the seething mass of dancers. For a few minutes we danced together, and then I lost sight of her, and a throng of strangers closed in around me. I tried to find a gap in the bodies to worm through and escape, but the moment one appeared it closed up again just as quickly. Several times I noticed that each time my glass was empty it was refilled as if by invisible servers.

By now I was feeling light-headed and unsteady on my feet. I blamed it on my being unused to loud music and crowds. I sipped at my drink, hoping it would refresh me. Gabriel was always going on about the importance of keeping our bodies hydrated.

I was just finishing my third cocktail when I felt an over-whelming desire to sink down to the floor. But I didn't reach it. Instead, I felt a strong hand take hold of me and lead me away from the throng. The grip around my arm tightened when I stumbled. I let my weight be supported and allowed the stranger to guide me outside. There, I was helped onto a garden bench where I sat doubled over, still holding the empty glass.

"You might want to go easy on that stuff."

The face of Xavier Woods came slowly into focus. He was wearing faded jeans and a fitted long-sleeved gray top. It made his chest look broader than it appeared in his school uniform. I pushed the hair out of my eyes and felt that my forehead was damp with sweat.

"Go easy on what?"

"Um . . . what you're drinking . . . because it's pretty strong," he said as if stating the obvious.

The liquid was starting to churn in my stomach now and my head was throbbing. I knew I wanted to say something, but the words failed to form, interrupted by waves of nausea. Instead I leaned weakly against Xavier, feeling close to tears.

"Does your family know where you are?" he asked.

I shook my head, which made the garden spin dangerously.

"How much of that have you had to drink?"

"I don't know," I mumbled groggily. "But it doesn't seem to agree with me."

"Do you drink often?"

"This is my first time."

"Oh, jeez." Xavier shook his head. "That would explain why you're such a lightweight."

"A what . . ." I lurched forward, nearly tumbling onto the ground.

"Whoa." Xavier caught me. "I think I'd better drive you home."

"I'll be fine in a minute."

"No, you won't. You're shaking."

I realized with some surprise that he was right. Xavier went back inside for his jacket, which he placed around my shoulders. It smelled of him and was comforting.

Molly stumbled her way over to us.

"How's it going?" she said, too cheerful to be bothered by Xavier's presence.

"What was Beth drinking?" he demanded.

"Just a cocktail," Molly replied. "Mostly vodka. Aren't you feeling well, Beth?"

"No, she's not," said Xavier flatly.

"What can I get her?" Molly said, sounding at a loss.

"I'll make sure she gets home safely," he said, and even in my state I couldn't miss the accusatory tone.

"Thanks, Xavier, I owe you one. Oh, try not to say too much to her brother, he doesn't seem like the understanding type."

The smell of the leather seats in Xavier's car was soothing, but I still felt like there was a furnace burning inside of me. I was vaguely aware of a bumpy car trip and of being carried to the door. I was conscious enough to hear what was going on around me but too drowsy to keep my eyes open. They seemed to shut of their own volition.

Because my eyes were shut I didn't see the look on Gabriel's face when he opened the door. But I couldn't miss the alarm in his voice.

"What happened? Is she hurt?" I felt him cup my head in his hands.

"She's okay," Xavier said. "She just had too much to drink."

"Where was she?"

"At Molly's party."

"Party?" Gabriel echoed. "We weren't told anything about a party."

"It wasn't Beth's fault—I don't think she knew either."

I felt myself transferred into my brother's capable arms.

"Thank you for bringing her home," Gabriel said in a voice designed to curtail further discussion.

"No problem," said Xavier. "She was out of it for a while; she might need to be checked out."

There was a pause while Gabriel considered what to say. I knew there was no need to call for a doctor. Besides, a medical examination would reveal some anomalies that couldn't be explained. But Xavier didn't know that, so he waited for Gabriel's answer.

"We'll take care of her," Gabriel said.

It came out sounding wrong, as if he were trying to hide something. I wished he could have at least tried to sound more appreciative. Xavier had rescued me, after all. If it hadn't been for him seeing that I was in trouble, I would still be at Molly's and who knew what might have happened.

"Fair enough." I could hear suspicion in Xavier's voice and sensed a reluctance to leave. But there was no reason for him to stay. "Tell Beth I hope she feels better soon."

I heard Xavier's retreating footsteps crunching on the gravel drive and the sound of his car pulling out. The last thing I remembered was Ivy's cool hands stroking my forehead and her healing energy flooding my body.

Phantom

I had no idea what time it was when I woke. I was only aware
of the relentless pounding in my head and that my tongue felt
like sandpaper. It took a while before I could put the events
of the previous night into coherent order, but when I did,
I wished I hadn't. I felt a rush of shame as I remembered my
disoriented state, my slurred speech, my failure to support
my own weight. I remembered Gabriel gathering me into his
arms and the concern mingled with disappointment in his
voice. I remembered having to be undressed and the look of
dismay on Ivy's face as she put me to bed like a small child.
As Ivy pulled the covers over me, I heard Gabriel's reiterate
his thanks to someone at the door.

Then I started to remember spending most of the time at
Molly's party slumped helplessly against the comforting body
of a stranger. I groaned aloud when the stranger's face flashed
vividly in my mind. Of all the gallant knights who could have
come to my rescue, why did it have to be Xavier Woods? What
was Our Father in His infinite wisdom thinking? I struggled
to recall the fragments of our brief conversation, but memory
refused to volunteer such details.

I was overcome with a mixture of regret and humiliation. I buried my burning cheeks under the quilt and curled myself into a ball, hoping I could stay that way forever. What must Xavier Woods, the school captain of Bryce Hamilton, think of me now? What must everyone think of me? I had barely been at the school a week and already I had disgraced my family and proclaimed to the world that I was a novice at life. How could I have not realized how powerful those cocktails were? On top of it all, I had proved to my brother and sister that I was incapable of looking after myself outside of their care.

I heard muted voices floating up to me from downstairs. Gabriel and Ivy were discussing something in hushed tones. The burning returned to my cheeks as I thought of the position I had put them in. How selfish of me not to consider that my actions would impact on them as well! Their reputations were on the line as well as mine, and mine was now undoubtedly in tatters. I considered the possibility of us packing up and starting afresh in a new location. Surely Gabriel and Ivy wouldn't expect me to stay in Venus Cove after the spectacle I'd made of myself. I half expected that in a moment they would come in to announce the news and we would quietly pack our bags and move on to a new town. There would be no time for farewells; the attachments I'd formed here would be reduced to nothing more than fond memories.

But no one came, and eventually I had no choice but to venture downstairs and face the consequences of what I had done. I caught a glimpse of myself in a hallway mirror. I looked fragile and there were bluish shadows under my eyes. The clock told me it was close to noon.

Downstairs, Ivy was working skillfully on a piece of embroidery at the kitchen table and Gabriel was standing at the window as straight as a pastor at his pulpit. He had his hands clasped behind his back and was looking thoughtfully out to sea. I went to the fridge and poured myself a tumbler of orange juice, which I gulped quickly to slake my raging thirst.

Gabriel didn't turn even though I knew he was aware of my presence. I shivered—an angry tirade would have been better than this silent recrimination. I cared too much for Gabriel's regard to lose it. If nothing else, his anger would have helped ease my guilt. I wished he would turn around so I could at least see his face.

Ivy put down her handiwork and looked up at me. "How are you feeling?" she asked. She sounded neither angry nor disappointed, and that confused me.

My hands moved involuntarily to my still-throbbing temples. "I've been better."

Silence hung in the air like a shroud.

"I'm really sorry," I continued meekly. "I don't know how that happened. I feel so childish."

Gabriel turned to look at me, his eyes the color of thunder. But in them I saw only his deep affection for me.

"There's no need to fret, Bethany," he said with his usual composure. "Now that we're human we're bound to make some mistakes."

"You're not angry?" I blurted, looking from one to the

other. Their mother-of-pearl skin was incandescent in the morning light.

"Of course we're not angry," said Ivy. "How can we blame you for something that was beyond your control?"

"That's just the point," I said. "I should have known. It wouldn't have happened to either of you. Why is it only me that makes mistakes?"

"Don't be too hard on yourself," Gabriel advised. "Remember this is your first visit to earth. You will learn from your experiences and in time, you will be able to avoid such situations."

"It's easy to forget that people are blood and bone. They're not indestructible," Ivy added.

"I'll try to keep that in mind," I said, feeling a little heartened. My head still felt ready to explode, so I sat down and rested it on the cool surface of the table.

"Don't worry, I have just the thing to get rid of that jackhammer in your head," said Gabriel.

Still in my fleecy pajamas, I went to his side and watched him gather ingredients from the fridge. He measured and tipped them into a blender with the precision of a scientist. Finally, he handed me a glass of murky red liquid.

"What *is* this?" I asked.

"Tomato juice, egg yolk, and a dash of chili," he said. "According to the medical encyclopedia I read last night it's one of the best-known cures for a hangover."

The mixture looked and smelled disgusting, but the throbbing in my head wasn't about to subside of its own accord. So I held my nose and gulped the drink down. It occurred to me later that Ivy could have cured my hangover with a touch to my temples, but perhaps my siblings were trying to teach me to accept the human consequences of my actions.

"I think we should all stay in today, don't you?" Ivy suggested. "Take some time to reflect."

I had never felt more in awe of my siblings than I did at that moment. The tolerance they displayed could only be described as superhuman, which of course it was.

Compared to the rest of the community we lived like Quakers: no television, computers, or cell phones. Our only concession to living on earth in the twenty-first century was the landline phone, which had been connected just after we moved in. We thought of technology as a sort of corrupting influence, promoting antisocial behavior and detracting from family values. Our home was a place where we spent time with one another, not whiling away time shopping on the Internet or watching mindless television programs.

Gabriel particularly hated the influence of television. During the preparation for our mission, he had shown us the beginning of a program to emphasize his point. It involved a group of people struggling with obesity being divided into groups and presented with tempting food to see if they were strong enough to resist. The ones who gave in were berated and shunned. It was disgusting, Gabriel said, to play with people's emotions and prey on their weaknesses. It was even more sickening that the general public considered such cruelty *entertainment.*

So that afternoon we didn't turn to technology to occupy our time but instead lazed on the deck reading, playing Scrabble, or simply lost in our own thoughts. Taking time to reflect didn't mean we weren't allowed to do other things; it just meant that we did them quietly and tried to spend some time evaluating our successes and failures. Or rather, Ivy and Gabriel evaluated their successes and I contemplated my failures. I stared at the sky and nibbled on slices of melon. Fruit, I'd decided, was my favorite food. The clean, sweet freshness of it reminded me of home. As I watched, I noticed that the sun appeared as a ball of blazing white in the sky—it was blinding and made my eyes hurt to look at it. I remembered the light in the Kingdom—our home was awash with mellow golden light that we could touch, and it dripped through our fingers like warm honey. It was much harsher here, but somehow more real.

"Have you seen this?" Ivy came out holding a platter of fruit and cheese and tossed a newspaper down on the table in disgust.

"Mmm." Gabriel nodded.

"What is it?" I sat up, craning my neck to get a look at the headline. I caught a glimpse of the photograph splashed across the page. People were running in all directions; men trying in vain to shelter the women; and mothers reaching out to children who had fallen in the dust. Some of them had their eyes squeezed shut in prayer; others had their mouths open in silent screams. Behind them flames licked at the sky and roiling smoke obscured the sun.

"Bombings in the Middle East," said my brother, turning the newspaper over with a flick of his wrist. It didn't matter—the image was burned into my brain. "More than three hundred dead. You know what this means, don't you?"

"Our Agents over there aren't doing their job properly?" My voice sounded shaky.

"*Can't* do their job properly," Ivy corrected.

"What could be stopping them?" I asked.

"The forces of darkness are overpowering the forces of light," Gabriel said gravely. "It's happening more and more."

"What makes you think Heaven is the only place sending out representatives?" Ivy sounded a little impatient with my lack of understanding. "We've got company."

"Isn't there anything we can do?" I asked.

Gabriel shook his head. "It's not for us to act without authorization."

"But there are three hundred dead!" I protested. "That must matter!"

"Of course it matters," said Gabriel. "But our services haven't been called for. We have been assigned our post, and we can't abandon it because of a tragedy in another part of the globe. We have been instructed to stay here and watch over Venus Cove. There must be a reason for that."

"What about those people?" I asked, their horror-struck faces flashing into my mind once again.

"All we can do is pray for divine intervention."

By mid-afternoon we realized we were running low on groceries. Although I was still feeling washed out, I offered to go into town for them. I hoped the errand would obliterate troubling images from my mind and distract me from dwelling on human calamities.

"What should I get?" I asked, picking up an envelope ready to scribble a list on the back.

"Fruit, eggs, and some bread from that new French bakery that's just opened," said Ivy.

"Would you like a lift?" Gabriel offered.

"No, thanks, I'll take my bike. I need the exercise."

I let Gabriel return to his reading and collected my bicycle from the garage, tucking a folded canvas bag into the front. Ivy had started cutting back the roses in the front garden and waved when I sailed past her.

The ten-minute ride down into town was refreshing after my zombielike sleep. The air was crisp with the scent of pine trees, which helped dispel my gloom. I refused to let my thoughts wander to Xavier Woods and blocked out any recollections of the previous night. Of course my mind had its own agenda, and I shivered as I remembered the feel of his strong arms holding me up, the fabric of his shirt against my cheek, the touch of his hand brushing my hair away from my face, just as he'd done in my dream.

I left my bike chained to the rack outside the post office and headed toward the general store. As I reached the door, I slowed to let two women come out. One was slightly stooped and elderly, the other robust and middle-aged. The younger woman helped her companion to a bench, then returned to the shop and taped a notice to its window. Sitting obediently on his haunches beside the older woman was a silver-gray dog. It was the strangest creature I'd ever seen, with an expression so thoughtful it might have been human. Even seated, it held its body upright and had a regal air. Its jowls were slightly droopy, its fur satin sleek, and its eyes as colorless as moonlight.

The older woman had a dejected air that piqued my attention. As I looked at the notice on the shop window, I was able to determine the cause of her misery. It was a poster offering the dog "Free to a Good Home."

"It's for the best, Alice, you'll see," said the younger woman in a brisk, practical tone. "You want Phantom to be happy, don't you? He can't come with you when you move. You know the rules."

The older woman shook her head sadly.

"But he'll be in a strange place, and he won't know what's going on. We have our own little routine at home."

"Dogs are very adaptable. Now let's get you home in time for dinner. I'm sure the phone will start ringing as soon as we walk through the door."

The woman named Alice didn't seem to share her companion's confidence. I watched her gnarled fingers anxiously twisting the dog's leash and stray to her hair, which was coiled in a flimsy bun at the nape of her neck. She seemed in no hurry to make a move, as if getting up would be an indication of sealing a deal she hadn't had time to think through.

"But how will I know he's being properly looked after?" she said.

"We'll make sure that whoever takes him agrees to bring him along to the new place for visits."

A note of impatience had crept into the younger woman's voice. I noticed too that her voice had grown progressively louder as the conversation continued. Her chest heaved and beads of sweat were beginning to form at her powdered temples. She kept glancing furtively at her watch.

"What if they forget?" Alice sounded petulant.

"I'm sure they won't," her companion said dismissively. "Now, is there anything you need before I drive you home?"

"Just a bag of dog treats for Phantom but not the ones with chicken, he doesn't like those."

"Well, why don't you wait here, and I'll pop in and get them?"

Alice nodded, then stared ahead with a resigned expression. She bent down to scratch Phantom behind the ears. He looked up at her with a puzzled expression. There seemed to be a tacit understanding between owner and animal.

"What a beautiful dog," I said by way of introduction. "What breed is he?"

"A Weimaraner," Alice replied. "But sadly not mine for much longer."

"Yes, I couldn't help overhearing."

"Poor Phantom." Alice sighed and bent to talk to the dog. "You know exactly what's going on, don't you? But you're being very brave about it all."

I knelt to pat Phantom's head, and he sniffed me cautiously before offering me his giant paw.

"That's strange," said Alice. "He's usually much more reserved around strangers. You must be a dog person."

"Oh, I love animals," I said, even though this dog was the first I'd encountered. "If you don't mind me asking, where are you going that he can't come?"

"I'm moving to Fairhaven, the retirement village in town. Have you heard of it? No pets allowed, unless you count goldfish."

"What a shame," I said. "But don't worry; I'm sure a dog as beautiful as Phantom will be snapped up in no time. Are you looking forward to going?"

She looked a little taken aback by the question. "You know, you're the first person to ask me that. I suppose I'm not fussed one way or the other. I'll be better once I know Phantom's settled. I had hoped my daughter would take him, but she lives in an apartment and that won't do."

As Phantom butted his spongy nose against my hand, I was struck by an idea. Perhaps this meeting was Providence offering me an opportunity to make amends for my recent lack of responsibility. Wasn't this what I was meant to be doing after all—making a difference to people wherever I could rather than focusing on my own egotistical obsessions? There wasn't much I could do about a crisis on the other side of the globe but here was a situation where I might be of use.

"Maybe I could take him?" I suggested impulsively. "We have a big garden." I knew that if I allowed myself time to think it through I would lose my nerve. Alice's face brightened instantly.

"Could you? Are you quite sure?" she said. "That would be wonderful. You'll never find a more loyal friend, I can promise you. Why, you've hit it off already. But what will your parents say?"

"They won't mind," I told her, hoping my siblings would view the decision the same way I did. "So it's settled then?"

"Here's Felicity." Alice beamed. "We'd better tell her the good news."

Phantom and I watched the two women drive away, one

dabbing at her eyes, the other looking visibly relieved. Apart from a piteous yelp at his mistress and a soulful look in his eyes, Phantom seemed unperturbed to find himself suddenly in my keeping. He seemed to understand instinctively that the new arrangement was the best that could be hoped for under the circumstances. He waited patiently outside while I shopped. Then I hung the shopping bag from one handlebar, tied his leash to the other, and walked the bike home.

"Did you find the place all right?" Gabe called out when he heard me come in.

"Sorry, forgot the bread," I said, striding into the kitchen with Phantom at my heels. "But I picked up a bargain instead."

"Oh, Bethany," Ivy gushed. "Where did you find *him*?"

"Long story," I replied. "Someone needed a helping hand." I gave them a summary of my encounter with Alice. Ivy stroked Phantom's head and he placed his muzzle in her hand. There was something unearthly in his pale, doleful eyes that made him look as though he belonged with us. "I hope we can keep him?" I finished.

"Of course," said Gabriel without further discussion. "Everyone needs a home."

Ivy and I busied ourselves gathering Phantom a makeshift bed and deciding which bowl should be his. Gabriel watched us, the corners of his mouth twitching with the beginnings of a smile. He smiled so rarely that when he did it was like sun bursting through cloud.

It was obvious that Phantom was going to be my dog. He looked at me as his adoptive mother and loped after me wherever I went in the house. When I flopped down on the couch, he curled up at my feet like a hot water bottle and fell asleep, snoring softly. Despite his size, Phantom had an indolent nature, and it didn't take him long before he was fully integrated into our little family.

After dinner I showered and settled on the sofa with Phantom's head in my lap. His affection had a therapeutic effect, and I was feeling so relaxed I'd almost forgotten the events of the previous night.

Then there came a knock at the front door.

No Boys Allowed

PHANTOM gave a territorial growl and bounded out of the room, sniffing furiously under and around the front door.

"What's *he* doing here?" Gabriel muttered under his breath.

"Who is it?" Ivy and I whispered simultaneously.

"Our heroic school captain."

Gabriel's sarcasm was wasted on me.

"Xavier Woods is outside?" I asked incredulously, sneaking a look at myself in the mirror above the mantelpiece. Although it was early I was already in my cow-print pajamas with my hair pulled up in a banana clip. Ivy noticed and looked amused at my display of vanity. "Please don't let him in—I look awful," I begged.

I shifted uncomfortably as my siblings deliberated. After the display I'd put on at Molly's party, Xavier Woods was the last person I wanted to see. In fact, he was the one person I wanted most to avoid.

"Has he gone?" I asked after a minute.

"No," said Gabriel. "And he appears to have no intention of going."

I gestured wildly at Phantom to move away from the door. "Come here, boy!" I whispered, trying to whistle softly through my teeth. "Stop that, Phantom!"

Phantom ignored me and shoved his nose farther under the door.

"What does he want?" I asked Gabriel.

My brother paused for a moment to tune into Xavier's thoughts and his face darkened.

"Well, I think that's rather presumptuous."

"What is?"

"How long have you known this young man?"

"Stop it, Gabe. That's a breach of privacy!" I snapped.

"Honestly." Ivy got up, shaking her head. "I think he's probably heard us by now. Besides, we can't just ignore him. He recently did Bethany a good turn, remember?"

"At least wait for me to go upstairs," I hissed, but she was already at the door, tugging Phantom back and commanding him to settle down. When she walked back into the room, Xavier Woods was right behind her, looking his usual self, apart from his hair, which was slightly wind ruffled. Satisfied that Xavier posed no threat, Phantom resumed his recumbent position on the sofa with a deep sigh. Gabriel acknowledged Xavier's presence with a mere incline of his head.

"I just wanted to check that Beth was feeling okay," Xavier said, unaffected by Gabriel's frosty reception.

I recognized this was my cue to say something but words eluded me.

"Thanks again for getting her home," Ivy jumped in, the

only one of us who had remembered good manners. "Would you like something to drink? I was just about to make some hot chocolate."

"Thanks but I can't stay long," Xavier said.

"Well, sit down at least," Ivy prompted. "Gabriel, can you give me a hand in the kitchen?"

Gabriel followed her out reluctantly.

Left alone with Xavier I was conscious of how ridiculously sedate we must appear, with no television in sight, my siblings making hot chocolate and me ready for bed at eight o'clock.

"Nice dog," Xavier said. He reached down, and Phantom cautiously sniffed his hand before nuzzling it enthusiastically. I had half hoped Phantom would growl, so I'd have at least one reason not to think Xavier was completely flawless. But he seemed to be passing every test with flying colors.

"I found him today," I said.

"Found him?" Xavier raised an eyebrow. "Do you make a habit of adopting stray pets?"

"No," I said indignantly. "His owner was moving to a retirement home."

"Oh, he must be Alice Butler's dog."

"How'd you know that?"

"Small town." Xavier shrugged. "You know, I was worried about you last night." His gaze was fixed intently on my face.

"I'm fine now," I replied shakily. I tried to meet his eyes but I felt giddy and looked away.

"You should be more careful about who you call your friends."

There was an intimacy in the way he spoke to me, as if we'd known each other a long time. It was unnerving and exciting at the same time.

"It wasn't Molly's fault," I said. "I should have known better."

"You're very different from the girls around here," he continued.

"How do you mean?"

"You don't get out much, do you?"

"I guess you could call me more of a homebody," I said, trying not to sound defensive.

"That's not a bad thing," Xavier said. "I think that makes a nice change."

"I wish I was more like everyone else."

"Why do you say that? There's no point pretending to be something you're not. You could have been in real trouble last night." He smiled suddenly. "Lucky I was there to rescue you."

I couldn't tell whether he was speaking in earnest or making a joke.

"How can I ever repay your kindness?" I said with a hint of what I hoped was flirtation in my voice.

"There is one thing you could do. . . ." His voice trailed off suggestively.

"What's that?"

"Go out with me. How about next weekend? We could catch a movie if you like."

I was too stunned to reply. Had I heard right? Was Xavier Woods, the most inaccessible boy at Bryce Hamilton, asking me out? What was the appropriate response? Where was Molly when I needed her? My hesitation lasted a fraction too long and he mistook it for reluctance.

"It's fine if you don't feel like it."

"No, I'd like to!"

"Great. Well, how about you give me your number and I'll put it in my phone. We can talk details later."

He withdrew a shiny black gadget from the pocket of his windbreaker. It lay twinkling in the palm of his hand. I could hear the clatter of crockery coming from the kitchen and knew there was no time to lose.

"It's easier if you give me yours and I call you," I said quickly.

He didn't argue. I spied a newspaper on the coffee table, tore off a corner, and handed it to him.

"I might need a pen," he said.

I found one marking the place in a leather-bound book one of my siblings had been reading. Xavier scribbled some digits, and I pocketed the slip just in time to give Gabriel and Ivy a beatific smile as they walked in, carrying a tray of mugs.

I walked Xavier to the front door, where his eyes lingered a moment on what I was wearing. The intensity had gone from his face and his characteristic half-smile had returned.

"By the way, nice jammies," he said and continued to look at me with an expression of curiosity. I found myself unable to wrench my gaze away. It would be easy, I thought, to look at his face all day and not get bored. Humans were supposed to have physical flaws but Xavier didn't seem to. I took in his features—his mouth shaped like an archer's bow, his smooth skin, the dimple in his chin—and struggled to believe he was real. He was wearing a casual shirt under the jacket, and I saw around his neck a silver cross threaded onto a leather cord that I hadn't noticed earlier.

"I'm glad you like them," I said, feeling more confident.

He laughed, and it sounded just like the peals of a church bell.

GABRIEL and Ivy tried hard to play down the alarm they must have felt when I informed them of my intention to see Xavier the following weekend.

"Do you really think that's a good idea?" asked Gabriel.

"Why wouldn't it be?" I challenged. I was relishing the idea of making my own decisions, and I didn't appreciate my independence being taken away from me so quickly.

"Bethany, please consider the repercussions of such an action." Ivy spoke calmly, but she was frowning and a rare look of apprehension had come over her face.

"There's nothing to consider. You two always overreact." I wasn't convinced myself by my breezy argument but refused to accept there was reason for caution. "What's the problem?"

"Only that *dating* is not and never was part of our assignment." Gabriel's voice was cutting and his gaze steely. I knew I was only fueling his doubts about my suitability for this mission. I was so susceptible to human whims and fantasies. A voice at the back of my mind told me I should take a step back and reflect—accept that a liaison with Xavier was dangerous and selfish given the circumstances. But there was a louder voice that drowned out all other thought, and it demanded to see him again.

"Perhaps keeping a low profile for a little while would be wiser," Ivy suggested less harshly. "Why don't we collaborate on some ideas designed to raise social awareness in the town?"

She sounded like a teacher trying to encourage enthusiasm for a school project.

"Those are your ideas, not mine."

"They can become yours," Ivy urged.

"I want to find my own way."

"Let's continue this discussion when you're thinking more clearly," Gabriel said.

"I won't be treated like a child," I snapped and turned away defiantly, clicking my tongue for Phantom to follow.

Together, we sat at the top of the stairs, me fuming and Phantom nuzzling my lap. Believing me to be out of earshot, my siblings continued the discussion in the kitchen.

"I find it difficult to believe she would jeopardize everything for a whim," Gabriel was saying. I could hear him pacing.

"You know Bethany would never deliberately do that." Ivy tried to defuse the situation. She hated any sort of friction between us.

"What is she doing then? Has she got any idea why we're here? I know we must make allowances for her lack of experience, but she's being deliberately rebellious and headstrong, and I don't recognize her anymore. Temptation is always here to test us. We have been here only weeks and Bethany cannot find the strength to withstand the charms of a pretty boy!"

"Be patient, Gabriel. It will go much further in. . . ."

"She tries my patience!" he said, but quickly collected himself. "What do you advise?"

"Put no obstacle in her path, and this will surely die a natural death; obstruct her, and it will give the situation an importance worth fighting for."

Gabriel's silence suggested he was weighing up the wisdom in Ivy's words.

"In time she will come to understand that what she seeks is impossible."

"I hope you're right," Gabriel said. "Do you see now why her part in this mission concerned me?"

"She does not defy us deliberately," Ivy said.

"No, but the depth of her emotion is unnatural for one of us," Gabriel said. "Our love for humankind is supposed to be impersonal—we love humanity, we do not form individual attachments. Bethany seems to love deeply, unconditionally—like a human."

"So I've noticed," said my sister. "Which means her love is much more powerful than ours, but also more dangerous."

"Exactly," said Gabriel. "Such emotion often cannot be contained—if we allow it to develop, it may soon be beyond our control."

I didn't wait to hear more and crept to my room, where I threw myself on my bed on the verge of tears. Such a powerful reaction surprised me, and the rush of pent-up emotion left me gasping for breath. I knew what was happening; I was embracing flesh and the feelings that came with it. It felt precarious and unsteady like being on a rickety roller coaster. I could feel the blood pulsing through my veins, the thoughts ricocheting around my head, my stomach clenching with frustration. I deeply resented being discussed as if I were nothing more than a laboratory experiment. And their implication that I was doing something wrong, not to mention their lack of faith in me, was disturbing. Why were they so determined to bar me from the human interaction I craved? And what exactly did Ivy mean by "impossible"? They were behaving as if Xavier was a suitor who didn't meet their criteria. Who were they to sit in judgment of something that hadn't even begun? Xavier Woods liked me. For whatever reason he saw me as worthy of his attention, and I was not about to let the paranoid fears of my family drive him away. I was amazed at my willingness to embrace my human attraction to Xavier. My feelings for him were escalating dangerously fast, and I was allowing it to happen. It should have scared me, but instead I was intrigued by the hollow ache in my chest when I thought about letting him go, the clenching of every muscle in my body when I recalled my brother's words. What was happening to me? Was I losing my divinity? Was I becoming human?

I slept fitfully that night and had my first nightmare. I had become accustomed to the human experience of dreaming, but this was different. This time I saw myself brought before a Heavenly Tribunal, with a jury made up of faceless, heavy-robed figures. I couldn't distinguish one from the other. Ivy and Gabriel were there, but they were looking down from a gallery. Their faces were impassive. They stared ahead and wouldn't look at me even though I cried out to them. I was waiting for the verdict to be announced, and then I realized it had already happened. There was no one to speak for me, no one to plead my case.

The next thing I was aware of was falling. Around me, all that was familiar crumbled into dust, the columns of the courtroom, the robed figures, and finally the faces of Gabriel and Ivy. And still I fell, tumbling on an endless journey to nowhere. Then all was motionless and I was imprisoned in a void. I had dropped to my knees, my head bowed, my wings broken and bleeding. I couldn't lift myself off the ground. The light began to fade until a suffocating darkness surrounded me, so dense that when I held my hands before my face, I couldn't make them out. In this sepulchral world I was left alone. I saw myself as the ultimate figure of shame, an angel fallen from grace.

A shadowy figure with blurred features was approaching. At first my heart leapt with hope at the possibility that it might be Xavier come to rescue me. But any hope was dashed when I sensed instinctively that whatever it was should be feared. Despite the pain in my limbs, I crawled as far from it as possible. I tried spreading my wings but they were too damaged to comply. The figure was closer now and hovering above me. Its features materialized just enough for me to see that the smile on its face was one of ownership. There was nothing left to do but allow myself to be consumed by the shadows. This was perdition. I was lost.

BY morning things seemed different, as they often do. A new feeling of stability now flooded through me.

Ivy came in to rouse me, the scent of freesias following her like handmaidens.

"Thought you could use some coffee," she said.

"I'm developing a taste for it," I said and sipped from the proffered cup without making a face. She sat stiffly on the edge of my bed.

"I've never heard Gabriel sound so angry," I said, eager to smooth things over with her. "I've always thought of him as . . . sort of . . . infallible."

"Have you ever thought that he might be under stresses of his own? If things don't go well, he and I will assume responsibility for it."

Her words struck me like a physical blow, and I felt the sting of tears welling.

"I don't want to lose your good opinion."

"You haven't," she reassured me. "It's just that Gabriel wants to protect you. He wishes only to spare you from anything that might cause you pain."

"I just can't see how spending time with Xavier could be a bad thing. Do you really think he would hurt me?"

"Not intentionally."

Ivy wasn't hostile like Gabe, and when she came to take my hand, I knew she had already forgiven my transgression. But her rigid posture and the hard line of her mouth told me that her position on the matter would not change. "You must be careful not to start things you can't continue. It wouldn't exactly be fair, would it?"

The tears I'd been restraining came flooding then. I sat there racked with misery as Ivy put her arms around me and stroked my head.

"I've been stupid, haven't I?"

I allowed the voice of reason to take over. I barely knew

Xavier Woods, and I doubted he would react with a deluge of tears if he found out he couldn't see me for whatever reason. I was behaving as if we'd sworn ourselves to each other, and suddenly it all seemed a little absurd. Maybe it was *Romeo and Juliet* rubbing off on me. I felt like there was a deep, unfathomable connection between Xavier and me, but maybe I was wrong. Could it be possible it was all just a figment of my imagination?

It was within my power to forget about Xavier. The question was did I want to? There was no denying that Ivy was right. We were not of this world and had no claim to it or what it could offer. I had no right to meddle in Xavier's life. Our role was to be messengers, harbingers of hope, and nothing more.

When Ivy had gone, I fished out Xavier's number from my pocket where it had stayed all night. I unrolled the tight wad of paper and slowly tore it into fragments the size of confetti. I went out onto my narrow balcony and threw the fragments into the air. I watched sadly as they were carried away by the wind.

Rebel

IGNORING Xavier's invitation proved easier than I expected when he wasn't at school the whole of the following week. After making a few discreet inquiries, I discovered that he was away at rowing camp. With the danger of running into him averted, I felt more relaxed. I wasn't sure I'd have the courage to renege on the date if he were standing right in front of me, nutmeg hair fringing those limpid blue eyes. In fact, I wasn't sure I'd be able to say anything much at all given my past attempts at conversation.

At lunchtime I sat with Molly and her friends in the quadrangle, listening halfheartedly to their litany of complaints about school, boys, and parents. Their conversations mostly followed a set pattern, and I felt I already knew the lines by heart. Today the prom was the subject of discussion—no surprise there.

"Oh my God, there's so much to think about," Molly said, stretching out on the asphalt like a cat. Her friends were scattered around her, some on the garden benches, their skirts hitched up to maximize the impact of the early spring sun.

I sat cross-legged beside Molly, tugging at my skirt so that it modestly covered my knees.

"Oh my God, I know!" agreed Megan Judd. She repositioned her head in Hayley's lap and pulled her top up so that her midriff was exposed to sunlight. "Last night I started making a to-do list." Still on her back she flipped open her school planner, emblazoned with designer labels that she'd stuck on for decoration. "Get this," she continued, reading from a dog-eared page. "Book French manicure. Look for sexy shoes. Buy clutch. Decide on jewelry. Find celebrity hairstyle to copy. Decide between Hawaiian Sunset and Champagne spray tan. Book limo. The list goes on. . . ."

"You forgot the most important thing—find dress," said Hayley.

The others laughed at the omission.

It baffled me that they could discuss in such detail an event that was so far away, but I refrained from commenting. I doubted my input would be appreciated.

"It's going to cost so much." Taylah sighed. "I'm going to end up blowing my budget and spending every dollar I've made working at that crappy bakery."

"I'm cashed up," Molly said proudly. "I've been saving from working at the drugstore since last year."

"My parents are paying for everything," bragged Megan. "They've agreed to pay for the whole thing as long as I pass all my exams—even a party bus if we want one."

The girls were clearly impressed.

"Whatever you do, don't screw up any exams," Molly said.

"Hey, she's not a miracle worker." Hayley laughed.

"Does anyone have a date yet?" someone else asked.

A few of the girls did, and those in steady relationships didn't have to worry about it. Everybody else was still desperately waiting for someone to ask them.

"I wonder if Gabriel will go," Molly mused, turning to me. "All the teachers get invited."

"I'm not sure," I said. "He tends to steer clear of those sorts of things."

"You should ask Ryan," Hayley suggested to Molly, "before he's taken."

"Yeah, the good ones always go first," Taylah agreed.

Molly looked affronted. "It's the formal, Haylz," she said. "The guy has to do the asking."

Taylah snorted. "Good luck with that."

"Molly, you're so stupid sometimes," Hayley sighed. "Ryan's six-two, built, blond, and plays lacrosse. He might not be the sharpest tool in the shed, but still, what are you waiting for?"

"I want him to ask me," Molly pouted.

"Maybe he's shy," Megan suggested.

"Uh, have you seen him?" Taylah rolled her eyes. "I doubt he has self-esteem issues."

A debate about floor-length gowns versus cocktail dresses followed. The conversation became so banal that I needed an escape. I mumbled something about going to the library to check if a book had come in.

"Ewww, Bethie, only losers hang out in the library," Taylah said. "Someone might see you."

"And we already have to spend fifth period there to finish that stupid research assignment," Megan moaned.

"What was that about again?" Hayley asked. "Something to do with politics in the Middle East?"

"Where is the Middle East?" asked a girl named Zoe, who always wore her blond hair piled on top of her head like a crown.

"It's a whole area near the Persian Gulf," I said. "It spans southwest Asia."

"I don't think so, Bethie." Taylah laughed. "Everybody knows the Middle East is in Africa."

I wished I could seek out Ivy's company, but she was busy working in town. She had joined the church group and was already recruiting members. She had made badges promoting fair trade and printed pamphlets that preached about the injustice of working conditions in the Third World. Given her goddess status within Venus Cove, the numbers at the church group were growing. The young males in the town had taken to seeking her out and buying far more badges than anyone could use in the hope of being rewarded with her phone number or even just an appreciative pat on the head. Ivy had made it her mission to play Mother Earth at Venus Cove—she wanted to bring people back to nature. I guess you could call it an environmentalist mentality—organic food, community spirit, and the power of the natural world over material things.

So I headed in the direction of the music wing instead, in search of Gabriel.

The music wing was in the oldest part of the school. I heard singing coming from the main hall, so I pushed open its heavy paneled doors. The hall was vast with a high ceiling and portraits of grim-faced headmasters lining the walls. Gabriel stood in front of a music stand, conducting the junior choristers. All the choirs had grown in popularity since Gabriel's arrival; in fact, there were so many new female recruits to the senior choir that they had to rehearse in the auditorium.

Gabriel was teaching the juniors one of his favorite hymns in a four-part harmony, accompanied by the music captain, Lucy McCrae, on the piano. My entrance interrupted the singing. Gabriel turned to determine the source of the distraction, and when he did, the light from the stained-glass window merged with his golden hair so that for a moment he looked ablaze.

I waved to him and listened as the choir resumed their singing.

> Here I am, Lord. Is it I, Lord?
> I have heard You calling in the night.
> I will go, Lord, if You lead me.
> I will hold Your people in my heart.

Even with some of the singers out of tune and the accompanist a little loud, the purity of the voices was transporting. I stayed until the bell signaled the end of lunch. By then I felt I'd been given a well-timed reminder of the bigger picture.

The next few days blurred into one another, and before I knew it, it was Friday and the end of another week. The rowers had reportedly gotten back after lunch, but I hadn't seen any sign of them and decided they must have gone straight home. I wondered whether Xavier had concluded that I'd lost interest as he hadn't heard from me. Or was he still awaiting my call? It bothered me that he might wait for a call that wasn't coming. Now I wouldn't even get the chance to see him and explain.

Packing my schoolbag at the end of the day, I noticed that someone had wedged a little scroll of paper into one of the metal louvers at the top of my locker. It fell to the ground when I opened the door. I picked it up and read the message, written in a loping, boyish hand.

> In case you change your mind, I'll be at
> the Mercury Cinema at 9pm on Saturday.
> X

I read it several times. Even via a piece of paper, Xavier managed to have the same dizzying effect on me. I handled the note as delicately as if it were an ancient relic. He wasn't easily deterred; I liked that about him. So this, I thought, is what it feels like to be pursued. I wanted to leap around in excitement, but I managed to remain calm. Nevertheless, I was still grinning when I met up with Gabriel and Ivy. I couldn't seem to force my face into a mask of serenity.

"You looked pleased with yourself," Ivy said when she saw me.

"Good result on a French test," I lied.

"Did you expect anything else?"

"No, but it's still nice to see it in black and white."

I was surprised to find how easily I could lie. I must be getting better at it and that wasn't a good thing.

Gabriel looked pleased to see my previous mood had lifted. I knew he'd been feeling guilty. He hated to witness distress, much less be the cause of it. I didn't really blame him for his sternness. It was hardly his fault he couldn't relate to what I was experiencing. His focus was overseeing our mission, and I couldn't imagine the strain that must accompany that task. Ivy and I depended on him, and the powers in the Kingdom were relying on his wisdom. It was only natural that he should try to avoid complications, and that's exactly what he feared contact with Xavier might bring.

The elation of receiving Xavier's message lasted through the rest of the afternoon and the evening. But by Saturday I was again wrestling with my conscience over what to do about it. I desperately wanted to see Xavier, but I knew it was reckless and selfish. Gabriel and Ivy were my family and they trusted me. I couldn't willingly do anything that might compromise their position.

Saturday morning was relatively uneventful and made up of chores and taking Phantom for a run along the beach. When I got home and looked at the clock, I saw that it was already mid-afternoon and I started to feel edgy. I managed to hide my agitation through dinner, and afterward Ivy sang to us with her melodic voice, accompanied by Gabriel on an old acoustic guitar. Ivy's voice could have reduced a hardened criminal to tears. As for Gabriel, every note he played was smooth and hummed like a living thing.

Around eight thirty I went up to my room and pulled everything out of my closet to rearrange it. No matter how hard I tried, thoughts of Xavier pushed themselves into the foreground of my mind with the force of a speeding train. By five minutes to nine, all I could think of was him waiting for me, the minutes ticking by. I visualized the moment when he realized I wasn't coming. In my mind's eye I saw him shrug his shoulders, walk out of the cinema, and go on with his life. The pain of this thought proved too much, and before I knew it, I had grabbed my purse, pulled the balcony doors open, and was climbing down the lattice to the garden below. I was overcome by a burning desire to see Xavier, even if I didn't speak to him.

I stumbled along the dark street, took a left, and kept going, heading straight for the lights of the town. A few people in cars turned to stare at me, a pale, ghostlike girl streaking down the street, hair flying like streamers. I thought I saw Mrs. Henderson peering out through the blinds in her living room, but I hardly gave her a second thought.

It took me about ten minutes to find the Mercury Cinema. I passed a café called the Fat Cat, which seemed to be full of students. Music was pumping from a jukebox and kids were sitting in deep couches, drinking milk shakes or sharing bowls of nachos. Some of them were dancing on the checkered floor. I passed the Terrace, one of the ritzier restaurants in town, set up on the first floor of an old Victorian hotel. The best tables were on the balcony that ran along the front of the building, and I could see candles glinting in their holders. I sped past the new bakery and the general store where I had met Alice and Phantom just weeks earlier. When I reached the Mercury Cinema, I was going at such a speed that I ran straight past it and had to double back when I realized the street had come to an end.

The cinema dated from the 1950s and had recently been redecorated in keeping with the fashion of that time. It was full of retro memorabilia. The floors were polished black-and-white linoleum; there were sofas in burnt orange vinyl with chrome legs and lights like flying saucers. I caught sight of myself in the mirror behind the candy bar. My breathing was ragged from excitement, and I looked flustered from my run.

The foyer was empty when I got there, and no one was milling around the coffee lounge. The movie posters advertised a Hitchcock marathon. It must have already started. Xavier had either gone in alone or gone home.

I heard someone behind me clearing his throat exaggeratedly, the way someone does when trying to get your attention. I turned.

"It's no longer fashionably late when you miss the movie." Xavier was wearing his wry smile, navy chino shorts, and a cream polo shirt.

"I can't make it," I said between breaths. "I just came to let you know."

"You didn't have to run all the way over here to tell me that. You could have called."

Xavier's eyes were playful. I struggled to think of a reply that wouldn't make me look ridiculous. My first impulse was to say I'd lost his number, but I didn't want to lie to him.

"Since you're here," he continued, "how about a coffee?"

"What about the movie?"

"I can see that anytime."

"All right, but I can't stay long. No one knows I'm out," I confessed.

"There's a place just two blocks down, if you don't mind walking."

The café was called Sweethearts. Xavier put his hand between my shoulder blades to steer me inside, and I felt the heat of his palm seep through to my skin. A strange warmth bubbled up inside of me until I realized his hand was directly on the place where my wings were carefully folded. I quickly edged away with a nervous laugh.

"You're a strange girl," he said, looking bemused.

I was grateful when he asked for a booth as I wanted privacy from prying eyes. We had attracted a fair bit of attention just walking down the street together. Inside the café were some faces I recognized from school, but I didn't know the students personally so no acknowledgment was required. I saw Xavier nodding in various directions before we sat down. Were these his friends? I wondered whether our outing would fuel the rumor mill come Monday.

The place was inviting and I started to feel more relaxed. The lighting was low, and the walls were lined with old movie posters. On the table were free postcards advertising the work of local artists. The menu offered a variety of milk shakes, coffees, cakes, and sundaes. A waitress wearing black-and-white sneakers took our order. I ordered a hot chocolate and Xavier asked for a latte. The waitress gave him a flirtatious smile as she scribbled on her pad.

"Hope this place is okay with you," he said when she'd gone. "I usually come here after training."

"It's nice," I said. "Do you train a lot?"

"Two afternoons and most weekends. What about you? Have you got involved in anything yet?"

"Not yet, I'm still deciding."

Xavier nodded. "These things take time." He folded his arms comfortably across his chest and leaned back in his seat. "So, tell me about yourself."

It was the question I'd been dreading.

"What would you like to know?" I asked cautiously.

"Firstly, why you've chosen Venus Cove. It's not exactly high profile."

"That's why," I said. "Let's call it a lifestyle decision—we were tired of jet-setting, wanted to settle down somewhere quiet." I knew this would be an acceptable answer; there was no shortage of families who had relocated for similar reasons. "Now, tell me about yourself."

I think he knew I was hoping to fend off more questions, but it didn't matter. Xavier was comfortable talking and didn't need encouragement. Unlike me, he was forthcoming with personal information. He told anecdotes about family members and gave an abridged version of the Woods's family history.

"I come from a family of six kids and I'm the second eldest. Both parents are doctors, Mom's a local GP and Dad's an anesthesiologist. Claire, the eldest, is following in my parents' footsteps, and she's in her second year of a med degree. She lives at college but comes home every weekend. She just got engaged to her boyfriend Luke—they've been together four years. Then there are three younger sisters—Nicola's fifteen, Jasmine's eight, and Madeline's about to turn six. The youngest is Michael and he's four. Bored yet?"

"No, it's fascinating. Please go on," I urged. I found the details of a normal, human family intriguing and was thirsty to hear more. Was I envious of his life? I wondered.

"Well, I've been at Bryce Hamilton since kindergarten because my mom insisted I go to a Christian school. She's a conservative—been with my dad since they were fifteen. Can you believe that? They've practically grown up together."

"They must have a very strong relationship."

"They've had their ups and downs, but nothing's ever happened that they haven't been able to deal with."

"Sounds like a close family."

"Yeah, we are, although Mom can be a little overprotective."

I imagined Xavier's parents having high aspirations for their eldest boy.

"Will you pursue medicine as well?"

"Probably." He shrugged.

"You don't sound too excited about it."

"Well, I was interested in design for a while but that was, let's say, *discouraged*."

"Why's that?"

"Isn't considered a serious career, is it? The idea of having invested all this money into my education only to have it end in unemployment doesn't thrill my parents."

"What about what you want?"

"Sometimes parents know best."

He seemed to accept the decisions made by his parents with good grace, happy to be guided by their expectations. His life was pretty much mapped out for him, and I imagined that any diversion from the set course wouldn't be looked upon kindly. I could relate to him in that way—my human experience came with strict boundaries and guidelines and straying from the path was out of the question. Lucky for Xavier, his mistakes wouldn't incur the wrath of Heaven. Instead they would be chalked up to experience.

Halfway through our drinks Xavier decided we needed "a sugar hit" and ordered chocolate cake, which arrived as a slab layered with whipped cream and berries on a large white plate with two long spoons. Despite being urged to "go for it," I scooped daintily around the edges. When we'd finished, Xavier insisted on paying the check and looked offended when I tried to offer my share. He waved my hand away and dropped a bill into a tip jar labeled GOOD KARMA before we left.

It was only once we were outside that I realized the time.

"I know, it's late," Xavier said, reading my face. "But how about a short walk? I'm not ready to take you home yet."

"I'm already in serious trouble."

"In that case ten minutes more can't hurt."

I knew I should cut the night short; Ivy and Gabriel had surely realized I was gone and would be worried about me. It wasn't that I didn't care—I just couldn't bear to tear myself away from Xavier a moment sooner than I had to. When I was around him, I was filled with an overpowering happiness that made the rest of the world fade away to nothing more than background noise. It was like the two of us were locked in a private bubble that nothing short of an earthquake could burst.

I wanted the night to last forever.

We walked to the end of the strip toward the water. When we got there, we saw a traveling carnival setting up on the boardwalk—a popular activity for families with restless children who needed a change from a winter spent indoors. A Ferris wheel rocked in the wind, and we could see bumper cars scattered around the track. A jumping castle glowed yellow in the twilight.

"Let's check it out," said Xavier with childlike enthusiasm.

"I don't think it's even open," I said. "We won't be able to get in." There was something about the tired-looking carnival that made me reluctant to explore it further. "Besides, it's almost dark."

"Where's your sense of adventure? We can always jump the fence."

"I don't mind a quick look, but I'm not jumping any fences."

As it turned out there weren't any fences to jump and we walked straight in. There wasn't much to see. Some men hauling ropes and driving machinery ignored us. On the steps of a trailer, a tanned woman sat smoking. She wore a colorful dress and jangly bracelets up to her elbows. She had deep creases around her eyes and mouth, and her dark hair was graying at the temples.

"Ah, young love," she said when she saw us. "Sorry, kids, but we're closed."

"Our mistake," Xavier said politely. "We were just leaving."

The woman took a long drag of her cigarette. "Like your fortunes read?" she asked in a rasping voice. "Since you're here."

"You're a psychic?" I asked. I didn't know whether to be skeptical or intrigued. It was true that some humans had a heightened awareness and could experience premonitions of sorts, but that was about the extent of it. Some humans could see spirits or feel their presence, but the term *psychic* seemed a little presumptuous to me.

"Sure am," said the woman. "Angela Messenger at your service." Her name threw me somewhat—that it should be so close to *angel* was unnerving. "Come on in, no charge," she added. "Might liven up the evening."

Inside, the trailer smelled of take-out food. Candles flickered on the table and fringed tapestries hung from the walls. Angela indicated we should sit down.

"You first," she said to Xavier as she took his hand and began to study it intently. The expression on his face told me he thought the whole thing was a joke. "Well, you have a curved heart line, which means you're a romantic," she said. "Short head line means you think directly and don't beat around the bush. I'm sensing a strong blue energy from you that indicates that heroism is in your blood but also means you are destined to experience great pain, of what sort I can't be sure. But you should be prepared for it as it's not far away."

Xavier tried to look as though he was taking her advice seriously.

"Thank you," he said. "That was very insightful. Your turn, Beth."

"No, I'd rather not," I said.

"The future is not to be feared but confronted," said Angela. The way she said it was almost a challenge.

I held my hand out reluctantly for her to read. Although her fingers were rough and calloused, her touch was not unpleasant. The moment she stretched out my palm she seemed to stiffen slightly.

"I can see white," she said, her eyes shut as if in a trance. "I feel an indescribable happiness." She opened her eyes. "What an amazing aura you have. Let me check your lines. Here we have a strong unbroken heart line, which suggests you will only love once in your lifetime. . . . Then let's see—Good Lord!" She straightened my fingers and pushed them back to stretch out the skin.

"What?" I asked in alarm.

"It's your life line," the woman said, her eyes wide with alarm. "I've never seen anything like it before."

"What about my life line?" I asked impatiently.

"My dear"—Angela's voice dropped to a mere whisper—"you don't have one."

WE walked back to Xavier's car in awkward silence.

"Well, that was weird," he said finally as he opened the door and I climbed in.

"Sure was," I agreed, trying to sound lighthearted. "But who believes in psychics?"

Xavier's car suited him perfectly. He drove a sky blue 1957 Chevrolet Bel Air convertible. It had been lovingly restored down to the last detail, and made me feel like we'd traveled back in time. Its headlights gleamed in the darkness and its smooth leather seats were strangely comforting.

"Beth, meet my baby," he said. "She's a pretty sweet ride."

"Hello," I half raised my hand in an awkward wave and immediately felt like an idiot.

"You do know cars are inanimate objects?" I teased.

"Take it easy," Xavier said. "You'll hurt her feelings."

"I didn't know cars had feelings."

"This one does. She's got a life of her own." Xavier patted the hood before pulling open my door. "Don't be jealous of Beth, baby. You can't be the only woman in my life."

He switched on the ignition and put the car into gear before turning the dial to a commercial radio station. The dulcet tones of the announcer welcomed listeners to his show, *Jazz After Dark*. I noticed Xavier's car had a comforting smell—a combination of leather seats and a crisp woody scent that might have been his cologne.

After riding only briefly in our hybrid Jeep, I wasn't prepared for the noise of the vintage engine roaring to life and flattened myself against the passenger seat. Xavier glanced across at me with raised eyebrows.

"You all right there?"

"Is this car completely safe?"

"Do you think I'm a bad driver?" He smirked.

"I trust you," I said. "I'm just not sure about cars."

"If you're worried about safety, you might like to follow my example and put on that seat belt."

"The what?"

Xavier shook his head in disbelief.

"You worry me," he muttered.

"ARE you going to be in trouble?" he asked when we pulled up outside Byron. I saw that the front porch light had been left on so my escape must have been noticed.

"I don't really care," I said. "I had fun."

"So did I." The moonlight glinted briefly on the cross at his neck.

"Xavier . . ." I began tentatively. "Can I ask you something?"

"Sure."

"Well, I'm just wondering . . . why did you ask me out tonight? It's just that Molly told me about . . . well . . . about . . ."

"Emily?" Xavier sighed. "What about her?" A defensive note had crept into his voice. "People just can't leave it alone, can they? That's the thing about small towns—they get off on gossip."

I found it difficult to meet his gaze. I felt as if I'd crossed a boundary, but I couldn't go back.

"She said you've never really wanted to spend time with any other girl. So I guess I'm just curious . . . why me?"

"Emily wasn't just my girlfriend," Xavier said. "She was my best friend. We understood each other in a way that's hard to explain, and I thought I'd never be able to replace her. But then when I met you . . ." He trailed off.

"Am I like her?" I asked.

Xavier laughed. "No, nothing like her. But I get the same feeling when I'm around you that I used to have with her."

"What sort of feeling?"

"Sometimes you meet a person and you just click—you're comfortable with them, like you've known them your whole life, and you don't have to pretend to be anyone or anything."

"Do you think Emily would mind?" I asked. "That you feel that way with me?"

Xavier smiled. "Wherever she is, Em would want me to be happy." I knew exactly where she was but thought better about sharing this information with Xavier just then. It was bad enough that I had struggled with the seat belt and my palm was minus a life line. I thought that might be enough surprises for one evening.

We sat in silence for a few minutes, neither of us wanting to break the mood.

"Do you believe in God?" I said eventually.

"You're the first girl to ask me that," Xavier said. "Most people think of religion as some kind of fashion statement."

"So you do?"

"I believe in a higher power, a spiritual energy. I think life's too complex to be an accident, don't you agree?"

"Absolutely," I replied.

I stepped out of Xavier's car that night with the certainty that the world as I knew it had changed irrevocably. All I could think about as I climbed the steps to the front door was not the lecture that awaited me but how long before I could see him again. There were so many things I wanted to talk to him about.

{ 11 }

Head over Heels

THE front door opened before I had a chance to knock. Ivy stood there, concern knitting her brow. Gabriel sat stony faced in the sitting room. He might have been a figure in a painting so still was his bearing. Ordinarily it would have prompted overwhelming remorse, but I was still hearing Xavier's voice and remembering his strong hand on my back as he ushered me into Sweethearts, as well as the fresh scent of his cologne.

Deep down I'd known when I clambered down my balcony that Gabriel would have sensed my absence almost immediately. He would also have guessed where I'd gone and who I was with. I knew the idea of coming to look for me would have crossed his mind, only to be dismissed. Neither he nor Ivy would have wanted to draw attention to us so publicly.

"You shouldn't have waited up, I was perfectly safe," I said. The words unintentionally came out sounding too offhand, impudent rather than apologetic. "I'm sorry if I worried you," I added as an afterthought.

"No, you're not, Bethany," said Gabriel softly. He still

hadn't lifted his head. "You're not sorry or you wouldn't have done it." I hated that he wouldn't look at me.

"Gabe, please," I began, but he silenced me by raising his hand in protest.

"I was apprehensive about having you with us on this mission, and now you have proven yourself to be completely erratic." He looked as if the words had left a bad taste in his mouth. "You're young and inexperienced—your aura is warmer and more human than any other angel's I have known, and yet you were chosen. I sensed we would encounter problems with you, but the others believed all would be well. But now I see you've made your decision—you've chosen a passing fancy over your family." He rose abruptly.

"Can we at least talk about it?" I asked. It was all sounding very dramatic, and I was sure it didn't need to be if only I could get Gabriel to understand.

"Not now. It's late. Whatever you want to say can wait till morning." And with that he left us.

Ivy looked at me, her eyes wide and sad. I hated to end the night on such a sour note, especially seeing as moments ago, I couldn't have been happier.

"I wish Gabriel wouldn't do that prophet-of-doom routine," I said.

Ivy looked suddenly tired.

"Oh, Bethany, don't say things like that! What you did tonight was wrong even if you can't see that yet. Our counsel may not make sense to you right now, but the least you can do is think about it before things get out of hand. You will realize this is nothing but an infatuation. Your feelings for this boy will pass."

Ivy and Gabriel were talking in riddles. How did they expect me to see a problem when they couldn't even articulate it? I knew my outing with Xavier was a minor deviation from the agenda, but what was the harm in that? What was the point of being on earth and having human experiences if we were going to pretend they didn't matter? Despite what my siblings thought was best, I didn't want my feelings for Xavier to *pass*. That made him sound like a cold or a virus that would eventually work its way out of my system. Never had I experienced such an all-consuming desire for someone's presence. An expression I'd read somewhere crossed my mind: "The heart wants what the heart desires." I couldn't remember where it came from, but whoever wrote it had been right. If Xavier was an illness, then I didn't want to recover. If my attraction to him constituted an offense that might incur divine retribution, then so be it. Let it rain down. I didn't care.

Ivy went up to her room and I was left alone with Phantom, who seemed to know instinctively what I needed. He came and nuzzled behind my knees, knowing it would force me to bend down and stroke him. At least one member of the household didn't hate me.

I went upstairs and peeled off my clothes, leaving them in a heap on the floor. I wasn't sleepy; instead I was weighed down by a feeling of being trapped. I stepped into the shower and allowed the hot water to pummel my shoulders and loosen my tight muscles. Even though we'd agreed never to do this in the house in case we could be seen, I partially released my wings until they pressed up against the glass of the shower screen. They were stiff from hours of being folded, and I felt them double in weight as they absorbed water. I tipped my head back, letting the water run down my face. Ivy had asked me to think about what I was doing, but for once I didn't want to think, I just wanted to *be*.

I dried myself hastily and with my wings still damp climbed into bed. The last thing I wanted was to hurt my brother and sister, but my heart seemed to turn to stone whenever I thought of never seeing Xavier again. I wished he was in my room right then. I knew what I would ask of him: to escort me from my prison. And I knew he wouldn't hesitate. In my imagination I was the maiden tied to the train tracks, and the face of my tormentor alternated between that of my brother's and sister's. I realized I was being irrational, turning the situation into a melodrama, but I couldn't stop myself. How could I explain to my family that Xavier was much more than a boy I'd developed a crush on? We'd only had a few short encounters and one date, but that was irrelevant. How could I make them see that a similar encounter was unlikely even if I lingered on the earth for a thousand lifetimes? I still possessed my celestial wisdom, and I knew it with the same certainty that I knew my days on this verdant planet were numbered.

What I couldn't determine and didn't dare to ask was what would happen once the powers in the Kingdom learned of my transgression. I didn't imagine the reaction would be mild. But was a little compassion and understanding too much to ask for? Wasn't I as deserving of these as any human being who would be pardoned without a second thought? I wondered what would happen next. Would I be recalled in disgrace? I felt a chill run through me at the thought, but then the memory of Xavier's face filled me with warmth once again.

The matter was not raised the next morning or during the rest of weekend. On Monday morning Gabriel went through the ritual of making breakfast in silence. The silence continued until we reached the gates of Bryce Hamilton and parted company.

Molly and her friends offered a welcome distraction. I let their conversation wash over me; it stopped me thinking. Today their source of entertainment was dissecting the latest fashion faux pas of their least favorite teachers. According to the girls, Mr. Phillips looked as though his hair had been cut by a lawnmower; Miss Pace wore skirts that would work better as carpet; and Mrs. Weaver, with her tailored slacks tucked under her breasts, had been dubbed Harry High-Pants. Most of them saw teachers as an alien species, undeserving of common courtesy, but despite their laughter, I knew there was no real malice intended in their jibes; they were just bored.

Soon the conversation turned to matters of more importance.

"Get excited, 'cause we're going shopping soon!" said Hayley. "We thought we'd get the train to the city and check out the boutiques in Punch Lane. Molly, are you coming?"

"Count me in," Molly replied. "What about you, Beth?"

"I don't even know if I'm going to the prom," I said.

"Why would you even think about missing it?" Molly looked aghast, as if only an apocalypse might serve as a valid reason for not attending.

"Well, for one I don't have a date."

I didn't confess this to Molly, but several boys had already broached the subject, seizing the opportunity of finding me alone in between classes. I had fended them off with non-committal responses. I told everyone who asked that I wasn't sure if I'd be going, which wasn't entirely a lie. I was buying time and secretly hoping Xavier would ask me.

A girl called Montana rolled her eyes. "Don't worry about that. The dress is way more important. If you get desperate, you can always find someone.

I was about to say something about checking my planner when I felt a strong arm slip around my shoulders. The group froze, their gazes fixed on the space above my head.

"Hi, girls, you don't mind if I steal Beth for a minute, do you?" Xavier asked.

"Well, we *were* in the middle of an important conversation," Molly objected. Her eyes narrowed in suspicion and she looked at me expectantly.

"I'll bring her right back," Xavier said.

There was something familiar about his manner toward me, which they didn't fail to notice. Although I liked it, I was also uncomfortable to suddenly be the center of attention. Xavier guided me to an empty table.

"What are you doing?" I whispered.

"I seem to be making a habit of rescuing you," he replied.

"Or did you want to spend the rest of lunch talking about spray tans and eyelash extensions?"

"How do you even know about that stuff?"

"Sisters," he said.

He seated himself comfortably at the table, ignoring the sidelong glances being aimed at us now from all directions of the crowded cafeteria. Some looked envious, others simply curious. Xavier had chosen to sit with me when almost any table in the room would have welcomed him and coveted his company.

"We seem to be drawing attention," I said and squirmed.

"People like to gossip, we can't help that."

"Why aren't you with your friends?"

"You're more interesting."

"There's nothing interesting about me," I said, a note of panic creeping into my voice.

"I disagree. Even your reaction to being called interesting is interesting."

We were interrupted by two younger boys approaching our table.

"Hey, Xavier." The taller of the two greeted him with a respectful nod. "The swim meet was awesome. I won four out of six heats."

"Good job, Parker," Xavier said, slipping easily into his role as school captain and mentor. "I knew we were going to kick Westwood's butt."

The boy beamed with pride.

"Reckon I'll make the nationals?" he asked eagerly.

"I wouldn't be surprised—Coach was pretty pleased. Just make sure you show up to training next week."

"You got it, man," the boy said. "See you Wednesday!"

Xavier nodded and they knocked their fists together. "See you, kiddo."

I saw right away that Xavier was good at dealing with people; he was affable without inviting familiarity. When the boy had gone, his expression changed back to one of concentration, as if what I had to say really mattered. It made my skin prickle and the corners of my lips twist into a smile. I could feel a blush starting in my chest, and soon it traveled to spread across my face.

"How do you do that?" I asked to cover my confusion.

"Do what?"

"Talk to people so easily."

Xavier shrugged. "It comes with the territory. Hey, I almost forgot, I dragged you over here to return something." He pulled a long, white, iridescent feather, flecked with rose, from the pocket of his blazer. "I found this in my car last night after I drove you home."

I snatched the feather from his hand and slipped it between the covers of my planner. I had no idea how it had ended up in Xavier's car. My wings had been firmly tucked away.

"Good luck charm?" Xavier asked, his turquoise eyes watching my face with curiosity.

"Something like that," I replied guardedly.

"You look upset; is something wrong?"

I shook my head quickly and looked away.

"You know you can trust me."

"Actually, I don't know that yet."

"You'll find out once we spend more time together," he said. "I'm a pretty loyal guy."

I didn't hear him. I was too busy scanning the faces in the crowd in case one of them belonged to Gabriel. His fears didn't seem so unfounded now.

"Don't overwhelm me with your enthusiasm." Xavier laughed. His words brought me back to the present with a jolt.

"I'm sorry," I said. "I'm a little preoccupied today."

"Anything I can help with?"

"I don't think so but thanks for asking."

"You know, keeping secrets is unhealthy for a relationship." Xavier folded his arms comfortably across his chest and settled back in his chair.

"Who said anything about a relationship? Besides, we're not required to share everything; it's not like we're married."

"You want to marry me?" Xavier asked, and I saw some faces turn toward us in curiosity. "I was thinking we'd start slow and see where things went, but hey, what the hell!"

I rolled my eyes. "Be quiet or I'll be forced to flick you."

"Ooh," he mocked. "The ultimate threat. I don't think I've ever been flicked before."

"Are you suggesting I can't hurt you?"

"On the contrary, I think you have the power to do great damage."

I looked at him quizzically and then blushed deeply when his meaning dawned.

"Very funny," I said curtly.

His arm lying across the table brushed against mine. Something inside me stirred.

THERE was nothing I could do about it. My attachment to Xavier Woods was instant and all-consuming. Suddenly my old life seemed far away. I certainly didn't yearn for Heaven as I knew Gabriel and Ivy did. For them, life on earth was a daily reminder of the limitations of flesh. For me, it was a reminder of the wonders of being human.

I became adept at masking my feelings for Xavier in front of my brother and sister. I knew they were aware of it, but if they disapproved, they must have made a pact to keep it to themselves. For that, I was grateful. I sensed a rift between us now that hadn't been there before. Our relationship seemed more fragile, and there were uncomfortable silences at the dinner table. Every night I fell asleep to the sound of their whispered conversations and felt certain that my disobedience was the subject of discussion. I elected to do nothing about the increasing distance between us even though I knew I might come to regret the decision later.

For now, I had other things to think about. I suddenly looked forward to getting up in the morning and leapt out of bed without needing Ivy to wake me up. I lingered in front of the mirror, trying different things with my hair, seeing myself as Xavier might see me. In my head I replayed snippets of conversation, trying to determine the impression I'd made. Sometimes I'd be pleased by a witty remark I'd delivered; other times I berated myself for saying or doing something clumsy. I made a pastime of thinking up sharp one-liners and memorized them for future use.

I was envious of Molly and her group now. What they took for granted, I could never have: a future on this planet. They would grow up to have families of their own, careers to explore, and a lifetime of memories to share with the partners they'd choose. I was just a tourist living on borrowed time. For this reason alone I knew I should curb my feelings for Xavier rather than allow them to develop. But if I'd learned anything about teenage romance, it was that intensity wasn't dictated by duration. Three months was the norm, six months marked a turning point, and if a relationship lasted a year, the pair was more or less engaged. I didn't know how long I had on earth, but whether it was a month or a year, I wasn't going to waste a single day of it. After all, every minute spent with Xavier would form the basis of memories I would need to sustain me for eternity.

I had no trouble collecting such memories because soon there wasn't a day that passed without me having some form of interaction with him. We looked for each other routinely at school whenever we had free time. Sometimes our contact was nothing more than a brief conversation at the lockers or sitting together at lunch. When I wasn't in class, I found myself on full alert, looking over my shoulder, trying to spy him coming out of the locker rooms, waiting for the moment when he came onto the stage during assemblies or squinting to make him out among the players on the rugby field. Molly sarcastically suggested I might need to get glasses.

On afternoons when he didn't have training, Xavier would walk me home, insisting on carrying my bag. We made sure to extend the walk by taking a detour through town and stopping at Sweethearts, which quickly became "our place."

Sometimes we talked about our day; other times we sat in comfortable silence. I was content to just look at him, something I never tired of doing. I could become mesmerized by his floppy hair, his eyes the color of the ocean, the habit he had of raising one eyebrow. His face was as entrancing as a piece of art. With my keen senses, I learned to identify him by his distinctive scent. I always knew when he was close by, before I could actually see him, by the clean, woody fragrance in the air.

Sometimes during those sun-kissed afternoons, I would look around furtively, expecting heavenly retribution. I imagined being watched by secret eyes gathering evidence of my misconduct. But nothing happened.

It was largely because of Xavier that I went from being an outsider to an integral part of life at Bryce Hamilton. Through my association with him, I made the discovery that popularity could be transferred. If people could be guilty by association, they could achieve recognition in exactly the same way. Almost overnight I became accepted simply because I numbered among Xavier Wood's friends. Even Molly, who had initially discouraged my interest in him, seemed appeased. When we were together, Xavier and I turned heads, but now it was more as a result of admiration than surprise. I noticed the difference even when I was alone. People gave me friendly waves as I passed them in the corridor, made small talk in the classroom while waiting for a teacher to arrive, or asked me how I'd done on the latest test.

My contact with Xavier at school was limited by the fact that we mostly took different classes. Otherwise I might have run the risk of following him around like a puppy. Apart from the French class we shared, his forte was math and science while I was drawn to the arts.

"Literature's my favorite subject," I announced to him one day in the cafeteria as if it were a vital discovery. I was carrying my booklet of literary terms, and I let it fall open at a random page. "Bet you don't know what enjambment is."

"I don't but it sounds painful," said Xavier.

"It's when one line of poetry runs into the next."

"Wouldn't it be easier to follow if you just put in full stops?" That was one of things I liked about Xavier; his view of the world was so black and white. I laughed.

"Possibly, but it might not be as interesting."

"Honestly, what is it you like so much about literature?" he asked with genuine interest. "I hate how there's no right or wrong answer. Everything's open to interpretation."

"Well, I like the way each person can have a completely different understanding of the same word or sentence," I said. "You can spend hours discussing the meaning behind a poem and have reached no conclusion by the end of it."

"And that doesn't frustrate you? Don't you want to know the answer?"

"Sometimes it's better to stop trying to make sense of things. Life isn't clear-cut, there are always gray areas."

"My life is pretty clear-cut," Xavier said. "Isn't yours?"

"No," I said with a sigh, thinking of the ongoing conflict with my siblings. "My world is messy and confusing. It gets tiring sometimes."

"I think I might have to change your world," Xavier replied.

We looked at each other in silence for a few moments, and I felt as if his brilliant ocean eyes could see right into my head and pull out my thoughts and innermost feelings.

"You know, you can always pick the lit students," he continued, grinning.

"Is that so? How?"

"They're the ones who walk around wearing berets and that I-know-something-you-don't expression."

"That's not fair!" I objected. "I don't."

"No, you're too genuine for that. Don't ever change, and don't under any circumstances start wearing a beret."

"I'll do my best," I laughed.

The bell sounded, signaling the start of the next class.

"What have you got now?" Xavier asked.

I cheerfully waved my glossary of literary terms under his nose by way of answer.

I was always happy to be going to literature with Miss Castle. It was a diverse class despite there being only twelve of us. There were two sullen-looking goth girls, who wore black eyeliner and whose cheeks were powdered so chalk white they looked like they'd never seen the sun. There was a group of diligent girls with neat hair ribbons and well-equipped pencil cases, who were obsessed with grades, and they were usually too busy taking notes to contribute to class discussion. There were only two boys: Ben Carter, who was cocky but astute, and loved an argument; and Tyler Jensen, a brawny rugby player, who invariably arrived late and sat through the lesson wearing a stunned expression and chewing gum. He never contributed anything and his presence in the class was a mystery to everyone.

Due to the small size of the group, we'd been relegated to a cramped classroom in the old part of the school that adjoined the administration offices. As the room wasn't used for any other purpose, we were allowed to shift the furniture and put up posters. My favorite was one of Shakespeare depicted as a pirate wearing an earring. The room's only advantage was that it came with a view of the front lawns and palm-lined street. Unlike other subjects, literature class could never be described as lackluster. Instead, the very air seemed to be charged with ideas all vying to be heard.

I sat next to Ben and watched him look up his favorite bands on his laptop, an activity he kept up even once the class had started. Miss Castle arrived carrying a mug of coffee and an armful of handouts. She was a tall, slender woman in her early forties with masses of dark curly hair and dreamy eyes. She always wore heavy-framed glasses on a fine red cord around her neck and pastel blouses. Judging by the way she carried herself and the way she spoke, she would have been more comfortable in a Jane Austen novel, in which women rode in carriages and witty repartee flew across a drawing room like sparks. She was passionate about language, and it didn't matter what text we were studying, she identified vividly with the heroine every time. Her teaching was so animated, people sometimes stopped to look into the classroom, where they'd see Miss Castle thumping the teacher's desk, firing off questions or gesticulating wildly to illustrate a point. I wouldn't have been surprised to walk in one day and find her standing on top of her desk or swinging from the light fixtures.

We'd started the term studying *Romeo and Juliet* in conjunction with Shakespeare's love sonnets. Now we were assigned the task of writing our own love poems, which would be recited to the class. The studious girls, who'd never had to rely on their own imaginations before, flew into a panic. This was something they couldn't look up on the Internet.

"We don't know what to write about!" they wailed. "It's too hard."

"Just think about it for a while," said Miss Castle in her floaty voice.

"Nothing interesting happens to us."

"It doesn't have to be personal," she coaxed. "It can be a total figment of your imagination."

The girls remained uninspired.

"Can you give us an example?" they persisted.

"We've been looking at examples all term," said Miss Castle in a dejected tone. Then an idea for a starting point came to her. "Think about qualities you find attractive in a boy."

"Well, I think intelligence is very important," a girl named Bianca volunteered.

"Obviously, he should be a good provider," her friend Hannah piped up.

Miss Castle looked at a loss. She was spared having to comment by a contribution from a different quarter.

"People are only interesting if they're dark and disturbed," said Alicia, one of the goths.

"Chicks shouldn't talk so much," drawled Tyler from the back of the room. It was the first thing we'd heard him say all term, and Miss Castle was graciously prepared to overlook its derogatory nature.

"Thank you, Tyler," she said with underlying sarcasm. "You have just proved that the search for a partner is a very individual thing. Some say we can't choose who we fall in love with; love chooses us. Sometimes, people fall for the complete antithesis of everything they believe they're looking for. Any other thoughts?"

Ben Carter, who had been rolling his eyes and wearing a martyred expression throughout the discussion, put his face in his hands.

"Great love stories have to be tragic," I said suddenly.

"Go on," encouraged Miss Castle.

"Well, take Romeo and Juliet for example: It's the fact that they're kept apart that makes their love stronger."

"Big deal—they both end up dead," snorted Ben.

"They'd have ended up divorced if they'd stayed alive," announced Bianca. "Did anyone else notice that it took Romeo all of five seconds to switch from Rosaline to Juliet?"

"That's because he knew Juliet was *the one* from the moment he met her," I said.

"Puh-lease," Bianca retorted. "You can't know that you love someone after two minutes. He just wanted to get in her pants. Romeo is just like every other horny teenage boy."

"He didn't *know* anything about her," Ben said. "All his praise is for her physical attributes: 'Juliet is the sun' and blah blah blah. He just thinks she's a babe."

"I think it's because after he met her everyone else became insignificant," I said. "He knew right away that she was going to be his whole world."

"Oh God," groaned Ben.

Miss Castle gave me a meaningful smile. Being a hopeless romantic, she couldn't help but take Romeo's side. Unlike most of the teachers at Bryce Hamilton, who competed to see who could get to the parking lot first after the final bell rang, she wasn't jaded. She was a dreamer. I suspected that if I told Miss Castle I was a celestial being on a mission to save the world, she wouldn't have even blinked.

{ 12 }

Saving Grace

I'D never seen God. I'd felt His presence and heard His voice but never actually come face to face with Him. His voice wasn't what people imagined, booming and reverberating as depicted in epic Hollywood movies. Rather it was as subtle as a whisper and moved through our thoughts as gently as a breeze through tall reeds. Ivy had seen Him. An audience in Our Father's court was reserved for the seraphim alone. As an archangel, Gabriel had the highest level of human interaction. He saw all the greatest suffering, the sort that was shown on the news; war, natural disasters, disease. He was guided by Our Father and worked with the rest of his covenant to point the earth in the right direction. Although Ivy had a direct line of communication with Our Creator, she could never be induced to talk on the subject. Gabriel and I had attempted many times to glean information from her to no avail. So, strangely enough, I ended up imagining God in much the same way as Michelangelo had: a wise old man with a beard, sitting on a throne in the sky. My mental picture was probably inaccurate, but there was one thing that couldn't be disputed: No matter what his appearance, Our Father was the complete embodiment of love.

Much as I savored every day spent on earth, there was one thing I sometimes missed about Heaven: how everything there was clear. There was no conflict, no dissension apart from that one historic uprising that resulted in the Kingdom's first and only eviction. Although it had altered the destiny of humankind forever, it was rarely talked about.

In Heaven I was dimly aware of the existence of a darker world, but it was removed from us and we were usually too busy working to think about it. We angels each had assigned roles and responsibilities: Some of us welcomed new souls into the Kingdom, helping to ease the transition; some materialized at deathbeds to offer comfort to departing souls; and others were guardians assigned to human beings. In the Kingdom, I looked after the souls of children when they first entered the realm. It had been my job to comfort them, to tell them that in time they would see their parents again if they let go of their doubts. I was a sort of celestial usher for preschoolers.

I was glad I wasn't a guardian angel; they were usually overworked. It was their job to listen to the prayers of their many human charges and guide them out of harm's way. It could get fairly hectic—I'd once seen a guardian try to come to the aid of a sick child, a woman going through a messy divorce, a man who'd just been laid off, and the victim of a car accident all in the same instant. There was so much work to do and never enough of us to go around.

———

XAVIER and I sat under the shade of a maple tree in the quadrangle, eating lunch. I couldn't help but be aware of his hand, resting just inches from my own. It was slender but masculine. He wore a simple silver band around his index finger. I was so engrossed in looking at him that I hardly noticed when he spoke to me.

"Can I ask a favor?"

"What? Oh, of course. What do you need?"

"Could you proofread this speech I've written? I've done it twice, but I'm sure I've missed things."

"Sure. What's it for?"

"A leadership conference next week," he said offhandedly, as if it were something he did every day. "You don't have to do it now. You can take it home if you like."

"No, it's fine."

I was flattered that he valued my opinion enough to ask me. I spread the pages flat on the grass and read through them. Xavier's speech was eloquent, but he'd missed some minor grammatical errors that I spotted easily.

"You're a good editor," he commented. "Thanks for doing it."

"It's no trouble."

"Seriously, I owe you one. Let me know if there's anything I can do for you."

"You don't owe me anything," I said.

"Yes, I do. By the way, when's your birthday?"

I was taken aback by the question.

"I don't like presents," I said quickly, in case he got any ideas.

"Who said anything about presents? I'm just asking for your date of birth."

"Thirtieth of February," I said, throwing out the first date that came to mind.

Xavier raised an eyebrow.

"Are you sure about that?"

I panicked. What had I said wrong? I ran through the months in my head and realised my mistake. Oops—there were only twenty-eight days in February!

"I mean thirtieth of April," I corrected and grinned sheepishly.

Xavier laughed. "You're the first person I've ever known to forget her own birthday."

Even when I made a fool of myself, my conversations with Xavier were always engaging.

He could talk about the most mundane of things and still manage to make them fascinating. I loved the sound of his voice and would have been happy listening to him read names from a phone book. Was this a symptom of falling in love, I wondered?

As Xavier scribbled notes in the margins of his speech, I bit into my roast vegetable focaccia and made a face as a strangely bitter flavor assaulted my taste buds. Gabriel had introduced us to most food products, but there were still plenty of things I had yet to try. I lifted the top cautiously and peered at the substance smeared under the vegetables.

"What's that?" I asked Xavier.

"I believe it goes by the name of eggplant," he replied. "Sometimes called aubergine in fancy restaurants."

"No, the other stuff." I pointed at the layer of crumbly, green paste.

"Dunno, pass it over." I watched him take a tentative bite and chew thoughtfully. "Pesto," he announced.

"Why does everything have to be so complicated," I said irritably, "including sandwiches?"

"You're so right," Xavier mused. "Pesto does make life much more complicated." He laughed and took another bite, pushing his own untouched salad wrap toward me.

"Don't be silly," I said. "Eat your lunch, I can cope with pesto."

But he refused to return my sandwich despite my whining. I gave up and ate his instead, enjoying the familiarity between us.

"Don't feel bad," he said. "I'm a guy, I'll eat anything."

ON our way to class after lunch, we came across a commotion in the corridor. People were talking agitatedly about some kind of accident. No one was too sure who was involved, but students were moving en masse toward the main doors, where a crowd had gathered outside around something or somebody. I sensed human pain and felt a wave of panic rise in my chest.

I followed Xavier through the crowd, which seemed to part instinctively to let the school captain through. Once outside my eyes found the shattered glass littering the pavement, and I followed the trail to a car with its hood completely smashed in, smoke curling from the engine. There had been a head-on collision between two seniors. One of the drivers was standing by his car, looking dazed and disoriented. Thankfully, he seemed to have suffered only minor scratches. My gaze shifted from his mangled Volkswagen to linger on the car now entangled with it. I realized with a jolt that the other driver was still inside, slumped in the seat, her head lolling against the steering wheel. Even from where I stood, I could see that she was seriously hurt.

The crowd watched with open mouths, unsure what was required of them. Only Xavier managed to keep his wits about him. He vanished from my side to call for help and alert the teachers.

Not entirely sure what I should be doing, acting more on impulse than anything else, I moved toward the car, coughing as thick smoke filled my throat. The driver's door had been crushed from the impact and had almost completely detached from the body of the vehicle. Ignoring the hot metal that dug into my palms, I pulled it free and froze when I saw the girl close up. Blood was flowing freely from a cut on her forehead, her mouth was open, but her eyes were closed and her body was limp.

Even in Heaven I had always felt faint watching scenes involving bloodshed unfold on earth, but today I hardly thought about it. I looped my arms under the girl's shoulders and, as carefully as I could, began to pull her from the wreckage. She was heavier than me, so I was grateful when two well-built boys, still in their gym gear, sprinted over to help. We laid the girl on the pavement at a safe distance from the smoking vehicle.

I realized that was the extent to which the boys could help. They both kept looking nervously over their shoulders, waiting for assistance to arrive. But there wasn't time to wait.

"Keep the crowd back," I instructed them and turned my attention to the girl. I knelt down and placed two fingers against her neck, as Gabriel had once shown me. I couldn't find a pulse. If she was breathing at all, it wasn't obvious through any visible sign. In my head I called out for Gabriel to come and help me. There wasn't a chance I could get through this on my own. I was already losing the battle. The warm blood oozing from the gash on her forehead had become matted in her hair. There were bluish rings under her eyes and she was deathly pale. I suspected internal injuries but couldn't put my finger on exactly what they were.

"Hold on," I whispered close to her ear. "Help is coming."

I cradled her head, sticky blood staining my hands, and focused on sending my healing energy through her. I knew I had only minutes to help her. Her body had almost surrendered the fight, and I could feel her soul trying to detach itself. Soon she would be looking at her inert body from outside it.

I concentrated so hard I felt I too might lose consciousness. I fought back the light-headedness and focused even more deeply. I imagined a power source surging from a deep well within me, traveling through my blood and arteries to charge my fingertips and flow into the body on the ground. As I felt the power draining from me, I thought that maybe, just maybe, the girl might survive.

I heard Gabriel before I saw him, urging the crowd to let him through. In the presence of authority the students breathed a collective sigh of relief. They had been absolved of further responsibility. Whatever happened now was out of their hands.

While Xavier went to the aid of the other driver, Gabriel knelt beside me and used his power to close the girl's wounds. He worked quickly and quietly, feeling for the broken ribs, the punctured lung, the twisted wrist that had snapped as easily as a twig. By the time the paramedics arrived, the girl's breathing had returned to normal although she hadn't regained consciousness. I noticed that Gabriel had left her minor cuts unhealed, probably to prevent arousing suspicion.

As the paramedics were lifting the girl onto a stretcher, a cluster of her hysterical friends rushed over to us.

"Grace!" one cried. "Oh my God, is she okay?"

"Gracie! What happened? Can you hear us?"

"She's unconscious," Gabriel said, "but she's going to be fine."

Although the girls continued to sob and cling to one another, I could see that Gabriel had calmed them.

After directing the students back to class, Gabriel took me by the arm and led me up the front steps, where Ivy was waiting for us. Xavier, who had not followed the others inside, ran over when he saw my face.

"Beth, are you all right?" His walnut-colored hair was ruffled by the wind, and his tension showed by the veins pulsing in his neck.

I wanted to answer, but I was struggling for breath and the world was starting to spin. I sensed that Gabriel was anxious for us to be alone.

"You'd better get to class," he said to Xavier, adopting his teacher voice.

"I'm waiting for Beth," Xavier replied. His eyes swept over my untidy hair, the bloodstained sleeves of my shirt, and my fingers clutching at Gabriel's arm.

"She just needs a minute," Gabriel said more coldly. "You can check on her later."

Xavier stood his ground.

"I'm not leaving unless Beth tells me to."

I wondered what kind of look was on Gabriel's face, but when I twisted my head to see, the steps I was standing on felt as though they were about to give way. Or was it my knees that were giving way? Black spots appeared across my field of vision, and I leaned against Gabriel more heavily.

The last thing I remembered was saying Xavier's name and seeing him take a step toward me before I fainted quietly in Gabriel's arms.

I woke up to the familiarity of my room. I was curled under the patchwork quilt on my bed, and I knew the balcony doors were not completely shut because I could feel a breeze carrying the briny scent of the ocean inside. I lifted my head and focused on comforting details like the peeling paint on the window-sill and the pockmarked floorboards softened by the amber glow of dusk. My pillow was soft and smelled of lavender. I buried my face in it, reluctant to stir. Then I saw the time on my alarm clock—seven p.m.! I'd been asleep for hours. My limbs felt like lead. I panicked momentarily when I couldn't move my legs before realizing that Phantom was lying across them.

He yawned and stretched when he saw that I was awake. I stroked his silky head, and he looked at me with his doleful, colorless eyes.

"Come on," I murmured. "It's not your bedtime yet."

I must have sat up too suddenly because a wave of fatigue hit me like an avalanche and I nearly fell back again. I swung my legs over the side of the bed and tried to muster the effort required to stand. It wasn't easy, but I managed to slip on my robe and stumbled downstairs, where Schubert's "Ave Maria" was playing in the background. I sank into the nearest chair. Gabriel and Ivy must have been in the kitchen; the smell of garlic and ginger filled the room. They stopped what they were doing and came out to greet me. Ivy was wiping her hands on a dish towel, and they were both smiling. This took me by surprise as it felt like a long time since we'd been on anything more than civil terms.

"How are you feeling?" Ivy's cool, slender fingers stroked my head.

"Like I've been hit by a bus," I replied honestly. "I really don't know what happened. I was feeling fine."

"Surely you know why you fainted, Bethany," Gabriel said.

I gave him a blank look. "I've been eating properly and taking all your advice."

"It's got nothing to do with that," my brother said. "It was because you saved that girl's life."

"That sort of thing can really take it out of you," Ivy added.

I almost laughed aloud. "But, Gabe, *you* saved that girl's life," I said.

Ivy looked at our brother to indicate that he should explain and discreetly moved off to set the table for dinner.

"I only healed her physical wounds," Gabriel said. I gave him a stupefied look, wondering if this was his idea of a joke.

"What do you mean *only*? That's what constitutes saving someone. If a person gets shot and you remove the bullet and heal the wound then you've saved them."

"No, Bethany, that girl was going to die. If you hadn't given her your life force, nothing I could have done would have saved her. Closing wounds can't bring someone back once they've reached that point. You spoke to her; it was your voice that called her back and your strength that kept her soul from leaving her body."

I couldn't believe what he was telling me. *I* had saved a human life? I hadn't even known I had the power to do that. I'd believed the extent of my powers on earth to be only good for soothing bad tempers or helping retrieve lost belongings. How was it possible that I had found it in me to save a girl on the brink of death? Power over the sea, over the sky, over human life, that was Gabriel's gift. It had never occurred to me that my powers might be greater than I was aware of.

Ivy looked across at me, her eyes bright with praise. "Congratulations," she said. "This is a big step for you."

"But how come I feel so bad now?" I asked, suddenly alerted to my aching body.

"The effort of reviving someone can be very debilitating," Ivy explained, "especially the first couple of times. It sends your human form into shock. It won't always be like that;

you'll grow accustomed to it and eventually you'll be able to recover more quickly."

"You mean I'll be able to do it again?" I asked. "It wasn't a fluke?"

"If you've done it once, you can do it again," Gabriel answered. "All angels have the ability, but it develops with practice."

Despite my exhaustion I felt suddenly buoyant and ate my dinner with appetite. Afterward Gabriel and Ivy refused my offer of help with the cleaning up. Instead Ivy steered me onto the deck and pushed me into the hammock.

"You've had a very tiring day," she said.

"But I hate not being useful."

"You can help me in a minute. I have a whole lot of hats and scarves to knit for the thrift shop." Ivy always found time to connect with the community, through small earthly tasks. "Sometimes it's the little things that count most," she said.

"You know, the whole idea of those places is that you donate your old clothes, not make new ones," I teased.

"Well, we haven't been here long enough to have old things," replied Ivy. "And I have to give them something; I'd feel just awful if I didn't. Besides, I can whip them up in no time."

I sat in the hammock with a mohair blanket around my shoulders, trying to process the events of the afternoon. In one way, I felt I understood the purpose of our mission better than before, but at the same time I'd never been more confused. Today had been a prime example of what I should be doing—protecting the sanctity of life. Instead I'd been spending my time absorbed in a teenage obsession with a boy who didn't really know anything about me. Poor Xavier, I thought. He would never be able to understand me, no matter how hard he tried. It wasn't his fault. He could only know as much as I allowed him to know. I was so busy trying to keep up my façade that I hadn't considered that sooner or later it would all have to come undone. Xavier was tied to a human life and an existence I could never be part of. The satisfaction I felt at my success that afternoon faded, and I was left feeling strangely numb.

13

His Kiss

SUNDAY mass was the only time I felt I could truly reconnect with my home. Kneeling in the pews and listening to the chords of "Agnus Dei" brought me back to my former self. There was an airy tranquility inside the church that couldn't be found anywhere else. It was cool and calm, like being at the bottom of the ocean, and I always felt that as soon as I stepped through its doors, I was in a safe place. Ivy and I were altar servers on Sunday, and Gabriel helped Father Mel in giving out Holy Communion. After the service, we always stayed behind to chat with him.

"The congregation is growing," he observed one day. "Every week, I see new faces."

"Maybe people are starting to realize what's important in life," Ivy said.

"Or maybe they are following your example." Father Mel smiled.

"The Church should need no advocates," Gabriel said. "It should speak for itself."

"It doesn't matter what brings people here," said Father Mel. "It only matters what they find here."

"All we can do is lead them in the right direction," Ivy agreed.

"Indeed, we cannot force them to have faith," Father Mel said. "But we can demonstrate its great power."

"And we can pray for them," I said.

"Of course," Father Mel winked at me. "And something tells me the Lord will listen when you call."

"He listens to us no more than to others," Gabriel said. I could tell he was concerned about giving away too much. Although we'd never so much as hinted to Father Mel about where we came from, there was a tacit understanding between us. It was only natural, I thought. He was a priest—he spent all his time trying to connect with the forces above. "We can only hope that He will bless this town," Gabriel added.

Father Mel's blue eyes flickered over us all. "I believe He already has." .

The next day Xavier had a sports meeting at morning break, so I spent the time listening to Molly and Taylah talk animatedly about a clothing outlet just out of town. There they could buy fake designer labels that looked so authentic no one would guess they weren't the "real deal." When they asked me to go with them, I was so preoccupied that I agreed without hesitation. Even when they invited me to a beach bonfire that Saturday night, I nodded my consent without really registering the details of the invitation.

I was glad when fifth period finally came around and Xavier and I had French together. I felt a rush of relief to be in the same room as him even though I could barely focus. I desperately needed to talk to him now, even if I hadn't decided what I was going to say. I just knew that it couldn't wait.

He was less than a handsbreadth away, and I had to sit on my fingers to keep them from reaching out and touching him. Partly because I wanted to reassure myself that I hadn't imagined him but also because it felt as if we were two magnets drawn to each other; resisting was more painful than succumbing. The minutes crawled by, and it seemed as if time had slowed deliberately just to spite me.

Xavier sensed my strange mood and stayed seated after the bell, watching everyone else file past. While I put on a charade of packing up my books and pencils, he sat very still without fidgeting. A few curious onlookers cast glances in our direction, probably hoping to pick up some threads of the conversation that they might report back to their friends as juicy gossip.

"I tried to call you last night but there was no answer," he said, seeing that I was struggling to start. "I was worried about you."

I fiddled nervously with the zipper of my pencil case, which seemed to be jammed. I must have looked uncomfortable because Xavier stood up and put his hands on my shoulders.

"What's up, Beth?" There was a familiar crease between his eyebrows, which always appeared when he was concerned.

"I guess yesterday's accident just drained me," I said. "But I'm better now."

"That's good. But something tells me there's more."

Even in the short time I'd known him, Xavier was always able to read my moods, yet his own eyes betrayed nothing of what he might be feeling. He didn't look away; his turquoise gaze was like a laser boring into me.

"My life is pretty complicated," I began tentatively.

"Why don't you try explaining it? I might surprise you."

"This situation," I said, "you and I spending time together, it's turning out to be harder than I thought. . . ." I paused. "It's better than I ever imagined, but I have other responsibilities, other duties that I can't ignore."

My voice rose in volume and pitch as I felt a wave of emotion explode in my chest. I stopped and took a deep breath.

"It's okay, Beth," Xavier said. "I know you have a secret."

I felt a sudden icy fear take hold of me, but at the same time a flooding relief. If Xavier already knew I was a fraud and a liar, it meant I'd failed completely in all aspects of our mission. Rule number one for all Agents of Light was to keep our identity a secret as we worked to piece the world back together—exposure could result in all kinds of chaos. But then again, it could also mean that Xavier had chosen to accept me anyway and the truth might not drive him away.

"You do?" I whispered.

He shrugged. "It's obvious you're hiding something. I don't know what it is, but I know it's upsetting you."

I didn't answer immediately. More than anything I wanted to tell him everything, to let all my secrets and fears pour out like wine from a spilled bottle, staining everything in their path.

"I understand that for one reason or another you can't or won't talk about it," Xavier said. "But you don't have to. I can respect your privacy."

"That's not fair to you," I said, feeling more torn than ever. The idea of walking away from him left a physical pain in my chest, like my heart was slowly breaking in two.

"Isn't that for me to decide?"

"Don't make this harder. I'm trying to protect you!"

"Protect me?" Xavier laughed. "From what?"

"From me," I said quietly, realizing how ridiculous that must sound.

"You don't look very dangerous to me. Unless you turn into a werewolf at night. . . ."

"I'm just not what I seem." I shrank away from him, as if trying to hide myself from the truth. My whole body felt weak and drained of energy. I sagged against a wall, unable to meet his gaze.

"No one is. Look, you think I haven't figured out there's something different about you? All I have to do is look at you."

"What is it?" I asked curiously.

"I'm not sure," he said. "But I know it's what I like about you."

"What I'm trying to tell you is that just because you like me doesn't make me what you want or need."

"What do you think I need?"

"Someone you can have an honest relationship with. What's the point otherwise?"

"Are you trying to tell me that person can't be you?" Xavier's expression was unreadable. His face appeared completely impassive—wiped of all emotion. I supposed that after everything he'd been through, he wasn't the type to wear his heart on his sleeve.

I knew he was trying to make it easier for me, but the bluntness of his question had the opposite effect. Now that the idea was out in the open, it sounded far too final. I was still struggling to find the right words, and I worried that my silence might come across as indifference.

"It's okay," Xavier continued. "I know it can't be easy for you, and I don't want to make things harder. Would it be helpful if I kept my distance for a while?"

How fickle and contradictory were human emotions! I'd spent the last few minutes trying to suggest this very idea but now found myself devastated by his readiness to walk away, even if his motivation was my well-being. I wasn't sure what reaction I'd expected, but this wasn't it. Did I want to see him drop to his knees and declare his undying love? Of course he wasn't going to do that, but I couldn't let him walk away. I didn't think I'd be able to stand it.

"So that's it then?" I choked out. "I won't see you anymore?"

Xavier looked confused. "Hang on—isn't that what you want?"

"Is that *all* you're going to say?" I demanded. "You're not even going to try and change my mind?"

"Do you want me to try and change your mind?" His quizzical, affectionate smile was back.

I paused to think. I knew what I should say. A simple no would end it all and return things to how they'd been before the moment we met in the corridor outside the chemistry lab, when I'd been trying to avoid glowing in the dark. But I couldn't bring myself to say it. It would be a lie.

"Maybe that's exactly what I want you to do," I said slowly.

"Beth, it sounds to me like you don't know what you want," Xavier said softly. He reached up and used his thumb to wipe away a tear that was snaking its way down my cheek.

"I don't want to complicate your life," I sniffed, realizing how irrational I must be sounding. "You're the one who said you preferred things to be clear-cut."

"I was talking about subjects, not people. Maybe I wouldn't mind a bit of complication," he said. "Straightforward relationships are overrated."

I groaned in frustration. "You really do have an answer for everything."

"What can I say? It's a gift." He took my hand between both of his. "I have an idea. How about I give you something to help make the decision easier?"

"Okay," I agreed. "If you think it'll help."

Before I knew what was happening, Xavier had brought his hands up to my face and was tilting my chin toward him. His lips brushed over mine with a feather touch, but it was enough to make me shiver. I liked the way he held me; as if I were fragile and likely to break if he held too tight. He rested his forehead against mine as though we had all the time in the world. A delicious heat started to spread through my body, and I strained toward him, reaching for his lips again. I returned his kiss with passionate urgency and clung to him. I allowed myself to melt into his embrace and pressed our bodies together. His warmth was seeping through my flimsy shirt, and I could feel his heart beating fast.

"Easy, now," he murmured into my ear, but he didn't break away. We stood locked in our embrace until Xavier gently but firmly detached himself. He tucked a stray lock of hair behind my ear and gave his dreamy half-smile. "Well?" he asked, folding his arms across his chest. My mind was a blur.

"Well what?"

"Did that help you make up your mind?"

By way of an answer, I twisted my fingers into his soft nut-brown hair and pulled him toward me.

"I guess it did," he said with undisguised pleasure.

That day taught me that I wanted more than his company; I craved his touch. There wasn't a doubt left in my mind. I could feel my face burning where he had touched me, and all I wanted was for him to do it again. Just hours earlier I had truly believed there was no option but to cut myself off from him because I could see no way to make him understand who I really was. Now I saw that there was another way. It would be seen as a serious transgression and punishable by who knew what, but it felt less frightening than parting from him. If it meant sparing us the pain of separation, I would face the consequences.

All that was required of me was to let down my guard and let Xavier in.

"I want us to be together," I said. "I don't think I've ever wanted anything more."

Xavier stroked my palm and entwined our fingers. His face was so close the tips of our noses were touching. He leaned in to whisper in my ear. "If you want me . . . you've got me."

I couldn't stop myself from sighing aloud as he kissed a path from my ear down to my neck. The physical surroundings of the classroom melted like snow in the sun.

"There's just one thing," I said, pushing him away with some difficulty. He was watching me with those piercing blue eyes, and I almost lost my train of thought. "This isn't going to work unless you know the truth." If I cared about Xavier as much as my beating heart told me I did then he deserved the truth. If it turned out that the truth was too much for him to deal with, then maybe it meant my feelings weren't returned and I would have to accept that. Either way it was time for the charade to end. Xavier had to see the uncensored version of me; not the idealized version in his head. In other words, he had to know me, warts and all.

"I'm all ears," he said looking at me expectantly.

"Not now. This isn't going to be easy, and I need more space than we've got here."

"Then where?" he asked, mystified.

"Are you going to the beach bonfire this weekend?" I asked quickly as students began to drift in for the next class.

"I was going to ask if you wanted to go together."

"Okay," I agreed. "I'll tell you everything then."

Xavier kissed me swiftly and left the classroom. I gripped the edge of the nearest desk feeling short of breath, as though I'd just run a marathon.

14

Defying Gravity

ALL week long the beach bonfire loomed in my mind. What I planned to do terrified me, but I was also strangely excited. Once the decision was made, it felt as though a great weight had lifted from my mind. After all the time I'd spent in internal debate, I now felt surprisingly sure of myself. In my head I rehearsed over and over the words I would use to tell Xavier the truth, making subtle adjustments each time.

Xavier was now behaving as though we were a couple, which I loved. It put us in our own exclusive world that no one else had access to. It meant that we took our relationship seriously and believed it had a future. It wasn't some infatuation we were likely to outgrow. We were making a commitment to each other. Every time I thought about this, I couldn't keep my face from cracking into a broad smile. Of course I remembered Ivy and Gabriel's warning and their belief that there was no chance of a future for us, but somehow that didn't matter anymore. I felt like the skies could open and rain fire and brimstone, but nothing could wipe the smile from my face. That was the effect he had on me—an explosion of happiness in my chest, scattering like little beads and making my whole body shiver and tingle.

A life with Xavier was full of promise. But would he still want that when I revealed my identity to him?

I tried to conceal my elation from Ivy and Gabriel. It had taken them long enough to recover from my last escapade with Xavier, and I didn't think they could handle another one. Whenever I sat down with them I felt like a double agent and kept wondering whether my face might betray me. But just because my siblings could read human minds, didn't mean they could read mine, and my acting skills must have improved because my new enthusiasm passed without comment. It struck me that I finally had an understanding of the expression "the calm before the storm." Everything seemed to be going smoothly, but I knew that appearances could be deceptive. There was an explosion waiting to happen. Tension, anger, and guilt were bubbling below the surface of our happy-family act, ready to erupt the moment Ivy and Gabriel discovered my betrayal.

"One of my juniors asked me today if there's such a thing as Limbo," Gabriel said over dinner one night. I found it ironic that the conversation had turned to punishment for sins.

Ivy put down her fork. "What did you say?"

"I said nobody knows."

"Why didn't you say yes?" I asked.

"Because good deeds have to be voluntary," my brother explained. "If a person knows for sure they'll be judged, then they'll act accordingly."

I couldn't argue with that. "What's Limbo like anyway?"

I knew enough about Heaven and Hell, but no one had ever told me about the eternal midpoint.

"It comes in several different forms," said Ivy. "It can be a waiting room, a train station."

"Some souls say it's worse than Hell," Gabriel added.

"That's ridiculous," I scoffed. "What could be worse?"

"Eternal nothingness," said Ivy. "Year upon year of waiting for a train that's never coming, waiting for someone to call your name. People start to lose all sense of time, it blurs into one never-ending stretch. They beg to go to Heaven, try to throw themselves into Hell, but there is no way out. The souls wander aimlessly. And it never ends, Bethany. Centuries can go by on earth and they will still be there."

"Sounds like crap," was all I could think to say. Gabriel and Ivy looked surprised for a moment before bursting into laughter.

I wondered if an angel could be exiled to Limbo.

AT Tuesday lunchtime I sat with Molly and the girls on the lawn in the afternoon sunshine. Around us green buds tipped the branches of the trees, bringing everything back to life. The imposing main building of Bryce Hamilton loomed behind us, casting a shadow over the benches arranged in a circle around the broad trunk of an ancient oak with ivy twining around its trunk in an amorous embrace. If we looked west, we had a view of the ocean in the distance stretching to the horizon, clouds drifting lazily overhead. The girls lounged on the lush grass, letting the sun warm their faces. I was feeling bold and ventured to tug my skirt up above my knees.

"Way to go, babe!" The girls applauded my progress, commenting that I was becoming "one of them" before falling into their usual routine of gossiping about teachers and absent friends.

"Miss Lucas is such a cow," Megan complained. "She's making me redo my Russian Revolution assignment because it was too 'sloppy.' What's that supposed to mean?"

"I think it means you did it in the half hour before it was due," Hayley said. "What did you expect—an A plus?"

Megan shrugged. "I reckon she's just jealous because she's hairy as a yeti."

"You should write a letter of complaint," a girl named Tara said with a serious expression. "She's totally discriminating against you."

"I agree she's defs picking on you," Molly began, and then fell suddenly silent, her gaze locked on a figure striding across the lawn.

I turned to identify the source of her fixation and saw Gabriel making his way toward the music center, some distance from where we sat. He cut a solitary figure with his faraway look and a guitar case slung over one shoulder. He had abandoned school protocol regarding dress sense some time ago, and today he was wearing his torn jeans with a white T-shirt under a pin-striped vest. No one had dared to query it. And why would they? Gabriel was so popular there would have been uproar among the students if he resigned. I noticed that Gabe looked so at ease with his surroundings. He had an easy gait and his movements were fluid. He seemed to be coming in our direction, which made Molly sit bolt upright and frantically smooth down her wild curls. Gabriel, however, suddenly cut across in a different direction. Lost in his own thoughts, he hadn't as much as glanced in our direction. Molly looked crestfallen.

"What can we say about Mr. Church?" Taylah speculated when she spotted him, eager to resume their usual sport. I had been quiet for so long, absorbed in my fantasy of being stranded on a secluded island somewhere in the Caribbean or held captive on a pirate ship, waiting for Xavier to come and rescue me, that it seemed they had temporarily forgotten I was there. Otherwise they might have reconsidered discussing Gabriel in my presence.

"Nothing," said Molly defensively. "He's a legend."

I could almost see the wheels turning in her head. I knew her fascination with Gabriel had grown in recent times, fueled by his remoteness. I didn't want Molly to suffer the rebuff that would inevitably follow from this infatuation. Gabriel was made of stone, metaphorically speaking, and was incapable of reciprocating her feelings. He was as detached from human life as the sky is from the earth. When he looked at humankind, he saw only souls in peril, barely even distinguishing men from women. I could see that Molly was under the delusion that Gabriel operated like the other young men she knew; full of hormones and unable to resist feminine allure if the girl in question played her cards right. But Molly had no idea what Gabriel was. He might have taken human form, but unlike me, he was far removed from anything human. In Heaven he was known as the Angel of Justice.

"He's a little uptight," Tara said.

"He is not!" Molly snapped. "You don't even know him."

"And you do?"

"I wish I did."

"Well, keep wishing."

"He's a teacher," Megan interrupted, "and in his twenties."

"Music teachers are kind of on the fringe," said Molly optimistically.

"Yeah, on the fringe *of the staff*," said Taylah. "Get over it, Molls, he's out of our league."

Molly narrowed her eyes as if she'd been issued a challenge. "I don't know about that," she said. "I like to think he's in a league of his own."

There was a sudden awkward silence as they remembered my presence. The subject was quickly dropped.

"So," said Megan a little too brightly. "About the prom . . ."

WHEN Xavier dropped me off at home that afternoon, I found Ivy icing cupcakes. There was a smudge of flour across the bridge of her nose, and her eyes sparkled as though she was captivated by the whole process. She had lined up all her ingredients neatly in assorted measuring cups, and now she was arranging her sprinkles so they formed perfectly symmetrical designs. It was something that no human hand could have managed. They looked like miniature artworks rather than something designed to be eaten. She presented me with one as soon as I came in.

"They look great," I said. "Can I talk to you about something?"

"Of course."

"Do you think there's any chance Gabriel will let me go to the school dance?"

Ivy stopped what she was doing and looked up.

"Xavier asked you, didn't he?"

"What if he did?" I was suddenly defensive.

"Calm down, Bethany," my sister said. "He'd look very handsome in a tuxedo."

"You mean you don't see a problem with it?"

"No, I think you'd make a lovely couple."

"Maybe, if I make it there at all."

"Don't be so negative," Ivy chided. "We'll have to see what Gabriel thinks, but it is a school event and it would be a shame to miss it."

I was impatient to hear the verdict. I dragged Ivy outside, and we scoured the beach for Gabriel, where he was taking a walk. The shoreline wound in one direction up to the main beach, where bodysurfers rode the waves and ice cream vans set up shop beneath the palms. In the other direction, if your eye traveled far enough, were the jagged cliffs of the wild Shipwreck Coast and a rocky outcrop known as the Crags. The area was famous for its dangerously high winds, choppy seas, and fierce rips. Divers occasionally searched for wreckage from the many ships that had gone down there over the years, but usually the only visitors were the gulls bobbing harmlessly on the water.

We spotted our brother seated on a prominent rock, looking out to sea. With the sun reflecting off his white T-shirt, he seemed to be surrounded by an aura of light. He was too far away for me to see his face, but I imagined his expression as one of deep longing. Sometimes there was an inexpressible sadness about Gabriel that he struggled to conceal. I thought it must be due to the burden of knowledge that couldn't be shared. He was more attuned to human suffering than Ivy and I, and this couldn't have been easy for him to bear alone. He knew all the horrors of the past, and I imagined he could see tragedies that were yet to occur. No wonder he was somber. But there wasn't anyone he could confide in. His service to the Creator of the universe resulted in his own isolation. This gave him an austerity of manner that made those who didn't know him uncomfortable. The young adored him, but adults invariably felt as if they were being judged.

Sensing that he was being observed, Gabriel turned his face in our direction. I took a step back, feeling that we were intruding on his solitude, but as soon as he saw us, the clouded expression vanished and he waved, indicating we should join him.

When we reached him, he helped us both up onto the rocks, and we all sat together for a while. In that moment I thought he seemed more at ease than he'd been in a long time.

"Why do I feel an ambush coming on?" Gabriel joked.

"Please can I go to the prom?" I chimed.

Gabriel shook his head in amusement. "I didn't realize you wanted to go. I didn't think you'd be interested."

"It's just that everybody's going," I said. "It's all they've talked about for months. They'd be so disappointed if I skipped it. It means a lot to them." I tapped him lightly on the arm. "Don't tell me you're planning on missing it."

"I'd love to miss it, but I've been asked to supervise," he replied, looking less than pleased at the prospect. "I don't know how they come up with these ideas. The whole thing seems an extravagant waste of time and money to me."

"It's still part of being at school," Ivy said. "Why not look at it as research?"

"Exactly," I said. "We'll be in the thick of things. If we wanted to watch from the outskirts, we might as well have stayed in the Kingdom."

"This wouldn't have anything to do with *dressing up* now, would it?" Gabriel asked.

"Never!" I said, sounding shocked. "Well, maybe just a little."

He sighed. "I suppose it's just for one night."

"And you'll be there to keep an eye on things," I added.

"Ivy, I was hoping you'd accompany me," Gabriel said.

"Of course." My sister clapped her hands. It was just like her to get excited once a consensus had been reached. "It'll be great!"

SATURDAY evening was balmy and clear, perfect for a beach bonfire. The sky was blue velvet, and a gentle breeze from the south swayed the trees, making them look as though they were bowing to one another. I should have been feeling on edge, but in my head everything made perfect sense. I was about to cement my connection with Xavier by bringing our conflicting worlds together.

I paid special attention to what I should wear that night and chose a loose-fitting dress made of soft white crepe with a bow at the back. Gabriel and Ivy were in the living room when I went downstairs. Gabe was reading the minuscule print of a religious text with the aid of a magnifying glass. It was such an incongruous sight given his youthful physique that I had to suppress a giggle. Ivy was vainly attempting to train Phantom to obey basic commands.

"Sit, Phantom," she said in the kind of gooey voice people usually reserve for infants. "Sit for Mommy."

I knew Phantom wouldn't obey so long as she adopted that tone with him. He was a very intelligent dog and didn't like being patronized. I imagined the expression on his face to be one of disdain.

"Don't be too long," Gabriel cautioned me.

He knew I was going to take an evening walk along the beach with some friends, and he also knew that Xavier would be among them. He'd raised no objection to this, so I figured he must be mellowing on the topic of my social life. The weight of our mission meant that sometimes each of us simply needed to escape from the task. Nobody protested when he went for a solitary run or when Ivy locked herself away in the guesthouse with only her sketchbook for company. So there was no reason why I shouldn't be allowed the same courtesy when I needed time out.

They trusted me enough not to ask too many questions, and I hated myself for the way I was about to betray them. But there was no question of backing out now—I wanted to invite Xavier into my secret world, I craved the intimacy. Mingled with my determination was a nagging fear that such a contravention would result in serious punishment. But I forced the worry from my mind and filled it instead with an image of Xavier's face. After tonight we would face everything together.

I didn't intend staying out long—just long enough to tell Xavier my secret and deal with whatever his reaction might be. I had been over and over the possible outcomes in my head and had finally narrowed them down to three. He could be enthralled, appalled, or frightened. Would he think I belonged in a museum? Would he even believe the truth when I finally mustered the nerve to say it aloud or would he think it was an elaborate hoax? I was about to find out.

"Bethany's quite capable of looking after herself," said Ivy. "Sit, Phantom! Sit down!"

"It's not Bethany—it's the rest of the world I'm worried about," said Gabriel. "We've seen some of the stupid things that go on. Just be careful and keep your eyes open."

"Will do!" I said, giving him a military salute and ignoring the sharp pang of guilt in my chest. Gabriel wasn't going to forgive this one in a hurry.

"Sit, Phantom!" Ivy cooed. "On your bottom!"

"Oh, for goodness' sake!" Gabriel put down his book and pointed a long finger at Phantom. "Sit," he commanded in a deep voice.

Phantom looked sheepish and sank straight to the floor.

Ivy scowled in frustration. "I've been trying to get him to do that all day! What is it with dogs and male authority?"

I ran lightly down the narrow steps to the scrubby track leading to the beach. Sometimes there were snake tracks in the sand and the occasional lizard darted across the path.

Twigs snapped underfoot and the trees grew so dense in places that they formed a canopy over my head through which only slivers of the setting sun's light managed to slip. An orchestra of cicadas drowned out all sound save for the roaring of the ocean. I knew that if I lost my way I could always follow the sound of the sea.

I reached the silky, white sand of the beach, which squeaked under my feet. The location for the bonfire was out near the cliffs because everybody knew it would be deserted. I headed along the beach, thinking how much more rugged the landscape looked at night. There was nobody around save for a lone fisherman casting his line from the shore. I watched him reel in and inspect his catch before throwing its thrashing body back to the waves. I noticed that the ocean varied in color: inky blue at its deepest point where it met the horizon; closer to aquamarine in the middle; and the waves that lapped at the shore were pale green and glassy. In the distance I could see a promontory jutting out, and at its top was perched a white lighthouse. It looked about the size of a thimble from where I stood.

By now it was getting dark. Up ahead I heard the sound of voices and then saw figures piling notes, exam papers, worksheets, and other flammable items into a large mound in preparation for the bonfire. There was no blaring music or a mass of seething bodies as there had been at Molly's party. Instead the few present lay around on the sand, taking swigs from bottles of beer and sharing crumpled cigarettes. Molly and her friends hadn't arrived yet.

Xavier was sitting on a fallen log half buried in the sand. He wore jeans, a floppy pale blue sweatshirt, and the silver cross around his neck. He held a half-empty bottle and was laughing at an impersonation by one of the boys. The firelight dancing across his face made him look more entrancing than ever.

"Hey, Beth," someone called out, and the others acknowledged me with waves and nods. Had people finally stopped treating us as "newsworthy" and just accepted that we now came as a package deal? I smiled shyly at everyone and quickly slid in beside Xavier where I felt secure.

"You smell amazing," Xavier said as he bent to kiss the top of my head. A few of his friends whistled and nudged him or rolled their eyes.

"Come on." He helped me up. "Let's go."

"Leaving already?" one of his friends joked.

"Just going for a walk," Xavier said in good humor. "If that's okay with you."

A few catcalls followed us as we strolled away from the group and the warmth of the fledgling bonfire. They came from Xavier's closest circle of friends so I knew their intention was not to offend. Soon their voices had petered to a distant hum.

"Xavier, I can't stay out long."

"I figured that much."

He slung an arm casually around my shoulders as we headed up the beach in silence, toward the jagged cliffs, now nothing more than serrated silhouettes against the midnight sky. The warm pressure of Xavier's arm made me feel safe and protected from everything. I knew as soon as I left him that cold uncertainty would return.

When I cut my foot on the sharp edge of a shell, Xavier insisted on carrying me. I was grateful that in the darkness he couldn't see the cut heal of its own accord. Even though the pain in my foot had subsided, I continued to cling to him, enjoying his attention. I relaxed my body, allowing it to meld with his. In my enthusiasm to get close, I accidentally poked him in the eye. I felt as clumsy as a schoolgirl when I should have been as graceful as an angel. I apologized profusely.

"It's okay, I've got another one," he joked, his eye watering from the jab. He squinted and blinked, trying to clear it.

He put me down when we reached a sandy inlet shadowed by the looming cliff face. The jagged rocks formed an ancient archway, like a portal to another world, and the moonlight turned the sand a pearly blue color. A steep flight of steps led to the top of the cliff, which offered the best view of the lighthouse. In the water scattered rock formations rose like monoliths. People hardly ever ventured out this way except for the occasional group of tourists. Most were happy to hang around the main beach, where the cafés and souvenir shops were a short stroll away. The spot was completely secluded—there wasn't anything or anybody within view. The only sound was the pounding of the sea, like a hundred voices speaking in a mysterious tongue.

Xavier sat down and rested his back against the cool rock. I hovered next to him, not wanting to delay the inevitable any longer but without the faintest idea how to start. We both knew why we'd come: I had something I wanted to get off my chest. I imagined it had been on Xavier's mind as well as mine, but he had no idea what was coming.

He waited for me to speak, but my mouth felt as dry as a cracker. This was supposed to be my moment. I'd planned to reveal my true identity to him tonight. All week I'd felt as if time was moving slowly, the hours inching by at a snail's pace. But now that the moment had finally arrived, I seemed to be buying more time. I was like an actor who'd forgotten her lines, even though the rehearsal had been flawless. I knew the gist of what I was supposed to say, but I had forgotten how I was meant to say it, the gestures that should accompany it, the timing of the delivery. I paced up and down the sand, twisting my hands and wondering where and how to begin. Despite the warmth of the night, I shivered. My hesitation was starting to make Xavier uncomfortable.

"Whatever it is, Beth, just get it over with. I can handle it."

"Thanks, but it's a little more complicated than that."

I'd been over the scene in my head a hundred times, but now the words died on my tongue.

Xavier stood up and put both hands reassuringly on my shoulders. "You know, whatever you're about to tell me won't change my opinion of you. It can't."

"Why can't it?"

"I don't know if you've noticed, but I'm crazy about you."

"Really?" I said, pleasantly sidetracked by his pronouncement.

"So you hadn't noticed? That's not a good thing—I'm going to have to be more demonstrative in future."

"That's if you still want us to have a future after tonight."

"Once you get to know me better, you'll learn that I don't run away. I take a long time to make decisions about people, but once I do, I stick by them."

"Even when you're wrong?"

"I don't believe I'm wrong about you."

"How can you say that when you don't know what I'm about to tell you?" I muttered.

Xavier opened his arms wide, as though inviting me to hit him with the truth.

"Let me prove it to you."

"I can't," I said, my voice catching. "I'm scared. What if you never want to see me again?"

"That isn't going to happen, Beth," he said more forcefully. He lowered his voice and spoke seriously. "I know this is hard for you, but you're going to have to trust me."

I looked into his eyes, like two blue pools, and knew that he was right. And I did trust him.

"First tell me something," I said. "What's the scariest thing that's ever happened to you?"

Xavier thought for a moment.

"Well, being at the top of a hundred-foot rappel drop was pretty scary, and once when I was traveling with the under-fourteen state water-polo team, I broke one of the rules and Coach Benson took me outside. He's a pretty scary guy when he wants to be and ripped me to shreds. He banned me from the game against Creswell the next day."

For the first time I was struck by Xavier's human innocence; if this was his definition of a frightening experience, what chance was there of him surviving the bombshell I was about to drop?

"Is that it?" I asked. The words came out sounding harsher than I intended. "That's your scariest moment?"

He looked me in the eye. "Well, I guess you could count the night I got a phone call telling me my girlfriend had died in a fire. But I don't really want to go there. . . ."

"I'm sorry." I looked at the ground. I couldn't believe I'd been so stupid as to forget about Emily. Xavier knew about loss and grief and pain that I'd never experienced.

"Don't be." He took my hand. "Just listen to me; I saw the family after it happened. They were all standing on the road, and I thought for a moment that everything was okay. I expected to see her with them. I was ready to comfort her. But then I saw her mom's face—like she didn't have a reason for living anymore—and I knew. It wasn't just their house that was gone, Em was gone too."

"That's awful," I whispered, feeling my eyes brim with tears. Xavier wiped them away with his thumb.

"I'm not telling you to upset you," he said. "I'm telling you because I want you to know that you can't scare me. You can tell me anything. I won't run away."

So I took a deep breath and began the speech that would change both our lives forever.

"I want you to know that if you still want me after tonight, then there's nothing that would make me happier." Xavier smiled and started to reach for me but I stopped him. "Let me get this over with first. I'm going to try and explain in the best way I can."

He nodded, crossed his arms, and gave me his undivided attention. For a split second I saw him as a schoolboy at the front of the class, eager to please and awaiting the teacher's instructions.

"I know this might sound crazy," I said, "but I want you to watch me walk."

I saw a flicker of confusion cross his face, but he didn't question me.

"Okay."

"But don't look at me, look at the sand."

Without taking my eyes from his face, I moved in a slow, deliberate circle around him. "What did you notice?" I asked.

"You don't leave footprints," Xavier replied, as though it were the most obvious thing in the world. "Cool party trick, but you probably need to eat more."

So far so good—he wasn't easily fazed. I smiled grimly and sat down beside him, turning my foot around so he could see the sole. The soft, peach-colored skin was unbroken.

"I cut my foot before. . . ."

"But there's no cut," Xavier said, his forehead creasing into a frown. "How did that . . ."

Before he could finish I took his hand and placed it on my stomach.

"Notice the difference?" I said with a hint of bluntness in my voice.

His fingers gently traced their way across my abdomen. His hand stopped when he reached dead center, and he pressed down lightly, his thumb searching for the indentation of my navel.

"You won't find it," I said before he could speak. "It's not there."

"What happened to you?" Xavier asked. He must have imagined that I'd been in some kind of accident from which I'd never fully recovered.

"Nothing happened to me, this is who I am."

I could almost see him trying to put the pieces together in his mind.

"Who are you?" It was barely a whisper.

"I'm about to show you. Would you mind closing your eyes? And don't open them till I tell you."

When I was sure his eyes were shut tight, I sprinted, three at a time, up the steep steps in the cliff face. I tiptoed my way along until I stood precariously close to the edge, with Xavier directly below me. The ground was lumpy and uneven but I kept my balance. It was roughly about a thirty-foot drop, but the height didn't deter me. I just hoped I would be able to go through with my plan. I could feel my heart thumping, almost turning somersaults in my chest. I could hear two voices shouting over each other in my head. *What are you doing?* one cried. *Have you lost your mind? Get down, go home! It's not too late to do the right thing!* The other voice had different ideas. *You've gone this far,* it said. *You can't back out now. You know how much you want him—you'll never be with him if you don't do this. Fine, be a coward and walk away, let him move on and forget all about you. I hope you enjoy eternal solitude.*

I clapped a hand over my mouth to stop myself from

crying out in frustration. There was no point dwelling on it any longer. I had made my decision.

"You can open your eyes," I called down to Xavier.

When he did, he looked around in surprise to find me gone before turning his gaze upward. I waved when he spotted me.

"What are you doing up there?" I heard a splinter of panic in his voice. "Beth, that's not funny. Come down right now before you hurt yourself."

"Don't worry, I'm coming down," I said. "My way."

I took a step forward so that I was teetering on the cliff's edge and shifted my weight to balance on the balls of my feet. The uneven rock scraped my skin but I hardly noticed. I felt like I was already flying, and more than anything I wanted to feel the rush of wind in my hair again.

"Cut that out, Beth! Don't move, I'm coming up to get you!" I heard Xavier yell, but I wasn't listening to him anymore. As the wind whipped my clothes, I spread my arms and let myself fall from the cliff. If I had been human, my stomach might have shot up into my throat, but the drop only made my heart soar and my body buzz with exhilaration. I plummeted toward the ground, relishing the sharp sting of the air against my cheeks. Xavier cried out and ran to catch me, but his efforts were futile. This was one time when I didn't need rescuing. Midway to the ground, I dropped my arms and allowed the transformation to take place. A blinding light shot from inside my body, shining from every pore and making my skin glow like white hot metal. I saw Xavier shield his eyes and draw back. I felt my wings burst from behind my shoulder blades. They exploded through the confines of my dress, tearing the light fabric to ribbons. Fully expanded, they cast a long shadow across the sand as though I were some sort of majestic bird.

Xavier had dropped to a crouch, and I knew that the pulsing light was blinding him. I felt exposed and naked hovering there, my wings beating the air to hold me up but also strangely elated. I felt the tendons in my wings stretch, eager for more exercise. They spent so much time cramped beneath my clothes these days. I resisted the urge to fly higher and dive through the clouds. I allowed myself to hover a moment before I swooped to the ground where I landed gently on the sand. The blazing incandescence that surrounded me dimmed once my feet reconnected with solid earth.

Xavier rubbed his eyes and blinked, trying to regain his vision. Finally he saw me. He took a step back, face stunned, hands hanging limply by his sides as if they should be doing something but he couldn't think what. I stood before him, light still clinging to my skin. The remnants of my dress hung like tentacles and from my back arched a pair of towering wings, feather-light but suggesting enormous power. My hair streamed behind me, and I knew that the ring of light around my head would be brighter than ever.

"Holy crap!" Xavier blurted.

"Would you mind not blaspheming?" I asked politely. He stared at me, grappling for the right words. "I know." I sighed. "Bet you didn't see this one coming." I waved a hand in the direction of the beach. "Feel free to leave now if you want."

Xavier stood motionless for a moment, staring at me wide-eyed. Then he circled me slowly, and I felt him brush his fingers ever so gently against my wings. Although they looked heavy, they were as thin as parchment and weighed next to nothing. I could see from his face that he was marveling at the fragile white feathers and tiny membranes that were visible beneath the diaphanous skin.

"Whoa," he said, lost for words. "That's so . . ."

"Freaky?"

"Incredible," he said. "But what *are* you? You can't be . . ."

"An angel?" I said. "Jackpot."

Xavier rubbed the bridge of his nose as though trying to make sense of everything in his head. "This can't be real," he said eventually. "I don't get it."

"Of course you don't," I said. "My world and yours are legions apart."

"Your world?" he asked incredulously. "This is insane."

"What is?"

"This stuff is all fantasy. It just doesn't happen in real life!"

"This *is* real," I said. "I'm real."

"I know," he replied. "The scariest part is that I believe you. Sorry I just need a minute. . . ."

He sank down on the sand, his face contorted like someone trying to solve an impossible riddle. I tried to imagine what was going on in his head. It must be chaotic. He must have so many questions.

"Are you angry?" I asked.

"Angry?" he repeated. "Why would I be angry?"

"Because I didn't tell you sooner?"

"I'm just trying to get my head around this," he said.

"I know it can't be easy. Take your time."

He was silent for a long while. The convulsive rise and fall of his chest suggested that an internal struggle was taking place. He stood and slowly passed his hand in a semicircle around my head. I knew his fingers would pick up the warmth emitted by my halo.

"Okay, so angels exist," he conceded eventually, speaking slowly as though trying to explain things to himself. "But what are you doing here on earth?"

"Right now there are thousands of us in human guise spread right across the globe," I answered. "We're part of a mission."

"A mission to achieve what?"

"It's hard to explain. We're here to help people reconnect with one another, to love one another." Xavier looked confused so I tried to elaborate. "There's too much anger in the world, too much hatred. It's stirring the dark forces and raising them up. Once they're unleashed, it's near impossible to tame them. It's our job to try and counteract that negativity, to prevent any more disaster from happening. This place has been pretty badly affected."

"So you're saying the bad things that have happened here are because of dark forces?"

"Pretty much."

"And by dark forces I take it you mean the devil?"

"Well, his representatives at least."

Xavier looked like he was about to laugh, but then stopped himself.

"This is crazy. Who's supposed to have sent you on this mission?"

"I thought that part might be obvious."

Xavier gazed at me in disbelief.

"You don't mean . . ."

"Yes."

Xavier looked shaken, like he'd been tossed around by a hurricane and thrown back down to earth. His fingers scraped the hair back from his forehead.

"Are you telling me that God really exists?"

"I'm not allowed to talk about it," I said, thinking it best to cut this conversation off before it went any further. "Some things are beyond human understanding. I'd get into a lot of trouble for trying to explain it. We shouldn't even speak his name."

Xavier nodded.

"But there is an afterlife?" he said. "A heaven?"

"Without a doubt."

"So . . ." He rubbed his chin pensively. "If there's a Heaven, it stands to reason that . . . there must also be . . ."

I finished his thought. "Yes, there's that too. But please, no more questions for now."

Xavier massaged his temples as though trying to figure out the best way to process all this information.

"I'm sorry," I said. "I know it must be overwhelming."

He dismissed my concern, more focused on getting a cogent picture in his head. "Just let me get this straight," he said. "You're angels on a mission to help mankind and you've been assigned to Venus Cove?"

"Actually Gabriel's an archangel," I corrected. "But otherwise, yes."

"Well, that explains why he's so hard to impress," said Xavier flippantly.

"You're the only person that knows this," I said. "You can't breathe a word of it to anyone."

"Who am I going to tell?" he asked. "Who would believe me anyway?"

"Good point."

He laughed suddenly.

"My girlfriend is an angel," he said and then repeated it more loudly, changing the emphasis, testing out how the words sounded. "My *girlfriend* is an *angel*."

"Xavier, keep your voice down," I warned.

Spoken aloud it sounded so outrageous and yet so simple at the same time that I couldn't help but giggle as well. To anyone else, Xavier's use of the word *angel* would have sounded like nothing more than a lovesick teenager professing his admiration. Only the two of us knew differently and now we both shared a secret—a dangerous secret that brought us closer than ever. It was as if we had just sealed the bond between us, closed the gap, and made it final.

"I was so worried that you wouldn't want to know me once you found out." I sighed, relief flooding through me.

"Are you kidding?" Xavier reached out and curled a lock of my hair around his finger. "Surely I've got to be the luckiest guy in the world."

"How do you figure that?"

"Isn't it obvious? I've got my own little piece of Heaven right here."

He wrapped his arms around me, pulling me closer to him. I nuzzled against his chest, breathing in his scent.

"Can you promise not to ask too many questions?"

"If you answer just one," Xavier replied. "I suppose this makes you and me a big no-no?" He clicked his tongue and wagged his finger to emphasize the point. I was happy to see that the shock had passed and that he was behaving a little more like his old self.

"Not just big," I said. "The biggest."

"Don't worry, Beth; there's nothing I love more than a challenge."

15

The Covenant

"SO what happens now?" Xavier asked.

"How do you mean?"

"Now that I know about you?"

"I honestly can't tell you. We've never had a situation like this before," I admitted.

"So you being an angel doesn't mean . . ." He hesitated.

"Doesn't mean I have an answer for everything," I concluded for him.

"I just assumed it would be one of the perks."

"Sadly, no."

"Well, it seems to me that so long as no one else knows, you should be safe. And when it comes to secrets, I'm a vault. Ask my friends. "

"I know I can trust you. But there is one more thing you should know." I paused. This was going to be the hardest part—more difficult even than what I'd just done.

"Okay . . ." Xavier seemed to be steeling himself this time.

"You have to understand that sooner or later this mission is going to end, and we'll be going home," I said.

"Home as in . . ." He turned his eyes upward to the sky.

"Exactly."

Even though he must have been expecting the answer, signs of strain suddenly materialized on his face. His ocean eyes darkened, and his mouth turned into an angry scowl.

"If you leave, will you ever come back?" he asked in a tight voice.

"I don't think so," I said quietly. "But if I do, it's not likely to be anytime soon or even to the same place."

Xavier's body stiffened beside me. "So you don't get a say?" he said with a note of disbelief in his voice. "Whatever happened to free will?"

"That gift was given to humankind, remember? It doesn't apply to us. Look, if there's a way for me to stay I haven't figured it out yet," I continued. "I knew when I came here that it wasn't going to be permanent, that eventually we'd have to leave. But I didn't expect to find you, and now that I have . . ."

"Well, you can't go," Xavier said simply. By his tone he might have been giving a weather report: *Today there will be late showers.* He spoke with a confidence that challenged anyone to defy the decision.

"I feel the same way," I said, kneading my fingers into his shoulders in an attempt to smooth out the visible tension, "but it's not up to me."

"It's your life," Xavier countered.

"No, that's not quite true. I'm kind of on a lease arrangement."

"We'll just have to renegotiate the terms then."

"How do you propose doing that? It's not like making a phone call."

"Let me think about it."

I had to admit his determination was impressive and so typically human. I wriggled closer to snuggle under his arm.

"Let's not talk about it anymore tonight," I suggested, reluctant to ruin the moment by discussing things we didn't have the power to change. For now, it was enough that he wanted me to stay and that he was prepared to take on heavenly powers to make that happen. "We're here together right now, let's not worry about the future. Okay?"

Xavier nodded and responded when I pressed my lips against his. After a moment the tension seemed to slip away, and we fell back onto the sand. I could feel the contours of our bodies fitting perfectly together. His arms wound around my waist as I ran my fingers through his soft hair, stroking his face. I'd never kissed anyone before him, but I felt as if a stranger had taken over my body—a stranger who knew exactly what she was doing. I tilted my head to plant kisses along his jawline, down to the base of his neck and along his collarbone. He stopped breathing for a moment. His hands came up to hold my face, stroking my hair and tucking it behind my ears.

I wasn't sure how long we stayed that way, tangled together on the sand, sometimes locked in an embrace, sometimes looking up at the moon or the rugged cliffs above us. All I knew was that when I became aware of the hour, more time had passed than I'd thought. I pulled myself up, dusting sand from my clothes and skin.

"It's getting late," I said. "I have to get home."

The sight of Xavier, sprawled on the sand, his hair ruffled, a dreamy half-smile on his lips, was so alluring that I was tempted to sink back down beside him. But I managed to compose myself and turned to head back the way we'd come.

"Uh, Beth," Xavier said, getting up. "You might want to um . . . cover up."

It took me a moment to realize that my wings were still fully visible through my torn dress. "Oh right, thanks!" He tossed me his sweatshirt, which I pulled over my head. It was way too big for me and reached halfway down my thighs, but it was warm, comfortable, and smelled deliciously of him. When we finally parted, I ran the rest of the way home feeling like he was still beside me. I knew I would sleep with his shirt on that night and commit the scent to memory.

When I reached the overgrown backyard of Byron, I raked my fingers hastily through my hair and rearranged my clothes in an attempt to look like I'd been for an innocent social stroll rather than a secret tryst on a moonlit beach. Then I slumped down in the heavy wooden swing, which creaked under my weight. I rested my cheek against the rough rope that was looped around a gnarled branch of the oak tree in our yard and looked toward the house. I could see through the window to the living room, where my brother and sister were sitting in the lamplight, Ivy knitting a pair of gloves and Gabriel strumming his guitar. Looking at them, I felt the icy tendrils of guilt wrapping around my chest.

There was a full moon and the garden was awash with blue light, illuminating a crumbling statue that stood among the high grass. It was of a severe angel, looking Heavenward, its hands folded over its chest in a gesture of devotion. Gabriel thought it a poor replica and somewhat offensive, but Ivy said it was sweet. Personally I had always thought it was a little eerie. I wasn't sure if it was the light playing tricks on me or just my imagination, but as I gazed at the statue in the semidarkness, I thought I saw one of its stone fingers twitch in accusation and its eyes roll forward to look directly at me.

The illusion lasted but a second, long enough for me to leap off the swing, causing it to collide with the tree trunk with a resounding *thwack*. Before I could examine the angel again and determine whether my sanity was in question, I was distracted by the sound of the glass doors sliding open. Ivy came out onto the deck, looking like a wraith. The moonlight pooled across her snowy skin, highlighting the blue-green veins in her arms and chest.

"Bethany, is that you?" Her voice poured out like honey, and the expression on her face was painfully trusting. My stomach twisted into a knot and I felt sick. She spotted me half hidden by the shadow of the tree. "What are you doing over there?" she asked. "Come inside."

Everything was reassuringly familiar in the house. The yellow lamplight reflected off the floorboards, Phantom's pawprint-patterned bed was in its usual place beside the sofa, and Ivy's carefully arranged selection of classical art books and interior-decorating magazines sat on the low coffee table.

Gabriel looked up when I came in.

"Have a good night?" he asked with a smile.

I tried to return the smile but found that the muscles in my face were frozen. I felt as though the weight of what I'd done was pressing down on me, like a wave crashing over me, forcing my head underwater so I couldn't breathe. When I was with Xavier, it was easy to forget that I had any other place in the world, that I owed allegiance to anyone else.

I didn't regret revealing the truth to Xavier, but I hated subterfuge, especially where my family was concerned. I was terrified of how my siblings would react when they found out what I'd done. Could I somehow make them understand why I'd done it? But most of all I was afraid that the powers in the Kingdom would end our mission or demand my immediate withdrawal. Either way, I would be taken away from earth, away from the one person who mattered most to me.

Gabriel must have noticed I was wearing Xavier's sweatshirt, but he refrained from comment. Although part of me wanted to confess everything on the spot, I forced myself to stay silent. I apologized for being late, said I was tired and excused myself, refusing the offer of cocoa and cookies that Ivy had baked that afternoon.

Gabriel called to me as I reached the foot of the stairs, and I waited as he strode over. My heart fluttered in my chest. My brother was frighteningly observant, and I was sure he'd noticed that I wasn't myself. I waited for him to examine my face, ask awkward questions, or make some accusation, but all he did was lay one hand against my cheek so that I felt the cool metal of his rings and gently kiss my forehead. His exquisite face looked so at ease that night. His blond hair had escaped from the band he sometimes used to tie it up. His rain-colored eyes had lost some of their sternness, and he was looking at me with brotherly affection.

"I'm proud of you, Bethany," he said. "You've made great progress in such a short time, and you are learning to make better decisions. Take Phantom up with you—he was fretting for you earlier."

It took all my resolve to hold back my tears.

Upstairs, as I lay in bed with Phantom's warm body beside me, I let them spill freely. I swore I could feel my lies slithering inside me like snakes, wrapping themselves around me and constricting. I felt they were squeezing the air from my lungs, tightening around my heart. Aside from the raking guilt that was coursing like a poison through my body, there was also a terrible fear. When I woke up, would I still be on earth? I didn't know. I wanted to pray but I couldn't. I was too ashamed to speak to Our Father after the sins I'd committed. I'd only held on to my secret for a few hours and already I was undone.

Mingled with my guilt and shame was a new latent anger at the thought that my fate wasn't mine to determine. Xavier had put that idea into my head. My relationship with him would be decided for me, and the worst part of it was that I didn't know when it would happen. My time on earth came with an unknown expiration date. What if I didn't even get to say good-bye to him? I kicked off my bedclothes, even though my skin felt as cold as ice. I was beginning to think I couldn't envisage an existence without Xavier. I didn't want to.

Hours later my thoughts were still raging, and nothing had changed except that my pillow was damp with tears. I drifted in and out of sleep. Sometimes I woke and sat bolt upright, scanning the darkness for a sign of something or someone come to deal out my punishment. *Vengeance is mine; I will repay, saith the Lord.* At one point I woke to see a hooded figure that I imagined had come to seek retribution, but it turned out to be my coat hanging from a stand next to my door. I was afraid to close my eyes after that, as if doing so would make me more vulnerable. It was irrational to feel that way. I knew that if they did come for me, it wouldn't make any difference whether I was asleep or awake. I would be utterly powerless.

By the time morning came I was an emotional ruin. When I washed up and glanced in the mirror, I realized that I looked it too. My normally pale face was even whiter, and the circles under my eyes had deepened. I now even looked the part of an angel that had fallen from grace.

When I found the kitchen empty I knew immediately that something was wrong. I couldn't remember a morning when Gabriel hadn't been waiting to greet me with breakfast already cooking. I had repeatedly told him I could make it myself, but like a doting parent, he insisted that he enjoyed doing it. Today the table was empty and the room was quiet. I told myself that this was nothing but a minor deviation from routine. I went to the fridge to pour myself a glass of orange juice, but my hands were trembling so much that I spilled half of it across the counter. I mopped up the mess with a paper towel, fighting against the fear that was clutching at my throat.

I felt the presence of Ivy and Gabriel before I saw them or heard them come in. They stood together in the doorway, united in silent condemnation, their faces immobile and expressionless. I didn't need them to say the words aloud. They *knew*. Was it my restlessness that had betrayed me? I should have expected their reaction, but it still stung like a slap in the face. For several long minutes I couldn't bring myself to speak. I wanted to run and hide my face in Gabriel's shirt, beg forgiveness, and feel his arms close around me; but I knew that I would find no comfort there. Despite the common portrayal of angels as endlessly loving and compassionate, I knew there was another side to them, one that could be harsh and unforgiving. The forgiveness was reserved for humans. They were always let off the hook. We had a tendency to regard them as infants, to conclude that the "poor things" didn't know any better. But for me, the expectations were higher. I wasn't a human, I was one of them, and there was no excuse.

There was no sound but the dripping of the tap in the sink and my ragged breathing. I couldn't bear the silence. It would have been easier had they attacked me outright, berated me, or thrown me out; anything but the deafening silence.

"I know how this must look to you, but I had to tell him!" I blurted.

Ivy's face was frozen in a mask of horror but Gabriel's had turned to stone.

"I'm sorry," I continued. "I can't help the way I feel about him. He means so much to me."

No one spoke.

"Please, say something," I begged. "What's going to happen now? We'll be recalled to the Kingdom, won't we? I'll never see him again."

I broke into a wave of tearless sobs and clutched at the edge of the counter to support myself. Neither of my siblings made any move to comfort me. I didn't blame them. It was Gabriel who broke the silence. He turned his steel gray gaze on me, eyes blazing. When he spoke I could hear that his voice was flooded with anger.

"Do you have any idea what you've done?" he asked. "Do you realize the danger you have put us all in?" His anger was mounting, the signs were evident. Outside, a fierce wind began to blow, rattling the windowpanes, and a glass on the counter shattered into tiny fragments. Ivy put her hands on Gabriel's shoulders. Her touch recalled him, and he let her guide him to the table where he sat with his back to me. His shoulders heaved as he tried to bring his rage under control. Where was his endless patience now?

"Please," I said in barely more than a whisper. "This isn't an excuse, but I think . . ."

"Don't say it." Ivy turned to me, a warning look on her face. "Don't say you love him."

"Do you want me to lie to you?" I asked. "I've tried not to feel like this, I really have, but he's not like other humans. He's different . . . he understands."

"Understands?" Gabriel's voice was tremulous, so different from his usual calm. I'd always thought nothing could ruffle his composure. "Only a handful of mortals throughout history have ever come *close* to understanding the divine. Are you suggesting that your school friend is one of them?"

I shrank back. I'd never heard Gabriel speak in that tone before.

"What can I do?" I said softly, tears spilling out and pouring down my face. "I'm in love with him."

"That may be, but your love is futile," Gabriel said unsympathetically. "It is your duty to show understanding and compassion to all of humankind and your exclusive attachment to this boy is wrong. You are from different worlds. It cannot be. Now you have endangered your own life and his."

"His?" I asked in panic. "What do you mean?"

"Calm down, Gabriel," Ivy said. She gripped his shoulder. "This situation has arisen and now it must be dealt with."

"I have to know what's going to happen!" I cried. "Will they call us back to the Kingdom? Please, I have a right to know."

I hated to be seen like this, so desperate, so completely lacking in control, but I knew that if I wanted to keep my entire world from falling apart, I would have to keep Xavier.

"It seems to me that you have forfeited any rights you had. There is only one thing now that can be done," said Gabriel.

"What?" I asked, trying to keep the hysteria out of my voice.

"I need to speak with the Covenant."

I knew he meant the circle of archangels that were called upon to intervene only in the direst of situations. They were the strongest and most powerful of our kind—together, they could bring the world to its knees. Gabriel obviously felt the need to call for reinforcements.

"Will you explain how it happened?" I asked.

"There will be no need," Gabriel replied. "They will already know."

"What'll happen then?"

"They will give their verdict and we will obey."

Without another word, Gabriel swept from the kitchen, and moments later, we heard the front door close behind him.

THE wait was excruciating. Ivy brewed cups of chamomile tea and sat with me in the living room, but it seemed a black cloud had descended over us both. We were in the same room but there was an ocean between us. Phantom too became uneasy, sensing that things weren't right, and burrowed his face in my lap. I tried to block out the thought that, depending on the verdict, I might never see him again either.

We didn't know where Gabriel had gone, but Ivy said it was most likely somewhere desolate and empty where he could communicate with the archangels without human interference. It was a bit like using wireless Internet—you had to find the best place to connect and the fewer humans around the better the connection. Gabriel needed somewhere he could meditate easily and contact the forces in the universe.

I didn't know much about the other six in Gabriel's arch. I knew them only by name and reputation. I wondered if any of them would be sympathetic to my cause.

Michael was the leader of the arch. He was a Prince of Light, angel of virtue, honesty, and salvation. Unlike the others, Michael was the only one who served duties as Angel of Death. Raphael was known as the Medicine of God because he was a healer and it was his duty to oversee the physical well-being of his charges on earth. He was talked of as the warmest of the archangels. Uriel was called the Fire of the Lord as he was the Angel of Punishment and was one of those called upon to devastate Sodom and Gomorrah.

Raguel's purpose was to watch over the others in the arch and ensure they behaved in compliance with the code set by the Lord. Angel of the sun, Zerachiel, kept constant watch over Heaven and earth. Ramiel's role was to oversee divine visions given to the chosen ones on earth. It was also his duty to lead souls into judgment when their time came.

And of course there was Gabriel. He was known as the Hero of God, chief warrior of the Kingdom. But unlike the others, who were distant and removed, I looked upon Gabriel as my brother, protector, and friend. I recalled a human saying about the power of blood ties. I felt that way about Gabe and Ivy—we were of the same spirit. I hoped I hadn't destroyed that bond through one careless action.

"What do you think they'll say?" I asked Ivy for the fifth time, and she let out a heavy sigh.

"I honestly don't know, Bethany." Her voice sounded far away. "We were given clear instructions not to allow ourselves to be exposed. Nobody expected that rule to be violated, and so the consequences were never discussed."

"You must hate me," I said in a small voice.

She turned to look at me. "I can't pretend to understand what you were thinking," she said. "But you're still my sister."

"I know I can't justify what I've done."

"Your incarnation is different from ours. You feel things so passionately. To us, Xavier is like every other human; to you, he is something completely different."

"He's everything."

"That's just reckless."

"I know."

"To make one person the center of your world is bound to end in disaster. There are too many factors outside your control."

"I know," I repeated with a sigh.

"Is there any chance you can retract your feelings?" Ivy asked. "Or is that out of the question?"

I shook my head. "It's too late."

"That's what I thought you'd say."

"Why am I so different?" I asked after a moment. "Why do I have these *feelings*? You and Gabe can command what you feel. It's like I have no control at all."

"You are young," said Ivy slowly.

"It's not that." I twisted my hands. "There must be something else."

"Yes," my sister agreed. "You are more human than any angel I've ever known. You have identified strongly with earth. Your brother and I are homesick—this place is foreign to us. But you, you fit in here. It's like you've always belonged."

"Why?" I asked.

My sister shook her head. "I don't know." For a moment I caught a wistful look on her face and wondered if in some small recess of her mind, she wished she could understand my all-consuming love for Xavier. But the look vanished before I could dwell on it.

"Do you think Gabriel will ever forgive me?"

"Our brother inhabits a different plane of existence," Ivy explained. "He is less used to mistakes. He feels that your errors become his. He will see this as his failure, not yours. Can you understand that?"

I nodded and didn't bother asking any more questions. There was nothing to do now but wait, and we could do that in silence.

The seconds ticked by slowly and the minutes stretched into hours. My fear welled up and subsided at various intervals, like ocean waves. I knew that if I went back to the Kingdom, I would be with my brothers and sisters again, but also alone, with the rest of eternity to yearn for what I'd had on earth. But that was assuming I would be allowed back into the Kingdom. Our Creator, gracious and loving as he was, didn't respond well to defiance. There was a chance I could be excommunicated. I refused to let myself picture what Hell might be like. I had heard stories and that was enough. Legend said sinners were hung from their eyelids, burned, tortured, torn to pieces, and stitched up again. They said the place reeked of seared flesh and singed hair and the rivers ran blood. Of course I didn't believe any of it, but the thought still gave me shivers.

I knew that many people on earth didn't believe there was such a place as Hell, but they didn't know how wrong they were. Angels like me didn't really have a clue what Hell was like, but I knew I didn't want to find out for myself. An archangel like Gabriel would know more about the dark kingdom but was barred from speaking about it.

I jumped when I heard the front door slam, and my heart hammered against my rib cage. A moment later Gabriel was standing before us, arms folded across his chest, his face careworn but as usual inscrutable. Ivy got up to stand beside him, showing no eagerness to hear the verdict.

"What's been decided?" I blurted, unable to stand the suspense.

"The Covenant regrets recommending Bethany for this mission," Gabriel said, his sharp eyes focused on me. "More was expected from an angel of her standing."

I felt myself begin to shake. This was it; it was all over. I was going back where I had come from. I considered trying to make a run for it but knew there was no point. There was no corner of the earth that could hide me. I stood up, bowed my head, and made for the stairs.

Gabriel's eyes narrowed. "Where do you think you're going?"

"I'll get ready to leave," I replied, trying to muster enough strength to look him in the eye.

"Leave to go *where*?"

"Back home."

"Bethany, you're not going home. None of us are," he said. "You haven't let me finish. There is great disappointment at your actions, but the Covenant's suggestion to terminate your mission has been overruled."

My head flew up. "By who?"

"A higher power."

I snatched wildly at this shred of hope. "You mean we're staying? They're not going to take me away?"

"It appears that too much has been invested in this mission to allow it to be thrown away because of a minor setback. Therefore, the answer is yes, we are staying."

"What about Xavier?" I asked. "Am I allowed to see him?"

Gabriel looked annoyed, as though the decision that had been reached on that subject was irrelevant in the extreme.

"You are permitted to continue seeing the boy while we are here. As he already knows our identity, there is more harm than good in preventing you from seeing him."

"Oh, thank you!" I began, but Gabriel interrupted me.

"As the decision was not mine, I deserve no thanks."

We all fell into a painful silence that lasted several long minutes until I ventured to break it.

"Please don't be angry with me, Gabriel. Actually you have every right to be angry, but at least understand that I didn't do it intentionally."

"I have no interest in hearing what you have to say, Bethany. You have your *boyfriend*, now be satisfied." He turned his back on me. A moment later I felt Ivy's hands comfortingly on my shoulders.

"I need to go to the supermarket," she said, in an attempt to return to normality. "I could use a hand."

I looked at Gabriel for approval.

"Go and help Ivy," he said more agreeably, an idea taking root in his head. "There will be four of us at dinner tonight."

{ 16 }

Family Ties

GABRIEL'S pronouncement that Xavier was to have the honor of being our first dinner guest made me suspicious. I couldn't help but question the motive behind the invitation. So far the only feelings Gabriel had expressed toward Xavier had wavered between disdain and indifference.

"Why are you inviting him over?" I asked.

"Why shouldn't he come?" Gabriel replied. "He knows about us now, so I don't see the harm in it. Besides, there are some ground rules we need to cover."

"Such as?"

"Such as the importance of confidentiality for a start."

"You don't know Xavier, he's as likely to blab as I am," I said and realized the irony as soon as the words were out.

"Well, that really doesn't inspire confidence, does it?" Gabriel remarked.

"Don't worry, Bethany, we just want to get to know him," said Ivy, giving my arm a maternal pat. She looked pointedly at Gabe. "We want him to feel comfortable. If we're going to trust him, he has to be able to trust us."

"What if he's busy tonight?" I parried.

"We won't know if you don't ask him," Gabriel replied.

"I don't even have his number anymore."

Gabriel went to a closet in the hall and returned with a hefty phone directory, which he dropped unceremoniously onto the table.

"I'm sure it's listed," he said darkly.

It was evident that Gabriel wasn't going to be talked out of this idea, so I didn't argue further and trudged off to call Xavier. The only protest I made was making sure to stomp up the stairs as loudly as possible. I'd never called Xavier's house and an unfamiliar voice answered.

"Hello, Claire speaking."

The voice was confident and impeccably polite. I had been secretly hoping that no one would pick up. If there was one thing that I felt might drive Xavier away, it was a night with my bizarre family. I considered hanging up the phone and telling Gabriel I couldn't get through, but I knew there was little point—he'd know I was lying and make me call back. Or worse, he might insist on making the call himself.

"Hello, it's Bethany Church calling," I said in a voice so meek I barely recognized it as my own. "May I please speak to Xavier?"

"Sure," the girl replied. "I'll just get him for you." I heard the clang of the receiver being put down, then her voice calling through the house. "Xavier! Phone!" I picked up a rustling noise and then the sound of children squabbling. Finally I heard footsteps, and Xavier's dreamy voice echoed through the receiver.

"Hello, Xavier speaking."

"Hi, it's me."

"Hello, me." His voice lifted a notch. "Is everything all right?"

"Well, that depends on how you look at it," I replied.

"Beth, what's happened?" His voice was suddenly serious.

"My family knows that you know. I didn't have to tell them."

"Jeez, that was quick. How'd they take it?"

"Not well," I admitted. "But then Gabriel met with the Covenant and . . ."

"I'm sorry . . . the what?"

"It's a circle of powers—it's too complex to explain now, but they're consulted whenever things go, um, off course."

"Right . . . and what was the outcome?"

"Well . . . nothing."

"What do you mean *nothing*?"

"They said that for now things can stay as they are."

"What about us? What happens there?"

"Apparently I'm allowed to keep seeing you."

"Well, that's good news, isn't it?"

"I think so but I'm not sure. Listen, Xavier, Gabe's behaving strangely—he wants to have you over tonight *for dinner*."

"Well, that sounds positive." I remained silent, not sharing his optimism. "Relax, Beth, I think I can handle it."

"I'm not sure *I* can."

"We'll get through it together," Xavier said. "What time do you want me there?"

"Is seven okay?"

"No problem. See you then."

"Xavier . . . ," I said, nibbling at a fingernail. "I'm worried. We're being thrown in the deep end here. What if this goes badly? What if he has bad news? Do you think it'll be bad news?"

"No, I don't, now quit stressing. Please—for me?"

"Okay. I'm sorry. It's just that our whole relationship is kind of hanging by a thread and they've been merciful so far, but this dinner could make or break it and I'm not sure why Gabe . . ."

"Oh, man," Xavier groaned. "See what you've done—now I'm stressing."

"You can't! You're the stable one!"

Xavier laughed and I realized his distress had been feigned to illustrate a point. He wasn't worried in the slightest.

"Just relax. Go and run a bath or have a shot of brandy."

"Okay."

"That second bit was a joke. We both know you can't hold your liquor."

"You seem very relaxed about this."

"That's because I am. Beth, isn't serenity meant to be, you know, your *thing*? You worry too much. Honestly, it'll be fine. I'll even dress to impress."

"No, no, just come as you are!" I begged into the phone, but he had already hung up.

Xavier showed up right on time, wearing a pale gray pin-striped suit and blue silk tie. He'd done something to his hair so that it no longer flopped but was slicked back away from his face. Under his arm he carried a bunch of long-stemmed yellow roses, wrapped in green cellophane and tied with raffia.

I did a double take when I opened the door. Xavier grinned when he saw my face.

"Too much?" he asked.

"No, it's great!" I said, genuinely pleased with his efforts. But my face clouded again almost immediately.

"Then why do you look so terrified?" He gave me a self-assured wink. "They're gonna love me."

"Just don't make any jokes—they don't really get them." I felt jittery and my knees were starting to shake.

"Okay—no jokes. Should I offer to say grace?" I had to giggle then; I couldn't help myself.

Although I should have been playing host and showing him into the living room, we lingered at the door like co-conspirators. Not knowing what the evening had in store, my instinct was to delay it as long as possible. Besides, at that moment all I could think was that Xavier was mine and that we belonged to each other. He might have been overdressed for a casual impromptu dinner, but he cut a pretty striking figure with his broad shoulders, fathomless blue eyes, and smoothed-back hair. He was my very own fairy-tale hero. And, like a fairy-tale hero, I knew I could rely on him not to run for cover when the going got tough. Xavier would stand his ground, and any decisions he made would be based on reasoning of his own. If nothing else, I knew I could depend upon that.

Ivy adopted the role of host effortlessly. She was charmed by the flowers and made small talk as well as every effort to make Xavier feel comfortable throughout dinner. Judgment didn't sit easily with Ivy, and her heart melted once she deemed a person to be sincere. Xavier's sincerity was authentic. It was this genuineness that had earned him the role of school captain as well as his widespread popularity. Gabriel, on the other hand, watched Xavier with a wary eye.

My sister had gone to a good deal of trouble with the menu—she'd made an aromatic potato and leek soup followed by whole baked trout and a tray of roasted vegetables. I knew there'd be crème brûlée for dessert as I'd seen them in the fridge, wobbling in ramekins. Ivy had even sent Gabe out in search of a kitchen blowtorch to caramelize the sugar topping. She'd also set the table with our silverware and best china. The wine in the decanter tasted of berries, and there was sparkling water in a crystal jug.

The candles on the table cast a glow over all our faces. We ate in silence at first and the tension was palpable. Ivy looked from me to Xavier and smiled too much, while Gabriel sliced up his food savagely, as though he were imagining the potatoes on his plate to be Xavier's head.

"Great meal," Xavier said eventually, loosening his tie, his cheeks flushed from the wine.

"Thank you." Ivy beamed with satisfaction. "I wasn't sure what you might like."

"I'm pretty easygoing but this is top class," Xavier said, earning another wide grin from my sister.

For my part, I was still trying to work out the purpose of this unorthodox get-together. Surely Gabriel's agenda included more than just socializing. Was he trying to gain an insight into Xavier's personality? Did he still mistrust him? I wasn't sure, and Gabriel still hadn't spoken more than two words to any of us.

Eventually, even Ivy ran out of steam and the conversation died entirely. I caught Xavier staring intently at his plate as though the unfinished vegetables there might reveal the mysteries of the universe. I tried to nudge Ivy under the table with my foot, hoping to prompt further comment from her, but by accident got Xavier's shin instead. It startled him and he jumped in his chair, almost spilling his drink. I retracted my foot with an apologetic smile and sat still.

"So, Xavier," said Ivy, laying down her fork although her plate was still full. "What sort of things are you interested in?"

Xavier swallowed uneasily. "Er . . . just the usual . . ." He cleared his throat. "Sports, school, music."

"What sports do you play?" Ivy asked, with a little too much enthusiasm.

"Water polo, rugby, baseball, and lacrosse," Xavier rattled off.

"He's really good," I added helpfully. "You should see him play. He's actually captain of the water-polo team." I couldn't seem to stop babbling. "He's also captain of the school . . . but you already know that."

Ivy decided on a safer topic. "How long have you lived here at Venus Cove?"

"My whole life—I've never lived anywhere else."

"Do you have brothers and sisters?"

"I come from a family of six kids."

"I imagine that must be fun, being part of a big family."

"Sometimes," Xavier agreed. "Sometimes it's just noisy. There's never much privacy."

Gabriel chose this moment to tactlessly cut in. "Speaking of privacy, I believe you recently made an interesting discovery?"

"Interesting isn't quite the word I'd use," Xavier replied, not at all caught off guard by the sudden attack.

"What word would you use?"

"Something more along the lines of mind-blowing."

"However you want to describe it, we need to get some things clear."

"I'm not going to tell anyone, if that's what you're worried about," Xavier responded immediately. "I want to protect Beth as much as you do."

"Bethany thinks very highly of you," Gabriel said. "I hope her affection is not undeserved."

"All I can say is that Beth's very important to me, and I intend to look after her."

"Where we come from, people are not judged by their words," Gabriel said.

Xavier was unfazed. "Then you'll have to wait and judge me by my actions."

Although he made no attempt to relax the mood, I could see from the expression in Gabriel's eyes that he was surprised by how well Xavier was handling the situation. He hadn't allowed himself to be intimidated, and his greatest armor was his honesty. Anyone could see that Xavier was driven by his ethics. Even Gabriel had to admire that.

"You see, you and I have one vital thing in common," Xavier continued. "We *both* love Beth."

An impenetrable silence settled over the room. Gabriel

and Ivy had not expected such a declaration and were taken aback. Perhaps in their own minds they had underestimated the strength of Xavier's feelings for me. Even I couldn't quite believe he had spoken those words out loud. I tried hard to keep my composure and continue eating quietly, but I couldn't keep the smile from spreading across my face, and I reached for Xavier's hand across the table. Gabriel looked pointedly in the opposite direction, but I only tightened my grip. The word *love* echoed in my brain, reverberating as though someone had screamed it through a loudspeaker. He *loved me*. Xavier Woods didn't care that I was ghostly white, seriously lacking in understanding of his world, and had a tendency to molt white feathers. He still wanted me. *He loved me*. I was so happy that if Xavier's grasp hadn't been anchoring me, I might have floated away.

"In that case, we can fast-forward to the second point on tonight's agenda," said Gabriel, unexpectedly ill at ease now. "Bethany tends to walk straight into situations, and at the moment she has only us to look out for her."

I was annoyed by how he spoke about me in the third person, as though I wasn't present, but I decided that now wasn't a good time to interrupt.

"If you're going to be spending time with her, then we need to know that you can protect her," Gabriel went on.

"Hasn't Xavier proved himself already?" I demanded impatiently. I was eager to bring the dinner ordeal to an end. "He rescued me from Molly's party, and nothing's ever gone wrong when he's been around."

"Bethany lacks understanding about the ways of the world," Gabriel said as though I hadn't spoken. "She still has much to learn and that makes her vulnerable."

"Do you have to make me sound like a full-time babysitting project?" I snapped.

"I happen to be an experienced babysitter," Xavier joked. "I can show you my résumé if you'd like."

Ivy was forced to smile behind her napkin at that, but when I searched Gabriel's face for a change of expression, I didn't find one.

"Are you sure you know what you're getting yourself into?" Ivy asked, looking straight at Xavier.

"No," he admitted. "But I'm prepared to find out."

"You can't turn back once you've placed your allegiance with us."

"We're not going to war," I muttered under my breath. Everyone ignored me.

"I understand," Xavier said, returning Ivy's gaze.

"I don't think you do," Gabriel said softly. "But you will."

"Is there anything else you think I should know?" asked Xavier.

"All in good time," said Gabriel.

FINALLY, I found myself alone with Xavier. He sat on the edge of the bathtub while I brushed my teeth. I brushed them after every meal; it was a habit I'd gotten into.

"That wasn't so bad." Xavier leaned against the wall. "I was expecting worse."

"You mean they haven't scared you off?"

"Nah," Xavier said causally. "Your brother's a bit intense, but your sister's cooking makes up for it."

I laughed. "Don't worry about Gabe—he's always like that."

"I'm not worried—he kind of reminds me of my mom."

"Don't tell him that," I giggled.

"I thought you didn't use makeup," Xavier said, picking up a stick of eyeliner from the counter.

"I bought it to make Molly happy," I said, rummaging around for the mouthwash. "She's turned me into her project."

"Is that so?" Xavier said. "Well, I happen to like you the way you are."

"Thanks," I said. "But I think *you* could do with a touch-up."

I grinned and waved the eyeliner at him.

"No, you don't," said Xavier ducking out of my reach. "No way."

"Why not?" I sulked.

"Because I'm a man," Xavier said. "And men don't wear makeup unless they're emo or play in a boy band."

"Please?" I wheedled.

His brilliant blue almond-shaped eyes seemed to sparkle. "Okay . . ."

"Really?" I brightened.

"No! I'm not that much of a pushover."

"Fine," I pouted. "I'll just have to make you smell like a girl. . . ."

Before he could stop me, I grabbed a bottle of perfume and squirted him in the chest. He sniffed his shirt curiously.

"Fruity," he concluded, "with a hint of musk."

I collapsed into laughter. "You're ridiculous."

"I think you mean irresistible," Xavier said.

"Yes," I agreed, "ridiculously irresistible."

I leaned forward to kiss him, just as there came a knock at the door. Ivy poked her head into the room and Xavier and I sprang apart.

"Your brother sent me to check on you," she said with a raised eyebrow. "To make sure you aren't up to no good."

"Actually," I began indignantly, "we were just—"

"Heading outside," Xavier cut in. I opened my mouth to argue, but he shot me a sharp look. "It's their house, we play by their rules," he murmured. As he steered me out of the room, I noticed Ivy looking at him with a new respect.

OUTSIDE, we sat on the garden swing with our arms around each other. Xavier disentangled himself long enough to roll up his shirtsleeves and then throw Phantom's frayed tennis ball across the grass. Phantom always retrieved but then refused to relinquish, so the soggy ball had to be pried from between his teeth. Xavier stretched back to throw the ball again and then rinsed his hands under the garden tap. I breathed in his clean, woody scent. All I could think was that we had survived our first test relatively unscathed. Xavier had been true to his word and had not allowed himself to be intimidated. On the contrary, he had held his ground with unswerving conviction. Not only did I admire him more than ever, but I also relished that he was in my house, this time as a legitimate guest rather than an intruder.

"I could stay here all night," I murmured into his shirt.

"You know what's so strange?" he said.

"What?"

"How normal this feels."

He twisted my hair around his fingers and I saw, reflected in his gesture, our lives entwined.

"Ivy was being dramatic when she said there's no turning back," I said.

"It's okay, Beth. I don't want my life to go back to the way it was before I met you. I thought I had it all, but really I was missing something. I feel like a completely different person now. This might sound corny, but I feel like I've been asleep for a long time, and you've just woken me up . . ." He paused. "I can't believe I just said that. What are you doing to me?"

"Turning you into a poet," I teased.

"Me?" Xavier growled in mock anger. "Poetry's for girls."

"You were great back there. I'm so proud of the way you handled yourself."

"Thank you. Who knows, maybe a few decades from now your brother and sister might actually like me."

"I wish we had that long." I sighed and immediately regretted the words. They had just slipped out. I could have kicked myself for being so stupid; what a perfect way to ruin the mood.

Xavier was so silent, I wondered if he'd even heard me. Then I felt his warm fingers under my chin, and he tilted my face up so we were looking eye to eye. He leaned down and kissed me softly, the sweet taste of his lips lingering after he pulled away. He bent forward and murmured in my ear, "We *will* find a way. That's a promise."

"You can't know that," I said. "This is different. . . ."

"Beth." Xavier put a finger against my lips. "I don't break my promises."

"But . . ."

"No buts . . . just trust me."

WHEN Xavier left, no one wanted to go to bed even though it was already past midnight. Gabriel we knew was an insomniac. It wasn't unusual for him or Ivy to stay up till the early hours of the morning. But this time all three of us were restless and alert. Ivy suggested a hot drink and was already pulling milk out of the fridge when Gabriel cut in.

"I have a better idea," he said. "I think we all deserve to unwind."

Ivy and I guessed his meaning immediately and didn't even bother trying to hide our excitement.

"Do you mean right now?" Ivy said, the milk carton almost slipping from her grasp.

"Of course, right now. But we have to hurry; it'll be light in a few hours."

Ivy let out a squeal. "Just give us a moment to change! We'll be right back."

I too could hardly contain my anticipation. This would be the perfect way to express the exhilaration I was feeling about the direction my relationship with Xavier had taken. It had been so long since I'd had a chance to really stretch my wings. My cliff-diving performance for Xavier hardly qualified as exercise. If anything, it had only served to whet my appetite and remind me how stiff and cramped my wings really felt. I had tried spreading them out and floating around my bedroom with the curtains pulled tight shut, but I'd only crashed into the ceiling fan and bumped my legs on the furniture. As I changed into a loose T-shirt, I felt a bolt of adrenaline shoot through my body. I was going to really savor this predawn flight. I went downstairs, and the three of us made our way silently out to the black Jeep parked in the garage.

It was a different experience driving along the coastal road that unfurled like a ribbon in the early morning. The air was fragrant with the scent of pine, and the trees were tipped with green. The sea looked solid, like a velvet mantle that had been draped over part of the earth. Along the residential streets, the shutters were all closed, and the streets were deserted as if the occupants had suddenly packed up and evacuated. The township, when we drove through it, was also deserted. I'd never seen Venus Cove asleep. I was so used to seeing people everywhere: riding bikes, eating fries on the pier, or buying jewelry from local craftsmen who set up their stalls on the pavement. But at that hour of the morning, there was a stillness that made me imagine we were the only living beings in the world. I wondered why people referred to the early hours of the morning as "ungodly" when in fact that was the very best time to connect with the forces above.

Gabriel drove for about an hour along a straight stretch of

road, then turned onto a bumpy scrub-lined track that seemed to wind toward the sky like a corkscrew. I knew where we were. Gabriel was taking the route to White Mountain, named because of the snow that sometimes coated its peak, despite its coastal location. You could see the mountain's outline from Venus Cove, like a pale gray monolith rising against a star-studded night sky.

There was fog up on the mountain, and the higher we drove the thicker it became. When Gabriel could no longer distinguish the road ahead he parked and we climbed out. We were standing on a narrow and winding road that continued uphill; tall fir trees, like soldiers, surrounded us on all sides, almost completely blocking out the sky. The tips of the trees were studded with beads of dew, and we could see our breath materialized in the cold air when we exhaled. The ground underfoot was sodden with leaves and bark, muffling our foot-steps. Moss-covered branches and tendrils of ferns brushed against our faces. We veered off the road, disappearing into the dense forest. Shafts of moonlight sliced through the canopy in places, like little spotlights illuminating our way. The trees whispered softly to one another and we could hear gentle rus-tling and the scampering of small paws. Despite the darkness none of us felt afraid. We knew the mountain was completely secluded. No one would find us there.

Ivy was the first to cast off her jacket and do what we were all waiting to do. She stood facing us, her back straight and her head thrown back so that her pale hair cascaded like a golden nimbus around her face and shoulders. In the moonlight she glowed like a lamp, and her sculpted figure looked like marble, white and flawless. Her body curved perfectly, each limb as long and elegant as a sapling.

"See you up there," she said like an excited child. She closed her eyes briefly, took a deep breath, and then sprinted away from us. She ran swiftly and nimbly through the trees, her feet barely touching the ground and gathered speed until she was almost a blur. Then she became suddenly airborne. There was a breathtaking artistry in it—Ivy made it look as easy as a swan taking flight. Her wings, slender but powerful, sliced through the loose T-shirt she wore and reared Heavenward like living entities. The wings that looked as solid as stone when stationary shone like satin in full flight.

I broke into a run and felt my own wings begin to pulse and then tear through their cage of cloth. Once released, their beating grew faster, and I too was lifted into the air to join Ivy. We flew in synchronization for a while, gliding slowly upward, then dipping suddenly, and finally coming to land on the soles of our feet on the branches of a nearby tree. From there we looked down at Gabriel with radiant faces. Ivy bent and let herself topple from the tree. The span of her wings broke her fall, and she swooped upward again with a gasp of pleasure.

"What are you waiting for?" she called down to Gabriel before she disappeared into a cloud.

Gabriel, who never did anything in a hurry, methodically peeled off layers and tossed aside his boots. He pulled his T-shirt over his head, and we watched his wings unfurl until the genteel music teacher had disappeared and he looked like the majestic celestial warrior he was created to be. This was the angel who, eons ago, had singlehandedly reduced a city to ash and stone. His entire figure shone like burnished brass. Even in flight his style was different from ours, lacking in urgency, more structured and meditative.

Above the treetops I was enveloped by mist and cloud. Droplets of water gathered on my back, and I felt their crisp bite. My wings beat furiously and lifted me higher. I abandoned thought and soared, letting my body twist and turn, looping around the trees. I felt the release of energy that had been pent up for so long. I saw Gabriel stop midair once to ascertain that I hadn't lost control. Ivy I only spotted every now and then as an amber glow through the mist.

For the most part interaction was kept to a minimum. This was our own personal time to feel whole again and embrace the kind of freedom that could only ever truly be felt in the Kingdom of Heaven. Our oneness was beyond the power of language to convey. Our humanity dropped away as we experienced our true selves.

We flew like this for what must have been several hours, until Gabriel emitted a low melodic hum, like the note of an oboe, which we knew was the signal to come down.

As we climbed into the Jeep, I thought there was no chance of my going to sleep once we got home. I was too jubilant, and it would be hours before I came down from my high. But I was wrong. The car trip back along the winding road was so rhythmic that I fell asleep curled on the backseat like a kitten long before Byron came into view.

17

Calm Before the Storm

MY relationship with Xavier seemed to deepen after the dinner with my family. We felt we had been given permission to express our emotions without fear of reprisal. We began to think and move in sync with each other, like one entity occupying different bodies. Although we made a conscious effort not to disconnect from everyone around us, at times it just couldn't be helped. We even tried allocating specific times to spend with other people, but when we did, the minutes seemed to drag and our behavior felt so contrived that we inevitably gravitated back together within the hour.

During lunch Xavier and I had taken to sitting together at our own private table at the back of the cafeteria. People drifted over from time to time to share a joke or ask "Woodsy" about details of a swim meet, but rarely did anyone attempt to join us nor were references made to our relationship. Instead people orbited around us, keeping a respectful distance. If they sensed there were secret issues between us, they at least had the manners not to pry.

"Let's get out of here," Xavier said, packing up his books.

"Not until you've finished your essay."

"I'm done."

"You've written three lines."

"Three carefully considered lines," Xavier objected. "Quality over quantity, remember?"

"I'm just making sure you stay focused. I don't want to be responsible for distracting you from your goals."

"Bit late for that," Xavier joked. "You're a huge distraction and a very bad influence."

"How dare you!" I teased. "It's impossible for me to be a bad influence on anyone."

"Really? And why is that?"

"Because I'm goodness personified—I'm so clean I squeak!"

Xavier's brows furrowed as he pondered this admission. "Hmmm," he said after a moment. "We're going to have to do something about that."

"Any excuse to get out of homework!"

"Maybe it's more that I have the rest of my life for achieving my goals. Who knows how long I've got with you."

I felt the lightheartedness seep from the conversation as soon as those words were spoken. We usually skirted around this topic—it mostly led to confusion as things do when they're outside our sphere of control.

"Let's not think about that."

"How can I not think about it? Doesn't it keep you awake at night?"

The conversation was going down a road I didn't like.

"Of course I think about it," I said. "But I don't see the point in spoiling our time together now."

"I just feel like we should be doing something," he said

angrily. I knew the anger wasn't directed at me. The fact that there was no one to blame made things even harder. "We should at least be trying."

"There's nothing we can do," I said quietly. "I don't think you realize what you're dealing with here. You can't just mess around with the forces of the universe!"

"What ever happened to free will? Or was that just a myth?"

"Aren't you forgetting something? I'm not like you so those rules don't apply to me."

"Maybe they should."

"Maybe . . . but what are we going to do about it, start a petition?"

"That's not funny, Beth. Do you *want* to go home?" Xavier asked, his eyes locked with mine.

I knew he wasn't referring to Byron.

"I can't believe you even have to ask me that question."

"Then why doesn't this bother you as much as it bothers me?"

"If I thought there was any way I could stay here, do you think I would hesitate?" I cried. "Do you think I'd willingly walk away from the most important thing in my life?"

Xavier turned to look at me, his turquoise eyes dark, his mouth narrowed into a hard line. "They, whoever they are, shouldn't have control over our lives," he said. "I'm not about to lose you. I've been through that before, and I'll do whatever it takes to make sure it doesn't happen again."

"Xavier . . . ," I began, but he silenced me by putting a finger lightly over my lips.

"Just answer me one question. If we were to fight this, what are our options?"

"I don't know!"

"But are there options, someone we can ask for help, something we can try, even if it's a long shot?" I looked into his eyes and saw an urgency that had never been there before. Xavier was always so calm and relaxed. "Beth, I need to know," he said. "Is there a chance? Even a small one?"

"There might be," I said. "But I'm afraid of finding out."

"Me too, but we can't think that way. We have to have faith."

"Even if it all comes to nothing?"

"You said yourself there was a chance." Xavier laced his fingers with mine. "That's all we need."

OVER the last weeks I'd felt a little guilty about distancing myself from Molly, but she had resigned herself to spending time with me whenever Xavier was otherwise occupied. I knew she must be resentful of his monopoly of my time and attention, but Molly was a realist and held the view that friendships had to take a backseat when relationships started—especially if the relationship was as intense as mine and Xavier's. She seemed to have overcome her previous irritation with him, and although she was far from willing to acknowledge him as her friend, she was much more prepared to accept him as one of mine.

Xavier and I were walking into town one afternoon when we spotted Ivy under an oak tree with a dark-haired senior from Bryce Hamilton. The boy was wearing a backward baseball cap, the sleeves of his shirt were rolled up to show off his muscular arms, and he kept smirking suggestively as he spoke. I'd never seen my sister look so flustered. The boy had her cornered; she clutched a shopping bag with one hand and nervously tucked her hair behind her ear with the other, clearly seeking a means of escape.

I nudged Xavier. "What's going on over there?"

"Looks like Chris Bucknall finally worked up the nerve to ask her out," Xavier said.

"You know him?"

"He's on my water-polo team."

"I don't think he's Ivy's type."

"I'm not surprised," Xavier said. "He's a total sleaze."

"What should we do?"

"Hey, Bucknall," Xavier called out. "Can I have a word?"

"Little busy here, dude," the boy replied.

"Did you hear the news?" Xavier said. "Coach wants to see everyone in his office tonight after the game?"

"Yeah? What for?" Chris said without turning around.

"Not sure. Something about taking names for next season's tryouts. Anyone who doesn't show doesn't get in."

Chris Bucknall looked alarmed. "I gotta go," he told Ivy. "I'll catch *you* later."

Ivy gave Xavier a grateful smile as Chris sprinted away.

GABRIEL and Ivy finally seemed to have accepted Xavier. He didn't intrude on our space but rather became a regular fixture within it. I began to suspect they actually liked having him around: first, because he was so reliable in terms of keeping an eye on me; and second, because he was useful when it came to working technical gadgets. Gabriel had found his students giving him strange looks when he didn't know how to work the DVD player, and Ivy wanted to promote her social service program via the school e-mail system. Both had enlisted Xavier's help. Knowledgeable as my siblings were, technology was a bit of a minefield for them, because it changed constantly. Gabriel had also grudgingly allowed Xavier to show him how to send e-mails to his fellow colleagues at Bryce Hamilton and teach him the workings of an iPod. It seemed to me that Xavier spoke a whole different language sometimes, using alien terms like *Bluetooth*, *gigabyte*, and *WiFi*. If it had been anyone else, I would have switched off, but I loved the sound of his voice, no matter what he was talking about. I could occupy myself for hours watching the way he moved, listening to the way he spoke, committing it all to memory.

Aside from being our tech angel, Xavier took his responsibility as my "bodyguard" so seriously that I found myself having to remind him that I wasn't made of glass and had managed quite adequately before his arrival. Entrusted to look after me by Gabriel and Ivy, Xavier was determined to keep his word and convince them of his moral fiber. He was the one who reminded me to drink plenty of water and the one who deflected questions about my family from curious classmates. He even took it upon himself to answer for me one day when Mr. Collins asked why I hadn't managed to finish my homework by the due date.

"Beth has a lot of other commitments at the moment,"

he explained. "She'll get the assignment in by the end of the week."

I knew that if it slipped my mind, Xavier would complete it for me and hand it in without my knowledge.

He became fiercely protective whenever anybody he didn't approve of came within a two-foot radius of me.

"Uh-uh." He shook his head at me when a boy named Tom Snooks asked if I wanted to "hang" with him and his friends one afternoon.

"What's wrong with him?" I asked crossly. "He seems nice enough."

"He's not your type of person."

"Why?"

"You ask a lot of questions, don't you?"

"Yes. Now tell me why."

"Well, because he's off with the green fairy most of the time."

I stared at him blankly so that he was forced to elaborate.

"He's good friends with Puff the Magic Dragon," Xavier hinted and waited for me to register, rolling his eyes when I didn't. "You're a *dope*."

If it hadn't been for Xavier acting as a buffer, my life at Bryce Hamilton would have been a lot more difficult. I had a tendency to get myself into sticky situations. Trouble seemed to seek me out even though I did my best to avoid it. It found me one day as I was crossing the parking lot to get to English.

"Hey there, sweetheart!" I spun around when I heard the voice behind me. It was a lanky senior with slick blond hair and pock-marked skin. He was in my biology class, but he was rarely there. I had seen him out behind the Dumpsters smoking cigarettes and doing burnouts in his car. He was flanked by three other boys, all grinning nastily.

"Hello," I said nervously.

"I don't think we've been properly introduced." He smirked. "I'm Kirk."

"Nice to meet you." I didn't meet his gaze. Something about his attitude made me uneasy.

"Anyone ever told you you've got a pretty sweet rack?" Kirk asked. The boys behind him sniggered.

"Excuse me?" I didn't understand what he meant.

"I'd like to get to know you better—if you know what I mean." Kirk took a step toward me. I immediately darted away from him. "Don't be shy, honey," he said.

"I have to get to class."

"Sure you can't spare a few minutes?" He said in a leering drawl. "I'm only after a quickie." He took hold of my shoulder.

"Don't touch me!"

"Ooh, feistier than she looks." Kirk laughed and tightened his grip.

"Take your hands off her." I breathed a sigh of relief as Xavier stepped in front of me, tall and reassuring. I drew instinctively closer to him, relishing the safety of his presence. His hair was pushed away from his face. His familiar turquoise eyes were narrowed with anger.

"I wasn't talking to you," said Kirk, dropping his hand. "This isn't any of your business."

"Her business *is* my business."

"Oh, yeah? You think you can stop me?"

"Touch her again and see what happens," Xavier warned.

"You wanna make something of this?"

"That's your call." Xavier pulled off his blazer and rolled up his sleeves. His school tie hung loose, and I saw the crucifix sitting just in the hollow of his throat. The fabric of his school shirt strained against the sculpted muscles in his arms. He was significantly broader in the chest than Kirk, and I saw the other boy do a quick evaluation of his strength.

"Let it go, man," one of his friends advised and then lowered his voice. "That's Xavier Woods."

This seemed to act as a deterrent for Kirk.

"Whatever." He spit on the ground, threw me a filthy look, and stalked away.

Xavier wrapped an arm around my shoulder, and I drew close to him, breathing in his clean, crisp scent.

"Some people really need to be taught some manners," he said disdainfully. I stared up at him.

"Would you really have gotten into a fight for me?"

"Of course." He didn't hesitate.

"But there were four of them."

"Beth, I'd take on Megatron's army to protect you."

"Who?"

Xavier shook his head and laughed.

"I keep forgetting we have different reference points. Let's just say, I'm not scared of four little punks."

XAVIER didn't know much about angels, but he knew about people. He knew what they wanted far better than I did and therefore could better judge who to trust and who to keep at a safe distance. I knew that Ivy and Gabriel still worried about the ramifications of our relationship, but I felt that Xavier supplied me with a strength and belief in myself that made me stronger for whatever my role in our mission was meant to be. Although he didn't really understand the nature of our job on earth, he was suddenly conscious of not distracting me from it. At the same time, his concern for my well-being bordered on obsession as he worried about even the littlest things, like my energy level.

"You don't have to worry about me," I reminded him one day in the cafeteria. "Despite what Gabriel thinks, I can take care of myself."

"I'm just doing my job," he replied. "By the way, have you had lunch today?"

"I'm not hungry. Gabriel always cooks a big breakfast."

"Here, eat this," he commanded and pushed a health bar across the table. As an athlete, he always seemed to have an endless supply at any given time. The label told me this one contained cashews, coconut, apricots, and seeds.

"I can't eat this; it's got birdseed in it!"

"Those are sesame seeds and they're full of energy. I don't want you burning out."

"Why would I do that?"

"Because your blood sugar is probably low—so don't argue."

Sometimes it was easier not to argue with Xavier when his objective was taking care of me.

"All right, Mother," I said, biting into the chewy bar. "By the way, this tastes like cardboard."

I rested my head on his strong tanned arms, reassured as always by his solidity.

"Sleepy?" he asked.

"Phantom snored right through the night, and I didn't have the heart to kick him out."

Xavier sighed and patted my head. "You're too nice for your own good sometimes. Don't think I haven't noticed you've only taken one bite out of that bar. Now eat up."

"Xavier, please, someone might hear you!"

He picked up the bar and waved it through the air making a whistling noise with his mouth. "It'll be a lot more embarrassing if we have to start playing airplanes."

"What's airplanes?"

"A game mothers play to get stubborn children to eat."

I laughed, and he seized the opportunity of flying the health bar straight into my mouth.

Xavier loved to tell stories about his family and I loved to listen. Whenever he spoke, I found myself enormously distracted by him. Lately his anecdotes revolved around his eldest sister's upcoming wedding. I often interrupted with questions, hungry for the details he omitted. What color were the bridesmaids' dresses? What was the name of the young cousin who had been recruited as ring bearer? Who was in favor of a band over a string quartet? Would the bride's shoes be white satin? Whenever he couldn't answer, he would promise to find out for me.

As I ate, Xavier explained how his mother and sister were currently butting heads over the wedding arrangements. His sister Claire wanted a ceremony in the local botanical gardens, but his mother said it was too "primitive." The Woods family were parishioners of Saint Mark's, and had a long-standing association with the church. Mrs. Woods wanted the wedding held there. During the recent spat, she had threatened not to attend at all if it wasn't going to be celebrated in a House of God. According to her, vows not exchanged in a sanctified place weren't even valid. So they'd compromised—the ceremony would be held at the church and the reception at a beachside pavilion. Xavier chuckled as he told me the story, amused by the irrational antics of the females in his family. I couldn't help thinking how well his mother would get along with Gabriel.

Sometimes I felt removed from this part of Xavier's life. It was like he was living a double life: one he shared with his family and friends, and then his deep attachment to me.

"Do you ever think we don't belong together?" I asked, propping my chin on my hands and trying to read his face.

"No, I don't," he said without a second's hesitation. "Do you?"

"Well, I know this wasn't supposed to happen. Someone upstairs slipped up big time."

"We are *not* a mistake," Xavier insisted.

"No, but I'm saying that we've gone against fate. This wasn't what they planned for us."

"I'm glad about the mix-up, aren't you?"

"I am for me. . . ."

"But?"

"But I don't want to become a burden for you."

"You're not a burden. You're infuriating sometimes and you don't listen to advice, but you're never a burden."

"I *am not* infuriating."

"I forgot to add that you aren't the best judge of character either, including your own."

I ruffled his hair, relishing its silkiness on my fingers. "Do you think your family would like me?" I asked.

"Of course. They trust my judgment about most things."

"Yes, but what if they thought I'm weird."

"They're not like that, but why don't you find out? Come over and meet them this weekend. I've been meaning to ask you."

"I'm not sure," I hedged. "I'm not comfortable around new people."

"They're not new," he said. "I've known them my whole life."

"I meant new to me."

"They're a part of who I am, Beth. It'd mean a lot to me if they got to meet you. They've heard enough about you."

"What have you told them?"

"Just how good you are."

"I'm not that good or we wouldn't be in this situation."

"Girls who are all good have never really appealed to me. So you'll come?"

"I'll think about it."

I had hoped he would ask and I wanted to say yes but part of me feared feeling different from them. After what I'd heard about his conservative mother, I didn't want to be judged. Xavier read my face.

"What's the problem?" he asked.

"If your mother's religious, she might recognize a fallen angel when she sees one." It sounded pretty stupid once I'd said it aloud.

"You aren't a fallen angel. Do you have to be so melodramatic?"

"I'm fallen compared to Ivy and Gabriel."

"Well, I hardly think my mother's going to notice. I had to face the God squad, remember? And I didn't try to squirm my way out of it."

"You have a point there."

"Then it's settled. I'll pick you up Saturday around five. Your lit class is about to start—I'll walk over with you."

As I was gathering my books, a peal of thunder echoed through the cafeteria and the sunlight streaming through the windows vanished. The sky had darkened and was threatening rain. We had all known the blissful spring weather wouldn't last, but it was disappointing just the same. The rainy season could be bitter along this part of the coast.

"The rain's about to hit," Xavier observed looking at the skies.

"Good-bye, sun," I moaned.

No sooner had I spoken than the first fat drops began to fall. The skies opened and soon rain was falling in steady sheets, drumming on the cafeteria roof. I watched students sprinting across the quad, shielding their faces with folders.

A couple of junior girls stood in the open, allowing themselves to be drenched and laughing hysterically. They would be in trouble when they finally turned up to class soaked. I saw Gabriel heading to the music wing, a troubled expression on his face. The umbrella he held was slanted by the strong wind that had blown up.

"Coming?" Xavier asked.

"Let's stay and watch the rain for a while. There's not much going on in lit right now."

"Is this bad Beth speaking?"

"I think we need to revise your definition of 'bad.' Can't I stay with you for this lesson?"

"And have your brother accusing me of being a bad influence? Not on your life. By the way, I hear there's a new student, on exchange from London. I think he's in your class. Aren't you a bit curious?"

"Not especially. I have everything I need right here." I ran my finger along his cheek, tracing its smooth contours.

Xavier removed my finger and kissed the tip before planting it firmly back in my lap. "Listen, this kid might be right up your alley. According to the grapevine, he's been expelled from three schools already, and he's been sent here to *sort himself out.* I guess because it's far away from anything that might get him into trouble. His dad's some media mogul or something. Interested now?"

"Maybe—just a little."

"Well, go to class and check him out. Maybe you can help him."

"Okay, Xavier, but I already have a conscience and it gives me enough of a hard time. I don't need another one."

"Love you too, Beth."

WHEN I looked back on this day later, I would remember the rain and Xavier's face. That change in the weather also marked a change in our lives; one that none of us could have seen coming. My life on earth up till then had been filled with minor drama and the angst of youth, but I was about to learn that these troubles had been child's play compared with what found us next. I suppose it served to teach us a lot about what was important in life. I don't think we could have avoided it; it was part of our story from the very beginning. After all, things had been running relatively smoothly; we were bound to hit a bump. We just didn't expect it to hit so hard.

The bump came all the way from England and had a name: Jake Thorn.

18

Dark Prince

EVEN though it was my most interesting class by a long shot, I wasn't in the mood for lit. I wanted to spend more time with Xavier; to be separated from him always gave me physical pain, like a cramp in my chest. When we got to the classroom, I tightened my grip on his fingers and pulled him toward me. No matter how much time we spent together, it never seemed to be enough—I always wanted more. When it came to him, I had a ravenous appetite that could never be satisfied.

"It won't matter if I'm just a few minutes late," I wheedled.

"Nope," Xavier said, prying away my fingers that were now clutching his shirtsleeve. "You're going to be on time."

"You've turned into such a grandma," I grumbled. He ignored my comment and deposited my books into my arms. These days, he rarely allowed me to carry anything for longer than was necessary. I must have looked so lazy to everyone else, always walking around with Xavier by my side, dutifully carrying my belongings.

"You know, I can carry my own stuff, Xav, I'm not an invalid," I said.

"I know," he replied, flashing his adorable half-smile. "But I enjoy being at your disposal."

Before he could stop me, I locked my arms around his neck and pulled him into an alcove between the lockers. It was his own fault really, standing there with his soft hair flopping over his eyes, his school shirt coming untucked, and the plaited leather band hugging his smooth tanned wrist as if it were a part of him. If he didn't want to be mauled, he shouldn't have put himself right in my path.

Xavier dropped his own books and kissed me back forcefully, his hands holding my neck, his body pressed close against mine. The few students hurrying by to classes stared openly at us.

"Get a room," someone sniped, but I ignored them. For that moment space and time didn't exist—there was only the two of us in our own personal dimension, and I couldn't remember where I was or even who I was. I couldn't distinguish where my being stopped and his began. It made me think of a line from *Jane Eyre* when Rochester tells Jane he loves her as if she were his own flesh. That was exactly how it felt loving Xavier.

Then he broke away.

"You are very bad, Miss Church," he said, breathing heavily, a smile playing around his lips. He put on a genteel voice. "And I am powerless when it comes to your charms. Now I believe we are *both* late for class."

Luckily for me, Miss Castle wasn't the sort of teacher to be bothered about punctuality. She handed me a folder as I came in and took a seat at the front of the room.

"Hello, Beth," she said. "We're just discussing the introduction to third quarter. I've decided to allocate you all a creative writing task to be done with a partner. Together you'll need to come up with a poem to read to the class on the subject of love, to preface our upcoming study of the great Romantic poets Wordsworth, Shelley, Keats, and Byron. Does anyone have a favorite poem they'd like to share before we start?"

"I do," said a well-spoken voice from the back of the room. I scanned the faces to identify the speaker who had a distinct English accent. An awed silence fell over the rest of the class. It was the newcomer. Brave of him, I thought, to go out on a limb on his first day. Either that or he was enormously conceited.

"Thank you, Jake!" Miss Castle said enthusiastically. "Would you like to come up here to recite it?"

"Certainly."

The boy that sauntered to the front of the room was not what I had expected. Something about his appearance made my heart plunge into my stomach. He was tall and lean, and his straight dark hair reached his shoulders. His cheekbones were sharp, giving him a gaunt, hollow look. His nose drooped slightly at the tip, and his brilliant jade-green eyes gazed out from beneath low-set brows. His lips curled in a permanent sneer. It made him look intolerant of his surroundings.

He was dressed in black jeans and a black T-shirt, and a dark tattoo of a serpent wound around his forearm. He was totally unselfconscious about not being in school uniform on his first day. In fact, he had the confident swagger of someone who considers himself above the rules. There was no denying it—he was beautiful. But there was something about him that suggested more than beauty. Was it grace, poise, charm, or something more dangerous?

Jake's smoldering gaze swept across the classroom. Before I could duck my head, his eyes locked with mine and lingered there. He gave a self-assured smile before beginning.

"'Annabel Lee,' a ballad by Edgar Allan Poe," he announced smoothly. "It might interest you to know that Poe married his thirteen-year-old cousin, Virginia, when he was twenty-seven. She died two years later from TB."

The class stared at him entranced. When he began to speak, his voice seemed to flow out like rich syrup and filled the room. It was the cultured, confident voice of someone used to having things his own way.

> It was many and many a year ago,
> In a kingdom by the sea,
> That a maiden there lived whom you may know
> By the name of Annabel Lee;
> And this maiden she lived with no other thought
> Than to love and be loved by me.
>
> I was a child and she was a child,
> In this kingdom by the sea:
> But we loved with a love that was more than love
> I and my Annabel Lee;
> With a love that the winged seraphs of heaven
> Coveted her and me.

And this was the reason that, long ago,
In this kingdom by the sea,
A wind blew out of a cloud, chilling
My beautiful Annabel Lee;
So that her high-born kinsmen came
And bore her away from me,
To shut her up in a sepulchre
In this kingdom by the sea.

The angels, not half so happy in heaven,
Went envying her and me—
Yes!—that was the reason (as all men know,
In this kingdom by the sea)
That the wind came out of the cloud by night,
Chilling and killing my Annabel Lee.

But our love it was stronger by far than the love
Of those who were older than we—
Of many far wiser than we—
And neither the angels in heaven above,
Nor the demons down under the sea,
Can ever dissever my soul from the soul
Of the beautiful Annabel Lee,

For the moon never beams without bringing me dreams
Of the beautiful Annabel Lee;
And the stars never rise, but I feel the bright eyes
Of the beautiful Annabel Lee;
And so, all the night-tide, I lie down by the side

Of my darling—my darling—my life and my bride,
  In the sepulchre there by the sea,
  In her tomb by the sounding sea.

When Jake finished, I couldn't help but notice that every female in the room, including Miss Castle, was enraptured, gazing at him as if their knight in shining armor had just arrived. Even I had to admit it was an impressive delivery. His recitation of the poem had been poignant, as though Annabel Lee truly had been the love of his life. By the look of some of the girls, they were ready to jump up and console him for his loss.

"That was a very expressive rendition," Miss Castle breathed. "We must keep you in mind when Jazz and Poetry night comes along. All right, everyone, I hope that's inspired you to come up with some poetry of your own. I'd like you to get into pairs and brainstorm ideas. The form is entirely up to you. Give yourselves free rein—complete poetic license!"

The class began to rearrange themselves so they sat in pairs around the room. On his way back to his seat, Jake stopped in front of my desk.

"Want to be partners?" he purred. "I hear you're new as well."

"I've been here for a while now," I said, not appreciating the comparison.

Jake interpreted my response as an acceptance of his offer and slid easily into the seat beside me. He leaned back in his chair, hands resting comfortably behind his head.

"I'm Jake Thorn," he said, looking at me with his hooded, dark eyes. He held out a hand, the epitome of good manners.

"Bethany Church," I replied, gingerly proffering my own hand.

Instead of shaking it, as I had expected, he turned it over and brought it to his lips in a ridiculous gesture of gallantry. "Delighted to make your acquaintance."

I nearly laughed outright. Did he expect me to take him seriously? Where did he think he was? I *would* have laughed had I not found myself looking into his eyes. They were dark green with a burning intensity, and yet there was a jaded expression on his face that suggested he had seen more of the world than most his age. His gaze swept over me, and I got the feeling he didn't miss a thing. He wore a silver pendant around his neck: a half-moon etched with strange symbols.

He drummed his fingers casually on the desk. "So," he said. "Any thoughts?"

I stared at him blankly.

"For the poem," he reminded me with a raised eyebrow.

"You start," I replied. "I'm still thinking."

"Very well," he said. "Any preference for particular metaphors? Rain forests or rainbows, anything like that?" He laughed at some private joke. "I'm partial to reptiles myself."

"What's that supposed to mean?" I asked curiously.

"To be partial to something means you like it."

"I know what *partial* means; but why reptiles?"

"Tough skinned and cold-blooded," Jake said, flashing a smile.

He turned away from me suddenly and scrawled a note

on a scrap of paper, scrunched it into a ball, and flicked it at the two goth girls, Alicia and Alexandra, who were sitting in front of us, bent over their notebooks, writing rapidly. They looked across in irritation, which soon faded when they saw who their correspondent was. They quickly scanned the contents of the note, whispering excitedly to each other. Alicia peeked at Jake from under her heavy bangs and nodded almost imperceptibly. Jake winked and, seeming pleased with his efforts, settled back in his chair.

"So the theme is love," he resumed.

"What?" I asked stupidly.

"For our poem." He slid his gaze over me. "Have you forgotten again?"

"I was just distracted."

"Wondering what I was saying to those girls?" he asked me slyly.

"No!" I said a little too quickly.

"I'm just trying to make friends," he said, his face suddenly very open and honest. "It's tough being the new kid in town."

I felt a sudden pang of sympathy for him. "I'm sure you'll make friends quickly," I said. "Everyone was really welcoming when I came. And I'm always here if you need someone to show you around."

His lip curled up in a smile. "Thanks, Bethany. I'll be sure to take you up on that offer."

We considered ideas in silence for a while until Jake spoke again. "So what do you do for kicks around here?"

"Most people just hang out with friends, go to the beach, stuff like that," I replied.

"No, I meant what do *you* do for kicks?"

"Oh." I paused. "I spend most of my time with my family . . . and my boyfriend."

"Ah, there's a boyfriend? How wholesome." Jake smiled. "Not that I'm surprised. Of course you have a boyfriend—with a face like that. Who's the lucky guy?"

"Xavier Woods," I said, embarrassed by his compliment.

"Will he be joining the priesthood anytime soon?"

I scowled at him. "It's a beautiful name," I said defensively. "It means light. Haven't you ever heard of Saint Francis Xavier?"

Jake grinned. "Wasn't he the one that went psycho and moved into a cave."

"Actually I think it was more of a conscious decision to live simply," I corrected.

"I see," said Jake, "my mistake."

I shifted uncomfortably in my seat.

"How do you like your new home?" Jake asked finally.

"Venus Cove is a nice place to live and the people are genuine,'" I said, "but someone like you might find it dull."

"I don't think so," he said, staring at me. "Not now—not with people like you around."

The bell rang, and I packed up my books quickly, eager to go and meet Xavier.

"See you soon, Bethany," said Jake. "Perhaps we'll work more productively next time."

I was seized by a sudden wave of insecurity when I caught up with Xavier at the lockers. For some reason I felt unsettled and wanted nothing more than to feel his protective arms around me, even though they had already spent most of the day in that position. As he put his books away, I ducked under his arm and clung to him like a limpet.

"Whoa," he said, his arms closing around me. "It's good to see you too. You okay?"

"Yes," I said, burying my face in his shirt and inhaling his familiar scent. "Just missed you."

"We've been apart an hour." Xavier laughed. "Come on, let's get out of here."

We made our way to the parking lot together. Gabriel and Ivy had granted Xavier permission to drive me home occasionally, which he saw as great progress. His car was parked in its usual spot under the shade of a row of oak trees, and he opened the door for me. I wasn't sure what he thought might happen if I was permitted to open my own door. Maybe he was worried it would fly off its hinges and flatten me or I might sprain my wrist trying to open it. Or maybe he was just brought up with good old-fashioned manners.

Xavier didn't switch on the ignition until I had put my seat belt on and stowed my bag safely in the backseat. Gabriel had told him I was susceptible to pain and injury and that my human form could be damaged. Xavier was taking it all very much to heart and pulled out of the parking lot with an expression of intense concentration.

But even Xavier's careful driving wasn't able to prevent what happened next. As we were turning onto the main road, a shiny black motorcycle shot out from nowhere and cut across us. Xavier slammed on the brakes, sending the Chevy lurching forward and narrowly avoiding a collision. We veered to the right, hitting the curb. I was flung forward, my seat belt catching me and throwing me painfully back against the seat. The motorcycle screamed away down the street, leaving a cloud of exhaust in its wake. Xavier stared dumbfounded after it, before quickly turning to make sure I was all right. Once he was satisfied that I was unharmed he was able to unleash his anger.

"What the hell was that?" he fumed. "What an idiot! Did you see who was driving? If I ever find out who that was, so help me God, I'll introduce his head to a pole."

"It was hard to see his face under the helmet," I said quietly.

"We'll find out soon enough," Xavier growled. "You don't see too many Yamaha V Star 250s around here."

"How do you know the bike model?" I asked.

"I'm a boy. We like engines."

Xavier drove me home, glaring suspiciously at passing cars as though the incident was likely to be repeated. By the time we pulled up in front of Byron, he seemed to have calmed down a little.

"I made lemonade," Ivy said as she opened the front door. She looked so domestic in her apron that both of us had to smile. "Why don't you come in, Xavier?" she asked. "You can do your homework with Bethany."

"Uh, no, thanks, I've got some chores I promised Mom I'd do," Xavier hedged.

"Gabriel's not here."

"In that case, sure, thanks."

My sister ushered us both inside and shut the door. Phantom charged from the kitchen when he heard our voices and knocked against our legs by way of greeting.

"Homework first, walk later," I said.

We spread our books out on the dining room table. Xavier had to finish a psychology report, and I had to analyze a political cartoon for history. The cartoon was of King Louis XVI standing beside a throne and looking very pleased with himself. I was supposed to be interpreting the significance of the objects around him.

"What do you call that thing he's holding?" I asked Xavier. "I can't see it properly."

"It looks like a fire poker to me," Xavier said.

"I highly doubt that Louis XVI poked his own fires. I think it's a scepter. And what's he's wearing?"

"Mmm . . . a poncho?" Xavier suggested.

I rolled my eyes.

"I'll get top grades with your help."

In truth, the homework I had been assigned and the grades I would be awarded for my effort, didn't interest me in the slightest. The things I wanted to learn didn't come from textbooks; they came from experiences and interactions. But Xavier was concentrating on his psych report, and I didn't want to distract him any further so I put my head down and peered at the cartoon. My attention span turned out to be unnaturally short.

"If you could take back one thing you've done in your life, what would it be?" I asked, tickling Phantom's nose with my fluffy-tipped pen. He caught the pen between his teeth, thinking it was some kind of furry animal and trotted off victoriously.

Xavier put down his own pen and looked at me quizzically. "Don't you mean: What is the independent variable in the Stanford Prison Experiment?"

"Yawn," I said.

"I'm afraid some of us aren't blessed with divine knowledge."

I sighed. "I can't believe that stuff really interests you?"

"It doesn't. But I have no choice, Beth," he said. "I have to get into college and get a decent job if I want to succeed—it's reality." He laughed. "Well, I guess it's not your reality, but it sure as hell is mine."

I didn't have an answer for that. The idea of Xavier getting older, of having to work the same job day in and day out to provide for a family until the day he died, made me want to cry. I wanted his life to be easy, and I wanted him to spend it with me.

"I'm sorry," I said quietly.

He slid his chair closer to me. "Don't be," he said. "I'd much rather be doing this . . ." And he leaned across and kissed my hair, his lips moving along until they found my chin and finally my mouth.

"I'd much rather spend all of my time talking to you, being with you, discovering you," he said. "But just because I've walked into this crazy fantasy, doesn't mean I can just abandon my other plans, much as I might want to. My parents still expect me to get into a top college." He frowned. "It's important to them."

"Is it important to you?" I asked.

"I suppose," he replied. "What else is there?"

I nodded—I knew what it was like to have to live up to family expectations.

"You have to do what makes you happy as well," I said.

"That's why I have you."

"How am I supposed to study if you go on saying things like that?" I complained.

"There's more where that came from," Xavier teased.

"Is that what you spend your spare time doing?"

"You got me. All I do is write down lines to impress women."

"Women?"

"Sorry—one woman," he rectified as I scowled at him. "One woman who is worth a thousand women."

"Oh, shut up," I said. "Don't try and dig yourself out of this one."

"So gracious." Xavier shook his head. "So forgiving and compassionate."

"Don't push it, buddy," I said, putting on a thuggish voice. Xavier hung his head.

"I apologize . . . jeez, I'm whipped."

I continued with the history task while he finished writing his report. He still had a stack of homework left, but in the end I proved too much of a distraction. He had just completed his third trig problem when I felt his hand wander over to my lap. I slapped it gently.

"Keep studying," I said when he looked up from the page. "No one said you could stop."

He smiled and scrawled something at the bottom of the answer sheet. The solution now read:

Find x if $(x) = 2\sin 3x$, over the domain $-2\pi < x < 2\pi$

$X = Beth$

"Stop goofing around!" I said.

"I'm not! I'm stating a truth. You're my solution to everything," Xavier replied. "The end result is always you. X always equals Beth."

19

Into the Woods

I was nervous about meeting Xavier's family on Saturday. He'd invited me several times already, and it had become impossible to refuse without looking as though I wasn't interested. Besides, he wasn't going to take no for an answer.

It wasn't that I didn't want to meet them; I was just terrified about how they might react to meeting me.

At school, after the first-day nerves had evaporated, I'd never been too bothered about how I was perceived by my peers. But Xavier's family was different; they actually mattered. I wanted them to like me, and I wanted them to think that Xavier's life had been enhanced by our relationship. In short, I wanted their approval. Molly had told me no end of stories about her ex-boyfriend Kyle, whom her parents had thoroughly disapproved of, even going so far as to refuse him entry into the house. I was sure the Woods clan couldn't object to me that strongly, but if they didn't like me, their influence might be strong enough to affect Xavier's feelings for me.

When Saturday came, Xavier's car pulled into our driveway at precisely two minutes to five as arranged. We headed off toward his house, which was on the other side of town, about a ten-minute drive away. By the time we pulled into his street, I had a hundred negative thoughts whirring through my brain. What if they thought my pale complexion was due to illness or a drug addiction? What if they thought I wasn't good enough for Xavier and that he could do better? What if I accidentally said or did something embarrassing, as I often did when I was nervous? What if his doctor parents noticed there was something different about me. Wasn't it their job to notice? What if Claire or Nicola thought my clothes were unfashionable? Ivy had helped me choose my outfit: a sleeveless navy dress with cream buttons down the front and a round collar. It was, as Molly would say, classy and very Chanel. But everything else was still one big question mark.

"Would you just relax!" said Xavier as I ran my hands through my hair and smoothed down my dress for the tenth time since we'd left home. "I can almost hear your heart from here. They're good, church-going people. They're obliged to like you. Even if they don't, which is impossible, you'll never notice. But they're going to love you, they already do."

"What do you mean?"

"I've told them all about you, and they've been dying to meet you in person for ages," he said. "So you can stop acting like you're going to meet the executioners now."

"You could show a little more sympathy," I said testily. "I have a lot to be worried about. You are so horrid sometimes!"

Xavier burst into laughter. "Did you just call me horrid?" he asked.

"I certainly did. You don't even care that I'm nervous!"

"Of course I care," he said patiently. "But I'm telling you that there's nothing to worry about. My mom is already your biggest fan, and everybody else is excited about meeting you. For a while they suspected I was making you up. I'm telling you this to make you feel better, because I *care*, and now I demand that you retract your insult. I can't live with the stigma of being labeled *horrid*."

"I take it back." I said, smiling. "But you are a dunce."

"My self-esteem is taking a serious bashing today," he said, shaking his head. "First I'm horrid, now a dunce. . . . I guess that makes me a horrid dunce."

"I'm just worried." My smile faded. "What if they compare me with Emily? What if they don't think I measure up to her?"

"Beth"—Xavier cupped my face in his hands and made me look at him—"you're incredible. They're going to see that right away. And besides, my mom didn't like Emily."

"Why not?"

"She was too impulsive."

"Impulsive how?" I asked, puzzled.

"She had some issues," Xavier said. "Her parents were divorced, she didn't see her dad, and sometimes she did things without thinking them through. I was always there to keep her safe, thank God, but it didn't make her too popular with my family."

"If you could change things and have her back, would you?" I asked.

"Emily's dead," Xavier said. "And that's how life played out for us. Then you came along. I might have been in love with her then, but I'm in love with *you* now. And if she came back today, she'd still be my oldest friend, but you'd still be my girlfriend."

"I'm sorry, Xav," I said. "I just feel sometimes like you're only with me because you lost the one you were meant to be with."

"But can't you see, Beth?" he insisted. "I was never meant to be with Em. I was destined to love her and lose her. You're the one I'm meant to be with."

"I think I understand now." I took his hand and squeezed it lightly. "Thanks for explaining it to me. I know I sound like a baby."

Xavier winked. "An adorable baby."

EVERYTHING about Xavier's home suggested comfort. It was a big, recently built neo-Georgian house with neat hedges and pillars by the shiny front door. Inside, the walls were painted white and the floors were wood parquet. The front of the house, with its plush living room, was reserved for guests, while the open area at the back, which overlooked the deck and pool, was where the family of eight spent most of their time. Deep sofas draped with fluffy throws faced a flat-screen TV mounted on the wall. The dining table was cluttered with a collection of girlie paraphernalia, a basket of folded laundry sat in one corner, and several pairs of sneakers were lined up by the back door. Opposite the TV was a toy corner, with a collection of Barbie dolls, trucks, and puzzles designed to keep the youngest children occupied.

A ginger cat lay curled in a basket. I noticed a whiteboard on one wall where family members had scrawled messages for one another.

Maybe it had something to do with the smell of cooking in the air, or the voices calling to one another from all around the house, but the place had a welcoming feel despite its size.

Xavier led me into the large kitchen where his mother was frantically trying to finish up her cooking and tidy the house at the same time. She seemed to be doing everything at super-speed but still managed to give me a warm smile when I came in. I could see Xavier's face in hers, right away. They both had the same straight nose and vivid blue eyes.

"You must be Beth!" she said, putting a saucepan down to simmer on the stove and coming over to hug me. "We've heard so much about you. I'm Bernadette—but you can call me Bernie, everyone does."

"It's lovely to meet you, Bernie. Do you need any help?" I asked immediately.

"Now, that's something I don't hear very often around here," Bernie said.

Taking my arm, she showed me a stack of napkins to fold and plates to dry. Xavier's father wandered in from where he'd been lighting the barbecue on the deck under the shade provided by triangular white sails. He was tall and lanky with a thatch of brown hair, and wore round glasses like a professor. I could see where Xavier got his stature from.

"Got her doing housework already," he said with a chuckle, shaking my hand and introducing himself as Peter.

Giving my shoulder a reassuring squeeze, Xavier went to

help his father with the barbecue. While I helped Bernie set the table, I looked around at the wonderful domestic disorder of this house. A baseball game was playing on the TV; I could hear the sounds of running feet upstairs as well as someone rehearsing a very basic piece on the clarinet. Bernie bustled around me, carrying platters to the table. It was all so gloriously normal.

"I'm sorry the place is such a mess," Bernie said apologetically. "It was Jasmine's birthday a few days ago, and it's been chaos around here."

I smiled. It didn't matter to me how messy the place was—I felt surprisingly at home.

"I told you not to touch my razor blades," someone shouted, and I heard the sound of feet stomping downstairs.

Xavier, who had come in to collect some plates, gave an exaggerated sigh. "Now would be a good time to make your escape," he murmured to me.

"For God's sake, you have a whole pack, stop your whining," another voice replied.

"That was my last one, and now it's got your gross skin cells all over it." A door slammed and a girl with brown curls pulled back from her face with a headband appeared. She was wearing a red tank top and lycra shorts, as though she had been exercising. "Mom, can you make Claire stay out of my room?" she demanded.

"I didn't go in your room. You left them in the bathroom," Claire called through the door.

"Why don't you just move out and live with Luke already?" her sister yelled back.

"Believe me, I would if I could."

"I hate you! This is so unfair." The girl seemed to suddenly notice my presence and took a break from shouting to look me up and down. "Who's this?" she asked brusquely.

"Nicola!" Bernie snapped at her. "Where are your manners? This is Beth. Beth, this is my fifteen year old—Nicola."

"Nice to meet you," she said grudgingly. "I don't know what you'd want to date *him* for anyway," she added, jerking her head in Xavier's direction. "He's a total loser and his jokes suck."

"Nicola's going through her angsty teen phase, and she's lost her sense of humor," Xavier explained. "Otherwise she'd appreciate my sharp wit."

Nicola looked daggers at him. I was spared having to formulate some sort of response by the entrance of Xavier's eldest sister, Claire. Her hair was straight like Xavier's and hung loose around her shoulders. She was wearing a knitted cardigan, black jeans, and high boots. Despite the previous shouting match, I could see that her face was friendly.

"Wow, Xav, you didn't tell us Beth was so stunning," Claire said, coming over and giving me a hug.

"Actually, I think I did," Xavier replied.

"Well, we didn't believe you." Claire laughed. "Hi, Beth, welcome to the zoo."

"Congratulations on your engagement," I said.

"Thanks, but it's so stressful at the moment, I don't know if Xavier's filled you in. Just yesterday I got a call from the catering company who said . . ."

Xavier smiled and left us to talk. I didn't have much to say, but Claire chatted easily about the wedding arrangements, and I was more than happy to listen to her. I wondered why such a happy occasion should be so difficult. According to her, everything that could go wrong was going wrong, and she wondered whether she had broken a mirror or something to bring about such bad luck.

Bernie came back into the kitchen, looking for Xavier, who stuck his head through the back door, holding a pair of tongs.

"Xavier, hon, run upstairs and get the little ones down here to meet Beth. They're watching *The Lion King*." Bernie turned to me. "It's the only way I can get them to be quiet for half an hour."

Xavier winked at me and disappeared into the hallway. A few minutes later I heard him coming down the stairs, followed by the sound of little bare feet slapping against the floor.

Jasmine, Madeline, and Michael burst into the room. They stopped dead when they saw me and stared openly in the way only small children can get away with. Madeline and Michael were the two youngest ones, and they both had blond hair, big brown eyes, and smudged faces from eating chocolate cookies not too carefully. Jasmine, who had just turned nine, was a very serious-looking child with big blue eyes. She had long Alice in Wonderland hair held back with a satin ribbon.

"Beth!" Michael and Madeline yelled, overcoming their initial shyness. They sprinted over and took a hand each, pulling me toward the toy corner. Bernie looked a little worried about the onslaught, but I didn't mind. I liked spending time with the souls of children in the Kingdom, and this was much the same, only messier.

"Will you play with us?" they pleaded.

"Not now," said Bernie. "Wait till after dinner before you go annoying poor Beth."

"I'm sitting next to Beth at the table," announced Michael.

"No, I am," said Madeline, shoving him. "I saw her first."

"Did not!"

"Did so!"

"Hey, hey, you can both sit next to Beth," said Claire, wrapping her arms around them and tickling them.

I was suddenly aware of a little figure at my side. Jasmine was looking up at me with her wide, pale eyes. "They're very noisy," she said softly. "I like quiet better."

Xavier, who had come to stand next to me, laughed and ruffled her hair.

"She's very thoughtful, this one," he said. "Always away with the fairies."

"I believe in fairies," said Jasmine. "Do you?"

"I certainly do," I replied and kneeled down beside her. "I believe in all those things, fairies and mermaids and angels."

"Really?"

"Yes. And just between you and me, I've seen them."

Jasmine's eyes widened, and her little rosebud mouth fell open in surprise. "You have? I wish I could see them."

"Oh, but you can," I told her. "You just have to look very carefully. Sometimes you find them in places where you least expect them."

When it was time to eat, I saw that Bernie and Peter had cooked up a feast. I looked at the platters of barbecued pork and sausages and ribs and felt suddenly very worried. Xavier must have forgotten to tell them that I didn't eat meat. It wasn't ethics so much as that our constitution didn't handle meat well. It was difficult to digest and made us sluggish. Even if this hadn't been the case, I wouldn't have wanted to eat it anyway. The very idea made my stomach churn. But they had gone to so much trouble, and I didn't have the heart to tell them. Luckily, I didn't have to.

"Beth doesn't eat meat," Xavier said casually. "Did I mention that?"

"Why not?" Nicola demanded.

"Look up *vegetarian* in the dictionary," Xavier said sarcastically.

"That's okay, sweetheart," said Bernie, taking my plate and piling it high with baked potatoes, grilled vegetables, and rice salad. "That's not a problem." She went on scooping, even though the dish was full.

"Mom . . ." Xavier took the almost overflowing plate away from her and set it down in front of me. "I think she's got enough now."

When everyone had been served, Nicola picked up her fork and was about to take a mouthful of rice when Bernie glared pointedly at her.

"Xavier, hon, would you say grace?"

Nicola purposely dropped her fork with a loud clatter.

"Shh," Jasmine said, and the whole family bowed their

heads. Claire kept a hand on both Madeline and Michael to keep them still.

Xavier made the sign of the cross.

"For what we are about to receive, may the Lord make us truly thankful. And may we always be mindful of the needs of others, for Jesus' sake. Amen."

He finished and looked up, his gaze locking with mine for a split second before he broke away and took a sip of soda. In his eyes I could see so much understanding, a connection of faith between us, and in that moment I couldn't have loved him more.

"So, Beth," said Peter, "Xavier tells us you moved here with your brother and sister."

"That's right." I nodded, feeling the food stick in my throat as I waited for the inevitable question: What about your parents? But it didn't come.

"I'd love to meet them," was all Bernie said. "Are they vegetarian as well?"

I smiled. "We all are."

"That's weird," said Nicola.

Bernie shot her a furious stare, but Xavier only laughed.

"I think you'll find there are a lot of vegetarians in the world, Nic," he said.

"Are you Xavier's girlfriend?" interrupted Michael, pushing his beans around on his plate and prodding them with his fork.

"Don't play with your food," Bernie said, but Michael wasn't listening, he was looking at me waiting for answer.

I turned to Xavier, unsure what I should or shouldn't say in front of his family.

"Aren't I lucky?" Xavier said to his little brother.

"Oh, spare us," Nicola started but Claire elbowed her into silence.

"I'm getting a girlfriend soon," said Michael in a serious tone, and everyone laughed.

"You've got plenty of time for that, kiddo," said his father. "No need to rush."

"Well, I don't want a boyfriend, Daddy," said Madeline. "Boys are dirty, and they make a mess when they eat."

"I'd imagine the six-year-old ones would." Xavier chuckled. "But don't worry, they get better at it."

"Even if they do, I still don't want one," said Madeline crossly.

"I'm with you," said Nicola.

"What are you talking about? You have a boyfriend," Xavier said. "Although that's the same as being single for you."

"Shut up," Nicola told him. "And I don't have a boyfriend as of two hours ago."

Nobody except me seemed particularly concerned to hear this.

"Oh, that's very bad news!" I said. "Are you all right?"

Claire laughed. "She and Hamish break up at least once a week," she explained. "They're always back together by the weekend."

Nicola pouted. "It's over for good this time. And I'm fine, Beth, thanks for asking." She glared around at the others.

"Nic's going to be an old maid," Michael said, giggling.

"What?" she snapped. "How do you even know what that means? You're like, four years old."

"Mommy said it," Michael answered.

Bernie coughed, nearly choking on her food as Peter and Xavier laughed into their napkins.

"Thank you, Michael," Bernie said. "What I meant was, you *might* like to reconsider the way you treat people if you want them to stick around. There's no need to get so angry all the time."

"I never get angry!" Nicola banged her glass down on the table, spilling some of its contents.

"You threw a tennis ball at Hamish's head," Claire said.

"He said my dress was too short!" Nicola cried.

"Your point being?" Xavier asked.

"He should have kept it to himself. He was totally out of line."

"And for that he deserves to have his brains bashed out by a tennis ball." Xavier nodded. "Makes perfect sense."

"I think it's so nice to finally have a girl over for dinner," Bernie said over the mounting argument. "We have Luke and Hamish here all the time, but it's so special for Beth to be with us."

"Thank you," I said. "I'm very glad to be here."

Claire's cell phone rang, and she excused herself from the table to take the call. Seconds later she was back, her hand cupped over the mouthpiece.

"It's Luke. He's running late, but he should be here soon."

She paused. "It would be so much easier if he could just stay the night."

"You know how your father and I feel about that," said Bernie. "We've had this conversation before."

Claire turned imploringly to her father, who pretended to be engrossed in his dinner.

"It's not up to me," he mumbled sheepishly.

"Isn't it time to ease up on all that?" Xavier said to his mother. "They have set a date, you know."

Bernie was adamant. "It's not appropriate. Just think what example that would be setting."

Xavier put his head in his hands. "He could sleep in the spare room."

"Are you offering to keep vigil all night? No, I didn't think so. So long as you kids are living under this roof, your parents will make the house rules," Bernie replied.

Xavier groaned as if to indicate he'd heard this speech before.

"There's no need to react like that," said Bernie. "I've raised my children to adhere to certain values, and sex before marriage is not something this family condones. I hope you haven't changed your position on that, Xavier?"

"Of course not!" Xavier declared with mock seriousness. "The very idea disgusts me."

His sisters couldn't hold back then, and their explosion of laughter lightened the mood. They were immediately joined by their younger siblings, who had no idea what they were laughing about but didn't want to feel left out.

"Sorry, Beth," said Claire once she found her breath.

"Mom gets on her soapbox sometimes, and there's no telling when it might happen."

"There's no need to apologize, Claire. I'm sure Beth understands what I'm saying. She seems a very responsible person. Is your family religious at all?"

"Very," I said with a smile. "I think you'd really get along with them."

For the rest of the night, we talked about safer topics. Bernie asked a lot of noninvasive questions about my interests at school and dreams for the future. Xavier had predicted the turn the conversation would take, and I had carefully rehearsed my answers beforehand. Claire brought a thick copy of *Brides* to the table and asked for my opinion on countless gowns and wedding cake designs. Nicola sulked and made sarcastic remarks whenever spoken to. The youngest ones came to sit on my lap when it was time to eat dessert, and Peter cracked what Jasmine called "Dad jokes." Xavier just sat with his arm around me, looking very content and dropping comments into the conversation at random intervals.

That night was as close to earthly normality as I had ever experienced, and I loved every minute of it. Xavier's family, despite their petty disputes, were so close-knit, so loving, so human, and I wanted more than anything to share what they had. They knew one another's strengths and flaws, and they accepted one another regardless. It amazed me how open they were and how much they knew about each other—even little things like favorite ice cream flavors and movie preferences.

"Should I see the new Bond film?" Nicola asked at one point during the night.

"You won't like it, Nic," Xavier replied. "Too much action for you."

Gabriel, Ivy, and I shared a bond of trust, but we didn't really know one another in the same way. Most of our reflections were internal and never expressed. Perhaps it was because we weren't required to have personalities that were distinctly our own; so we never spent time developing them. As spectators rather than players, there were no decisions to be made, no moral dilemmas to be solved. Having achieved oneness with the universe meant that we had no need for personal connections. The only love we were supposed to experience was a generic one, which encompassed all living things.

I realized with a pang that I was beginning to identify with humans more strongly than with my own kind. Humans seemed to want to be deeply connected to one another. They both feared and craved intimacy. In a family, it was impossible to keep secrets. If Nicola was in a bad mood, everyone knew about it. If their mother was disappointed, they only had to look at her face to see it. Pretense was a waste of time and energy.

At the end of the evening, I felt enormously grateful to Xavier. Allowing me to meet his family was one of the greatest gifts he could have given me.

"How do you feel?" he asked when he pulled into my drive.

"Exhausted," I admitted. "But happy."

That night I thought about something that had never occurred to me before. Bernie's comment about sex before marriage had struck a chord. I knew it was possible for Xavier and me to have sex because I had taken human form and could engage in any physical human interaction—but what would be the consequences of such a decision?

I made up my mind to broach the subject with Ivy—but not tonight. I didn't want to ruin my buoyant mood.

20

Warning Sign

I opened the door of the Literature classroom to find Jake Thorn sitting casually on the edge of Miss Castle's wooden desk, his eyes fixed on her reddening face. I realized they hadn't heard me come in when neither looked my way. Jake's glossy dark hair was combed smoothly away from his face. His cheekbones looked razor sharp, and his cat-green eyes watched Miss Castle intently with the hypnotic quality of a snake about to strike. A red rose lay on the desk, and I saw that his long, slim hand rested lightly over hers. There was no sound in the room other than Miss Castle's shallow breathing.

"This is inappropriate," she whispered.

"According to what laws?" Jake's voice was low and confident.

"The school's for one. You're my student!"

Jake gave a low chuckle. "I'm all grown up—old enough to make my own decisions."

"But what if we're caught? I'll lose my job, I'll never be able to work as a teacher again, I'll . . ." I heard her sharp intake of breath as Jake pressed a finger against her lips and then slid it teasingly down till it rested in the hollow of her throat.

"We can be discreet."

Just as he leaned toward her and Miss Castle closed her eyes, there was a loud bang from behind me, followed by a stream of cursing. Ben Carter had just arrived and accidently jammed his bag in the door. Jake sprang up from the desk with a feline grace while a flustered Miss Castle shuffled papers and tried to smooth her hair.

"Hi," Ben grunted as he pushed past me to his seat, oblivious of the exchange he had just interrupted. He threw himself into his chair and scowled at the clock. "I'm not even late."

I took a seat behind Ben as other students began to file into the classroom and stared studiously at my desk. Someone had scratched into the desktop, "English Is Death. Death Is Crap." I didn't want to look at Jake; I was shocked by what I'd seen. I knew I had no right to be. Jake was eighteen, he was entitled to make a play for whoever he liked. But Miss Castle was a teacher; surely she deserved more respect. I shook my head resolutely; it was absolutely none of my business.

I should have known he wouldn't let me get away with ignoring him. He slid into the seat beside me.

"Hello," he said, his voice slick as oil. His eyes were even more captivating than his voice. When I looked into them, it was hard to look away.

THINGS were starting to change at Bryce Hamilton. It was hard to pinpoint exactly what had changed or when, but the school felt different. There was cohesion where there had only been disparity when we first arrived. Involvement in school activities had never been so popular, and judging by some of the posters that had appeared around the place, there was a new awareness of global issues. I could claim no credit for these improvements; I'd been far too preoccupied with fitting in and getting to know Xavier to have given much thought to anything else. I knew the change was due entirely to the influence of Gabriel and Ivy.

From the outset, people in Venus Cove recognized Ivy's commitment to helping others. Although she didn't attend the school, she was busy gathering support for various causes from animal welfare to environmental issues. She campaigned for these in her usual soft-spoken manner—she didn't need to be loud to get her point across. Bryce Hamilton had asked her to speak at assemblies to inform the students of upcoming charity drives and fund-raisers being held in town. If there was a cake drive, car wash, or Miss Venus Cove competition to raise money for a good cause, Ivy was usually behind it. She seemed to have created an entire social service program within the town, and a small but growing number of volunteers opted to help out on Wednesday afternoons. The school had even introduced a volunteer program as an alternative to afternoon sports. This involved helping out at local charity groups, shopping for elderly members of the community, or working at the soup kitchen in Port Circe. Some people, admittedly, feigned interest as an excuse to get closer to Ivy, but most were genuinely inspired by her dedication.

However, with only two weeks left until the senior prom, all social service projects were temporarily abandoned. The mood of the girls at school was bordering on obsessive. It was hard to believe the time had passed so quickly. It seemed like only yesterday that Molly had circled the date in my planner and berated me for my lack of enthusiasm. To my surprise, I now found myself as eager as everyone else for the big night to arrive. I clapped and squealed along with the rest of the girls whenever the subject came up and didn't care how puerile it looked.

On Friday I met Molly and the girls out front after school for our long-anticipated shopping trip to Port Circe. Port Circe was a large town just a half-hour train ride south. With a population of some two hundred thousand, it was significantly larger than Venus Cove, and many of the people living in our sleepy town commuted there daily for work, while the teenagers went there to shop or to sneak into nightclubs using their fake IDs.

Gabriel had handed me a credit card along with instructions to be sensible and a reminder of the irrelevance of material goods. He knew how dangerous it was to let a pack of teenage girls loose with a credit card, but he had nothing to worry about; my chances of finding something I liked were slim. I was particular when it came to clothing and I had a very clear picture of how I imagined myself looking on the night of the prom. I had set my standards rather high. Just for that night, I really wanted to look as well as feel like an angel on earth.

I was nervous as we headed down the main street toward the station. This would be my first experience on public transportation. Much as I was looking forward to it, I couldn't help feeling a little apprehensive. When we got there, I followed the others through an underpass and up onto an old-fashioned platform. We lined up at the booth and bought tickets from a gruff man with gray whiskers behind the window. He shook his head at the racket the girls were making, and I gave him an apologetic smile as I tucked my ticket safely into my wallet.

We moved to sit on the wooden benches lining the platform and waited for the four-fifteen express to arrive. The girls continued to talk over one another and typed text messages at lightning speed, arranging to meet up with boys from Saint Dominic's school in Port Circe. Molly announced she was thirsty and bought a can of diet soda from a vending machine. As for me, I was relaxed and comfortable until the arrival of the train sent me into shock.

It started out as nothing more than a rumble in the distance, like a peal of thunder. But it grew steadily louder, and soon the platform was vibrating beneath my feet. From out of nowhere the train came barreling down the tracks, at such a speed, I wondered how the driver would manage to stop. I jumped up and pressed my back against the wall of the waiting bay as the train cars, which looked poorly secured, clattered noisily to a halt. The girls stared at me.

"What are you doing?" Taylah asked, looking around self-consciously to make sure nobody had witnessed my display.

I eyed the train suspiciously. "Is it supposed to make that noise?"

The metal doors opened and people spilled out in a wave. I watched one set of doors snap shut again, catching the hem of a man's overcoat. I gasped and the girls howled with laughter. The man banged angrily on the train doors until they sprang open again. He stalked off, throwing us a livid look as he passed.

"Oh, Beth," Molly sputtered, clutching her abdomen as she shook with laughter, "you'd think you've never seen a train before."

The heavy row of interlinked metal boxes looked to me more like a weapon of mass destruction than any form of reliable transportation.

"It doesn't look all that safe," I said.

"Don't be a baby!" Molly grabbed my wrist and hauled me toward an open door, "We're going to miss it!"

Inside the train wasn't so bad. Molly and her friends threw themselves down on a row of seats, ignoring the irritated glances they received from passengers whose space they had invaded. As we rattled toward Port Circe I sat perched on the edge of my seat and watched the people around me. I was surprised at the array of characters that mass transit attracted, from executives in business suits to sweaty schoolkids to an elderly bag lady wearing fur-lined moccasins. I wasn't very comfortable being surrounded by all those people and nearly being jolted from my seat each time the train jerked to a stop, but I told myself I ought to be grateful for every human experience I could get. All too soon it would come to an end.

When we reached our stop, we joined the crowd pushing their way off the train and into the main square of Port Circe. It was certainly a far cry from sleepy Venus Cove. The streets were wide, rectangular, and tree lined. Church spires and skyscrapers were silhouetted against the horizon. Molly insisted we weave our way across the congested roads rather than waste time finding the crosswalks. There were shoppers everywhere. We passed a homeless man with a white beard sitting on the cathedral steps; the wrinkles around his droopy eyes were as deep as crevices. He'd draped a gray army blanket over his shoulders and was banging a tin cup. I dug in my pocket for some change, but Molly stopped me.

"You can't just go up to strangers like that," she said. "It's not safe. He's probably a drug addict or something."

"Does he look like a drug addict?" I objected.

Molly shrugged and walked ahead, but I turned back to press a ten-dollar bill into the man's hand. He gripped my arm. "God bless you," he said. When he looked right past me, I realized that he was blind.

The girls decided we should split up. Some went to a little boutique in a cobbled lane off the main square, while Molly, Taylah, and I went to a big department store with a revolving glass door and a checkered marble floor. I was glad to get out of the frenzy of the street and turned my face up toward the air-conditioning vents on the ceiling.

"This is Madison's," Molly explained as if she were speaking to a Martian. "It's split over five levels and sells just about everything a girl could need."

"Thanks, Molly, I think I get the general idea. Where's ladies' wear?"

"We're not going anywhere near there. That's for losers. We need Mademoiselle, which is on the third floor. They've got some great stuff, and it's cheaper than those little exclusive places. Just because Megan's got cash coming out of her butt . . ."

It took two hours of combing through the racks and the help of some very tolerant sales assistants before Molly and

Taylah finally found dresses they were satisfied with. They went through rack after rack, discarding outfits because they looked too frumpy, too slutty, too middle-aged, too dorky, or not sexy enough. Forgetting that they'd debated this before, they launched into a drawn-out discussion about the perfect hemline. Apparently just above the knee was too schoolgirl, below the knee was geriatric, and mid-calf was only for people who bought their clothes at thrift shops. That left only two acceptable options—mini or floor-length. This they discussed as though it were a matter of national importance, until the discussion broadened to ruffle or no ruffle, strapless or halter, satin versus silk. I followed them around like a somnambulist, trying my best to keep up and not look as weary as I felt.

After what seemed like endless deliberation, Taylah settled on a short, backless taffeta dress in a peach color that kicked out at the hem. It served the purpose of showing off her toned legs even if, in my opinion, it made her look like a walking cream puff.

I spotted something I thought would suit Molly's coloring perfectly and pointed it out to her. The shop assistant instantly agreed with me. "That color would look great on you," she said to Molly.

"It is beautiful," Molly agreed.

"So?" said Taylah. "Try it on."

When Molly emerged from the dressing room, it was as though she'd undergone a transformation from gangly schoolgirl to goddess. Even other shoppers stopped to admire her. We made her spin around in order to appraise her from every angle. The dress was an off-the-shoulder, Grecian-style gown with a delicate gold chain over the bare shoulder. The fabric wound around her hourglass figure in soft layers, then pooled on the floor like liquid. But it was the color that was most incredible. It was a dazzling bronze that shimmered when the light caught it. It picked up the russet tones of Molly's curls and heightened her peaches-and-cream complexion.

"Wow . . . ," breathed Taylah. "I think we found your dress. You and Ryan are going to look stunning together."

"Wait, he asked you?" I said.

Molly nodded. "He took his time, but yeah."

"Why didn't you tell me?" I asked.

"It's not, like, major news or anything."

"Are you joking!" Taylah cried. "You've been going on about him for weeks. Everything is perfect now. You got everything you wanted."

"I guess so," Molly nodded, but her face was lacking its usual enthusiasm. Was she thinking about Gabriel? I wondered if maybe Molly was changing and Ryan Robertson with all his good looks and bulging muscles just wasn't enough to satisfy her anymore.

For Taylah and Molly the agonizing search was over and relief showed plainly on their faces. Shoes and accessories could wait; they had found dresses that suited them perfectly. I, on the other hand, had seen nothing even remotely appealing. The dresses were all more or less the same: either too busy, covered in sequins and bows or too nondescript. I wanted something simple yet striking, something that would allow me to stand out from the crowd and take Xavier's breath away. It was a tall order, and I didn't like my chances of finding it. Part of me felt ashamed of my newfound vanity, but my desire to impress Xavier was stronger.

"Come on, Beth!" Molly said, folding her arms obstinately. "There must be something here you like! We're not leaving till you've found it."

I tried to protest, but now that Molly had her outfit all organized, she threw herself magnanimously into helping me find one. On her insistence I tried on dress after dress, but none of them felt right.

"You're nuts," she said, after an hour had passed. "Everything looks stunning on you."

"Yeah, you're so thin," said Taylah through gritted teeth.

"Here's one!" cried Molly. She pulled out a white satin dress with pleats that opened like a fan. "A Marilyn Monroe replica. Try it on!"

"It's lovely," I agreed. "But not what I'm looking for."

She sighed and thrust the dress back onto the rack.

I left Madison's with the meager purchases of a bottle of nail polish called Whisper Pink and a pair of sterling silver hoop earrings. It had hardly been worth the time and effort.

We met up with the others at Starbucks. Various designer bags were scattered around their feet, and three boys in striped blazers had joined them. They were stretching back in their chairs, enjoying the girls' shameless flirting.

"I'm starving," Molly announced. "I'd kill for one of those giant cookies."

Taylah wagged a finger at her. "Salad until after the formal," she said.

"You're right," Molly groaned. "Is coffee allowed?"

"Skim milk, no sugar."

By the time I got home my despondency was hard to disguise. The shopping expedition had failed to deliver, and I didn't know where I was going to find a dress. I'd scoured the shops in Venus Cove weeks ago and all that remained were a couple of thrift stores.

"No luck?" Ivy didn't sound surprised. "Did you have fun at least?"

"Not really. It was a waste of time. There are only so many dresses you can try on before they all start to look the same."

"Don't worry—you'll find something. There's still plenty of time."

"It won't make any difference; what I want just isn't out there. I shouldn't even bother going."

"Come on now," said Ivy. "You can't do that to Xavier. I have an idea. Why don't you tell me the kind of dress you've got in mind and I can make it for you."

"I can't ask you to do that! You have more important things to think about."

"I'd like to do this for you," said Ivy. "Besides, it won't take me long, and you know I can make exactly what you want."

I knew she was right. Ivy could become a skilled seamstress in a matter of hours. There was nothing she and Gabriel couldn't do if they had a mind to.

"Why don't we spend some time this afternoon going through magazines and see if there's anything you like?" Ivy asked.

"I don't need a magazine. I can picture it in my head."

My sister smiled. "Okay, then close your eyes and send it to me."

I shut my eyes and imagined the night of the prom. I saw Xavier and me standing arm in arm under a canopy of fairy lights. He was wearing a tux and smelled fresh and sharp. A shock of hair fell across his eyes. I stood beside him, and in my mind's eye I saw the dress of my dreams. It was a shimmering ivory gown with an undergarment of soft cream silk and an overlay of antique lace. The bodice was studded with pearls and a row of satin buttons lined the fitted sleeves. It had a scalloped neckline with an intricate gold trim of tiny rosebuds. The material seemed to be woven with little fragments of light and emitted a faint pearly glow. On my feet I wore the daintiest, beaded satin slippers.

I looked at Ivy sheepishly. It wasn't exactly the simplest of requests.

"Piece of cake," said my sister. "I can whip that up in no time."

AT lunchtime on Monday I sat alone in the cafeteria. Xavier was at water-polo practice, and Molly and the girls were on the prom committee and had a meeting of their own to discuss the final decorations and seating arrangements. As I sat and picked at my wilted lettuce, people looked at me curiously, probably surprised to see me unaccompanied, but I hardly noticed them. As usual, Xavier occupied my thoughts, even more so when we were physically separated. When I found myself calculating how many more minutes needed to pass before I could see him again, I decided I should be making better use of my time and headed for the library. The senior library was the one space where solitary activity was considered acceptable. I planned to use the rest of the lunch break looking up the causes of the French Revolution.

I had just grabbed my books from my locker and was taking the short cut across a narrow walkway when a voice called out from behind me.

"Hello there."

I turned to see Jake Thorn leaning against a brick wall, his arms folded across his chest. His dark hair framed his pallid face, and his lips were curled in a sardonic smile. He now wore the Bryce Hamilton uniform but with a distinctive style of his own: He was tieless and the collar of his shirt was turned up. Instead of a blazer he wore a hooded gray windbreaker. His trousers hung loosely from narrow hips and he was wearing white oxfords instead of the regulation school shoes. I noticed for the first time that he wore a diamond stud in his left ear as well as the mysterious pendant around his neck. He took a long drag of his cigarette and blew a ring of smoke into the air.

"You shouldn't smoke here," I cautioned, wondering how anyone could so openly flout the school rules. "You'll get into trouble."

"Will I?" Jake feigned concern. "This happens to be known as smokers' corner."

"There are still teachers on duty."

"I've noticed they never come this far—they sort of hover near the staff-room steps counting the minutes until they can get back to their coffee and crosswords."

"I think you'd better put that out before someone notices," I said.

"If you say so," Jake replied.

He crushed the butt under the heel of his shoe then kicked it into a garden bed just as Miss Kratz, the ancient and crabby librarian, scuttled past, eyeing us both suspiciously.

"Thank you, Beth," he said when she was out of earshot. "I think you just saved my skin."

"You're welcome," I said, flushing at his dramatic expression of gratitude. "It's hard when you don't know the ropes. You must have had a lot of freedom at your old school."

"Let's just say I took some risks. Some didn't pay off—hence my exile here. You know, the ancient Romans preferred death to exile. At least mine isn't permanent."

"How long are you staying?"

"As long as it takes for my character to be reformed."

I laughed. "Is there much chance of that?"

"I'd say there was every chance given the right influence," said Jake meaningfully. He narrowed his eyes suddenly as though something had just occurred to him. "I don't often see you alone. Where's that smothering Prince Charming of yours? Not sick, I hope."

"*Xavier* is at practice," I said quickly.

"Ah, sports—the invention of pedagogues in an attempt to keep raging hormones in check."

"Sorry?"

"Never mind." Jake rubbed the stubble on his chin thoughtfully. "Tell me, I know your boyfriend is an athlete, but is he any good at poetry?"

"Xavier's good at most things," I boasted.

"Really? How lucky for you," Jake said, arching an eyebrow.

His behavior was confusing me, but I certainly wasn't going to make him aware of that. I decided the safest thing to do was change the subject. "So where are you staying?" I asked. "Close to school?"

"At the moment I'm living in the rooms above the tattoo parlor," said Jake. "Until more permanent accommodation can be organized."

"I thought you'd be with a host family," I said in surprise.

"Well, that would be like staying with boring relatives, wouldn't it? I prefer my own company."

"And your parents are okay with that?" I was uncomfortable with the idea of him living on his own. Even though he sounded mature and worldly, he was still a teenager.

"I'll tell you all about my parents if you tell me about yours." His dark eyes burned into mine like lasers. "I suspect we have a lot more in common than we realize. By the way, what are you doing Sunday morning? I thought we might work on our masterpiece."

"I have church on Sunday."

"Of course you do."

"You're welcome to come along."

"Thanks, but I'm allergic to incense."

"That's a shame."

"It's the bane of my existence."

"Well, I have to go and study," I said, moving past him, aware of the minutes slipping by.

He stepped casually in front of me. "Before you go, I have the opening line of our poem."

He dug a crumpled ball of paper from his pocket and tossed it lightly to me. "Don't be too hard on me—it's only a beginning. We can take it anywhere you like from here."

He flashed me a smile and sauntered away. I moved over to the closest bench and smoothed out the paper. Jake's handwriting was elegant and narrow, the letters elongated; nothing like Xavier's boyish print. Xavier hated cursive; it took too long and looked too fancy. Jake's writing was like calligraphy, the letters swirled across the page as though they were dancing. But it was the seven words he had written that sent my mind into a spin:

She had the face of an angel

21

Drowning

WHAT could Jake mean by that? *She had the face of an angel.* I felt as if the words had been burned into my brain, as though, in a split second, Jake had unzipped me and left me shivering and exposed. Could he possibly have guessed my secret? Was this his idea of a twisted joke?

Something snapped in me then; I felt overcome by a sudden anger. Forgetting all about my plans to catch up on the French Revolution, I bolted inside to find Jake. I tore through empty corridors, back to the cafeteria, where I scanned the groups gathered in little clusters. But he wasn't among any of them. A flutter of fear began in my chest and I knew it would soon swell if I didn't do something to stop it. I had to track Jake down and ask him about the poem before the beginning of the next class or it would eat away at me.

I found him at his locker.

"What's this all about?" I demanded, charging up to him and waving the paper under his nose.

"Pardon me?"

"This isn't funny."

"It wasn't supposed to be."

"I'm not in the mood for games. Just tell me what you meant by this."

"Hmmm, I'm guessing you don't like it," Jake said. "Don't worry, we can scrap it—no need to get worked up."

"What were you thinking when you wrote it?"

"I was just thinking it might be a good place to start." He shrugged. "Did I offend you or something?"

I breathed deeply and forced myself to remember how Miss Castle had introduced the assignment to the class. She had given us a brief rundown on the tradition of courtly love and read us some sonnets by Petrarch and Shakespeare. She'd talked about the idealization and worship of the woman from afar. Was it possible that Jake was merely sticking to the theme? My fury was suddenly redirected at myself for jumping to wild conclusions.

"I'm not offended," I said, feeling ridiculous. Both my anger and fear had subsided as quickly as they had arisen. It was hardly Jake's fault he'd come up with the word *angel* in rela-tion to a poem about love. I was just paranoid about all celestial references. Jake's use of the word had more than likely been innocent. It wasn't even original; how many poets over time had made similar comparisons?

"It's fine," I added. "We'll work on it some more in class. Sorry if I seemed a little loopy just now."

"That's okay, we all have our loopy days."

He gave me a smile, a proper one this time, without the curling lip and attitude. He reached out and touched my arm reassuringly.

"Thanks for being cool about it," I said gratefully, mirroring what Molly might say in a similar situation.

"It's what I do," he said.

I watched him stroll away to join a small group that included Alicia, Alexandra, and Ben from our literature class, along with some others I recognized as music students by their straggly hair and loose ties. They closed in around him like devotees as he approached and then seemed to dive immediately into a deep discussion. I felt pleased for him that he had found a group to belong to.

I went off to my own locker, still feeling as though something was amiss. It wasn't until I had gathered my books and was waiting for Xavier to come and meet me that I realized I felt physical discomfort. I focused for a moment and located the sensation. It wasn't real pain—more like a mild case of sunburn. The skin on my arm, just below the elbow, was stinging in exactly the place where Jake had touched me. But how could his touch possibly have hurt me? He had only put his hand very gently on my arm, and I hadn't experienced anything unusual at the time.

"You seem distracted," Xavier said as we walked together to French class. He knew me so well, he never missed a beat.

"Just thinking about the prom," I replied.

"And that makes you look sad?"

I decided to force Jake Thorn from my mind. The pain in my arm probably had nothing to do with him. I'd most likely scraped it on a locker or desktop without noticing. I needed to stop overreacting.

"I don't look sad," I said lightly. "This is my thoughtful expression. Honestly, Xavier, can't you read me by now?"

"I must be slipping."

"It's really not good enough."

"I know. Feel free to punish me in any way you see fit."

"Did I mention I've finally decided on a nickname for you?"

"I didn't know you were looking."

"Well, I've given the matter some serious thought."

"And what have you come up with?"

"Cookie," I announced proudly.

Xavier scrunched up his face. "No way."

"You don't like it? What about Bumblebee?"

"Worse."

"Snookie-wookie?"

"Do you have any cyanide?"

"Well, some of us are just a bit hard to please."

We walked past some girls poring over celebrity gowns in a magazine, and I remembered my other news. "Did I tell you that Ivy's making my dress? I hope it's not putting her out too much."

"What are sisters for?"

"I'm so happy we're going together." I sighed. "It's going to be perfect."

"You're happy?" Xavier whispered. "I'm the one going with an angel."

"Shh!" I clapped a hand over his mouth. "Remember what we promised Gabe."

"It's okay, Beth; no one around here has supersonic hearing."

He gave me a peck on the cheek. "And the prom is going to be great. Tell me about your dress."

I pursed my lips and refused to disclose any details.

"Oh, come on!"

"No. You'll have to wait till the night."

"Can I at least know the color?"

"Nope."

"Women can be so cruel."

"Xavier?"

"Yes, babe?"

"Would you write me a poem if I asked you to?"

Xavier looked at me quizzically. "Are we talking love poems?"

"I guess so."

"Well, I can't say it's my forte, but I'll have something for you by day's end."

"You don't have to do that," I laughed. "I was just wondering."

I was always taken aback by Xavier's willingness to oblige. Was there anything he wouldn't do for me if I asked?

Xavier and I were due to give a talk in French that lesson, and we'd chosen to do it on Paris, the city of love. In truth, we hadn't done very much research; Gabriel had given us all the information we needed. We hadn't even had to open a book or Internet page. When Mr. Collins called us up, Xavier spoke first, and I noticed other girls in the class eyeing him with interest. I tried to imagine myself in their place, watching him longingly from a distance but never really knowing him. I looked at his smooth tanned skin, his entrancing aqua eyes, his half-smile, his strong arms, and the locks of light brown hair falling across his forehead. He still wore his silver crucifix on a leather cord around his neck. He was so striking—and he was all mine.

I was so caught up in admiring him that I missed my cue to start talking. Xavier cleared his throat, recalling me to the present, and I quickly launched into my part of the presentation, focusing on the romantic sights and the cuisine Paris had to offer. As I talked, I realized that instead of making eye contact with the class and attempting to engage them, I was sneaking sidelong glances at Xavier. I couldn't seem to take my eyes off him for a minute.

With the talk concluded, Xavier spontaneously swept me up into his arms.

"Urgh, would you two just get a room already?" Taylah called out. "*C'est très* disgusting."

"Yes, that will do," said Mr. Collins, swatting us apart.

"I'm sorry, sir," Xavier said with a smile. "We were just trying to make our presentation as authentic as possible."

Mr. Collins glared at us but the class laughed.

News of our performance in French filtered through the grapevine, and Molly bailed me up about it at the first opportunity.

"So you and Xavier are really into each other?" she said enviously.

"Yes." I tried to keep from beaming, as I usually did when I thought of him.

"I still can't believe you're with Xavier Woods," Molly said, shaking her head. "I mean, don't get me wrong, I think you're really gorgeous and all, but girls have been chasing after him for ages, and he hasn't batted an eyelid. People thought he'd never get over Emily, and then you come along and . . ."

"I can't believe it either sometimes," I said modestly.

"You've got to admit it's pretty romantic, the way he looks after you, like some sort of knight in shining armor." Molly sighed. "I wish a guy would treat me like that."

"You've got heaps of guys that are madly in love with you," I said. "They follow you around like puppy dogs."

"Yeah, but it's not the same as with you and Xavier," Molly replied. "You two really seem connected. Other guys only want one thing." She paused. "Well, I'm sure you and Xavier get up to some good stuff, but it seems like there's more to it."

"What sort of stuff?" I asked curiously.

"You know, like, in the bedroom." Molly giggled. "You don't have to be embarrassed about telling me, I've pretty much done it all—well, almost."

"I'm not embarrassed," I said. "We just haven't really been up to anything."

Molly's eyes widened. "You mean you and Xavier haven't—?"

"Shh!" I flapped my hands at her when I saw the kids at the next table turn and stare. "No, of course not!"

"Sorry," she said. "You just surprised me. I mean, well, I just thought you would have. But you've done other stuff, yeah?"

"Sure. We go for walks, hold hands, share lunch . . ."

"My God, Beth, how old are you?" Molly groaned. "Do I have to spell everything out for you?" She narrowed her eyes. "Wait, have you even seen it?"

"Seen what?" I exploded.

"You *know*," she said emphatically. "*It!*" She gestured in the vicinity of her groin until I finally understood her meaning.

"Oh!" I exclaimed. "I'd never do anything like that."

"Well, hasn't he hinted that he wants more?"

"No," I said indignantly. "Xavier doesn't care about stuff like that."

"That's what they all say at first," Molly said cynically. "Just give it some time. Great as Xavier is, all guys want the same thing."

"Do they really?"

"Of course, hon." Molly patted my arm. "I just think you should be prepared."

I fell silent. If there was one subject I trusted Molly's opinion on it was boys. They were her area of expertise, and she'd had enough experience to know what she was talking about. I felt suddenly very uneasy. I'd assumed Xavier wasn't bothered by my inability to fulfill all aspects of our relationship. After all, he'd never brought it up, never hinted that it numbered among his expectations. But was there a chance he was keeping his true desires from me? Just because he never mentioned it, didn't mean it wasn't playing on his mind. He loved me because I was different, but human beings still had certain needs—some of which couldn't be ignored indefinitely.

"Oh my God, have you seen the new guy?"

Molly broke my train of thought, and I looked up to see Jake Thorn strolling past us. He didn't acknowledge me but instead crossed the cafeteria to sit at a table of about fifteen seniors who gazed at him with a strange combination of adoration and respect.

"He hasn't wasted any time recruiting friends," I commented to Molly.

"Are you surprised? That guy is seriously hot."

"Do you think so?"

"Yeah, in a dark, brooding kind of way. He could be a model with a face like that."

Jake's circle of supporters all had a similar air about them. They had dark shadows under their eyes. They tended to keep their heads down and didn't make eye contact with anyone outside their group. I watched the way Jake looked at them, with a self-satisfied smile on his face, like a cat with a saucer of cream.

"He's in my lit class," I said casually.

"Oh my God, you are so lucky!" Molly moaned. "So what's he like? He looks like a rebel to me."

"He's actually pretty intelligent."

"Damn." Molly pouted. "Those guys never go for me. I only get the dumb jocks. But hey, there's no harm in trying."

"I'm not sure that's such a good idea," I said.

"That's easy for you to say when you've got Xavier Woods," Molly replied.

We were distracted by a piercing scream coming from the kitchens, followed by the sound of panicked voices and running feet. The students exchanged nervous glances and a few got up hesitantly to investigate. One of them, Simon Laurence, froze in the doorway of the kitchen and his hand flew to his mouth. He backed away, his face was turning ashen, and he looked like he was about to retch.

"Hey, what happened?" Molly grabbed Simon as he came past us.

"Uh, one of the cooks," he said. "Deep fryer tipped over . . . burned her legs pretty bad. They're calling for an ambulance." He staggered off, looking shaken.

I stared down at my plate and tried to focus on sending healing energy in the direction of the kitchen, or at least something that might numb the pain. It was more effective if I could see the person who was hurt or touch them, but I knew that to go into the kitchen would look suspicious, and I'd probably get thrown out for interfering before I could get near the cook. So I stayed where I was and did my best. But there was something wrong: I couldn't channel properly. Every time I tried, something blocked me, and I felt my energy rebound before it reached the kitchen. It felt like another force was intercepting mine, as impenetrable as concrete, pushing the healing energy back. Maybe I was just tired. I pushed harder but only met with stronger resistance.

"Um, Beth . . . what are you doing? You look constipated," Molly said, snapping me out of my trance.

I shook my head to clear it and gave her a forced smile. "It's just warm in here."

"Yeah, let's go. There's not much we can do anyway," she said, pushing back her chair and standing up.

I followed her wordlessly out of the cafeteria.

As we passed the table where Jake Thorn and his new friends were seated, Jake looked up at me. Our eyes met, and for a split second I felt I was drowning in their depth.

{ 22 }

The "S" Word

ON the weekend, Molly visited Byron for the first time. She'd been making veiled remarks about coming over for a while, and finally I relented and invited her. It didn't take her long to make herself at home. She flopped down on the deep sofa and kicked up her feet.

"This is a great place," she said. "You could host a sick party here."

"I don't think that's likely to happen anytime soon," I said.

Ignoring my lack of enthusiasm, Molly leapt to her feet to examine a piece of artwork hanging above the fireplace. It was an abstract piece depicting an expanse of white with a circular symbol drawn in the center. Concentric blue circles widened around it, growing fainter as they moved closer to the edge of the canvas.

"What's this supposed to be?" she asked dubiously.

I looked at the inky blue circles against the stark white background and thought of a number of ideas they could represent. It seemed to me an expression of ultimate reality, a depiction of Our Creator's role in the universe. He was the source and center of all things. From Him the web of life unfolded, but it was all inextricably tied to Him. The circles could have represented the extent of His sovereignty, and the white, a depiction of space and time. His power, His very being extended to the edges of the canvas and hinted that it went beyond—filling every space. Not just the world belonged to Him, but the universe as well. It was an expression of infinity, encapsulating everything the human mind struggled to understand. The only true reality that could never be denied was Him.

Of course I wasn't about to try and explain any of that to Molly. I wasn't being arrogant in believing that it was beyond the comprehension of man. Humans feared life outside their world, and although some questioned what lay beyond, they never came close to enlightenment. One day human life would end, and even the earth itself would crumble to dust, but existence would continue.

Molly lost interest in the painting and instead picked up the acoustic guitar propped against a chair and held it gingerly.

"Does this belong to Gabriel?"

"Yes, and he loves that thing," I replied, hoping she would put it down.

I looked around furtively in case Gabriel and Ivy were lurking around a corner, but they were tactfully giving us some privacy. Molly held the instrument gently, running her fingers over the taut strings in fascination.

"I wish I was musical. I used to take piano when I was little but I never had enough discipline to practice. It just seemed like too much hard work. I'd love to hear your brother play."

"Well, we can ask him when he comes back. Feel like a snack?"

The thought of food distracted her, and I led her into the kitchen, where Ivy had thoughtfully laid out assorted muffins and a fruit platter. My siblings had finally recovered from the incident at the party and had accepted Molly as one of my friends. Although they didn't have much choice—I seemed to have developed an inexorable will of my own these days.

"Oh, yum!" said Molly, taking a bite of a blueberry muffin and rolling her eyes to emphasize her appreciation of Ivy's cooking. She froze suddenly and looked forlorn. "This doesn't count as salad, does it?"

At that moment Gabriel appeared at the back door, lugging a surfboard, his damp T-shirt clinging to his taut body. He had recently taken up surfing as a way of releasing pent-up tension. Of course, he hadn't needed to take lessons. Where was the need when the waves themselves would do his bidding? Gabriel was very active in human form; he needed physical activity like swimming, running, or lifting heavy objects in order to quell his restlessness.

Molly surreptitiously dropped her muffin onto her plate as Gabriel wandered into the kitchen.

"Hello, Molly," he said.

Nothing ever escaped Gabriel's notice, and his attention was drawn to the discarded muffin. He must have wondered what he'd done to make her lose her appetite. "Bethany, perhaps we can offer Molly something else," he said very politely. "She doesn't seem to be enjoying Ivy's muffins."

"No, they're delicious," Molly cut in.

"Don't worry, Gabe," I said with a laugh. "Molly's on a crash diet for the prom."

Gabriel shook his head. "Crash diets are very unhealthy for girls your age," he said. "Besides, I wouldn't recommend weight loss—in your case—it would be completely unnecessary."

Molly stared at him for a moment before speaking. "You're just being nice," she said. "I could afford to lose a few pounds." She pinched the flesh around her waist between thumb and forefinger to illustrate her point.

Gabriel leaned against the kitchen counter and studied her for a moment. "Molly," he said eventually, "the human form is beautiful regardless of size or shape."

"But aren't some forms more beautiful than others?" Molly asked. "Like, you know, supermodels?"

"There is nothing more alluring than a girl with a healthy appreciation of food," Gabriel said. The comment surprised me; I'd never heard him express any sort of opinion about what constituted feminine appeal. He was usually completely immune to any sort of female charm or attractiveness. It was just something he never noticed.

"I totally agree!" said Molly and she resumed nibbling at her muffin.

Gabriel looked pleased at having conveyed his point and headed out of the kitchen.

"Wait! Are you coming to the prom?" Molly called out after him.

Gabriel turned to look at her, an expression of mild amusement flickering around his silvery eyes.

"Yes," he replied. "Unfortunately it's part of my job description."

"You might enjoy it," she suggested coyly.

"We'll see."

Despite the noncommittal nature of Gabe's answer, Molly seemed hugely satisfied by it. "I guess I'll see you there then," she said.

We spent the rest of the afternoon thumbing through fashion magazines and Googling images on Molly's laptop, looking for hairstyles to replicate. Molly was definite that she wanted to wear hers up, either in a French roll or a crown of curls. I wasn't sure what I wanted but knew I could rely on Ivy to come up with something.

"I've been thinking about what you said," I blurted out suddenly as Molly was printing a photo of Blair Waldorf from *Gossip Girl*, "about Xavier and the . . . um . . . physical part of our relationship."

"Oh my God," Molly squealed. "Tell me everything. How was it? Did you enjoy it? It doesn't matter if you didn't. You can't expect the first time to be good. It gets better with practice."

"No, no, nothing's happened," I replied. "I was just wondering whether I should bring it up with Xavier."

"Bring it up? What for?"

"To find out what he's thinking."

"If it bothered him, he would have brought it up already. What are you stressing for?"

"Well, I want to know what he wants, what he expects, what would make him happy . . ."

"Beth, you don't have to do anything just to make a boy happy," Molly said. "If you're not ready, you should wait. I wish I'd waited."

"But I want to talk to him about it," I said. "I don't want to seem like a little kid."

"Beth." Molly closed the Web site she was exploring and swung around to face me wearing her sober counselor face. "This is something that all couples have to talk about eventually. The best way is just to be honest, don't pretend to be someone you're not. He knows you've had no experience, right?" I nodded mutely. "Okay, well, that's good, there won't be any surprises. You just need to tell him that it's been on your mind and ask him how he feels. Then you'll know where you both stand."

"Thanks." I grinned at her. "You're the best."

She laughed. "I know. By the way, did I tell you I've come up with an awesome plan?"

"No," I said. "What's the objective?"

"Getting Gabriel's attention."

I groaned inwardly. "Molly, not this again—we've been through this before."

"I know, but I've never met anyone like him. And things are different now . . . I'm different."

"How do you mean?"

"Well, I've realized something." She grinned. "The only way I can get Gabriel to like me is to be a better person. So . . . I've decided to develop a social conscience, you know, show more *community involvement.*"

"How exactly do you plan to do that?"

"By doing some volunteer hours at the nursing home. You have to admit, it's a great strategy."

"You know, most people don't take up community service as a strategy," I said. "You shouldn't do it as a ploy. Gabe wouldn't like that."

"Well, he doesn't know, does he? Anyway, I'm doing it for the right reasons," she said. "I know he doesn't see me the way I see him right now, but one day he might. I can't expect that out of the blue he'll suddenly just change his mind. I have to show him I'm worthy."

"But how will you be showing him that by faking it?" I asked.

"Maybe I really want to change."

"Molls," I began, but she cut me off.

"Don't try and talk me out of it," she said. "I want to follow this through and see where it goes. I have to try."

It won't go anywhere. It can't, I thought, remembering the warnings that had been issued to me not so long ago.

"You don't know anything about Gabriel," I said. "He's not what he seems. Gabriel has as much feeling as that stone angel in the garden."

"How can you say that?" Molly exclaimed. "Everyone has feelings—just with some people, they're harder to get in touch with. I don't mind waiting."

"You're wasting your time with Gabriel," I said. "He doesn't feel things like ordinary people."

"Well, if you're right, then I'll let it go."

"I'm sorry," I said. "I'm not trying to upset you. I just don't want to see you get hurt."

"I know it's risky to like him," Molly conceded. "But I think it's a risk I'm willing to take. Besides, it's too late for me to back out now. How am I supposed to look at anyone else after him?"

I looked at Molly closely. Her face was so open and genuine that I couldn't help but believe her. Her eyes were shining with anticipation.

"Has he given you any reason to think something might happen?" I ventured.

"Not yet," Molly conceded. "I'm still waiting for a sign."

"Why do you like him so much?" I asked. "Is it just the way he looks?"

"At first it was," Molly admitted. "But now it's something more. Whenever I see him, I get this weird sense of déjà vu—like I've been with him before. It's kinda scary but amazing. Sometimes I feel like I know what he's about to say or do." She shook her curls determinedly. "So, will you help me?"

"What can I do?"

"I want you to take me seriously. Let me come with you next time you visit Fairhaven."

Was Molly's interest in the nursing home part of the divine plan? We were trying to encourage a spirit of charity, even if the motivation was questionable. "I guess I can do that much, but promise not to get your hopes up."

BY the time Molly was ready to leave, it was getting dark. Gabriel politely offered to drive her home.

"No, it's okay," Molly said, not wanting to be an imposition. "I can walk. It's really not far."

"I'm afraid I can't allow that," Gabriel replied, picking up the keys to the Jeep. "The streets are no place for a young girl at this time of night."

He wasn't the sort of person one argued with, so Molly just winked as she hugged me good-bye. "A sign!" she hissed in my ear before following Gabriel to the car, walking as demurely as it was possible for Molly to walk.

Upstairs in my room, I tried to continue working on the poetry assignment but found myself with a serious case of writer's block. I couldn't come up with a single idea. I scribbled down a few possibilities, but they all seemed so stale they ended up in the wastepaper basket. As Jake had been the one to start it, I felt no sense of ownership over it and nothing I came up with seemed to fit. Eventually I gave up trying and went downstairs to call Xavier.

AS it turned out, my creative deficiency wasn't a problem.

"I've taken the liberty of completing the first stanza for us," Jake announced as we sat together at the back of the lit classroom the next day. "I hope you don't mind."

"No, I'm glad you did. Can I hear it?"

With a flick of his wrist, he opened his journal to the right page. His voice was like liquid as he read aloud.

> She had the face of an angel
> I saw mirrors in her eyes
> We were one and the same, she and I
> Both bound by potent lies.

I looked up slowly, unsure what I had been expecting. Jake's expression remained amicable.

"Awful?" he asked. His eyes were searching my face for a reaction. I could've sworn they were green the last time I checked, but today they were coal black.

"It's good," I said weakly. "You have a flair for this stuff."

"Thanks," he said. "I tried to imagine myself as Heathcliff writing about Cathy. Nobody meant as much to him as she did. He loved her so much that he had nothing left for anyone else."

"It was all consuming," I agreed.

I looked down, but Jake took my hand and began to run his finger in swirls across my wrist. His fingers were hot and I felt them burning into my skin. It was as if he were trying to send me a message without speech.

"You're very beautiful," he murmured. "I've never seen skin so delicate, like a flower. But I suppose you hear that all the time."

I pulled my wrist away. "No," I said. "Nobody's ever told me that."

"There's a whole lot more I'd like to tell you if you give me the chance." Jake was almost in a trancelike state now. "I could show you what it's really like to be in love."

"I *am* in love," I said. "I don't need *your* help."

"I could make you feel things you've never felt before."

"Xavier gives me everything I want," I snapped.

"I could show you pleasure on a scale you never thought possible," Jake persisted, his voice a low hypnotic hum, "things beyond your wildest imagination."

"I don't think Xavier would like that," I said coldly.

"Think about what *you* would like, Bethany. As far as Xavier goes, it sounds like you tell him far too much. I'd try operating on a *need-to-know* basis if I were you."

I was taken aback by his bluntness. "Well, you're *not* me and that's not how I operate. My relationship with Xavier is based on trust, something you don't seem to be familiar with," I snapped. I was trying to highlight the moral chasm that separated us.

I pushed back my chair and got up. Anticipating a scene, the other students turned to stare at me expectantly. Even Miss Castle looked up from the stack of papers she was marking.

"Don't be angry with me, Beth," said Jake, suddenly imploring. "Please, sit down."

Reluctantly I took my seat again but only because I didn't want to draw attention and add fuel to the Bryce Hamilton rumor mill.

"I don't think I want to continue this assignment with you," I said. "I'm sure Miss Castle will understand."

"Don't be like that. I'm sorry. Can we just forget I said anything?"

I huffed and folded my arms, but I was no match for the expression of innocence that had suddenly appeared on Jake's face.

"I need you as a friend," he said. "Give me one more chance?"

"Only if you promise never to say anything like that to me again."

"Okay, okay." Jake held up his hands in defeat. "I promise—not another word."

When I saw Xavier after class, I didn't mention the conversation with Jake. I suspected it would only make him angry and result in a confrontation. Besides, Xavier and I already had enough to think about without throwing Jake into the equation. Nevertheless, keeping things from him gave me an uneasy feeling. When I looked back on it later, I realized that was exactly what Jake Thorn had wanted.

"CAN I talk to you about something?" I asked Xavier as we lay on the sand after school.

We had intended to go straight home and study for our upcoming third-quarter exams, but we'd been distracted by the prospect of ice cream. We'd bought cones and taken the long route home via the beach, walking hand in hand. Inevitably I'd wanted to dip my feet in the water. Then we'd ended up chasing each other, until Xavier caught me and we'd both sprawled on the sand.

Xavier rolled around to face me, dusting the grains of sand from my nose. "You can talk to me about anything."

"Well," I began awkwardly, "I don't know how to say this . . . and I don't want it to come out sounding wrong. . . ."

Xavier sat up and pushed the hair out of his eyes, his face serious. "Are you breaking up with me?" he asked.

"What!" I cried. "No, of course not—just the opposite."

"Oh." He slid back down and smiled lazily. "Then you must be about to propose. You know, it's not a leap year. . . ."

"You're not making this any easier," I complained.

"Sorry." He looked at me earnestly. "What did you want to talk about?"

"I want to know what you think . . . how you feel about . . ." I paused and lowered my voice, "the S word."

Xavier rested his chin on his hand.

"I'm not good at riddles. You're going to have to be a bit more specific," he said.

I squirmed uncomfortably, not wanting to say it out loud.

"What's the second letter?" Xavier laughed, trying to help me along.

"E," I said. "Followed by X."

"You want to talk about sex?"

"Not talk about it," I said. "I'm just asking if . . . well, if you ever think about it?"

"Where is this coming from?" Xavier asked gently. "This doesn't sound like you at all."

"Well, I was talking to Molly," I said. "And she thought it was weird that we hadn't . . . you know, done anything."

Xavier scowled. "Is it really necessary for Molly to know every detail of our relationship?"

"Don't you think about me in that way?" I asked, feeling a sudden tension in my chest. That was a possibility I hadn't considered. "Is there something wrong with me?"

"Hey, hey, of course not." Xavier reached over and took my hand. "Beth . . . for so many guys sex is the only thing that keeps their relationships from falling apart, but we're not like that. We have so much more. I've never discussed it with you because I've never felt that we needed to." He gazed at me. "I'm sure it would be amazing, but I love you for you, not for what you can offer me."

"Did you and Emily have a physical relationship?" I was hardly listening to him.

"Oh God." Xavier flopped back onto the sand. "Not this again."

"Well, did you?"

"How is that important?"

"Just answer the question!"

"Yes—we did. Happy now?"

"There you go! That's another thing she could give you that I can't."

"Beth, a relationship isn't only based on the physical," he said calmly.

"But it's part of it," I protested.

"Sure—but it doesn't make or break it."

"But you're a boy, don't you have . . . *urges?*" I said in a lowered voice.

Xavier laughed. "When you meet a family of celestial messengers, you tend to forget about your *urges* and focus on the bigger picture."

"What if I told you I wanted to?" I said suddenly, surprised to hear the words come out of my mouth. What was I thinking? Did I have any idea what I was committing to? All I knew was that I loved Xavier more than anything in the world and that being separated from him caused me physical pain. I hated the idea that there was some part of him I hadn't discovered, a part of him that might be closed off to me. I wanted to know him inside and out, to memorize his body and burn it into my memory. I wanted to get as close to him as was physically possible, melded in body and soul.

"Well?" I asked him softly. "Would you say yes?"

"Definitely not."

"Why!"

"Because I don't think you're ready."

"Isn't that for me to decide?" I said stubbornly. "You can't stop me."

"I think you'll find it takes two to tango," Xavier said. He stroked my face. "Beth, I love you and nothing makes me happier than being close to you. You're intoxicating."

"So . . . ?"

"So if you really want to do this, then I'm in one hundred and ten percent, but not before we think it over carefully."

"When will that be?"

"When you're thinking clearly and when you haven't been speaking to Molly."

I sighed. "This has nothing to do with Molly."

"Beth, have you considered what the consequences of something like that might be?"

"I suppose—"

"And you still want to do it? That's crazy."

"Don't you see?" I said softly. "I don't care anymore." I turned my face up toward Heaven. "That's not my home anymore. You are."

Xavier wrapped his arms around me and pulled me close. "And you're mine. But I could never do anything that might hurt you. We have to play by the rules here."

"It's not fair. I hate that they rule my life."

"I know you do, but right now there's nothing we can do about it."

"We could do what we want." I tried to stop myself, but the words seemed to be spilling out uncontrollably. "We could run away, we could forget that anyone else exists." I realized that I had been holding this back for some time. "We could hide, they might never find us."

"They *would* find us, and I'm not going to lose you, Beth," said Xavier forcefully. "And if that means we abide by their rules, so be it. I know you're angry, but I want you to think about what you're suggesting. Just *think* for a little while."

"Like a couple of days?"

"Try a couple of months."

I sighed, but Xavier was adamant.

"I'm not going to let you rush into anything you might regret. Just slow down—we need to be calm and reasonable. Can you do that for me?"

I leaned my head against his chest and felt the pent-up anger drain from my body. "I can do anything for you."

"WHAT would happen if an angel and a human made love?" I asked Ivy that night as I was pouring myself a mug of milk.

She looked at me sharply.

"Why do you ask that?" she said. "Bethany, please tell me you haven't. . . ."

"Of course not," I cut in. "But I'm just curious."

"Well . . ." My sister was thoughtful. "The purpose of our

existence is to serve God by helping man, not mingling with him."

"Has it ever happened before?"

"Yes, with disastrous consequences."

"Meaning?"

"Meaning that the human and the divine were never meant to merge. If it happened, I believe the angel would lose his or her divinity. There could be no redemption after such a transgression."

"And the human?"

"The human would never be able to return to normal existence."

"Why?" I asked.

"Because the experience would surpass all human experiences," Ivy explained.

"So he would be damaged for life?"

"Yes," said Ivy. "I guess that's one way of putting it; a kind of outcast. I think it would just be cruel. It would be like giving a human a glimpse into another dimension and then barring him from it. Angels exist outside of time and space and can travel freely between worlds. For the most part our existence is incomprehensible to humans."

Although the concept was complex and unclear to me, I knew one thing—I couldn't rush into anything with Xavier, much as I might want to. Such a union was dangerous and forbidden. It would mean Heaven and earth coming together in an unnatural way, a collision of two worlds. And from what Ivy said, the impact could be potentially devastating.

———

"XAVIER and I have decided to wait," I told Molly, when she quizzed me in the cafeteria at school. Sometimes I thought she had an unhealthy interest in my love life. I couldn't explain to her what Ivy had told me, so I worded it the best way I could. "We don't need to do anything to prove how we feel about each other."

"But don't you want to?" Molly asked. "Aren't you curious?"

"I guess so, but we're not in a hurry."

"Oh boy, you guys really are living in a time warp." Molly laughed. "Everyone else is dying to do it every chance they get."

"Dying to do what?" Taylah asked, appearing behind Molly, sucking on a lollypop. I shook my head at her to indicate that we should change the subject, but Molly ignored me.

"Get down and dirty," she said.

"Oh, you want to lose your V-plates?" Taylah asked, flopping down beside us. I must have looked alarmed because Molly burst out laughing.

"Relax, hon, you can trust Taylah—maybe she can help you out."

"You got a sex question, I'm your girl," Taylah assured me. I was skeptical. I trusted Molly, but her friends all had big mouths and little discretion.

"It's okay," I said. "It's not important."

"You want my advice?" Taylah asked, not seeming to care whether her advice was wanted or not. "Don't do it with someone you love."

"What?" I stared at her. She had just thrown my entire system of beliefs into chaos with a few simple words. "Don't you mean exactly the opposite?"

"Oh, Tay, don't tell her that," Molly said.

"Seriously"—Taylah wagged a finger at me—"if you lose it to someone you really love, it all goes to hell."

"But why?"

"Because when it ends, you've given away something really special and you can't get it back. If you give it to someone you don't care about—it won't hurt so much."

"What if it doesn't end?" I asked, feeling a sickly lump rise in my throat.

"Trust me, Beth," said Taylah earnestly. "Everything ends."

As I listened, I felt a sudden, overwhelming urge to be as far away from them as possible.

"Bethie, don't pay any attention to her," Molly said as I pushed back my chair and stood up. "Now look, you've upset her."

"I'm not upset," I lied, trying to keep my voice level. "I have a meeting. I'll see you guys later—thanks for the advice, Taylah."

I picked up my pace as soon as I was outside the cafeteria. I needed to find Xavier. I needed him to hold me so that I could breathe again and his smell and touch would wash away the violent waves of nausea erupting inside me. I found him at his locker about to head to water-polo practice and skidded into him in my haste for reassurance.

"It's not going to end, is it?" I buried my face in his chest. "Promise me you won't let it end."

"Whoa, Beth, what's wrong?" Xavier detached me firmly but gently and made me look at him. "What's happened?

"Nothing," I said with an unsteady voice. "It's just that Taylah said . . ."

"Beth," Xavier sighed, "when are you going to stop listening to those girls?"

"She said everything ends," I whispered and felt Xavier's arms tense around me and knew the thought was just as painful to him. "But I couldn't stand it if that happened to us. Everything would fall apart; there wouldn't be anything to live for. If we end, I end"

"Don't talk like that," Xavier said. "I'm here and so are you. Nobody is going anywhere."

"And you won't ever leave me?"

"Not so long as I'm living."

"How do I know that's true?"

"Because when I look at you, I see my whole world. I'm not about to walk away; I wouldn't have anything left."

"But why did you choose me?" I asked. I knew the answer, I knew how much he loved me, but I needed to hear him say it.

"Because you bring me closer to God and to myself," Xavier said. "When I'm around you, I understand things I never thought I'd understand and my feelings for you seem to override everything. The world could fall apart around me, and it wouldn't matter if I had you."

"Do you want to hear something crazy?" I whispered. "Sometimes, at night, I think I can feel your soul next to me."

"That's not so crazy." Xavier smiled.

"Let's create a place," I said, as I pressed against him. "A place that's just ours; a place we can always find each other if things ever go wrong."

"Like under the cliffs off Shipwreck Coast?"

"No, I mean a place inside our heads," I said. "That we can visit if we're ever lost or apart, or just need to make contact with each other. It's the one place nobody else will ever know how to find."

"I like that," said Xavier. "Why don't we call it the White Place?"

"That's perfect."

23

R.I.P.

ACCORDING to the belief system of most humans, there are only two dimensions, the dimension of the living and that of the dead. But what they don't realize is that there are many more. Every day people on earth exist parallel to other beings; close enough to touch but invisible to the untrained eye. Some are called the Rainbow People, immortals who can travel between worlds and are made up of nothing but wisdom and understanding. People catch glimpses of them sometimes, shooting between realms. They appear as a streak of glittering white-gold light or the faint glow of a rainbow hanging in the air. Most humans think they're witnessing a trick of the light. Only very few can sense a divine presence. I liked to think Xavier was one of those few.

I found Xavier in the cafeteria, slid in beside him, and nibbled from the container of nachos he offered me. When he shifted position in his chair, his thigh brushed against mine and sent a tingling heat through my body. I couldn't enjoy it for long as the sound of raised voices reached us from the counter.

Two boys in their early teens were arguing over their place in line.

"Man, you just pushed in front of me!"

"Whatever, I've been here the whole time."

"That's bull! Ask anyone!"

With no teacher in sight, their disagreement escalated to the point of shoving and name calling. Some junior girls just behind them started to look worried when one of the boys seized the other in a headlock.

Xavier sprang to his feet to intervene but sat down again when someone beat him to it. It was Lachlan Merton, a boy with bleached blond hair who was permanently plugged into his iPod and hadn't handed in a single homework assignment all year. He was usually impervious to everything going on around him. Now he was pushing his way between the two boys and hauling them off each other. We couldn't hear what he said, but the boys reluctantly parted and even complied with his directive to shake hands.

Xavier and I exchanged looks. "Lachlan Merton behaving responsibly—now that's a first," remarked Xavier.

It occurred to me that what we'd witnessed was a prime example of the subtle shift in thinking at Bryce Hamilton. I immediately thought of how pleased Ivy and Gabriel would be to hear their efforts were paying off. Of course there were needier communities in the world than Venus Cove, but they weren't part of our mission. Other watchers had been assigned there. I was secretly glad I hadn't been sent to a part of the world ravaged by war, poverty, or natural disaster. The images of those places on the news were confronting enough. I tried to avoid the news as it often led to feelings of despair. I couldn't watch footage of children suffering from starvation and illness caused from lack of clean water. When I thought about the things humans could turn a blind eye to, it made me want to cry. What made one person more or less deserving than another? No one should be hungry or lonely or wishing for life to end. Although I prayed for divine intervention, sometimes the thought just made me angry.

When I talked to Gabriel about it, he said I wasn't ready to understand right now, but that one day I would. "Address the things you can address," was his advice.

The next morning the three of us set off to Fairhaven, the local nursing home. I'd visited Alice there once or twice as promised, but my visits had dropped off as I tended to devote most of my free time to Xavier. Gabriel and Ivy were regular visitors there, however, and made sure to take Phantom along with them. According to them, he always made a beeline for Alice without needing directions.

As Molly had also volunteered her services, we made a detour to pick her up. She was dressed and ready, despite the fact that it was nine o'clock on a Saturday morning, and I knew that she rarely surfaced before noon. We were surprised to find her dressed as if for a photo shoot in a denim miniskirt, high heels, and checked shirt. Taylah, who had stayed the night, couldn't understand Molly's decision to forfeit a *Gossip Girl* marathon to work with "old people."

"Why are you going to a nursing home?" I heard her say as I opened the car door for Molly.

"We'll all end up there one day," said Molly with a smile. She checked her lip gloss in the car window.

"I won't," Taylah vowed. "Those places stink."

"Call you later," said Molly and climbed in dutifully beside me.

"But, Moll," Taylah whined, "Adam and Chris were going to meet up with us this morning."

"Say hi from me."

Taylah stared after us as we pulled out of the drive, obviously wondering who had abducted her best friend and replaced her with this impostor.

When we arrived at Fairhaven, the nursing staff looked pleased to see us. They were used to Gabriel and Ivy coming regularly, but Molly's presence took them by surprise.

"This is Molly," said Gabriel. "She's kindly offered to help us out today."

"We're always grateful for an extra pair of hands," said Helen, one of the ward nurses. "Especially when we're as short staffed as we are today." She looked drawn and tired.

"I'm happy to help out," said Molly, enunciating her words clearly as if Helen was hard of hearing. "It's very important to give something back to your community." She cast a sidelong glance at Gabriel, but he was busy unzipping his guitar case and didn't notice.

"You're just in time for breakfast," said Helen.

"Thanks but I already ate," said Molly.

A doubtful look crossed Helen's face. "I meant the residents' breakfast. You can help with the feeding if you like."

We followed her down a dingy corridor and into the dining

hall, which was shabby and had a dismal air despite the Vivaldi filtering out of an old CD player. The floral carpet was worn and the curtains were patterned with faded fruit. The residents were seated on plastic chairs at Formica tables. Those who couldn't hold themselves upright were in deep leather chairs known as tub chairs. Despite the air fresheners plugged into the walls, there was a distinct smell of ammonia mixed with boiled vegetables. A portable television was switched on in one corner and was playing a wildlife documentary. The caretakers were mainly women, who went routinely about their tasks of folding napkins, clearing tables, and tying bibs on residents who couldn't manage themselves. Some faces looked up in anticipation when we came in. Others weren't aware enough of their surroundings to notice.

The breakfast trays were stacked on a cart and the meals were sealed in foil packs. On the second tier were rows of plastic drink mugs.

I couldn't see Alice anywhere, so I spent the next half hour feeding a woman named Dora, who sat in a wheelchair with a multicolored crocheted afghan over her knees. She sat slumped with her mouth slack and her eyes drooping. Her skin was sallow and her hands were liver spotted. On her face, a network of broken capillaries showed through the paper-thin skin. I wasn't sure what constituted "breakfast" at Fairhaven, but it looked like a pile of pale yellow sludge to me. I knew that some residents ate pureed meals to avoid the risk of choking.

"What is this?" I asked Helen.

"Scrambled eggs," she said before moving off with the cart.

One elderly gentleman tried to take a spoonful of food, but

his hands were so jittery, he ended up spilling it down his front. In an instant Gabriel was at his side. "I'll get it," he said, patting away the spilled food with a paper towel. Molly was so engrossed in watching him that she forgot to feed her charge who sat openmouthed and waiting.

After I'd finished helping Dora, I moved on to Mabel, who had the reputation of being the most truculent resident at Fairhaven. She pushed away the spoon I offered her and pressed her mouth shut firmly.

"Aren't you hungry?" I asked.

"Oh, don't worry about Mabel," said Helen. "She's waiting for Gabriel. If he's here she won't accept food from anyone else."

"Okay," I said. "I haven't seen Alice today. Where is she?"

"She's been moved to a private room," Helen replied. "I'm afraid she's deteriorated since you last saw her. Her eyesight's failing and she's getting over a pulmonary infection. Her room's just down the hall—first door on the right. I'm sure that seeing you will do her a world of good." Why hadn't Gabriel and Ivy told me? Had I been so engrossed in my own world that they'd concluded I wouldn't care? I made my way down the hall to Alice's room with a rising sense of dread.

Phantom had beaten me to it and was already there, keeping vigil in the hall. When I opened the door and we both went in, I almost didn't recognize the woman in the bed. She was nothing like the Alice of my memory. Illness had ravaged her face and transformed her. Her body looked as fragile as a bird's and her flimsy hair was uncombed. The colorful cardigans were gone and she was dressed in a plain white gown.

She didn't open her eyes when I said her name, but she did stretch out her hand toward me. Phantom pushed his nose into it before I could take it.

"Is that you, Phantom?" said Alice in a hoarse voice.

"It's Phantom and Bethany," I replied. "We've come to visit."

"Bethany . . . ," she repeated. "How good of you to come. I've missed you." Her eyes were still shut as though the effort of opening them was too great.

"How are you feeling?" I asked. "Is there something I can get you?"

"No, dear, I have everything I need."

"I'm sorry I haven't come for a while. It's just that . . ." I didn't know what explanation to give for my negligent behavior.

"I know," she said. "Life gets in the way. No need for apologies. You're here now and that's what's important. I hope Phantom has been behaving."

Phantom let out a short bark upon hearing his name.

"He's the perfect companion."

"Good boy," said Alice.

"What's all this I hear about you being sick?" I asked brightly. "We'll have to get you back on your feet!"

"I'm not sure I want to get back on my feet. I think it might be time. . . ."

"Don't say that," I said. "You just need some rest and . . ."

Alice's head suddenly rolled forward and her eyes flew open. They didn't focus on anything but rather stared wildly into space. "I know who you are," she croaked.

"That's good," I replied, feeling a knot of alarm in my chest. "I'm glad you haven't forgotten me."

"You've come to take me," she said. "Not yet but soon."

"Where are we going?" I asked. I didn't want to accept what she was telling me.

"To Heaven," she replied. "I can't see your face, Bethany, but I can see your light."

I stared at her, speechless.

"You will show me the way, won't you?" she said.

I touched her wrist and felt for her pulse. It was like a candle burned almost to the wick. I knew that I couldn't let my attachment to her stop me from doing my job. I closed my eyes and recalled the entity I had been in the Kingdom: a guide, a mentor for souls in transition. My domain had been to comfort the souls of children as they passed through.

"When the time comes you won't be alone."

"I'm a little frightened. Tell me, Bethany, will there be darkness?"

"No, Alice, only light."

"What about my sins? I haven't always been a model citizen, you know," she said, a hint of her old feisty self emerging.

"The Father I know is all forgiving."

"And will I see my loved ones again?"

"You will enter a much larger family. You will be as one with all the creatures of this world and beyond it."

Alice sank back on her pillows, looking satisfied but tired. Her eyelids fluttered.

"You should try to sleep now," I said.

I closed my fingers around her frail hand, and Phantom

laid his head against her arm. Together we watched over her until she slept.

On the drive home I was still thinking about Alice and what she'd said. Watching death from above was sad, but actually experiencing it on earth was heart wrenching. It was an intense pain for which there could be no remedy. I felt a sharp stab of guilt for letting myself become so fixated by my love for Xavier that I'd shirked my other responsibilities. Heaven had approved our relationship, for the time being, at least, and I must not allow it to be all consuming. At the same time, I wanted nothing more than to find him and breathe in his comforting scent. No other person I knew could make me feel so alive.

News reached us the next morning that Alice had passed away in her sleep. It didn't come as a surprise to me. I'd woken in the night to the sound of rain lashing at my window and when I'd slipped out of bed to close the curtains, Alice's spirit had been hovering outside. She was smiling and seemed utterly at peace. Alice had lived a full and enriching life and was ready to move on. The loss would be felt most by her family, who hadn't made the best of the time they'd shared together. They didn't know it yet, but one day they would be given a second chance.

I felt her spirit as it passed out of this world, buzzing with nervous anticipation. She was no longer afraid, only excited to see what lay beyond. I reached out to her in my mind in a final gesture of farewell.

24

Only Human

THE day of Alice's funeral was overcast. The sky was pewter, and the ground was damp from the light drizzle that had fallen overnight. There were only a handful of mourners, including staff members from Fairhaven and Father Mel who performed the service. Her gravesite was on a grassy knoll under an acorn tree, and I thought how she would have chuckled that her final resting place had a view.

Alice's passing stirred something in me. It brought my attention back to the purpose of our mission, and I decided to up my hours of community service. It was a very small gesture in the grand scheme of things, and I felt almost silly suggesting it, seeing as our purpose was to save the earth from the fallen and their forces of darkness. But it made me feel more like I was contributing to our cause and focusing on what was important. Often Xavier came with me. His family had been doing volunteer work for the church for years, so it was nothing new to him.

"You don't always have to come," I said to him one night as we waited for the train that would take us down to the soup kitchens in Port Circe.

"I know," he said. "But I want to come. I've been brought up to believe community's important."

"But you have so much more on your plate than I do. I don't want to add pressure."

"Quit worrying. I know how to manage my time."

"Don't you have a French oral tomorrow?"

"No, *we* have a French oral tomorrow—that's why I've brought this." He drew a textbook from his backpack. "We can study on the way."

I'd gradually become more comfortable with trains, and riding with Xavier certainly helped. We found seats on a car that was empty, save for a wizened old man who was nodding off and drooling onto his shirt. There was a bottle in a brown paper bag between his feet.

We opened the textbook and had only been reading a few minutes when Xavier looked up. "Heaven must be pretty big," he said. He spoke softly, so I didn't tell him off for bringing up the subject in public. "How much space would you need to fit all those souls? I guess it's just the concept of infinity that throws me."

"Actually there are seven realms of heaven," I said suddenly, wanting to share my knowledge with Xavier even though I knew it was against our laws.

Xavier sighed and flopped back in his seat.

"Just when I thought I was getting my head around it. How can there be seven?"

"There's only a throne in the First Heaven," I said. "And angels that preach the word of the Lord. The Father, the Son, and the Holy Spirit dwell in the Seventh Heaven—which is the ultimate realm."

"But what's the point?"

"Different realms have different functions. It's like working your way up to meet the CEO of a company."

Xavier massaged his temples.

"I've got a lot to learn, don't I?"

"There are just lots of rules to remember," I said. "The Second Heaven is the same distance as the First Heaven to earth, the angels on the right are always more glorious than the ones on the left; entry to the Sixth Heaven is quite complicated, and you have to travel into the air outside Heaven's door, and I know that seems confusing but you'll know which is which because the lower heavens are dark compared to the brilliance of the Seventh. . . ."

"Stop," Xavier said. "Stop before my brain explodes."

"Sorry," I said sheepishly. "I guess it is a lot to take in."

Xavier grinned at me. "Try to remember that I'm only human."

XAVIER invited me to watch his team play in the end-of-season rugby game. I knew it was important to him, so I arranged to go with Molly and her friends, who usually acted as the Bryce Hamilton cheer squad at games. What they called school spirit was really more of a thin excuse to watch boys in shorts run around a field and work up a sweat. The girls always made sure they had a supply of cool drinks to pass around during breaks, in the hope of being rewarded with a compliment or, better yet, a date.

It was a home game, so I made my way down to the field with Molly and the girls. The rugby team was already there when we arrived, warming up in their black-and-red-striped jerseys. The opposition, Middleton Preparatory School, stood at the other end of the field in green and yellow. They were listening intently to their beet-faced coach, who looked on the verge of an aneurism. Xavier waved for a second when he saw me, then resumed the warm-up. Before the game began the Bryce Hamilton team huddled together and chanted some motivational mantra about the *mighty red and black army*. They jogged on the spot and hugged while they waited for the referee to blow his whistle.

"Typical," Molly muttered. "Nothing like sports to drag some emotion out of them."

As soon as the game began, I realized that I would never be a fan of rugby. It was too aggressive. The sport mainly consisted of players smashing into one another in an attempt to wrestle the ball from the opposition's grasp. I watched one of Xavier's teammates charge up the field, the ball securely lodged under his arm. He dodged two of the Middleton players, who pursued him ruthlessly. When he was a few yards away from the goal, he threw himself forward into the air and landed sprawled on the ground, his arms stretched over his head. His hands, clasping the ball, lay just over the line. One of the players from Middleton, who had attempted a tackle in the hope of blocking the goal, landed on top of him. The Bryce Hamilton team broke into whoops and cheers, helping their player up and thumping him on the back as he staggered back to the center of the field.

I was shielding my eyes to avoid witnessing two players collide when Molly nudged me. "Who's that guy?" she said, pointing to a figure standing on the other side of the field. It was a young man in a long leather jacket. His identity was concealed by a fedora and a long scarf he'd wound around the lower half of his face.

"I'm not sure," I replied. "A parent maybe?"

"Pretty weird-looking parent," Molly said. "Why is he standing there by himself?"

We quickly forgot about the stranger and reverted to watching the game. I grew steadily more nervous as it progressed. The Middleton boys were merciless and most of them looked like tanks. I felt my heart rate increase and my breathing become more rapid whenever any of them went near Xavier. Given the nature of the game, this happened quite often and Xavier wasn't one to stick to the perimeter. He wanted to be in the thick of things and was just as competitive as the rest of them. I had to admit that as much as I disliked rugby, he was a skilled player. He was fast and strong, and best of all, he played fair. I watched him streak toward the goal and slam the ball into the ground. Whenever one of the other players grabbed him or knocked him to the ground, he was up again in a matter of seconds. He was unfaltering. Eventually I stopped wincing about potential scrapes and bruises, stopped worrying about his safety, and started feeling proud of him. I cheered and waved Molly's pom-poms in the air whenever he had the ball.

By halftime Bryce Hamilton was ahead by three points. Xavier jogged over to the sideline where I ran to meet him.

"Thanks for coming," he panted. "I know this probably isn't your thing." He gave me his endearing half-smile as he tipped a bottle of water over his head.

"You're amazing out there," I said, pushing back the wet hair that was plastered across his forehead. "But you've got to be careful, the Middleton boys are huge."

"Skill over size," he said.

I looked in anguish at a long scratch across his forearm. "How did this happen?"

"It's just a scratch." He laughed at my concern.

"It might be just a scratch to you, but it's a scratch on *my arm*, which I don't want to see damaged."

"So is everything marked as property of Bethany Church or just the arm?"

"Every inch of you, so be careful."

"Yes, Coach."

"I'm serious. I hope you realize you can't lecture me about safety ever again," I said.

"Babe, injuries are inevitable. It's all part of the game. You can play nurse afterward if you like." He threw me a wink over his shoulder as the horn sounded for play to resume. "Don't worry, I'm invincible."

I watched him jog lightly back to his teammates and noticed that the boy in the leather jacket was still standing by the opposite sidelines. His hands were dug deep in his pockets. I still couldn't see his face.

With ten minutes till the end of the game, the Bryce Hamilton boys looked as if they had victory in the bag. The opposition's coach was doing a lot of head shaking and had to keep mopping sweat from his brow. His players looked furious and desperate. It didn't take them long to employ dirtier tactics. Xavier had the ball and was running up the field when two of the Middleton players charged at him like freight trains from either side. Xavier swerved in an attempt to avoid a collision, but the others swerved with him and closed in. I cried out when one of them threw out his leg and caught Xavier around the ankle. It sent him tumbling forward so that the ball slipped from his grasp. I saw his head connect with the ground and his eyes snap shut as he winced in pain. The Bryce Hamilton players made a furious protest, and the referee blew his whistle to indicate foul play but it was too late.

Two boys ran over to help Xavier, who was still prostrate on the ground. He tried to get up but his left ankle was sticking out at a peculiar angle, and when he tried to put weight on it, he grimaced and slipped. His teammates supported him as they helped him over to a bench and the medic scurried over to examine the extent of the damage. He seemed unsteady— like he might be about to pass out.

From where I stood, I couldn't hear what they were saying. I saw the medic shine a light in Xavier's eyes and shake his head at the coach. Xavier gritted his teeth and dropped his head in frustration. I tried to push past the girls to get to him, but Molly restrained me.

"No, Beth, they know what they're doing. You'll just be in the way."

Before I could argue, Xavier was being helped onto a stretcher and into the ambulance that was always waiting in the event of an accident. I stood frozen as the game resumed now that the crisis had passed. The ambulance drove off the track and onto the road. I noticed vaguely through my panic that the boy on the sidelines had disappeared.

"Where are they taking him?" I asked.

"To the hospital, of course," Molly said. Her face softened when she saw my eyes fill with tears. "Hey, it didn't look too serious—probably just a sprain. They'll bandage him up and send him home. Look," she pointed at the scoreboard. "We're still going to beat them by six points."

But I felt no cause for jubilation now and excused myself to get home to Gabriel and Ivy so I could ask them to drive me to the hospital. I summoned them in my mind as I ran, in case they weren't at home. I was so distracted with worry for Xavier that I collided head-on with Jake Thorn in the parking lot.

"Well, somebody's in a hurry," he said, helping me up and brushing off the dust clinging to my coat. "What's the problem?"

"Xavier had an accident during the rugby game," I said, rubbing my eyes with my fists like a small child. At that point I couldn't have cared less what I looked like—I just needed to see that Xavier was okay.

"Dear me," Jake drawled. "That's unfortunate—is it serious?"

"I don't know," I said, my voice choked. "They've taken him to hospital to be checked out."

"I see," Jake replied. "I'm sure he'll be okay. It's the nature of the game."

"I should have known," I said angrily, more to myself than to him.

"Known what?" Jake asked, peering closely at my face. "This isn't your fault now, is it? Don't cry. . . ."

He stepped forward and closed his arms around me in a hug. His embrace wasn't anything like Xavier's; his body was too lean and thin to be very comfortable, but I sobbed into his shirt all the same and let him hold me. When I tried to pull away, I found his arms still locked tightly around me and had to wriggle to break free.

"Sorry," Jake said, a strange look in his eyes. "Just making sure you're all right."

"Thanks, Jake. But I really have to go now," I said, tears stinging my eyes and my words spilling over one another.

I ran up the main steps and down the deserted central corridor of the school and saw with flooding relief the figures of Ivy and Gabriel heading toward me.

"We heard you calling," Ivy said when I opened my mouth to tell her the story. "We know what happened."

"I need to get to the hospital right away. I can help him!" I cried.

Gabriel stepped in front of me and grasped my shoulders. "Bethany, calm down! You can't do that now, not if he's already being looked after."

"Why not?"

"*Think* for a moment, Bethany," said Ivy in exasperation. "He's already been taken to the hospital; his parents have already been notified. If his injury miraculously heals, how do you think everyone will react?"

"But he needs me."

"What he needs is for you to be sensible about this," replied Gabriel. "Xavier is young and healthy. His injury will heal naturally and no suspicions will be raised. If you want to speed up the process later, fine; but for now you need to keep your head. He's not in any real danger."

"Can I at least go and see him?" I asked, hating the fact that they were right, which also meant Xavier's recovery would be delayed.

"Yes," Gabriel replied. "We'll all go."

I didn't like the local hospital. It was gray and sterile and the nurses' shoes squeaked on the linoleum floor. I could feel grief and loss as I soon as I stepped through its automatic doors. I knew there were people there who would not recover; victims of car accidents or incurable diseases. At any given time someone could be in the process of losing a mother, father, husband, sister, or child. I could feel the pain contained within the walls like a stinging slap in the face. This was the place from which so many made their journey to Heaven. I was reminded of the many souls whose transition I had been able to ease—it was remarkable the number of people who reconnected with their faith in their last days on earth. There were so many souls here in desperate need of guidance, of reassurance, and it was my duty to attend to them. But, as usual, the moment I pictured Xavier's face, any feelings of responsibility or guilt dissolved from my mind, and I could think of nothing but finding him.

I followed Ivy and Gabriel quickly down the wide passageway with fluorescent lighting and hospital furniture.

Xavier was in a room on the fifth floor. His entire family were leaving as we arrived and they spilled out into the passageway.

"Oh, Beth!" exclaimed Bernie when she saw me, and suddenly I was surrounded by members of Xavier's family, all passing on pieces of information as to his condition. Gabriel and Ivy watched in amazement.

"Thanks for coming, hon," said Bernie. "Give her some space, everyone. He's fine, Beth, don't look so worried—although he could do with some cheering up."

She cast an inquiring look at Gabriel and Ivy. "This must be your brother and sister." She extended her hand by way of greeting, and my siblings shook it in turn. I left them to deal with introductions and slipped quietly into Xavier's room. One bed was empty; the other had its curtains drawn.

"Knock, knock," I said softly.

"Beth?" Xavier's voice came from inside. "Come in!" He was sitting propped up on the bed with a blue tag around his wrist. "What took you so long?" he said, his eyes lighting up when he saw me.

I ran to the side of the bed, grabbed his face in my hands and examined it. Gabe and Ivy waited outside, not wanting to intrude.

"So much for being invincible," I said. "How's your ankle?"

He lifted off an ice pack to reveal his ankle, which was swollen to twice its size. "They've taken X-rays and it's fractured. They'll have to put a cast on as soon as the swelling goes down. Looks like I'll be on crutches for a while."

"Well, that's a nuisance but not the end of the world. It'll give me a chance to look after you for a change."

"I'll be fine," Xavier said. "They're keeping me overnight for observation, but I'll be home in the morning. I just have to keep my weight off the foot for a few weeks. . . ."

"I'm just glad you're okay," I said, trying to keep my voice level.

"There's something else." Xavier looked uncomfortable, almost embarrassed to be admitting any sort of weakness.

"What is it?" I asked gently.

"*Apparently* I have a concussion," he said, emphasising the word "apparently" as though he didn't take it seriously. "I told them I'm fine, but they won't listen. I have to stay in bed for the next few days—doctor's orders."

"That sounds serious," I said. "Are you okay?"

"I'm fine," Xavier said. "I just have a killer headache."

"Well, I'll look after you," I said. "I don't mind."

"Beth, you're forgetting something."

"I know, I know," I said. "You don't like feeling like an invalid—but that's what you get for playing a rough game like—"

"No, Beth, you don't understand." Xavier shook his head in frustration. "The prom is this Friday."

I felt a sinking feeling in my stomach.

"I don't care about that!" I said, my voice falsely cheerful. "I just won't go."

"You have to go. You've been looking forward to this for weeks, Ivy made your dress, the limos are all booked, and everybody is expecting you."

"But I only want to go with you," I said. "It won't mean anything to me otherwise."

"I'm so sorry this happened," he said, clenching his hand into a fist. "I'm an idiot."

"Xavier, it wasn't your fault."

"I should have been more careful." The anger drained out of his face and his expression softened. "Please say you'll go," he said. "Then I won't feel so guilty. I don't want you to miss out because of me. We might not be there together, but you can still have a good time. This is the event of the year, and I want you to tell me all about it."

"I don't know . . ."

"Please? Do it for me?"

I rolled my eyes. "Well, if you're going to resort to emotional blackmail I can hardly say no." I knew Xavier would feel guilty for the next five years if I missed the prom on his account.

"Then it's settled?"

"All right, but just know that I'll be thinking about you all night."

He smiled. "Make sure someone takes photos."

"Will you come over before I leave?" I asked. "So you can see me in my dress?"

"I'll get someone to drive me. I'm not missing that for the world."

"I hate leaving you here," I said, sinking down in the chair beside his bed. "With no one to keep you company."

"I'll be fine," he reassured me. "If I know Mom, she'll probably set up a cot and spend the night."

"Yes, but you'll need something to keep you occupied."

Xavier nodded toward the small bedside table, where a thick black book with gold lettering lay half open. "I can always read the Bible and learn more about eternal damnation."

"Is that your idea of entertainment?" I asked sarcastically.

"It's a pretty dramatic story—good old Lucifer, spicing things up a bit."

"Do you know the whole story?" I asked.

"I know that Lucifer was an archangel," he said as I raised an eyebrow in surprise. "He went off the rails in a big way."

"So you were paying attention at Sunday school," I said jokingly. "His name actually means 'light giver.' In the Kingdom, he used to be Our Father's favorite. He was created to be elite in beauty and intelligence. He was consulted in times of trouble, and all the other angels held him in the highest esteem."

"But he wasn't satisfied," Xavier added.

"No," I said. "He became arrogant. He resented human beings, couldn't understand why Our Father thought they were His greatest creation. He believed that only angels should be exalted, and started to think he could overthrow God."

"And that's when he was booted out."

"Yes. Our Father heard his thoughts and cast him out, along with his followers. Lucifer got his wish and became Our Father's counterpart, ruler of the Underworld, and all the other fallen angels became demons."

"Do you know anything about what it's like down there?" Xavier asked.

I shook my head.

"I don't, but Gabriel does. He knew Lucifer. They were brothers—all the archangels were. But he never talks about it."

The conversation was cut short when Gabriel and Ivy poked their heads through the curtain to see how the patient was doing.

"ARE you serious?" Molly looked horrified. "I thought they were just taking him to a hospital as a precaution. He actually has a concussion? This is a disaster! You're going to be dateless for the prom!"

I was starting to regret having said anything. Her reaction wasn't doing anything to lift my spirits. The prom was supposed to be a magical night spent with Xavier that I would remember always. Now it was ruined.

"I don't want to go at all," I said. "I'm only going because Xavier wants me to."

She sighed. "That is so sweet of him."

"I know and that's why I don't care about being dateless."

"We'll think of something," Molly said reassuringly. "There must be someone who can step in at the last minute. Let me think about it."

I knew what she was thinking. She was imagining the start of the prom, when couples would make their entrance together and have their photos professionally taken. Turning up alone would be tantamount to social suicide.

As it turned out, Molly needn't have bothered trying to find a solution as one presented itself that very afternoon.

I was sitting with Jake Thorn in our usual place at the

back of the literature classroom. He was scribbling in his journal in silence as I struggled to focus on the final verse of our joint poem.

"You know this is quite difficult seeing as you've written it from a male perspective," I complained.

"My sincerest apologies," Jake replied with his usual exaggerated manners. "But feel free to take some creative license. The first verse may be from a man to a woman, but the next could easily be the reverse. Don't take forever about it, Beth. I'm over this assignment. Let's get it done so we can talk about more interesting things."

"I can't be rushed," I said brusquely. "I don't know about you, but I want to do well on this."

"Why? It's not like you need the grades."

"Excuse me? Why wouldn't I?"

"Doing well is pretty much a given—Miss Castle likes me." He smirked, and went back to writing in his notebook. I didn't ask what he was writing, and he didn't offer to divulge anything.

Jake's suggestion had freed my imagination, and it was a lot easier to come up with the next lines now that I could write them about Xavier. All I had to do was picture his face and the words flowed as though my pen had a life of its own. In fact, the four-line stanza I had been allocated hardly seemed enough. I felt as if I could fill every notebook in the world with my thoughts about him. I could devote pages to describing his voice, his touch, his smell, and every other detail of his person. And so before I knew it, my fluid script sat beneath Jake's swirling calligraphy. It now read,

She had the face of an angel
I saw mirrors in her eyes
We were the same, she and I
Both bound by potent lies.

In him I saw my future
In him I saw my friend
In him I saw my destiny
Both my beginning and my end.

"That works," Jake said. "There may be a poet in you after all."

"Thanks," I replied. "What have you been so busy working on?"

"Jottings . . . observations," he answered.

"What have you observed so far?"

"Just that people are *so* gullible and *so* predictable."

"Do you hold that against them?"

"I think it's pathetic." He sounded so bitter that I shrank away from him. "They're so easy to figure out," he continued. "It's not even challenging."

"People don't exist for your recreation," I protested. "They're not a hobby."

"They are for me. Most are an open book . . . except for you. You puzzle me."

"Me?" I feigned a laugh. "There's nothing puzzling about me. I'm just like everyone else."

"Not quite." There was Jake being cryptic again. It was getting unsettling.

"I don't know what you're talking about," I said, but I had to turn my face away so he wouldn't see the color spreading across my cheeks.

"If you say so." He let the subject drop just as Alicia and Alexandra timidly approached our desk and waited for Jake to acknowledge them.

"Yes?" he snapped, when he realized they weren't going to go away. I'd never heard him use such a cutting tone before.

"Are we getting together tonight?" Alicia whispered.

Jake glared at her in exasperation. "Didn't you get my message?"

"Yes."

"So what's the problem?"

"No problem," she said, looking mortified.

"Then I'll see you both later," he said smoothly.

The girls exchanged covert smiles before returning to their seats. Jake shrugged his shoulders in response to my puzzled look as if to say that he was as mystified by their attention as I was.

"Looking forward to Friday?" he asked, changing the subject. "I hear that due to a little sporting mishap you no longer have a partner. It's a terrible shame pretty boy won't be able to make it." His dark eyes shone and his lip curled in a snarl.

"News sure travels fast around here," I said in a flat voice, choosing to ignore his jibe. Now that I was dreading rather than anticipating prom night, I didn't welcome the reminder. "Who are you taking?" I asked out of politeness.

"I, too, am flying solo."

"Why? What about your fan club?"

"Fans are only acceptable in small doses."

I unconsciously let out a deep sigh. "Life's not very fair, is it?" I was trying my hardest to put a positive spin on things, but it just didn't seem to be working.

"It doesn't have to be like that," Jake said. "I know one would hope to attend such a function on the arm of a beloved, but sometimes one just has to be practical, especially when said beloved is otherwise engaged."

His exaggerated speech succeeded in making me smile.

"That's better," he said. "Gloom just doesn't suit you." He straightened in his chair. "Bethany, I know I'm not your first choice, but would you allow me the honor of accompanying you to the prom to help you out of your current predicament?"

It might have been a genuine gesture, but I didn't feel comfortable accepting.

"I'm not sure," I said. "Thanks for offering, but I'd have to discuss it with Xavier first."

Jake nodded. "Of course. Just know that the offer is on the table should you care to accept it."

WHEN I broached the subject with Xavier, he didn't hesitate: "Of course you should go with someone else."

Xavier was leaning back on the couch, facing the TV. I could tell he was bored—for someone used to being so active, daytime television was a poor substitute. He wore a gray sweatshirt, and his ankle was propped up on a pillow. He looked restless and kept shifting positions. He didn't complain, but I knew his head was still pounding from the impact of the collision. "It's a dance," he continued with a reassuring smile. "You're going to need a partner seeing as I'm useless to you."

"Okay," I said slowly. "And how do you feel about Jake Thorn as my partner?"

"Really?" Xavier's smile vanished, and his blue eyes narrowed almost indiscernibly. "There's something about that kid I don't like."

"Well, he's the one who's offered."

Xavier sighed. "Beth, any guy would jump at the chance to be your date."

"But Jake's my friend."

"Are you sure about that?" Xavier asked.

"What's that supposed to mean?"

"Nothing, just that you haven't known him for very long. Something about him doesn't feel right."

"Xavier . . ." I took his hand and pressed it against my cheek. "It's just one night."

"I know, Beth," he said. "And I want you to have the full prom experience; I just wish it was another guy . . . *any* other guy."

"It doesn't matter who I go with, I'll still be thinking of you the whole time," I said.

"That's good, try and sweet-talk me into this," Xavier said, but he was smiling now. "If you're sure about Jake, then go with him. Just don't act as if he's me."

"As if anyone could measure up to you."

He leaned down to kiss me, and as usual, one kiss wasn't enough. We fell back onto the couch, my hands running through his hair, his arms locked around my waist, our bodies pressed together. At the same moment we both caught sight of his plastered ankle sticking up at a strange angle and burst into laughter.

25

Substitute

"EXCELLENT!" said Jake when I told him the news. "We're going to make a stunning couple."

"Mmm." I nodded.

There was still a nagging doubt at the back of my mind, a feeling of foreboding that caused a slight shiver to run down my spine. When I was lying safe in Xavier's arms, the idea hadn't seemed so bad, but in the cold light of day I was beginning to regret my decision. I couldn't explain my uneasiness, so I chose to ignore it. Besides, I couldn't back out now and disappoint Jake.

"You won't regret this," he said in a silky voice, as if reading my thoughts. "I'll show you a good time. Shall I pick you up at seven?"

I hesitated a moment before answering. "Make it seven thirty."

MOLLY'S jaw dropped in disbelief when she heard about the change of plans.

"What is it with you?" she said, throwing her hands up in

exasperation. "You're just a magnet for the hottest guys in school. I can't believe you were going to turn him down."

"He's not Xavier," I said sulkily. "It won't be the same."

I knew I was starting to sound like a broken record, but my disappointment was overwhelming.

"But Jake's not a bad substitute!"

I gave Molly a stern look and she sighed.

"I suppose he'll just have to do," she amended. "You'll have to suffer in silence with your male model . . . I feel for you."

"Oh, stop it, Molly."

"Seriously, Beth, Jake's a great guy. Half the girls at school have fallen in love with him. He's giving Xavier a run for his money."

I snorted.

"All right, I know no one can measure up to Xavier Woods in your eyes, but he'd be upset if he thought you weren't going to enjoy yourself."

I didn't try to argue with that.

Knowing that prom fever would hit and hardly anyone in the senior year would turn up for classes, the school had given us Friday afternoon off to get ready. Naturally, nobody could focus on work during the morning and most of the teachers didn't even bother trying to be heard over the excited chatter that flew around the classrooms.

Molly and her friends had been busy the previous night and showed up at school looking like toasted almonds from their spray tans. They had French manicures and fresh highlights in their hair. Taylah's hair, which couldn't possibly get any blonder, was starting to look a little talcum powder white.

When the bell rang at eleven o'clock, Molly grabbed my wrist and hauled me out of the classroom. Her pace didn't slow, nor did she release me until we were safely strapped into the backseat of Taylah's car. I could tell from the expressions on their faces that they meant business.

"First stop, makeup," Molly said in her best commando voice. She stuck her head between the two front seats. "Let's roll!"

We drove down to Main Street and pulled up in front of Swan Aesthetics, one of the two local beauticians. The shop smelled of vanilla, and mirrors lined the walls along with displays of the latest beauty products. The owners had opted for a bohemian, back-to-nature feel, and there were beads hanging from the doorways, incense burning in little jeweled holders, and the calming sounds of a rain forest filtered from hidden speakers. In the waiting room were bright floor cushions and bowls filled with potpourri. Herbal teas were available from urns set on a low table.

The girls who greeted us didn't look at all in touch with the natural world, with their platinum blond hair, tight T-shirts, and theatrical makeup. Molly seemed to be on very friendly terms with them, and they embraced her warmly when we went in. She introduced them as Melinda and Mara.

"Tonight's the night!" they crooned. "Are you pumped or what? Okay, girls, let's get started so the makeup will have a chance to settle."

They seated us in high swivel chairs facing a wall of mirrors. I hoped their own makeup wasn't an indication of how we'd look once they were through with us.

"I want a baby-doll look," purred Taylah. "Sparkly eye shadow, pale pink lips . . ."

"I want classic sixties Catwoman. Lots of eyeliner and definitely fake lashes," Hayley announced.

"I want to look soft and smoky," said Molly.

"I just want to look like I'm not wearing makeup," I said when it came to my turn.

"Believe me, you don't need any," said Melinda, studying my skin.

I listened, trying not to wriggle in my seat, as the girls explained the beauty treatments for the afternoon. To me, it didn't even sound as though they were speaking English.

"First, we'll just strip your skin of any impurities, using an herbal mask and mild exfoliant," explained Mara. "Then pop on a layer of primer, use a formula-one ivory concealer stick to get rid of any spots or blemishes, and then apply base foundation with either a yellow or pink tone to match your own coloring. Then we'll talk blush, eyeshadow, lashes, and gloss!"

"You don't seem to have any blemishes or uneven skin tone," Melinda said to me. "What products are you using?"

"None really," I said. "I usually just wash my face at night."

Melinda rolled her eyes.

"Top secret, is it?"

"No, really, I don't use skin-care products."

"Whatever, suit yourself."

"It's true, Mel," said Molly. "Beth's family probably doesn't even believe in beauty products. They're kind of like the Amish."

"I guess reading the Good Book works miracles on your skin," muttered Melinda.

ALTHOUGH Melinda didn't seem to warm to me, I had to admit she knew what she was doing when it came to makeup. When she showed me the finished result in the mirror, I was rendered speechless. For the first time there was color in my face and my cheeks glowed a pale rosy pink. My lips looked full and red, if a little too glossy. My eyes were huge and bright, framed by long delicate lashes, the lids dusted with a fine silver shimmer and the rims outlined by a thin black line. I looked so glamorous I almost didn't recognize myself. The best part was that I still looked like me. Molly and the others had such thick layers of powder and bronzer, they might have been wearing masks.

From Swan Aesthetics the others went straight to the hairdresser, but I decided to go home and let Ivy deal with the issue of my hair. I was already weary from the first ordeal and didn't think I could sit through any more grooming rituals. Besides, there was no one I trusted more than Ivy to get it right.

By the time I got home, Gabriel and Ivy were already dressed and ready. Gabriel was sitting at the kitchen table wearing a tux. His blond hair was slicked back, making him look like a cross between dreamy Hollywood actor and eighteenth-century gentleman. Ivy was standing at the sink washing up in a long, emerald-colored gown. Her flowing hair was loosely coiled in a knot at the nape of her neck. It was incongruous to see her looking more like a mirage than a human being, and wearing a pair of pink rubber gloves. It just went to show how little she cared about physical beauty. She waved at me when I came in, still holding her sponge.

"You look beautiful," she said. "Shall we go upstairs and get that hair done?"

Ivy helped me into my gown first, smoothing and arranging the fabric so that it sat perfectly. In the dress I resembled a column of shimmering moonlight. My delicate silver slippers peeped out from beneath spools of fabric. My delight showed on my face.

"I'm glad you like it." My sister beamed. "I know things haven't gone exactly as you might have liked for tonight. But I still want you to look dazzling and have the time of your life."

"You're the best sister anyone could hope for," I said and hugged her.

"Well, let's not be hasty." She laughed. "First, we'd better see what I can do with your hair."

"Nothing complicated," I said as she began to free it and shake it loose. "I just want it to . . . reflect me."

"Don't worry." She patted my head reassuringly. "I know exactly what you mean."

It didn't take Ivy's nimble fingers long to fashion my hair perfectly. It fell in natural waves, and she took two sections from the sides and wound them into braids that joined across the top of my head like a band. The rest she allowed to fall gently down my back. She laced the braids with a string of tiny pearls that complemented my dress wonderfully.

"It's perfect," I said. "I don't know what I would have done without you."

At six o'clock Xavier arrived to see me in my dress so we could pretend, at least for a little while, that our perfect evening hadn't been ruined by one ill-timed tackle. I heard him downstairs chatting to Gabriel and instantly felt an armada of butterflies spring up in my stomach. I didn't know why I was so nervous when being around Xavier usually felt as easy as breathing. I suppose I just wanted to impress him, to reassure myself that he loved me by the look on his face when I came down the stairs.

Ivy squirted me with an atomizer, took my hand, and walked with me to the top of the stairs.

"Will you go first?" I asked, swallowing apprehensively.

"Of course," she smiled. "But I don't think it's me he wants to see."

I watched Ivy descend gracefully and wondered why I had asked her to go first. Nobody could look elegant next to her—it was an impossible task, and I might as well have conceded defeat immediately. I heard Xavier applaud softly and make complimentary remarks. I knew that Gabriel would have been waiting at the bottom to take her arm. Now it was my turn and my family waited expectantly at the foot of the stairs.

"Coming down, Bethany?" I heard Gabriel ask.

I drew a deep breath and began my shaky descent. What if Xavier didn't like the dress? What if I stumbled? What if he saw me and realized that I didn't measure up to the girl he had created in his mind? The thoughts rushed through my brain like small bolts of lightning, but as soon as I rounded the curve in the stairs and saw Xavier standing below, all of my worries and inhibitions slipped away like flour in the wind. His face was turned upward, alight with anticipation. His eyes widened into two vivid pools when he saw me, and his mouth opened slightly in surprise. He was resting against the banister, his left ankle in a brace. He looked dazed, and I wondered if it was me that inspired such a reaction, or just the concussion.

When I reached the bottom, he took my hand and helped me down the last step, never once taking his eyes off me. They traveled over the contours of my face and body, drinking everything in.

"What do you think?" I asked, biting my lip hesitantly.

Xavier opened his mouth, shook his head, and closed it again. His blue eyes gazed at me with an expression even I couldn't translate.

Ivy laughed. "Xavier, you're a man of few words."

"I think it's more that words have failed me," Xavier said, seeming to recover somewhat. The corner of his mouth crept up in his familiar half-smile. "They'd only be an understatement. Beth, you look incredible."

"Thanks," I murmured. "You don't have to say that."

"No, really," he said. "I can hardly believe that you're real.

I feel like you might disappear if I close my eyes. I wish I could be there with you tonight just to see everyone's face when you walk through the door."

"Don't be silly," I scolded. "Everyone is going to look amazing."

"Beth, have you seen yourself?" Xavier said. "You're radiating light. I've never seen anyone look more like . . . well, like an angel."

I blushed as he gently fastened a corsage of tiny white rosebuds around my wrist. I wanted to wrap my arms around his waist, wind my fingers into his schoolboy hair, trace the smooth skin of his face, and kiss his perfect, full lips. But I didn't want to ruin Ivy's careful work, so instead I leaned forward gingerly and gave him a single kiss.

I felt as though Xavier and I had barely spoken two words to each other when there came a knock at the front door. Gabriel went to answer it and came back with Jake Thorn at his elbow.

I wasn't sure if I was imagining it, but Gabriel, who had seemed perfectly at ease a moment before, now seemed to be standing straighter. His jaw was clenched, and I could see the veins in his neck throb. Ivy, too, seemed to stiffen when she saw Jake, and her rain gray eyes took on a rare glazed look that meant she was alarmed by something.

Their reactions were disturbing and brought my own doubts about Jake flooding back. I caught Xavier's eye. Something in his expression told me that the feeling of uneasiness was mutual.

Gabriel placed a hand heavily on my shoulder as he disappeared into the kitchen to get drinks. My siblings were usually wary of strangers; they'd warmed to Xavier and Molly but nobody else. Still, their guardedness toward Jake made me uncomfortable. What could they sense? What had he done in his lifetime to cause angels to flinch at his presence? I knew Ivy and Gabriel would never ruin the night by making a scene, and so I tried to dismiss silly notions from my head and enjoy the evening as best I could. Sensing I was on edge, Xavier stood close to my side, his warm palm pressed against the small of my back in a gesture of support.

Jake, on the other hand, seemed completely unaware of the effect he'd had on us. He wasn't wearing a tux as I'd expected but fitted black pants and a leather aviator jacket. Trust him, I thought, to choose the unconventional option. It was dramatic though, which was probably why he liked it.

"Good evening all," Jake said and strolled over to me. "Hello, baby, you look great."

"Hi, Jake."

I stepped forward to greet him, and he took my hand, bringing it to his lips. I saw a flicker of something close to anger cross Xavier's face, but in the next moment it was gone and he stepped forward to shake Jake's hand.

"Nice to meet you," he said, but there was a hard edge to his voice.

"Likewise," Jake replied. "This introduction has been a long time coming."

Unlike Xavier, Phantom made no effort to be sociable. He sank down on his haunches and gave a guttural growl.

"Hello, boy," said Jake bending, and proffering his hand.

Phantom sprang up, barking furiously and snapping his teeth. Jake withdrew his hand, and Ivy hauled a reluctant Phantom out of the room by his collar.

"I'm sorry," I said to Jake. "He's not usually like this."

"Don't worry about it," he replied, and withdrew a small box from his jacket. "This is for you. I think corsages are a little passé."

Xavier scowled but refrained from comment.

"Oh, thank you, but you shouldn't have," I said, taking the box.

Inside was a pair of fine white-gold hoop earrings. I was a little embarrassed by how expensive they looked.

"It's nothing," said Jake, "just a thought."

Xavier chose this moment to intervene. "Thanks for taking care of Beth tonight," he cut in with a pleasant voice. "As you can see, I'm a little indisposed."

"It's my pleasure to help Bethany out," Jake replied. As usual, his voice came out sounding affected and a little pretentious. "Sorry to hear about your accident. What a shame for it to happen just before the night of the prom. But don't worry; I'll make sure Bethany has a good time. It's the least a *friend* can do."

"Well, as her *boyfriend*, I would have liked to be there," Xavier said. "But I'll make it up to her somehow."

Now it was Jake's turn to scowl. Xavier turned his back on him and took my face in his hands, planting a soft kiss on my cheek before wrapping my silver shawl around me.

"Are you all set?" he asked.

In truth, all I wanted to do was stay home and curl up on the sofa with Xavier and completely forget about the prom. I wanted to take off my dress, put on sweatpants, and snuggle up to him where I felt safe. I didn't want to leave the house, and I certainly didn't want to leave on the arm of another boy. But I didn't tell him any of that; I just forced a smile and nodded.

"Take care of her," Xavier said to Jake. His face was friendly, but there was a note of warning in his voice.

"I won't let her out of my sight."

Jake offered me his arm, and we stepped out into the street where a limousine was waiting for us. I saw from Gabriel's expression that he thought it was excessive. Before I left, Ivy leaned down to fiddle with the strap of my dress. "We'll be close by all night if you need us," she whispered. I thought she was being a touch overdramatic. What could possibly go wrong in a ballroom filled with hundreds of guests? Still, her words were comforting.

The limousine looked like an alien spaceship with its sleek, elongated body and tinted windows. I found it vulgar rather than glamorous.

Inside, it was even more spacious than I'd imagined. A modular couch in white leather stretched around its walls. The lighting was purple and blue and came from halogen lights that studded the ceiling. To the right was a bar built into the wall, and blue lava lamps illuminated the rows of glasses and the bottles of liquor that had been brought along by the underage partygoers. A television screen formed part of one wall with speakers in the roof. A song about girls just wanting to have fun was blaring, and it made the whole interior vibrate. The limo was almost full when we climbed in as we were the last to be picked up. Molly's face split into a huge smile when she saw me, and she blew me kisses from the opposite end of the car in lieu of an embrace. A few of the other girls looked me up and down, and their smiles froze on their lips.

"Terrible affliction, jealousy," Jake whispered in my ear. "You're the most stunning by a mile. I'd say prom queen is in the bag."

"That doesn't mean anything to me. Besides, you haven't seen the rest of the competition."

"I don't need to," Jake replied. "I'm putting all my money on you."

26

Prom

THE prom was being held at the Pavilion Tennis Club. With its sweeping grounds and various function rooms overlooking the bay, it was indisputably the finest reception center in the area.

The limousine glided past its high bluestone fence and through the cast-iron gates onto a winding gravel driveway lined by manicured lawns and hedges. Stone fountains dotted the garden; one of them was in the shape of a majestic lion with one paw raised as if in attack, an arc of water cascading from each of its claws. There was even a small lake with a bridge and a gazebo, which looked better suited to an ancient castle somewhere in Europe rather than in a town as casual as Venus Cove. I couldn't help being overwhelmed by the lavishness. Jake, on the other hand, seemed unimpressed. He maintained his perpetually bored expression, his mouth twisting into a smirk whenever our eyes met.

As the limousine continued up the sweeping driveway we passed tennis courts that glowed like green pools under the lights and headed toward the pavilion itself: a large, circular glass building with a pitched roof and wide white balconies stretching around it. There was a steady stream of couples heading inside, the boys standing erect and the girls clutching their purses and constantly adjusting their straps. Although the boys looked dashing in their tuxedoes, they were only really there as escorts; the night clearly belonged to the girls, every face I saw wore the same expression of anticipation.

Some groups had arrived in limos and chauffeur-driven cars, while others had opted for the double-decker party bus, which now pulled in carrying its jubilant passengers. I noticed that the bus's interior had been redecorated to look like a nightclub, complete with strobe lights and booming music.

For this evening at least, feminist philosophy had been abandoned, and the girls, like fairy-tale princesses, allowed themselves to be led up the flight of steps and into the foyer. On my right, Molly was too engrossed in her surroundings to bother making conversation with Ryan Robertson, who admittedly, did look handsome in a suit. On my left, Taylah was taking hundreds of photographs, eager to make sure she recorded even the most minor details. She kept sneaking glances at Jake when she thought I wasn't looking. He caught her eye and rewarded her with a wink. Taylah's cheeks flamed so red I thought it was a wonder her makeup didn't melt right off.

Dr. Chester, Bryce Hamilton's principal, stood just inside the foyer, wearing a pale gray suit, surrounded by flower arrangements on pedestals. Other members of the staff had positioned themselves strategically in order to see the young couples as they made their entrance. I noticed a few beads of perspiration gathering on Dr. Chester's domed forehead, the only indication of stress. His smile might be wide, but his eyes said that he wanted to be at home in his favorite armchair rather than supervising a group of indulged seniors determined to make this the most memorable night of their lives.

Jake and I joined the line of glamorous couples waiting to make their entrance. Molly and Ryan were ahead of us, and I watched them closely to determine the protocol so I didn't slip up.

"Dr. Chester, my partner, Molly Amelia Harrison," said Ryan in a formal voice. It sounded odd coming from a boy who usually amused himself and his friends by drawing giant genitals on the asphalt outside the school entrance. I knew Molly had instructed him to be on his best behavior for the night.

Dr. Chester smiled benevolently, shook his hand, and ushered the couple inside.

We were next. Jake laced my arm through his. "Dr. Chester, my partner, Bethany Rose Church," he said gallantly, as though presenting me at an imperial court.

Dr. Chester gave me a warm smile of approval.

"How do you know my middle name?" I asked him once we were inside.

"Haven't I mentioned that I'm psychic?" Jake replied.

We followed the wave of people into the ballroom, which was more lavish than I had imagined. The walls were glass from floor to ceiling, the lush carpet was a deep burgundy, and the parquet dance floor gleamed under the crystal chandeliers, which threw off little crescents of light. Through the glass walls I could see an undulating expanse of ocean and a small pillar of white resembling a salt and pepper shaker. It took me a moment to identify it as the lighthouse. Tables were set up around the room, covered in white linen and set with fine china. The table centerpieces were bunches of pale pink and yellow rosebuds, and silver sequins were scattered across the tablecloths. At the back of the room, the band was tuning their instruments. Waiters bustled around us, carrying trays of nonalcoholic punch.

I spotted Gabriel and Ivy alone on the fringe of the action, looking so unearthly it almost hurt to gaze at them. Gabriel's expression was unreadable, but I could tell that he wasn't enjoying the evening. Students stared at Ivy in awed silence as they passed, but no one had the nerve to approach her. I saw Gabriel's eyes sweep across the room until he found Jake Thorn. His laser gaze watched him with penetrating intensity for a few seconds before he turned away.

"You're at our table!" Molly cried, hugging me from behind. "Let's go sit down, my shoes are already killing me." She caught sight of Gabriel. "On second thought, I'd better go and say hello to your brother first . . . don't want to seem rude!"

We left Jake to find our seats and headed over to my brother. Gabriel had his hands clasped behind his back and was wearing a grim expression as he surveyed the scene.

"Hi!" said Molly, tottering up to him in her strappy shoes with pencil-thin heels.

"Good evening, Molly," replied Gabriel. "You're looking fetching tonight."

Molly glanced at me uncertainly.

"He means you look good," I whispered, and her face brightened.

"Oh . . . thanks!" she said. "You look very *fetching* too. Having fun?"

"Fun may not be the most accurate description," Gabriel said. "I've never much liked social events."

"Oh, I know what you mean," said Molly. "The ball part is always a bit boring. Things really kick off at the after-party. Are you coming?" Gabriel's stone face seemed to soften for a moment, and the corners of his mouth twitched in the beginning of a smile. But in a matter of seconds he recollected himself and the smile was gone.

"As a teacher I'm afraid it's my duty to pretend I didn't hear anything about an after-party," said Gabriel. "Dr. Chester has made his thoughts on the subject very clear."

"Yeah, well, there's not much the doc can do about it, is there?" Molly laughed.

"Who's your partner?" Gabriel changed the subject. "I don't believe I've met him."

"His name's Ryan. He's sitting over there."

Molly pointed to where Ryan and his friend were arm wrestling on the carefully set table. One of them knocked over a glass and sent it rolling across the floor. Gabriel eyed the two boys censoriously.

Molly's face flushed with embarrassment, and she looked away. "He's a bit immature sometimes, but he's a good guy. Well, I better get back before he destroys something valuable and we get thrown out! I'll see you later though. I've saved you a dance."

I almost had to steer Molly back to our table, and she kept

looking back at Gabriel in unashamed rapture. Ryan seemed not to notice.

I soon realized that despite the magical surroundings, I wasn't enjoying myself either. My conversations with people were trifling, and several times I caught myself looking around for a clock. I started wondering whether I could legitimately excuse myself long enough to phone Xavier. But even if I borrowed Molly's cell, there was nowhere private to call from. Teachers were stationed at the front doors to prevent anyone escaping into the gardens, and the bathrooms would be full of girls touching up their makeup.

The night seemed lackluster after all the buildup. It wasn't Jake's fault. I could see that he was trying. He was an attentive escort, and when he wasn't asking me whether I was enjoying myself, he was cracking jokes and exchanging anecdotes with the others at our table. But as I looked around at the girls picking daintily at their food and brushing imaginary lint off their dresses, I couldn't help thinking that there seemed little purpose to the event apart from sitting there looking pretty. Once everybody had given one another the once-over, there wasn't much left to do.

Even when he was conversing with the others, Jake's eyes rarely left my face. He seemed intent on following my every move. Sometimes he tried to draw me into the conversation by asking pointed questions, but I answered mostly in monosyllables and kept looking at my hands. I didn't want to spoil the night for anyone or appear sulky, but my thoughts kept creeping back to Xavier. I found myself wondering what he was doing, imagining how the night would be if he were here by my side. I was in the right place, wearing the right dress, but with the wrong boy, and I couldn't help but feel a little melancholy about it.

"What's the matter, princess?" Jake asked when he caught me staring longingly out at the ocean.

"Nothing," I answered quickly. "I'm having a lovely time."

"Filthy lies," he joked. "Shall we play a game?"

"If you like."

"All right . . . how would you describe me in one word?"

"Driven?" I suggested.

"Wrong. Driven is the last thing I am. Fun fact: I never do my homework. What else makes me unique?"

"Your hair gel? Your suave nature? Your six toes?"

"Now that was uncalled for. I had number six removed years ago." He flashed a smile. "Now describe yourself in one word."

"Oh . . ." I hesitated. "I don't really know . . . that's difficult."

"Good," he said. "I'd never like a girl who could sum herself up in one word. There's no complexity in that. And without complexity, there's no intensity."

"You like intensity?" I asked. "Molly says all guys want a girl who's chill."

"Chill just means easy to get into bed," Jake replied. "But I suppose there's nothing wrong with that."

"Isn't that the opposite of intense?" I said. "Make up your mind!"

"A game of chess can be intense."

"Er . . . yes, it can. Perhaps the idea of girls and chess pieces is interchangeable for you?"

"Never," Jake said. "Have you ever broken a heart?"

"No," I replied. "And I never want to. Have you?"

"Many but never without good reason."

"What sort of reasons?"

"They weren't right for me."

"I hope you ended it in person," I said. "And not over the phone or anything like that."

"What do you take me for?" Jake said. "They deserved that much. That little shred of dignity was all they had left in the end."

"What do you mean by that?" I asked curiously.

"Let's just say that you love and you lose," he replied.

We sat through a tedious speech by Dr. Chester about how this was our "special night" and how we were all expected to behave responsibly and not do anything to tarnish Bryce Hamilton's reputation. Dr. Chester said he trusted we were all going to go straight home when the prom ended. There were a few sniggers from the audience at this, which the principal chose to ignore. He reminded us instead that he had sent letters home discouraging after-parties and advising parents to think twice before offering their homes as a venue.

What Dr. Chester didn't know was that the after-party had been planned months ago, and the organizers hadn't been naïve enough to think they could get away with holding it at somebody's house with their parents just upstairs. It was going to be held at an old, abandoned factory just out of town. The father of one of the seniors was an architect who'd been working on converting the space into apartments. He'd encountered some objections from local environment groups, and the project was temporarily on hold while waiting for permits to be approved. The factory was spacious, dark and, most of all, secluded. Nobody would think to look for the after-party there. No matter how loud the music, there would be nobody to complain because there were no residential streets nearby. Somebody knew a professional DJ who had offered his services free for the night. The kids could hardly wait for the prom to finish so the "real party" could start, but I knew I'd never contemplate going, even if Xavier had been there with me. I'd been to one party in my human life, and that was enough.

Dinner followed the speeches, and when we'd finished eating, we lined up on a raised platform to have our photos taken for the school magazine. Most couples adopted a standard pose, arm around the other's waist, the girls smiling demurely, the boys standing rigid, terrified of making a wrong move and ruining the photo—a crime for which they knew they'd never be forgiven.

I should have known that Jake would do something different. When it was our turn, he dropped to one knee, plucked a rose from the table arrangement and clenched it between his teeth.

"Smile, princess," he whispered in my ear.

The photographer, who had been clicking mechanically, brightened when she saw him, grateful for the variation. As we stepped down from the dais, I saw other girls glaring pointedly at their partners. Their eyes said, "Why can't you be more like that romantic Jake Thorn?" I felt sorry for the boy who did try to mimic Jake's gesture and ended up pricking his lip on the rose's thorns. He was led away to the restroom by his lobster-faced date.

After the photos, a dessert of wobbling crème caramel arrived. This was followed by an interlude of dancing, and finally we were called back to our seats for the announcement of the awards. We watched as the prom committee, including Molly and Taylah, climbed onto the dais, carrying envelopes and trophies.

"It is our pleasure," began a girl named Bella, "to announce this year's award winners for the Bryce Hamilton Prom. We have put a lot of thought and effort into these decisions and before we start we want you to know that you're all winners inside!"

I heard Jake suppress a snort of laughter.

"We've added more categories to the list this year in rec- ognition of the effort you've all made tonight," the girl went on. "Let's start with the award for Best Hair."

It seemed to me that the world had gone mad. I returned Jake's look of dismay as we sat through awards for Best Hair, Best Gown, Most Transformed, Best Tie, Best Shoes, Best Makeup, Most Glamorous, and Most Natural Beauty. Finally, the minor awards were over, and it was time for the announce- ment that everybody had been waiting for: the winners of Prom King and Queen. Excited whispers flew around the room. This was the award most hotly contested. Every girl in the audience was holding her breath and the boys were pretending not to look interested. I wasn't sure what all the fuss was about. It wasn't exactly something to include on their résumés.

"And this year's winners are . . . ," began the speaker. She paused for dramatic effect and the audience groaned in frustration. "Bethany Church and Jake Thorn!"

The room burst into wild applause, and for a split second I scanned the crowd for the winners until I realized it was my name that had been called. I maintained my stony expression as I walked up onto the dais with Jake, although his disgust seemed to have morphed into amusement. Everything felt wrong as Molly placed the crown on my head and presented me with my sash. Jake, on the other hand, seemed to be enjoying the attention. We had to lead the crowd in a waltz, so I gave Jake my hand and he slipped his arm around my waist. Even though I'd practiced waltzing with Xavier, I didn't feel so confident now that he wasn't with me. Luckily angels have the advantage of catching on to things relatively easily. I followed Jake's lead, and soon the rhythm of the dance was bolstered in my mind. My limbs moved like water, and I was surprised to find that Jake was just as graceful.

Ivy and Gabriel passed by us, their bodies moving in sync, flowing like silk. Their feet hardly touched the floor, and they looked as if they were floating. Even with their somber expressions, they were so entrancing to watch that people stopped and stared, giving them a wide berth on the dance floor. My siblings soon got tired of being the entertainment for the evening and headed back to their table.

As the music changed tempo, Jake whirled me to the edge

of the dance floor. He leaned forward so that his lips brushed against my ear.

"You're dazzling."

"So are you." I laughed, trying to keep the mood light. "All the girls think so."

"Do *you* think so?"

"Well . . . I think you're very charming."

"Charming," he mused. "I suppose that'll do for now. You know, I've never met a girl with a face like yours. Your skin is the color of moonlight; your eyes are fathomless."

"Now you're just overdoing it," I teased. I could sense him about to launch into one of his tirades and wanted to prevent it at all costs.

"You're not good at accepting compliments, are you?" he said.

I blushed. "Not really. I never know what to say."

"How about a simple thank-you?"

"Thanks, Jake."

"That wasn't so hard. Now, I could use some fresh air. What about you?"

"It's a bit hard to get out," I said, nodding in the direction of the teachers standing guard at the exits.

"I've sussed out an escape route. Come on, I'll show you."

Jake's escape route was via a back door that had somehow been overlooked. It was past the restrooms and through a storeroom at the rear of the building. He helped me over the buckets and mops stacked against the walls, and suddenly I found myself alone with him on the balcony that wound around the whole exterior of the pavilion. It was a clear night, the sky was scattered with stars, and the breeze was cool on my skin. Through the windows we could see couples still dancing, the girls a little wilted now and appreciatively allowing their weight to be supported by their partners. At some distance from the others stood Gabriel and Ivy, shimmering as if they'd been sprinkled with stardust.

"So many stars," Jake murmured, so softly he might have been speaking to himself, "but none as beautiful as you."

He was so close that I could feel his breath on my cheek. I lowered my eyes, wishing he would stop offering me compliments. I tried deflecting the focus onto him.

"I wish I was as sure of myself as you are. Nothing seems to faze you."

"Why would it?" he replied. "Life's a game—and I happen to know how to play."

"Even you must make mistakes sometimes."

"That's exactly the sort of attitude that stops people from winning," he said.

"Everyone loses at some point; but we can learn from loss."

"Who told you that?" Jake shook his head, his emerald eyes boring into mine. "I don't like to lose and I always get what I want."

"So right now do you have everything you want?"

"Not quite," he replied. "One thing is missing."

"And what's that?" I asked warily. Something told me I was treading on dangerous ground.

"You," he said simply.

I didn't know how to respond. I didn't appreciate the new

turn the conversation was taking. "Well, that's flattering, Jake, but you know I'm not available."

"That's irrelevant."

"Not to me!" I took a step back. "I'm in love with Xavier."

Jake regarded me coolly. "Isn't it obvious to you that you're with the wrong person?"

"No, it's not," I retorted. "I suppose you're arrogant enough to think you're the right person?"

"I just think I deserve a chance."

"You promised not to bring this up again," I said. "You and I are friends, and you ought to value that."

"Oh, I do, but it's not enough for me."

"That's not for you to decide! I'm not a toy that you can just point your finger at and have."

"I disagree."

He sprang lightly forward, grabbing my shoulders, and pulled me toward him. He pressed our bodies together and his lips sought mine. I averted my face in protest, but he brought one hand up to force me to look at him and crushed his lips against mine. Something flashed in the sky, though there'd been no sign of rain. His kiss was hard and forceful, and his hands held my body in an iron grip. I struggled, pushing against his chest, and finally broke the contact between us.

"What do you think you're doing?" I shouted, my anger fomenting now.

"Giving us what we both want," he replied.

"I don't want this," I cried. "What have I done to make you think I wanted this?"

"I know you, Bethany Church. You're no mouse," Jake snarled. "I've seen the way you look at me, and I've felt the connection between us."

"There is no connection," I stressed. "Not with you. I'm sorry if you've been misled."

His eyes flashed dangerously. "Are you honestly turning me down?" he asked.

"I honestly am," I said. "I'm with Xavier. I've been trying to tell you that. It's not my fault you've chosen not to believe me."

Jake took a step toward me, his face dark with anger. "Are you quite sure you know what you're doing?"

"I've never been more sure about anything," I said coldly. "You and I can only ever be friends, Jake."

He let out a throaty laugh. "No, thank you," he announced. "Not interested."

"Can't you at least try to be mature about this?" I said.

"I don't think you understand, Beth. We're meant to be together. I've waited for you all my life."

"What do you mean?"

"I've been looking for you for centuries. I'd almost given up hope."

I felt a strange coldness grip my chest. What was he talking about?

"Never, in my wildest dreams, did I imagine that you would be . . . *one of them.* I struggled against it at first, but it was no use—our destiny is written in the stars."

"You've got the wrong idea," I said. "We have no destiny together."

"Do you know what it's like to wander the earth aimlessly in search of someone who could be anywhere? I'm not about to walk away from it now."

"Well, maybe you don't have a choice."

"I'm going to give you one more chance," he said in a low voice. "I don't think you realize this, but you're making a terrible mistake—one that will cost you dearly."

"I don't respond to threats," I said haughtily.

"Very well." Jake's whole face clouded over and he took a step away, his body giving a violent shudder as though he was enraged by the very sight of me. "I'm done making nice with the angels."

{ 27 }

Playing with Fire

IN the next moment Jake spun around and disappeared the way we'd come. I stood fixed to the spot, a chill permeating my body. I wondered if I could have misheard the threat in his parting words. But I knew I hadn't. I suddenly felt like the night was pressing down on me, suffocating me. There were two things I was now certain of: First, Jake Thorn knew about us; and second, he was dangerous. I realized I had been completely blind not to see it before. I had so badly wanted to see the good in him that I'd ignored the blatant warning signs that screamed at me to retreat. Now those signs were flashing as bright as neon lights.

Someone grabbed my elbow and I gasped. I was relieved to find it was just Molly.

"What's going on?" she demanded. "We could see you through the window! Are you with Jake now? Did you and Xavier have a fight or something?"

"No," I spluttered, "I'm not with Jake, of course not! He just . . . I don't know what happened . . . I have to go home."

"What? Why? You can't just leave. What about the after-party?" Molly said, but I had already started running.

I found Gabriel and Ivy seated at the teachers' table and pulled them away. "We have to leave," I said, tugging at Gabe's sleeve.

I wasn't sure if he already knew what had happened or if he just sensed the urgency in my voice, but he didn't ask any questions. He and Ivy silently collected their belongings and led me out of the pavilion and into the Jeep. They listened wordlessly on the trip home as I explained what had happened with Jake and repeated his parting words.

"I can't believe I've been so stupid," I moaned, putting my head in my hands. "I should have noticed . . . I should have realized."

"This is not your fault, Bethany," said Ivy.

"What's the matter with me?" I replied. "Why didn't I feel it? You felt something was wrong, didn't you? You knew it as soon as he set foot in our house."

"We felt a dark energy," Gabe admitted.

"Why didn't you say something?" I asked. "Why didn't you stop me from going with him?"

"We couldn't be sure," Gabriel said. "His mind was very guarded; it was nearly impossible to glean any information. It might have been nothing, and we didn't want to worry you for no reason."

"Troubled humans can also have dark auras," Ivy added. "The result of any number of things, tragedy, grief, pain. . . ."

"And evil intentions," I added.

"Those too," admitted Gabriel. "We didn't want to jump to conclusions, but if this boy knows what we are then there is every chance that he may be . . . well, stronger than your average human."

"How much stronger?"

"I don't know," Gabriel replied. "Unless . . . you don't think Xavier might have . . ." He trailed off.

I shot an angry glance in his direction.

"Xavier would never tell anyone our secret," I said. "I can't believe you'd even think that. You should know him by now."

"Okay. Say Xavier has nothing to do with this," said Gabriel. "There is something unnatural about Jake Thorn—I can feel it and so can you, Bethany."

"So what do we do now?" I asked.

"We have to bide our time," replied Gabriel. "These events will unfold naturally. We mustn't rush into anything. If he is truly dangerous, he will reveal himself in time."

When we got home, Ivy offered hot cocoa, but I declined. I went upstairs and took off my dress, feeling as though a great weight had just descended onto my shoulders. Things had been going so well, and now it seemed this one boy threatened to destroy it all. I tugged the pearls out of my hair and wiped off my makeup, feeling suddenly like nothing more than an imposter. It was too late to call Xavier, although I knew that speaking to him would make me feel better. Instead I put on my familiar pajamas and crawled into bed, clutching a stuffed toy Xavier had given me for comfort. I let the tears leak from my closed lids and soak into my pillow. I didn't feel angry or frightened anymore; I just felt sad. I wished so much that things could be straightforward and simple. Why was our mission fraught with so many complications? I knew it was childish, but all I could think was how unjust it all was. I was too weary not to allow myself to drift off to sleep, but I did so knowing that all too soon a storm was about to rage.

I didn't hear from Xavier all weekend. I assumed he hadn't heard about the incident at the prom, and I didn't want to stress him. I was so preoccupied worrying about Jake that I didn't even stop to wonder why Xavier hadn't called. We rarely went more than a few hours without talking.

On the other hand, I didn't have to wait long to hear from Jake Thorn. Monday morning at school when I opened my locker, a slip of paper fell out and drifted slowly to the ground, like a crinkled petal. I picked it up, expecting it to be a note from Xavier that would either make me sigh adoringly or giggle like a schoolgirl. But the handwriting didn't belong to Xavier; it was the same skillfully sharp calligraphy that I knew from my literature class. When I read what was written on the paper, I felt my blood freeze:

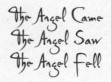

I showed the note to Gabriel, who read it and then crumpled it in frustration without speaking a word. I tried not to think about Jake for the rest of the day, but it wasn't an easy task. Xavier wasn't at school, and I desperately wanted to speak to him. It felt like an eternity since Friday, so much had happened.

The day passed in a gray haze. I came alive for about five

minutes during lunchtime when I borrowed Molly's cell phone to call Xavier, but I descended back into grayness as soon as it went to voice mail. Not having any contact with him made me feel lethargic and heavy. A cloud seemed to have filled my mind, and I couldn't catch any of the thoughts that skidded through my head because they disappeared too quickly.

At the end of the day, I went home with my brother and still hadn't heard anything from Xavier. I tried calling him again from home, but the sound of the voice mail only made me want to cry. I sat and waited all afternoon and all through dinner for him to call or for the doorbell to ring, but there was nothing. Didn't he want to know how the prom had gone? Had something happened to him? What was the reason behind his sudden silence? I didn't understand.

"I can't get through to Xavier," I managed to choke out over dinner. "He wasn't at school, and he won't answer my calls."

Ivy and Gabriel looked at each other.

"There's no need to panic, Bethany," said Ivy kindly. "There are plenty of reasons why he might not be answering his phone."

"What if he's unwell?"

"We would have sensed it," Gabriel reassured me.

I nodded and tried to swallow my dinner, but the food stuck like glue in my throat. I didn't want to speak to Ivy or Gabriel anymore; I just dragged myself up to bed feeling like the walls were closing in on me.

When I realized Xavier was absent from school the

following day, my eyes burned and I felt hot and dizzy. I wanted to crumple to the ground and just wait for someone to carry me away. I couldn't make it through another day without him; I could hardly make it through another minute. Where was he? What was he trying to do to me?

Molly saw me sagging against my locker. She walked up and put a hand gingerly on my shoulder.

"Bethie, are you okay, hon?"

"I need to speak to Xavier," I said. "But I can't get in touch with him."

Molly bit her lip. "I think there's something you need to see," she said softly.

"What?" I asked, panic edging into my voice. "Is Xavier okay?"

"He's fine," Molly said. "Just come with me."

She led me up to the third floor of the school and into one of the computer labs. It was a dull room with gray flecked carpet, no windows, and rows of computers, their blank screens staring at us. Molly flicked one on and pulled up a couple of chairs. She tapped her acrylic nails against the desk, humming in irritation. When the computer had finished loading, she clicked on an icon and rapidly typed something into the toolbar.

"What are you doing?" I asked and she turned to face me.

"You know how I told you about Facebook and how awesome it is?" she said.

I nodded blankly.

"Well, there are some parts that aren't so awesome."

"Like what?"

"Well . . . it's not very private, for one thing."

"What do you mean?" I asked.

I knew she was getting at something, but I couldn't figure out what, and judging from the look on her face, I wasn't sure I wanted to know. She was staring at me with a mixture of concern and dread. I knew Molly had a tendency to overreact so I tried not to panic. Her idea of disaster and mine were completely different.

Molly took a deep breath. "Okay . . . let me show you."

She tapped a key, and her Facebook page appeared on the screen. She read aloud the slogan that was written below the heading: "Facebook helps you connect and share with the people in your life. Except in this case, it was something we didn't really want to share," she said cryptically.

I was getting tired of the secrecy. "Just tell me what's happened. It can't be that bad."

"Okay, okay," she said. "Just be prepared." She clicked on a photo album titled "Prom Pics by Kristy Peters."

"Who's she?"

"Just a girl in our grade. She was taking photos all night."

"Wait, it says I'm tagged in this album," I said.

"That's right." Molly nodded. "You and . . . someone else."

Molly clicked on a thumbnail image, and I waited for the full-size picture to load on the screen. My heart thumped in my chest. Had Kristy somehow managed to capture my wings on camera? Or was it just a really unflattering photo that Molly had dubbed an "emergency." But when the picture flashed up on the screen, I realized that it wasn't either of those things. It was worse; much, much worse. A ripple of nausea washed through me and my vision tunneled so that all I could see were the two faces on the screen: mine and Jake Thorn's locked together in a kiss. I sat and stared for several long moments. Jake's hands were gripping my back, and my hands were on his shoulders, trying to push him away. I had my eyes closed in shock; but to anyone who hadn't been there to witness the full scene, it looked like I was lost in a moment of passion.

"We have to get rid of it," I cried, grabbing the mouse. "It has to go."

"We can't get rid of it," Molly said quietly.

"What do you mean?" I choked. "Can't we just delete it?"

"Only Kristy can delete it off her Facebook," Molly said. "We could un-tag you, but people will still see the picture on Kristy's page."

"But it has to go," I begged. "It has to go before Xavier sees it."

Molly looked at me sympathetically.

"Beth, sweetie, I think he's already seen it."

I ran out of the computer lab and right out of the school. I didn't know where Gabriel was, but I couldn't afford to wait for him. Xavier needed to hear the whole story and he needed to hear it right away.

His house wasn't far and I ran the whole way there, my faultless sense of direction guiding me. It was the middle of the day so Bernie and Peter were both at work, Claire was with her bridesmaids at a dress fitting, and the others were all at school. So when I rang the doorbell it was Xavier who answered. He was wearing a loose gray sweatshirt and a pair of sweatpants and hadn't shaved. He'd taken the brace off his ankle, but I could see he was still leaning on his right foot. His floppy hair was slightly ruffled, and his face looked as clear and beautiful as always, but there was something different in his eyes. Those familiar turquoise eyes that always seemed to sparkle for me now looked hostile.

Xavier didn't say anything when he saw me standing there; he just turned and walked away, leaving the front door open. I wasn't sure if he wanted me to follow him, but I did anyway. I found him in the kitchen, eating a bowl of cereal, even though it was almost lunchtime. He didn't look at me.

"I can explain," I said softly. "It's not what it looks like."

"Isn't it?" he asked in a low voice. "I think it's exactly what it looks like. What else could it be?"

"Xavier, please," I said, fighting back tears. "There's an explanation for this, just hear me out."

"You were trying to give him mouth to mouth?" Xavier asked sarcastically. "You were collecting saliva samples for research? He has a rare disease and that was his dying wish? Don't play with me, Beth; I'm not in the mood."

I ran over to him and took his hand, but he pulled it away. I felt sick; this wasn't the way things were supposed to be. What was happening? I couldn't stand the distance that I felt between us. Xavier seemed to have put up an invisible wall, a barrier. This cold, detached person was not the Xavier I knew.

"Jake kissed *me*," I said forcefully. "And that picture was taken a moment before I pushed him away."

"Very convenient," Xavier muttered. "How stupid do you

think I am? I may not be a messenger of God, but that doesn't make me a complete idiot."

"You can ask Molly," I cried. "Or Gabriel or Ivy—they'll tell you."

"I trusted you," Xavier said. "And it only took one night without me for you to move on to someone new."

"That's not true!"

"You could've at least had the decency to tell me this was over in person, instead of letting me find out from everyone else."

"It's not over." I choked. "Don't say that! Please . . ."

"Do you even realize how humiliating this is for me?" he said. "There's a photo of my girlfriend hooking up with some other guy while I was at home nursing a stupid concussion. All my friends have been calling to ask if I got dumped over the phone."

"I know," I said. "I know and I'm so sorry, but . . ."

"But what?"

"Well . . . you . . ."

"I'm an idiot, I know," Xavier cut in. "Letting you go to the prom with Jake. I guess I had too much faith in you. I won't make that mistake again."

"Why won't you listen?" I whispered. "Why are you so set on believing everyone but me?"

"I thought that we had something," Xavier said. He looked directly at me and I saw that his eyes were bright with unshed tears. He blinked them away angrily. "After everything we went through to be together, you just go and . . . Our relationship obviously didn't mean much to you."

I couldn't help myself and I burst into tears. My shoulders shook with each sob. I saw Xavier instinctively get up to comfort me, but then he thought better of it and stopped. His jaw was tight, as though it killed him to see me so upset and not do anything about it.

"Please," I cried. "I love you. I told Jake I loved you. I know I'm hard work but don't give up on me."

"I just need time alone," he said quietly. He wouldn't meet my gaze.

I ran from the kitchen and out of Xavier's house. I didn't stop running until I reached the beach, where I collapsed on the sand and sobbed myself into stillness. I felt like something inside me was broken, like I had literally shattered and nothing could make me whole again. I loved Xavier so much it hurt, and yet he had turned away from me. I didn't try to console myself; I just let myself ache. I don't know how long I lay there, but eventually I became aware of the tide lapping at my feet. I didn't care; I hoped it would sweep me away, toss me around, force me under the water, and pound the strength from my body and the thoughts from my head. The wind howled, the tide crept closer, and still I didn't move. Was this Our Father's way of punishing me? Had my crime been so severe that this was what I deserved: to experience love and then have it ripped away, like stitches out of a wound? Did Xavier still love me? Did he hate me? Or had he just lost all faith in me?

The water was lapping around my waist by the time Ivy and Gabriel found me. I was shivering, but I hardly noticed. I didn't move or speak, not even when Gabriel lifted me out of the water and carried me back to our house. Ivy helped me into the shower, and came to help me out half an hour later when I'd forgotten where I was and just stood under the pounding water. Gabriel brought me some dinner, but I couldn't eat it. I sat on my bed, staring into space and doing nothing but thinking of Xavier and trying not to think of him at the same time. The separation made me realize just how safe I felt with him. I craved his touch, his smell, even the awareness that he was nearby. But now he felt miles away, and I couldn't reach him, and that knowledge made me feel ready to crumble, to cease to exist.

When sleep finally came, it was a blissful relief, even though I knew that in the morning it would start all over again. But I was haunted even in my dreams. That night they took a darker turn.

I dreamed I was outside the lighthouse on Shipwreck Coast. It was dark and I could hardly see through the fog, but there was a figure crumpled on the ground. When he moaned and rolled over, I instantly recognized Xavier's face. I cried out and tried to run to him, but a dozen pairs of clammy hands reached out and held me back. Jake Thorn strode out from the lighthouse, his eyes as bright and sharp as broken glass. His dark hair was slicked away from his face, and he was dressed in a long black leather coat with the collar turned up against the wind.

"I didn't want it to come to this, Bethany," he crooned. "But sometimes we are left with no choice."

"What are you doing to him?" I sobbed as Xavier convulsed on the ground. "Let him go."

"I'm only doing what I should have done a long time ago," Jake snarled. "Don't worry, it will be painless. After all, he's half dead already. . . ."

With a flick of his wrist he hauled Xavier upright and pushed him toward the edge of the cliff. Xavier would have defeated Jake in an instant had they engaged in a physical fight, but he couldn't compete with supernatural powers.

"Sweet dreams, pretty boy," said Jake just as Xavier's feet slipped from the edge of the cliff.

My screams were swallowed up by the night.

THE next few days passed in a blur. I didn't feel as though I was really living, but just observing life from the sidelines. I didn't go to school, and Ivy and Gabriel didn't try to make me. I didn't eat much; I didn't leave the house; in fact, I hardly did anything except sleep. Sleep was the only way I could escape the pain of longing for Xavier.

Phantom was my only source of consolation. He seemed to sense my distress and spent all of his time with me, making me smile with his antics. He took underwear out of my open drawers and spread them around my room; he got tangled up in Ivy's knitting and I had to set him free; and he carried an entire packet of Meaty Treats up to my room in the hope of being rewarded with one. These little tricks offered me small reprieves from the interminable silence and emptiness that stretched before me, but once they were over I fell heavily back into my coma of emptiness.

Ivy and Gabriel became more worried by the day. I had

become the ghost of a person and an angel; I no longer contributed anything to the household.

"This can't go on," said Gabriel one afternoon when he got back from school. "This is no way to live."

"I'm sorry," I said flatly. "I'll try harder."

"No," he said. "Ivy and I are going to deal with this tonight."

"What are you going to do?" I asked.

"You'll see," he replied and refused to disclose anything else.

After dinner he and Ivy left the house together, while I lay on my bed, staring up at the ceiling. I didn't think there was anything they could do to solve the problem, although I appreciated them trying.

I dragged myself up and went to look at my reflection in the bathroom mirror. I certainly looked different. Even in my baggy pajamas I could see I'd lost weight in a matter of days, my face was sallow, and my shoulder blades protruded. My hair hung limply and looked dull, just like my eyes, which were wide, dark, and sad. Instead of standing straight, I stooped as if I could hardly support my own weight, and my face seemed shadowed. I wondered if I would ever be able to put together the pieces of my life on earth that had been blown apart when Xavier had left me. It occurred to me momentarily that he hadn't actually declared the relationship over, but that was what he'd meant. I had seen the expression on his face; we were through. I shuffled back to my bed and curled up under the comforter.

About an hour later there was a knock at my door, but I hardly heard it through the miasma that had enveloped me.

The knock came again, louder this time. I heard the door open and someone come into the room. I covered my head with my pillow; I didn't want to be coaxed downstairs.

"Jesus, Beth," said Xavier's voice from the doorway. "What are you doing to yourself?"

I lay still, not daring to believe that it was actually him. I held my breath, sure that when I lifted my head the room would be empty. But then he spoke again.

"Beth? Gabriel explained everything . . . what Jake did and how he threatened you. Oh God, I'm so sorry."

I sat up. There he was in a loose white T-shirt and faded jeans, tall and beautiful, just as I remembered. His face was paler than usual, and there were faint circles under his eyes— the only signs of distress. I saw him flinch when he saw how haggard and exhausted I looked.

"I thought I'd never see you again," I whispered, looking him up and down, proving to myself that he was real and that he had come to see me.

Xavier came over to the bed and took my hand, pressing it against his chest. I shivered at his touch and looked into his sapphire gaze, so filled with concern that I couldn't stop the tears from pouring down my face.

"I'm here," he whispered. "Don't cry, I'm here, I'm here." He repeated those words again and again, and I let him gather me into his arms and hold me. "I should never have let you leave like that," he said. "I was just upset. I thought . . . well, you know what I thought."

"Yes," I said. "I just wish you'd trusted me enough to let me explain."

"You're right," he said. "I love you, and I should have known you were telling the truth. I can't believe I was so stupid."

"I thought you were gone forever," I whispered, tears leaking from beneath my eyelids. "I thought you'd walked away from everything, because I failed, because I destroyed the only thing that ever mattered to me. I waited for you to come, but you didn't."

"I'm so sorry." I heard Xavier's voice break. He swallowed hard and looked at his hands. "I'll do whatever it takes to make it up to you, I'll—"

I silenced him with a finger against his lips. "It's over now," I said. "I want to forget that it ever happened."

"Of course," he said, "whatever you want."

We lay in silence on my bed for a little while, just happy to be back in each other's company. I kept a tight hold on his shirt, as if afraid that he might disappear if I let go. He told me that Gabriel and Ivy had gone into town to give us some space to sort things out.

"You know," Xavier said, "not speaking to you for a few days was the hardest thing I've ever done in my life."

"I know what you mean," I said softly. "I just wanted to die."

He let go of me quickly. "Never think that, Beth," he said. "No matter what. I'm not worth that."

"I think you are," I said and he sighed.

"I can't say I don't know what you mean," he admitted. "It feels like the end of the world, doesn't it?"

"Like the end of all happiness," I agreed. "Of everything you've ever known. That's what happens when you make one person your reason for living."

Xavier smiled. "I guess we weren't too smart then. But I wouldn't change it."

"Neither would I." I was quiet for a few minutes, and then I nudged his fingers with the tip of my nose. "Xav . . ."

"Yes?" He bowed his head and nudged me back.

"If a few days apart nearly killed us, what happens when . . . ?"

"Not now," he cut in. "I only just got you back; I don't want to think about losing you again. I won't let that happen."

"You won't be able to stop it," I said. "Just because you're a rugby player doesn't mean you can take on the forces of Heaven. There's nothing I want more than to stay with you, but I'm so scared."

"A man in love can do extraordinary things," Xavier said. "I don't care if you're an angel, you're my angel, and I won't let you go."

"But what if they give us no warning?" I asked desperately. "What if one morning, I wake up, and I'm back where I came from? Have you thought of that?"

Xavier narrowed his eyes. "What do you think my greatest fear is, Beth? Don't you know how much it scares me that one day I might go to school and you won't be there? That I'll come here looking for you, but nobody will answer the door. Nobody in town will know where you've gone except me, and I'll know it's a place where I can't go to get you back. So don't ask me if I've thought of that, because the answer is yes, every day."

He lay back and stared angrily at the ceiling fan, as if it were to blame for the whole situation.

As I watched him, I realized that my whole world was

right in front of me, just over six feet tall and lying on my bed. I realized at the same moment that I could never leave him. I could never go back to my home, because now, *he* was my home. And I was filled with a strange and overwhelming desire to be as close to him as I could possibly get, to meld with him in a promise to both of us that I would never let us be broken apart.

I got up off the bed and stood scrunching my toes on the floorboards. Xavier looked at me curiously. I returned his stare without speaking and slowly pulled my top up over my head and let it drop to the ground. I didn't feel any sort of self-consciousness; I just felt free. I slipped off my pajama bottoms and let them crumple around my feet so that I was standing before him, fully exposed and vulnerable. I was letting him see me at my most defenseless.

Xavier didn't speak, it would have broken the hum of silence that had fallen across the room. A moment later he stood and mimicked my motions, letting his shirt and jeans fall in a heap on the ground. He came over to me and ran his warm hands down my back. I sighed and let myself sink into his embrace. The feel of his skin on mine sent a warm glow flooding through my body, and I leaned against him, feeling whole for the first time in days.

I kissed his soft lips and ran my hands over his face, feeling the familiar nose and cheekbones. I would have recognized the shape of his face anywhere; I could read it like a blind person reading Braille. He smelled fresh and sweet, and I pressed my chest against his. In my eyes, he didn't have a single physical fault, but I wouldn't have cared if he did. I still would have loved him if he was scarred or dressed in rags, just because he was Xavier.

We lowered ourselves onto the bed and that was how we stayed—until we heard Ivy and Gabriel downstairs—just the two of us, holding each other. Molly would have thought it was crazy. But it was the contact we wanted. We wanted to feel like the same person rather than two separate individuals. Clothing concealed us. Without it, there was nowhere to hide, no way to mask any part of ourselves, and that was what we wanted—to be completely and utterly ourselves and feel completely safe.

} 28 {

Angel of Destruction

THE next morning Xavier came back to have breakfast with us before school. As we ate, Gabriel tried to talk some sense into him. We all knew that Xavier was furious about Jake's duplicity and was ready to take him on single-handedly. That was something Gabriel wanted to avoid at all costs, especially as we didn't know the extent of Jake's power.

"Whatever you do, you mustn't confront him," Gabriel said soberly.

Xavier looked at him over the rim of his coffee mug. "He threatened Beth," he said, his shoulders tightening. "He forced himself on her. We can't just let him get away with it."

"Jake is not like the other students. You mustn't try to deal with him alone," Gabriel said. "We don't know what he's capable of."

"Can't be too dangerous, he's pretty scrawny," Xavier muttered under his breath.

Ivy gave him a stern look. "You know that his appearance has nothing to do with it."

"So what do you want us to do then?" Xavier asked.

"We can't do anything," Gabriel said, "not without drawing

unwanted attention to ourselves. We can only hope that he means no harm."

Xavier let out a short laugh and then stared at Gabriel. "You're serious?"

"Deadly."

"But what about what he did at the prom?"

"I wouldn't call that evidence," Gabriel said.

"What about the accident with the cook and the deep fryer?" I said. "And the car crash at the start of term?"

"You think Jake might have had something to do with those things?" Ivy asked. "But he wasn't even at the school when the crash happened."

"He only needed to be in town," I replied. "And he was definitely there that day in the cafeteria—I walked right past him."

"I read about a boating accident at the jetty two days ago," Xavier added. "And there have been a couple of fires recently that the paper said were started by arsonists. That's never happened around here before."

Gabriel put his head in his hands. "Let me think about this," he said.

"That's not all," I cut in, feeling guilty to be the bearer of so much bad news. "He has *followers*, everywhere he goes, they're right behind him, acting like he's their ringleader, or something. It started off as just a few, but every time I see him, there are more."

"Beth, go and get ready for school," Gabriel said quietly.

"But . . . ," I began.

"Just go," he said. "Ivy and I need to talk."

———

AFTER the prom, Jake Thorn's popularity seemed to grow with alarming speed, and his followers doubled in number. When I went back to school, I noticed they all walked around with vacant looks, like drug addicts, their pupils strangely dilated, their hands thrust deep in their pockets. Their faces only came alive when they saw Jake, taking on a disturbing, adoring expression that suggested they would drown themselves in the ocean if he instructed them to do so.

Acts of random vandalism also seemed to be suddenly on the increase. The doors of Saint Mark's church were desecrated by obscenities, and the windows of the municipal offices were shattered by vandals, using homemade explosives. Fairhaven reported a virulent outbreak of food poisoning, and many of its residents had to be transferred to the hospital.

And it seemed that wherever disaster struck, Jake Thorn was there. He never allowed himself to be implicated in any way; he was always an observer, hovering at the sidelines. To me, it seemed he was bent on causing pain and suffering, and I couldn't help thinking that his motivation was revenge. Was he showing me the consequences of my rejection?

On Thursday afternoon I planned to leave school early and pick Phantom up from the dog groomer. Gabriel hadn't come to school that day because he called in sick; in truth, he and Ivy were replenishing their strength after a week spent cleaning up Jake's messes. They weren't used to having so much to do, and despite their strength, the constant effort had left them drained.

I had just grabbed my school bag and was heading out the front to meet Xavier at his car when I noticed a crowd of people a little way down the hall just outside the girls' bathroom. I felt something at the back of my mind, like a warning telling me to stay away, but instinct and curiosity drew me closer. The group of students were clutching one another and talking in hushed voices. I saw that some of them were crying. One girl was sobbing into the shirt of a senior hockey player who was still in uniform. He'd obviously been called away from practice in a hurry, and he was staring at the bathroom door with a mixture of distress and disbelief on his face.

I moved through the crowd as if in slow motion. I had a strange feeling of being disconnected from my body—as though I was watching the scene on a television set, rather than being physically present. Interspersed with the faces of ordinary students, I noticed members of Jake Thorn's crowd; they were easy to pick out these days by their trademark hollow faces and black clothing. Some of them stared at me as I passed, and I realized that they all had the same eyes: deep, wide, and black as pitch.

As I drew closer to the bathroom, I saw Dr. Chester standing by the door, along with two police officers. I saw one of the officers was talking to Jake Thorn. Jake's face was molded into a mask of earnestness and concern, but his cat's eyes glinted dangerously and his lip curled back ever so slightly as though he wished he could sink his teeth into the man's throat. I got the feeling it was only me who could see the menace behind his expression and that to everybody else he looked every bit an innocent teenager. I moved closer to hear what they were talking about.

"I can't think how it could have happened in a school like this," I heard Jake say. "It's come as a shock to us all."

Then he shifted his position, and I couldn't catch much else, just words here and there: "tragedy," "no one around," and "inform the family." Eventually the police officer nodded and Jake turned away. I noticed that his followers were looking at one another, laughter in their eyes, traces of smiles on their lips. They looked greedy, almost hungry, and they all seemed to be secretly satisfied by whatever was going on.

Jake signaled and they began to disperse, moving subtly away from the crowd. I wanted to shout out for someone to stop them, to tell everyone just how dangerous they were, but I couldn't find my voice.

I realized suddenly that I was edging closer to the open door of the bathroom, as if I'd been pulled there by some unseen force. Two paramedics were lifting a stretcher covered in a blue cloth. I saw that a red stain was starting to seep through, growing steadily larger and creeping across the fabric like a living thing. And hanging out from beneath the cloth was a long, pale hand. The fingertips were already bluish.

A rush of pain and fear took my breath away. But they weren't my own feelings—they belonged to someone else, to the girl on the stretcher. I felt her hands gripping the handle of a knife. I felt the fear in her mind mingled with helplessness as some mysterious compulsion guided the blade to her throat. She struggled against it, but it was as though she had no control over her own body. I felt the shock of pain as the cold metal sliced across her skin and I heard the cruel laughter echoing through her brain. The last thing I saw was her face—it flashed across my field of vision like a lightning bolt. I knew that face. How many lunchtimes had I sat and listened to her endless gossip? How many times had I laughed at her antics, or taken her advice? Taylah's face was burned into my brain. I felt her body lurch forward, felt her struggle for air as blood bubbled from the slit in her throat and poured down her neck. I saw the terror and panic in her eyes right before they turned glassy and she slumped down dead. I opened my mouth to scream, but no sound came out.

Just as my own body began to shake violently, someone stepped in front of me and took hold of my shoulders. I gasped and tried to break away, but his grip was firm. I looked up, expecting to see a pair of searing eyes and sunken cheeks, but instead it was Xavier, who wrapped his arms around me and pulled me away from the crowd and out into the open air.

"No," I said, more to myself than to him. "Please, no . . ."

He kept his arm around my waist and half carried me over to his car because I seemed to have forgotten how to use my legs.

"It's okay," he said, pressing a hand against my face and looking me in the eye. "It's going to be okay."

"This can't be happening . . . that was . . . that girl was . . ." My eyes were burning with tears.

"Get in the car, Beth," he said, yanking open the door and helping me inside.

"Jake's responsible for that!" I cried as he started the ignition. He seemed in a hurry to get home to Ivy and Gabriel. Come to think of it, so was I. They would know what to do.

"The police are treating it as a suicide," Xavier explained flatly. "It's tragic but it's got nothing to do with Jake. In fact, he's the one who noticed her missing and alerted the authorities."

"No." I shook my head vehemently. "Taylah would never do something like that. Jake had a hand in this."

Xavier was unconvinced. "Jake may be many things, but he's not a murderer."

"You don't understand." I wiped my tears away. "I saw it all—it was like I was there when it happened."

"What?" Xavier turned to look at me. "How?"

"When I saw her body, it was like I suddenly became the victim," I explained. "She slit her own throat, but she didn't want to do it—somebody made her. He was controlling her, and then he was laughing while she died. It was Jake, I know it."

Xavier squeezed his eyes shut and shook his head. "Are you sure about this?"

"Xav, I could sense him. He did this."

We both fell silent until I spoke again. "What happened after she died? I didn't see that far."

Xavier's expression was pained, but his voice came out sounding impassive. "She was found dead on the bathroom floor. That's all I know. One of the juniors came in and saw her lying in a pool of blood. There was nothing else there but a kitchen knife." He was gripping the steering wheel so tightly that his knuckles had turned white.

"Why do you think Jake chose her?"

"I guess she was just unlucky." Xavier said. "In the wrong place at the wrong time. I know she was your friend, Beth—I'm sorry this had to happen."

"Is this our fault?" I asked in a small voice. "Did he do this to get back at us?"

"He did this because he's sick," Xavier said. He was staring unblinking at the road ahead, as if he was trying to hold back everything he felt inside. "I just wish you hadn't been there to see it." Xavier sounded angry, but I knew it wasn't directed at me.

"I've seen worse."

"Yeah?"

"We see a lot of bad things where I come from," I said. I didn't tell him how different it was experiencing the loss first-hand on earth, when the victim was your friend and the pain was amplified tenfold. "Did you know her too?" I asked quietly.

"I've been at school with those kids since first grade. I know them all."

"I'm sorry." I put my hand on his shoulder, which was tense and rigid.

"So am I," Xavier said.

GABRIEL and Ivy had already heard what happened by the time we got home.

"We have to act now," Ivy said. "This has gone too far."

"And what do you propose we do?" Gabriel asked her.

"We have to stop him," I said. "Destroy him if that's what it takes."

"We cannot simply charge in and destroy him," Gabriel said. "We're not permitted to take life without reason."

"But he's taken someone else's life!" I cried.

"Bethany, we cannot harm him unless we know without a doubt who or what he is. So, much as we might wish it, confrontation is out of the question for the time being."

"Maybe you can't hurt him," Xavier said, "but I can. Let me fight him."

Gabriel's gray eyes were unyielding. "You will be no use to Bethany dead," he said sharply.

"Gabe!" I cried, distressed by the very idea of anyone touching Xavier. I knew he would jump headfirst into a fight if he thought he was protecting me.

"I'm stronger than him," Xavier said. "I know I am; let me do it."

Ivy put a hand on Xavier's shoulder. "You don't know what we're dealing with in Jake Thorn," she said.

"He's just a boy," Xavier replied. "How frightening can he be?"

"He isn't just a boy," Ivy said. "We have felt his aura—it is growing stronger now. He is aligned with dark forces that no human can understand."

"What are you saying? That he's a demon?" Xavier asked incredulously. "That's impossible."

"You believe in angels. Is it so difficult to consider we might have evil counterparts?" Gabriel asked.

"I've tried not to think about that," Xavier said.

"As surely as there is a Heaven, there is a Hell," Ivy said softly.

"So you think Jake Thorn is a demon?" I whispered.

"We believe he may be an agent of Lucifer," Gabriel said. "But we need proof before we can act to stop him."

The proof came when I unpacked my school bag a little later on that afternoon. A familiar coil of paper was tucked inside the zip. I unrolled it to reveal Jake's distinctive script:

When angels' tears do flood the earth,
The gates of Hell shall see rebirth.

When the demise of angels doth impend,
The human boy shall meet his end.

I felt a sudden lump stick in my throat. Jake had threatened Xavier. His vendetta was no longer against me alone. I clutched Xavier's arm. I could feel the muscles there beneath my fingers—but it was still only human strength.

"Is that proof enough for you?" Xavier asked in a low voice.

"That is a poem and nothing more," Gabriel said. "Listen, I believe that Jake is behind the murder and all of the accidents. I believe that he means to wreak havoc, but I need concrete evidence before I can act—the laws of the Kingdom demand it."

"And then what will you do?" Xavier wanted to know.

"Whatever is necessary to keep the peace," Gabriel said.

"Even if it means killing him?" Xavier spoke plainly.

"Yes," was Gabriel's icy response. "For if he is what we suspect him to be, then taking his human life will send him back where he came from."

Xavier considered this for a moment and then nodded. "But what does he want with Beth? What can she give him?"

"Beth turned him down," Gabriel replied. "Someone like Jake Thorn is used to getting what he wants. Right now his vanity is wounded."

I shuffled my feet uncomfortably. "He said he'd been looking for me for centuries. . . ."

"He said *what?*" Xavier exploded. "What does that mean?"

Gabriel and Ivy exchanged worried looks.

"Demons often search for a human to make their own," Ivy said. "It's their twisted version of love, I suppose. They lure the human to the underworld, and they're forced to stay there forever. Over time they're corrupted and even start to develop feelings for their oppressor."

"But what's the point of it?" Xavier asked. "Can demons even have feelings?"

"It's mainly done to spite Our Father," Ivy said. "The corruption of His creations causes Him great anguish."

"But I'm not even a real human!" I said.

"Exactly," Gabriel replied. "What better prize than an angel in human form? Capturing one of us would be the ultimate victory."

"Is Beth in danger?" Xavier moved closer to me.

"I think we may all be in danger," said Gabriel. "Just have patience. Our Father will reveal our path to us in due course."

I insisted that Xavier stay the night with us, and after Jake's message, Ivy and Gabriel did not object. Although they didn't say as much, I knew they were worried about Xavier's safety.

Jake was unpredictable, like a firework that could go off at any moment.

Xavier called his parents and told them he was staying the night at a friend's place so they could finish studying for an exam the next day. There was no way his mother would have allowed him to stay if she'd known he was at my house—Bernie was far too conservative for that. She and Gabriel would have gotten along famously.

We said good night to Ivy and Gabriel and climbed the stairs to my bedroom. Xavier stood on the balcony while I took my shower and brushed my teeth. I didn't ask what he was thinking or if he was as frightened as I was. I knew he would never admit it, at least not to me. To sleep, he stripped down to a pair of boxer shorts that said, "Don't sweat it!" across the back and a white tank that he had on under his shirt. I put on a pair of leggings and a loose T-shirt.

We didn't say much to each other that night. I lay still and listened to the sound of his steady breathing, felt the rise and fall of his chest. With his body curved around mine, his arms protectively wrapped around me, I felt safe and cocooned. Even though Xavier was only human, it seemed he could protect me from anything and everything. I wouldn't have been worried if a fire-breathing dragon had torn off the roof, because I knew that Xavier was there. I wondered fleetingly if I was expecting too much of him but dismissed the idea.

I woke in the middle of the night, frightened by a dream I couldn't remember. Xavier lay beside me. He looked so beautiful when he was asleep, his perfect lips slightly parted, his hair tousled on the pillow, his smooth, tanned chest rising and falling gently as he breathed. My anxiety got the better of me and I reached out to him. He woke easily, and his eyes were startlingly blue even in the moonlight.

"What's that?" I whispered, suddenly aware of shadows. "Over there, do you see that?"

Leaving his arm around me, Xavier sat up and looked around the room. "Where?" he asked, his voice thick with sleep. I gestured toward the far right corner of the room. Xavier swung himself out of the bed and walked across to where I was pointing.

"Here?" he asked when he reached the spot. "I'm fairly sure this is a coatrack." I nodded then remembered he couldn't see me in the dark.

"I thought I saw someone standing there," I said. "A man in a long coat and a hat." Spoken aloud it sounded ridiculous.

"I think you're seeing ghosts, babe." Xavier yawned and prodded the coatrack with his foot. "Yep, definitely a coatrack."

"Sorry," I said when he came back to bed. I wrapped myself around his warmth.

"Don't be scared," he murmured. "Nobody can hurt you while I'm here."

I trusted him and, after a while, let myself stop listening for noises and movements.

"Love you," Xavier said just before he drifted back to sleep.

"Love you more," I said playfully.

"Not a chance," Xavier said, fully awake now. "I'm bigger, I can contain more love."

"I'm smaller, therefore my love particles are more compressed, which means I can fit more in."

Xavier laughed. "That argument makes no sense. Overruled."

"I'm just basing it on how much I miss you when you're not around," I countered.

"How can you possibly know how much *I* miss *you?*" he said. "Have you got some sort of built-in miss-o-meter that can give us a reading?"

"I'm a girl; of course I have a built-in miss-o-meter."

I drifted off to sleep reassured by the feel of his chest pressed against my back. I could feel his breath on the back of my neck. I traced the smooth skin on his arms, made golden by time outdoors. In the moonlight I could see every hair, every vein, every freckle, and I loved it all. That was my last thought before I fell asleep that night, and I found that fear had abandoned me completely.

29

A Friend in Need

TAYLAH haunted my dreams. I saw her as a faceless ghost with a pair of bloodstained white hands that grasped aimlessly at the air. Then I was inside her body, lying in a pool of sticky warm blood. I heard the dull dripping of the taps in the girls' bathroom as she slipped into death. Then I felt the grief and overwhelming sorrow of her family. They were blaming themselves for not having noticed her depression, wondering if they could have prevented the outcome. Jake was there in the dream too, always at the edge of the frame, slightly out of focus and laughing softly.

In the morning I woke to find the covers rumpled and the place beside me empty. If I pressed my face into the pillow where his head had rested, I could still faintly catch Xavier's scent. I rolled out of bed and opened the curtains to let golden sunlight pour into the room.

In the kitchen, it was Xavier and not Gabriel cooking breakfast. He had pulled on his jeans and T-shirt, and his hair was tousled. He looked fresh faced and beautiful as he carefully cracked eggs into the sizzling pan.

"I thought a decent breakfast was in order," he said when he saw me.

Gabriel and Ivy were already seated at the dining table, plates heaped with scrambled eggs on sourdough toast in front of them.

"This is really good," Ivy said between mouthfuls. "How did you learn to cook?"

"I had no choice, I had to learn," Xavier said. "My whole family besides Mom are useless in the kitchen. When she works late at the clinic they order pizza or eat whatever they can find that says, 'add water and stir.' So I cook for them whenever Mom isn't around."

"Xavier's a man of many skills," I told Ivy and Gabe glowingly.

Xavier had stayed only one night yet I marveled at how easily he had become integrated into our little family. It didn't feel like we had a guest in the house—he was just one of us now. Even Gabriel seemed to have accepted him, and found him a clean white shirt to wear to school.

I noticed we were all carefully avoiding the subject of what had happened the previous afternoon. I knew I was certainly trying to block out the memory.

"I know yesterday came as an awful shock to us all," Ivy said eventually. "But we're going to deal with this situation."

"How?" I asked

"Our Father will show us the way."

"I just hope He does it soon, before it's too late," Xavier muttered, but I was the only one who heard him.

A shock wave had torn through the school after the

discovery of Taylah's suicide. Although classes continued in an attempt at maintaining normality, everything seemed to be operating tentatively. Letters had gone out to parents offering grief counseling and encouraging families to support their children in any way they could. People walked around as if on eggshells, not wanting to be too loud or insensitive. Jake Thorn and his friends were notably absent.

An assembly was called mid-morning, and Dr. Chester explained to the students that the administration didn't know exactly what had transpired, but they had placed the investigation in the hands of the police. Then his voice became less matter-of-fact.

"The loss of Taylah McIntosh is shocking and tragic. She was a great friend and student, and she will be greatly missed. If any of you would like to speak to someone about what has occurred, please book a time with Miss Hirche, our trusted school counselor."

"I feel sorry for the doc," said Xavier. "He's been getting phone calls all morning. The parents are up in arms about this."

"What do you mean?" I asked.

"Schools go down over incidents like this," he said. "Everyone wants to know what happened, why the school didn't do more to prevent it. People start to worry about their own kids."

I was outraged. "But this had nothing to do with the school."

"Well, the parents sure don't see it that way," Xavier said.

After the assembly, Molly caught up with me, her eyes red

and puffy from crying. Xavier saw that she wanted to talk in private and excused himself to go to a water-polo meeting.

"How are you holding up?" I asked, taking her hand. Molly shook her head, and fresh tears trickled down her cheeks.

"It just feels so weird being here at the moment," she said in a choked voice. "It's not the same without her."

"I know," I said softly.

"I don't get it," Molly said. "I can't believe she would do something like that. Why didn't she talk to me? I didn't even know she was depressed—I'm the worst friend!" She let out a sob, and I rushed forward to hug her. It seemed she might collapse if something wasn't holding her up.

"This isn't your fault," I said. "Sometimes things happen that no one could've predicted."

"But . . . ," Molly began.

"No." I cut her off. "Trust me—there was nothing you could have done to stop this."

"I wish I could believe that," Molly whispered. "Did you hear how they found her in all that blood? It's like something out of a horror movie."

"Yeah," I mumbled. The last thing I wanted was to relive the experience. "Molly, maybe you should talk to a counselor," I said gently. "It might help."

"No." Molly shook her head forcefully and then laughed. It sounded high-pitched and hysterical. "I just want to forget that it ever happened. I want to forget that she was ever here."

"But, Molly, you can't just pretend things are okay."

"Watch me," she said, her voice suddenly falsely cheerful

and bright. "Something good actually happened the other day." She smiled broadly, her eyes still shining with tears. It was frightening to watch.

"What?" I asked, wondering whether she might give up the charade if I played along.

"Well, it turns out that Jake Thorn is in my IT class."

"Oh," I said, amazed at how quickly the conversation was spiraling downhill. "That's great."

"Yeah, it really is," Molly said. "Because he asked me out."

"What!" I burst out, spinning around to face her.

"I know," she said. "I couldn't believe it either." It was obvious the shock had messed with her head. She was grasping at any sort of distraction that would take her mind off the pain of her loss.

"What did you say?" I asked.

She laughed harshly. "Don't be stupid, Beth. What do you think I said? We're going out this Sunday with some of his friends. Oh, I almost forgot, are you okay with it, after what happened at the prom? Because you said you didn't have feelings for him . . ."

"No! I mean, of course I don't have feelings for him."

"Then you don't mind?"

"Molly, I do mind, but not for the reasons you think. Jake's bad news—you can't go out with him. And would you please quit acting like everything's fine!" My voice had gone up an octave, and I knew I sounded stressed.

Molly looked confused. "What's the problem? Why are you being all weird about it? I thought you'd be happy for me."

"Oh, Molly, I would be if you were going out with anyone but him," I cried. "You can't trust him—surely you can see that. He's got trouble written all over him."

Molly got suddenly defensive.

"You just don't like him because he made trouble for you and Xavier," she said heatedly.

"That's not true. I don't trust him, and you're not thinking straight!" I said.

"Maybe you're jealous of his uniqueness," Molly spit out. "He said there are some people like that."

"What?" I spluttered. "That doesn't make any sense."

"Sure it does," Molly replied. "You think that you and Xavier are the only people who deserve to be happy. I deserve to be happy too, Beth, especially now."

"Molly, don't be crazy," I said. "Of course I don't think that."

"Then why don't you want me to go out with him?"

"Because he scares me," I said truthfully. "And I don't want to see you make a huge mistake because you're a mess over what happened to Taylah."

But Molly didn't seem to be listening to me anymore.

"Do you want him? Is that it? Well, you can't have all the guys in the world, Beth, you have to leave some for the rest of us."

"I don't want him anywhere near me or you. . . ," I began.

"Why not?"

"Because he killed Taylah!" I yelled.

Molly stopped and stared at me, her eyes wide. I couldn't believe I'd spoken those words aloud, but if they got Molly to come to her senses, if they could save her from falling prey to Jake, then it would be worth it. But a moment later Molly narrowed her eyes.

"You're out of your mind," she hissed and took a step back from me.

"Molly, wait!" I cried. "Just hear me out. . . ."

"No!" Molly interrupted. "I don't want to hear it. You can hate Jake as much as you want, but I'm still going to see him because I *want* to. He's the most amazing guy I've ever met, and I'm not going to pass up the opportunity to be with him just because you're having a little PMS freak-out." She narrowed her eyes at me. "And for your information, he says you're a bitch."

I opened my mouth to respond when a shadow fell across the pavement and a figure appeared at Molly's side. Jake leered at me as he draped an arm around Molly's shoulders and pulled her close. She nestled into his chest and giggled.

"Envy is a deadly sin, Bethany," Jake purred. His eyes were completely covered by a glistening black film, so I couldn't distinguish between pupil and iris. "You should know that. Why don't you just congratulate Molly and be gracious?"

"Or start writing her eulogy," I snapped.

"Now, now, that's below the belt," he said. "Don't you worry; I'll take care of your friend. It seems we have a lot in common."

Then he turned and swept Molly away. I watched her disappear from sight, russet curls bobbing.

I spent the rest of the afternoon desperately looking for Molly so I could explain things to her in a way she might understand, but I couldn't find her anywhere. I told Xavier what had happened and saw the muscles in his face tighten ever so slightly. Together we looked all over the school for Molly, and with every empty classroom I felt my insides twisting with anxiety. Xavier made me sit down on a bench when I began breathing loudly and erratically.

"Hey, hey," he said, lifting up my face so we were looking eye to eye, "calm down. She's going to be okay. Everything is."

"How?" I asked. "He's dangerous! He's completely unstable! I know what he's trying to do. He's trying to get to me through her. He knows she's my friend."

Xavier sat down beside me.

"Think about it for a moment, Beth," he said. "Jake Thorn hasn't hurt anyone in his inner circle yet. He wants to recruit people—it's what he does. So long as he has Molly on his side, she'll be safe."

"You can't know that. He's completely unpredictable."

"Unpredictable or not, he still won't hurt her," Xavier said. "We have to keep our wits about us now; we can't afford to lose our heads. It's easy to overreact given what's just happened."

"So what do you think we should do?" I asked.

"I think Jake might have given us a clue to finding that proof Gabriel is after."

"Really?"

"Did Molly say where he was taking her?"

"She just said it was going to be on Sunday . . . and his friends were going to be there," I said.

Xavier nodded. "Right, well, Venus Cove isn't that big a place—we'll find out where they're going and follow them."

We relayed our concerns to Ivy and Gabriel. The problem was working out where Jake might take Molly. It could be anywhere in Venus Cove, and we couldn't afford to miscalculate. This was our one chance to see what he was really up to, and we didn't want to blow it.

"Where would he go?" Ivy mused. "Of course there are all the normal places in town, like the movie theater or Sweethearts, the bowling alley. . . ."

"There's no point thinking normal," I said. "He's anything but that."

"Beth's right," said Xavier. "Let's try to think like him for a moment."

Asking an angel to get inside the head of a demon was a tall order, but Gabriel and Ivy tried to mask their disgust and complied with Xavier's request.

"It won't be somewhere public," Ivy said suddenly, "especially not if he plans to bring his friends along. They're too big a group, too conspicuous."

Gabriel agreed. "They'll go somewhere quiet and private, a place where they won't be interrupted."

"Are there any abandoned houses or factories around here?" I asked. "Like the one where the after-party was held? That would suit Jake."

Xavier shook his head. "Jake strikes me as a little more dramatic than that."

"So let's think exaggerated and over-the-top then," Ivy suggested

"Exactly." Xavier looked at me, his azure eyes sharp. "His followers . . . think about what they look like, how they dress."

"They look like goths," I replied.

"And what is the center of goth culture?" Gabriel said.

Ivy looked at him, her eyes wide. "Death."

"Yes." Xavier's face was grim. "So where would be the best place for a bunch of weirdos obsessed with death?"

The realization hit me, and I drew a sharp breath. It was overstated, it was grim, it was dark, and it was the perfect place for Jake to stage his show.

"The cemetery," I breathed and Xavier nodded.

"I think so."

He turned to my brother and sister, who were looking dour. Gabriel's ringed fingers tightened around his coffee mug.

"I think you might be on to something," he said.

"Honestly, you'd think the boy might be a little more original," Ivy snapped. "The cemetery indeed. Well, I suppose one of us is going to have to follow them there on Sunday."

"I will," Gabriel said immediately, but Xavier shook his head.

"That would be asking for a fight. Even I know you can't just throw an angel and a demon together like that. I think I should go," Xavier said.

"It's too dangerous," I argued.

"Beth, I'm not scared of them."

"You're not scared of anything," I shot back. "But maybe you should be."

"This is the only way," he insisted.

I looked up at my brother and sister.

"Fine but if he's going, I'm going with him."

"Neither of you are going anywhere," Gabriel cut in. "If

Jake were to turn on you with a group of others to support him . . ."

"I'll look after her," Xavier said. He seemed offended by Gabe's insinuation that he wouldn't be able to protect me. "You know I wouldn't let anything happen."

Gabriel looked skeptical. "I don't doubt your physical strength," he said. "But . . ."

"But what?" Xavier asked in a low voice. "I would lay down my life for her."

"I know you would, but you have no idea what you're facing here."

"I have to protect Beth—"

"Xavier." Ivy put a hand on his arm, and I knew she was sending a soothing energy through his body. "Please listen to us. We don't know what these people are . . . we don't know how strong they are or what they're capable of. From what we've seen so far, it's likely they have no reservations about killing. Brave as you are, you are still only one human facing . . . only Our Father knows what."

"So what do you propose we do?"

"I think we should do nothing until we've consulted a higher authority." Gabriel's face was expressionless. "I'll make contact with the Covenant right away."

"There isn't time for that!" I cried. "Molly could be in serious trouble."

"Our first concern is protecting the two of you!" The anger in Gabriel's voice caused a hush to fall over the room. Nobody spoke until Ivy looked at us with sudden decisiveness.

"Xavier, whatever we decide to do, you cannot go home

this weekend," she said. "It's not safe. You must stay with us."

THE scene at Xavier's house wasn't pretty. Gabriel and Ivy waited in the car while Xavier and I went inside to tell his parents he was staying with me for the weekend.

Bernie glared at him when he broke the news. "This is the first I've heard of it." She followed Xavier into his bedroom and stood in the doorway, hands on hips as he packed a bag. "You can't go—we have plans for this weekend."

She seemed to have missed the part where he'd *told* her he was going rather than asked.

"I'm sorry, Mom," he said, striding around the room and throwing clothes and underwear into his sports bag, "but I have to go."

Bernie's eyes widened. She threw me an accusatory look, evidently holding me responsible for her model son's transformation. It was a shame because we'd been getting along so well. I wished there was a way we could tell her the truth, but there was no chance she would have understood that it was too dangerous to leave Xavier unprotected.

"Xavier," Bernie snapped, "I *said* no."

But Xavier wasn't listening.

"I'll be back on Sunday night," he said, zipping up the sports bag and slinging it across his shoulder.

"That's it; I'm getting your father." Bernie whirled around and stormed down the hall. "Peter!" we heard her calling. "Peter, come and talk to your son—he's out of control!"

Xavier looked at me apologetically. "Sorry about this," he said.

"They're just worried," I replied. "It's natural."

A few moments later Xavier's father appeared in the doorway, his forehead creased with concern and his hands buried in his trouser pockets.

"You've got your mother in a bit of a state," he said.

"I'm sorry, Dad." Xavier put a hand on his father's shoulder. "I can't explain it all right now, but I have to go. Just trust me on this one."

Peter looked over at me. "Are you both all right?" he asked.

"We will be," I said. "After this weekend everything will be fine."

Peter seemed to sense the urgency in our voices, and he put his hand over Xavier's.

"I'll take care of your mother," he said. "You two worry about taking care of yourselves." He gestured to the bedroom window. "Go that way." We stared at him, wondering if it was some sort of joke. "Hurry up!"

Xavier smiled grimly, pushed open the window, and tossed his bag out before helping me through.

"Thanks, Dad," he said and hoisted himself up after me.

From outside, pressed against the cool bricks, we heard Bernie come back into the room.

"Where did they go?" she demanded.

"I'm not sure," replied Peter innocently. "They must have slipped past me."

"Are you okay?" I asked Xavier once we were safely in the

car. I knew how terrible I'd felt lying to Ivy and Gabriel, and I knew that Xavier had a lot of respect for his parents.

"Yeah, Mom will recover," he said, and smiled at me. "You're my top priority and don't you forget it." We drove home in pensive silence.

30

Raising Hell

HARD as I tried, I couldn't accept Gabriel's proposal of waiting for divine guidance. It seemed unlike him to respond in such a way, uncharacteristically cautious, which told me everything I needed to know; Jake Thorn was a serious threat, and that meant I couldn't sit at home while Molly was in his clutches.

Molly had been my first friend at Venus Cove. She had taken me under her wing, confided in me, and made every effort to ensure I felt included. If Gabriel, of all people, didn't feel confident enough to act alone, then something was seriously wrong. So I didn't think twice. I knew exactly what I had to do.

"I'm going out to pick up some groceries," I told Gabriel, careful to keep my face impassive so he wouldn't detect the lie.

My brother frowned. "We're not running low. Ivy stocked up yesterday."

"Well, I need something to get my mind off this whole business with Jake," I said, trying a different tact. Gabriel looked at me closely, his silver eyes narrowed, his chiseled features severe. I swallowed. Lying to him was never easy. "I just need to get out of the house."

"I'll come with you," he said. "I don't want you going out alone, given the current situation. . . ."

"I won't be alone," I insisted. "I'll be with Xavier. And besides, I'll only be gone ten minutes." I felt awful lying to his face, but I had no other choice.

"Don't be such a worrywart." Ivy patted my brother's arm. She was always so quick to trust in me. "Some fresh air will do them good."

Gabriel pursed his lips and folded his hands behind his back.

"All right. But come straight back."

I took Xavier's hand and tugged him out of the house. He started the Chevy in silence. I told him to make a left at the end of the street.

"You have a terrible sense of direction," he joked, but the smile didn't touch his eyes.

"We were never going to the grocery store."

"I know," Xavier said. "And I think you're crazy."

"I have to do something," I said quietly. "Lives have already been lost because of Jake. How will we live with ourselves if Molly's his next victim?"

Xavier was unconvinced. "Beth, do you really think I'm going to take you right into the path of a murderer? The guy's unstable. You heard what your brother said."

"This isn't about me anymore," I said. "I'm not worried."

"Well I am! Do you realize the danger you're putting yourself in?"

"It's my job! Why do you think I was sent here? Not just to sell badges and work in soup kitchens—this is it, this is our challenge! I can't turn my back on it because I'm too scared."

"Maybe Gabriel's right—sometimes it's smart to be scared."

"And sometimes you just have to bite the bullet," I insisted.

Xavier was exasperated. "Look, I'll go down to the graveyard and bring Molly back. You stay here."

"Great idea," I said sarcastically. "If there's one person Jake hates more than me, it's you. Look, Xav, you can either come with me or you can stay home. But either way I'm going to help Molly. I understand if you don't want to be a part of this. . . ."

Xavier made a sharp turn at the next corner and drove in silence. Ahead of us was an uninterrupted stretch of road. I noticed the houses growing sparser.

"Wherever you go, I go," he said.

The cemetery was located at the end of a long, wide road just out of town. Alongside it ran an abandoned railroad line, with neglected train cars weathered by the elements. The only buildings nearby were a row of derelict town houses, their balconies choked with vegetation and their windows boarded up.

The cemetery dated back to the town's first settlement but had expanded since then to reflect the waves of migration. The newest section contained shiny marble monuments and shrines, all meticulously maintained. In many of the shrines were photographs of the deceased surrounded by glowing votive lights in frosted glass. There were small altars, crucifixes, and statues of Christ and the Virgin Mary, her hands folded in prayer.

Xavier parked his car across the street, a little way from the main gates so we wouldn't draw attention. At this time of day the gates were open so we crossed the road and walked straight in. At first glance the place seemed peaceful. We saw a lone mourner, an elderly woman in black, tending one of the newer graves. She was cleaning its glass front and replacing the flowers that had shriveled with a new bunch of chrysanthemums, cutting them to size with a pair of scissors. She was so absorbed in her task that she barely noticed us. The rest of the place seemed deserted apart from the occasional raven circling overhead and the soft droning of bees that hovered around the lilac bushes. While there was no earthly disturbance, I sensed the presence of several lost souls who haunted their place of burial. I would have liked to stop and help them on their journey, but I had more pressing matters on my mind.

"I know where we might find them," said Xavier, and he steered me to the original section of the cemetery.

There, a very different scene greeted us. The graves were old and abandoned, their cast-iron railings rusted. Over time, a tangle of ivy had smothered all other vegetation and now ruled unchallenged, threading its tenacious tendrils through the iron railings like rope. These graves were more humble and at ground level; some had nothing more than a plaque to identify the occupant. I saw a patch of turf littered with small windmills and soft toys that had long lost their sheen and realized this was a section for infants. I stopped to read one of the tiny tablets: LUCY ROSE, 1949–1949, AGE 5 DAYS. Thinking about this little soul who had graced the earth for a mere five days filled me with an unspeakable sadness.

Xavier and I picked our way around the crumbling head-stones. Very few were still intact. Most had sunk into the grass, their inscriptions faded and barely legible. Others were nothing more than a jumble of broken stone and tangled weeds. Every so often we came across a statue of an angel, some towering and some small, but all grim faced with arms outstretched as if in welcome.

As we walked, I was aware of the bodies of the dead under the blankets of cracked stone. My skin prickled. It wasn't the sleepers beneath our feet that troubled me, but what we might discover around the next corner. I could sense Xavier's regret over the decision to come here. But he showed no signs of fear.

We stopped suddenly when we heard the sound of voices. They seemed to be chanting some kind of dirge. We crept forward until the voices became louder, and we took refuge behind a towering birch. Peering between its boughs, we could make out a small gathering of people. I thought there must have been about two dozen or so in total. Jake stood on a mossy grave facing them, his legs apart and his back arrow straight. He wore a black leather jacket and the inverted pentagram hung from a cord around his neck. On his head was a gray fedora. I paused—I recognized that hat from some-where. The sight of it stirred a memory in the back of my mind. And then it hit me—the strange, solitary figure at the rugby game. He'd appeared at the sidelines, his face shrouded from view, and after Xavier had been hurt, he'd vanished into thin air. So Jake had orchestrated the whole thing! The thought that he'd tried to injure Xavier sent a burning anger pulsing through me, but I tried to stifle it. I needed to keep my wits about me now more than ever.

Rearing up behind Jake was a ten-foot angel made of stone. It had to be one of the most chilling earthly things I'd ever seen. Despite looking like an angel, there was something sinister about it. It had narrow eyes, huge black wings that reared majestically behind it, and a powerful body that looked as though it could crush anyone and anything. A long stone sword was melded to its muscular waist. Jake stood under its shadow as though it was protecting him.

The group were gathered in a semicircle around him. They were dressed strangely, some in hooded garments that shrouded their entire faces and others in tattered black lace and chains, their cheeks powdered chalk white and their lips stained bloodred. They didn't seem to be interacting with one another, but they approached Jake in turn, each bowing in deference before removing some object from a drawstring pouch and depositing the offering at his feet. They made a woeful spectacle that afternoon, standing in the watery sunlight. I wondered by what means and through what promises Jake had lured these young people from their regular pursuits to join him here and disturb the departed.

And I wondered why I didn't see Molly.

Jake held up his hands and the group stilled. He threw off his hat, and I saw that his long, dark hair was uncombed and tangled. He looked almost wild. When he spoke his voice seemed to reverberate from the stone angel itself.

"Welcome to the dark side," he said, and laughed coldly. "Although I prefer to think of it as the *fun side*." There were murmurs of appreciation from his followers. "I can promise you that nothing feels better than sin. Why not turn to pleasure when life treats us with such indifference? We are here, all of us, because we want to feel alive!"

He ran a slender hand over the coarse stone of the angel's thigh and spoke again, his voice dripping like syrup. "Pain, suffering, destruction, death, these things are like music to our ears, sweet as honey on our tongues. We thrive on them. They are food for our souls. You must all learn to reject a society that promises everything and delivers nothing. I am here to show you how to create your own meaning, thereby freeing yourselves from this prison in which you are all chained like animals. Man was created to rule, but you have become simpering and soft. Let us reclaim our power over the earth!"

He looked around the group, and his voice became suddenly cajoling, like a parent coaxing a child. His hand gripped the hilt of the angel's stone sword. "You have done well so far, and I am pleased with your progress. But it's time to take more than baby steps. I urge you to do more, to be more, and to throw off those shackles that bind you to polite society. Let us invoke the twisted spirits of the night to assist us."

His words seem to incite a kind of fever in his followers, as if by mass hypnosis. They threw back their heads and cried incoherently into the air, some whispering, some screaming. It was a sound full of pain and vengeance.

Jake smiled approvingly then glanced at his gold watch. "We don't have much time. Let's get down to business." He peered into the crowd. "Where are they? Bring them to me."

Two figures were thrust forward so they fell at Jake's feet.

Both were wearing hooded cloaks. Jake took hold of the figure closest to him and pulled back the hood, revealing an ordinary-looking boy whom I recognized from school, a fairly unassuming student who kept a low profile and was a member of the chess club. There were no shadows under his eyes, and his eyes themselves were not black like the others' but a pale green. Despite his fresh-faced appearance, he looked shaken.

Jake placed his hand on the boy's head. "Don't be afraid," he purred in a seductive voice. "I'm here to help you."

Slowly he began to make swirling signs in the air above where the boy knelt. From where I was crouched, I saw the boy follow Jake's hand movements and scan the faces in the crowd, obviously trying to gauge the seriousness of the situation. Perhaps he was wondering if this was some elaborate prank, an initiation rite that must be endured before he was accepted into the group. I feared it was something much more sinister.

Then one of his followers handed Jake a book. It was bound in black leather, and the pages were yellowed from age. Reverentially, Jake held the book aloft and let it fall open. Instantly a gust of wind shook the trees and sent dust flying around the squatting headstones. I recognized the book from my teachings back home.

"Oh, no," I whispered.

"What?" Xavier sounded alarmed as he too, caught sight of it. "What's that?"

"It's a grimoire," I said. "A book of dark magic. It contains instructions on how to call on spirits and raise up the dead."

"You've got to be kidding me." Xavier looked like he was about to pinch himself to try to wake from the nightmare he had unexpectedly fallen into. I was struck for a moment by how innocent he was, and I felt almost sick with the guilt of having dragged him into this. But now wasn't the time to lose my head.

"This is a bad sign," I said. "Grimoires are powerful things."

Still atop the grave, Jake's chest began to heave. His chanting grew faster and more manic and he read from the book. He spread his arms wide. "*Exorior meus atrum amicus quod vindicatum is somes*" He was speaking Latin, but not like I'd ever heard it before. It had been altered, and somehow I knew it was the language of the Underworld. "*Is est vestri pro captus,*" Jake sang, his hands clutching at the empty air.

"What's he saying?" Xavier whispered. I was surprised to find that I could translate the meaning of the words exactly.

"Come forth, my dark friend, and claim this body. It is yours for the taking."

His followers watched with bated breath. No one moved, no one uttered a sound, not daring to interrupt whatever unnatural process was taking place.

Beside me, Xavier sat so transfixed that I had to touch his hand to reassure myself that he was still conscious. We both jerked when a sound like splitting stone filled the air and had to resist the urge to cover our ears. It was a screeching noise, like nails tearing down a blackboard. It stopped abruptly, and a cloud of black smoke poured from the mouth of the massive stone angel. It drifted down to where Jake was standing and seemed to be whispering in his ear. Jake grabbed the boy by the hair, tilting his head back and forcing his mouth open.

"What are you doing?" the boy cried.

The black cloud seemed to reel and spin for a moment in midair before plunging into the boy's open mouth and down his throat. Jake released him, and the boy instantly uttered a guttural scream. He clutched at his throat and clawed at his body as it convulsed on the ground. His face was contorted as though he were in agony. I felt Xavier's arm begin to shake with anger.

The boy lay still. A moment later he sat up and looked around him, his expression of confusion turning to one of pleasure. Jake offered him a hand and hoisted him to his feet. The boy flexed his body as if discovering it for the first time.

"Welcome back, my friend," Jake said, and when the boy turned around, I saw that his green eyes were black as tar.

"I can't believe I didn't see this before," I said and dropped my head in my hands. "I befriended him, I wanted to help him. . . . I should have sensed he was a demon."

Xavier put his hand on the small of my back. "This is not your fault." His eyes swept over the congregation gathered at Jake's feet. "Are they all demons?"

I shook my head. "I don't think so. Jake seems to be conjuring vengeful spirits to possess his followers."

"This just keeps getting better and better," Xavier muttered. "Where do the spirits come from? Are they the people in these graves?"

"I doubt it," I said. "They're probably the souls of the damned from the Underworld, quite different from demons. A demon is a creature created by Lucifer himself, and they worship none but him. It's the same concept as angels in

Heaven; there are millions of souls that go to Heaven, but they don't become angels. Angels and demons were never human. They're in a league of their own."

"Are these spirits still dangerous?" Xavier asked. "What will happen to the people they possess?"

"Their main purpose is to cause destruction," I said. "When they take over the body of a human, they can make that person do anything. It's like having two souls within the one shell. Most people can survive it unless the spirit intentionally damages their body. They aren't much of a threat to us, our powers are far greater than theirs. Jake is the only one we need to worry about."

Xavier and I fell silent as Jake led the next victim forward. But I was not prepared for what happened next. When he pulled back the hood, I saw a familiar cascade of russet curls and wide, frightened blue eyes.

"Don't worry, my dear," said Jake, tracing his finger lightly across Molly's neck and down to her chest. "It won't hurt much."

I gripped Xavier's arm. "We have to stop him," I said. "We can't let him hurt Molly!"

Xavier's face was pale. "I want to bring Jake down too, but if we intervene now, we don't stand a chance against all of them. We need your brother and sister." He shook his head, and I realized he was finally accepting that he couldn't defeat Jake alone.

Overcome with jealousy and desire, one of Jake's followers threw herself on the ground and began to writhe. Her eyes rolled back so that only the whites showed, her mouth opening and closing in silent moans. I recognized her immediately as Alexandra from my lit class. Jake bent down and stilled her thrashing by grasping her hair in one hand. He ran a finger suggestively along her exposed throat and let it linger over her mouth. She was breathing heavily and seemed to arch toward him in ecstasy, but he moved away from her and used the tip of his boot to trace a line down her body.

"We should leave," Xavier whispered. "This is more than we can handle."

"We can't go without Molly."

"Beth, we can't let Jake know we're here."

"I can't leave her, Xavier."

He sighed. "Okay, I think I have an idea for getting her back, but you have to trust me and listen to what I say. A wrong move could cost her safety."

I nodded and waited for Xavier to say more, but a blood-curdling scream commanded my attention. Molly was on her knees, Jake's hand gripping the back of her neck. Her own hands were tied behind her with rope. The black fog was erupting from the stone angel's mouth. Molly's face was white with pain and confusion, but her eyes fixed intently on Jake. I couldn't stand to see it. I stumbled out from behind the tombstone, ignoring Xavier's yell of protest.

"What are you doing?" I screamed. "Stop this! Jake, let her go!" When I looked at Jake's face, it was distorted with anger. I felt Xavier's presence by my side. He positioned himself protectively between me and Jake.

Upon seeing him, Jake's anger seemed to dissipate, and he

folded his arms and cocked one eyebrow in an expression of amusement.

"Well, well," he said. "What have we here? If it's not the Angel of Mercy and her . . ."

"Molly, get down from there," Xavier called out, and she obeyed dumbly, too stunned to argue or formulate any sort of response. Jake snarled.

"Don't move," he commanded her and Molly froze.

"You!" I pointed a finger at Jake. "We know what you are."

He clapped his hands slowly and mockingly. "Well done. What a first-rate detective you are."

"We're not going to let you get away with this," Xavier said. "There are four of us, and there's only one of you."

Jake laughed and waved a hand around him. "Actually there are many more of us, and the numbers increase daily," he snickered. "It seems I'm quite popular."

I stared at him in horror, feeling any confidence I'd had trickle away.

"You and your good deeds don't stand a chance," Jake said. "You might as well give up."

"That's not going to happen," Xavier growled.

"Oh my, how sweet," Jake said. "The human boy thinks he can defend the angel."

"Believe me, I can and I will."

"Do you actually think that you can hurt me?" Jake asked.

"You'll find out if you try and hurt her," Xavier replied.

Jake's lip curled back, revealing his small, sharp teeth. "You should know that you're playing with fire," he smirked.

"And I'm not scared of getting burned," Xavier spit out.

They glared at each other for a long moment, as if one was daring the other to act. I stepped forward.

"Just let Molly go," I said. "There's no need to hurt her; it doesn't gain you anything."

"I'll gladly release her," Jake smiled. "On one condition . . ."

"And what's that?" Xavier asked.

"Beth must take her place."

Xavier's body tensed with anger, and his blue eyes flashed. "Go to hell!"

"You poor, helpless human," Jake taunted. "You've already lost one love, and now you're about to lose another one?"

"What did you say?" asked Xavier, his eyes narrowing. "How do you know about her?"

"Oh, I remember her quite well." Jake smiled sickeningly. "Emily, wasn't it? Didn't you ever wonder why her whole family made it out alive, but not her?" Xavier looked like he was about to throw up. I gripped his hand as Jake continued. "It was almost too easy—tying her to her bed, while the house went up in flames. Everybody thought she slept through the alarm, they didn't hear her screaming over the roar of the flames."

"You son of a bitch." Xavier took several strides toward Jake but didn't get very far. Jake smirked and his fingers twitched and before he could reach him, Xavier doubled over in pain, clutching his abdomen. He tried to right himself, but Jake sent him to the ground with a flick of his wrist.

"Xavier!" I cried, rushing to his aid. I felt his shoulders

shuddering in pain. "Leave him alone!" I begged Jake. "Stop, please!"

In my head I tried to silently invoke God's help by issuing a mental prayer: *Almighty Father, Creator of Heaven and Earth, deliver us from evil. Send your spirit to help us, and call forth the angels of salvation. For the kingdom, the power, and the glory are yours, now and forever. . . ."*

But Jake's powers clouded my prayer like a thick, black fog descending on me, forcing the words to stick in my mind until I felt my head might burst. Jake Thorn thrived on misery and pain, and I knew I couldn't defeat someone like that alone. Xavier had been right. I wished I had listened. And, since no one was coming to my aid, there was only one way to help him and Molly, the only way I knew how.

"You can have me!" I shouted, opening my arms.

"No!" Xavier heaved himself to his feet, but he was no match for Jake's dark strength, and he crumpled once again.

I didn't hesitate; I ran forward, propeling myself into the circle. The group pressed forward, chanting in crazed voices until Jake raised a hand indicating they should retreat.

I reached out to Molly and managed to pry her away from his grasp.

"Run!" I gasped.

I felt the air being squeezed from my lungs as Jake closed in on me. The black fog overwhelmed me, and I slid to the ground, hitting my head hard on the corner of the stone angel's plinth. I must have cut myself because I felt a warm trickle of blood on my brow. I tried to get up, but my body refused to comply. It was as if every drop of energy had leaked out of me. I opened my eyes and saw Jake standing above me.

"My brother and sister will never let you get away with this," I murmured.

"I believe I already have," Jake snarled. "I gave you the choice to join me, and like a fool, you declined."

"You're evil," I said. "I'd never join you."

"But naughty can be oh so nice." Jake laughed.

"I'd rather die."

"And so you will."

"Get away from her," Xavier yelled, his voice thick with pain. He was still crippled on the ground and unable to move. "Don't you dare touch her!"

"Oh, shut up," Jake snapped. "Your pretty face can't save her now."

The last thing I remembered before everything went dark was the greedy glint in Jake's snake-green eyes and Xavier's voice calling out to me.

31

Deliverance

I woke up in the backseat of a long car. When I tried to move, I realized some invisible force was pinning me down. Jake Thorn was in the driver's seat and on either side of me were Alicia and Alexandra from my literature class. They watched me with chalky, expressionless faces as if I were a specimen in a laboratory. They kept their gloved hands folded in their laps. I struggled to move and almost succeeded, my elbow hitting Alexandra in the ribs.

"She's being difficult," she complained, and Jake tossed her a small package wrapped in foil.

"One of these should do the trick," he said.

Alicia forced open my mouth with her gloved hand while Alexandra dropped a pale green pill down my throat, washing it down with liquid from a silver flask. The liquid burned as it coursed down my throat and spilled out my mouth. It choked me until I had no choice but to swallow. I gagged and spluttered, and the two girls exchanged a satisfied smirk. Their white faces and hollow eyes started to blur into a haze of misty blue, and a ringing began in my ears that drowned out all other sound. The last thing I was aware of was my heart beating much faster than normal, before I sank down into their bony laps and everything went black.

WHEN I opened my eyes again, I was sitting on a faded rug on the floor with my back propped against a cold plaster wall. I knew I must have been slumped there for a while because the cold of the room had seeped through my clothes and into my skin. My hands were bound, and my fingers tingled when I wriggled them. My arms were aching from being in the same position for too long. Someone had wound a rope tightly around my waist and gagged me with a dirty rag, making it difficult to breathe. I thought I could smell gasoline.

I peered around the dim surroundings, trying to make out where Jake had taken me. It wasn't a dungeon as I had first imagined. Instead I appeared to be in the formal sitting room of a Victorian house. The room was large and airy and had high ceilings and light fixtures in the shape of twisted rosebuds. The rich tones of the carpet suggested it was Persian, but it smelled musty. The stale odor of cigar smoke also hung in the air. Two wide chesterfield couches, which had seen better days, sat opposite each other, with marble-topped side tables nearby. A deep mahogany sideboard held decanters so dusty you could barely make out the amber and plum liquids inside. In the middle of the room stood a long, polished cedar dining table with elaborately carved legs. The high-backed chairs positioned around it were upholstered in burgundy velvet, and in the center of the table sat an immense silver candelabra, its lighted candles casting elongated shadows across the room. Strange markings and symbols were scrawled on the walls, which were covered in peeling striped wallpaper. Portraits in heavy gilt frames hung above the marble mantelpiece, and their faces watched me archly as if they were in on a secret I had yet to discover. There was one of a Renaissance-looking gentleman in a ruffled collar, and another of a woman surrounded by five nymphlike daughters, all with Pre-Raphaelite hair and swirling dresses.

A film of dust lay over everything, including the paintings. I wondered how long it had been since anyone had lived in the house. It seemed to be frozen in time. A giant spider's web swooped gracefully across the width of the ceiling like a sheet of muslin. When I looked more closely, I saw that everything reeked of decay. The dining chairs looked moth-eaten, the picture frames were lopsided, the leather sofas sagged, and there were patches of damp on the ceiling where water had seeped through. Everything was still in place, as though the owners of the house had left in a hurry and never come back. The windows were boarded up so that only a few bars of natural light filtered into the room to fall in random beams across the carpet.

My whole body ached, and my head felt leaden and foggy. I could hear distant voices coming from somewhere, but no one appeared. I sat there for what felt like hours and started to realize what Gabriel had meant about the human body having certain requirements. I was feeling faint with hunger, my throat was dry and parched from lack of hydration, and I desperately needed to use the bathroom. I drifted into a semiconscious state, until eventually I was aware of someone coming into the room.

When I focused my eyes and sat up, I saw Jake Thorn seated at the head of the dining table. He was wearing a smoking jacket of all things and had his arms crossed. On his face he wore his trademark sneer.

"I'm sorry it had to end like this, Bethany," he said. He glided over to untie the gag from around my mouth. His voice was like honey. "I did try to offer you a chance at a life together."

"A life with you would be worse than death," I said in a hoarse whisper.

I saw Jake's face harden. His cat eyes, which were black again, seemed to glaze over.

"Your stoicism is admirable," he said. "In fact, I think it may be one of the things I like best about you. However, in this case I think you will come to regret the choice you have made."

"You can't hurt me," I said. "I'll only return to the life I knew."

"That's very true." He smiled. "What a shame your *other half* will be left behind. I wonder what will become of him when you're not here."

"Don't you dare threaten him!"

"Struck a nerve?" Jake asked. "I do wonder how Xavier will react when he finds his precious one dead. I hope he doesn't do anything rash—grief can make men behave in strange ways."

"Leave him out of this." I struggled against the rope. "We can settle this ourselves."

"I don't think you're in a position to bargain, do you?"

"Why are you doing this, Jake? What do you think you'll gain?"

"That depends on your definition of gain. I am but a servant of Lucifer. Do you know what Lucifer's biggest sin was?"

"Pride," I answered.

"Precisely, so you really shouldn't have wounded mine. I didn't appreciate it."

"I didn't mean to wound you, Jake . . ."

He cut me off. "That was your mistake, and this is the part where I get even. It will be quite a show watching the perfect school captain take his own life. My, my, what will everybody say?"

"Xavier would never do that!" I hissed, feeling my heart skip a beat.

"No, he wouldn't," Jake agreed, "not without a little help from me. I can get inside his head and offer some useful suggestions. It shouldn't be hard. He'll already have lost the love of his life, right? That ought to make him very vulnerable. What shall I make him do? Throw himself onto the rocks at Shipwreck Coast? Wrap his car around a tree, cut his wrists, walk into the ocean? So many choices to consider."

"You're doing this because you're hurt," I said. "But killing Xavier won't make you happy again. Killing me won't bring you satisfaction."

"Enough tiresome talk!"

He drew a sharp knife from inside his jacket and bent to slice through the ropes that held me with small, deft movements. My arms and hands ached even more once they were free. Jake pulled me up so that I was kneeling at his feet. I saw his polished black shoes with their pointed toes, and at that moment, I didn't care about the pain in my limbs or the pounding in my head or about feeling sick and weak from lack of nourishment. All I cared about was getting to my feet. I would not bow before an Agent of Darkness. I would rather die than betray my Heavenly allegiance by surrendering to him.

I put a hand out to the wall and used it to haul myself to my feet. It took all my energy, and I didn't know how long I could keep it up. My knees wanted to buckle beneath me.

Jake looked at me with mild amusement.

"Hardly the time for loyalty," he jeered. "You do realize I hold your life in my hands? Worship me if you want to live to see your Xavier again."

"I renounce you and all your works," I said calmly.

This seemed to enrage him, and he lifted me off my feet and threw me across the dining table. My head hit the surface with a crack before I careered onto the floor and landed in a heap. Something sticky was snaking its way down my forehead.

"All right down there?" Jake asked smugly from his position, leaning against the side of the table. He roughly stroked the wound on my face and his hands radiated heat.

"It doesn't have to be this way," he purred. He waited for a sign of agreement, but I remained mute.

"Well, if that's your answer, you leave me no choice. I'm going to have to rip every shred of goodness out of you," he said softly. "When I'm done there won't be a scrap of honesty or integrity left."

He bent over me so that his hair fell over his glistening eyes. He was just inches from me, and I could see every feature, the curve of his prominent cheekbones, the thin line of his mouth, the stubble on his chin.

"I'm going to blacken your soul and then claim it as my own."

My body began to shudder at his words. I grasped desperately at the table legs, looking for leverage, a way of escape. Jake ran a hand slowly along the length of my arm, savoring the contact. My skin burned and throbbed, and when I looked down, I saw a ribbon of red where his touch had scorched me.

"I'm afraid you won't be going back to Heaven, Bethany, because by the time I'm finished with you, they won't let you in."

He stroked my face with a single finger and then traced the outline of my lips. I felt my face turn into a burning mask.

I turned away and thrashed furiously, but Jake held me and forced me to look at him. I felt as though his fingers were boring right through my cheeks.

"Don't fret, my angel, we are very hospitable in Hell."

He kissed me roughly, the weight of his body pressing down on me before he pulled away. Spasms of heat seared through my entire body.

"It's time to say good-bye, Miss Church."

JAKE closed his eyes and concentrated so hard that I saw beads of sweat appear on his brow. A vein pulsated close to his temples. Then, slowly, he straightened, reached out, and clamped his hands around my head.

That was when it happened—an onslaught of tearing, hot

needles pierced my mind, and in a single moment, I saw all the evil perpetrated since the dawn of time concentrated in single moment. Every calamity known to man spliced into single disconnected images, a series of flashes so intense I thought my brain would shatter.

I saw children orphaned during wartime, villages turned to rubble by earthquakes, men blown apart by gunfire, families starving and weak from drought. I saw murders. I heard screams. I felt all the injustices of the world. Every illness known to humankind flooded through my body. Every feeling of terror, grief, and helplessness rushed at me. I felt every violent death acutely. I was in the car when Grace had the crash. I was a man in a boating accident, drowning in the ocean, crushed by the weight of the waves. I was Emily, swallowed alive by flames in her bed. And through it all I heard pitiless laughter, which I knew to be Jake's.

The pain of thousands, of millions, entered my earthly flesh like shards of glass. I was vaguely aware of my body convulsing on the floor, my hands at my temples. I was an angel, and I was being filled with all the agony and darkness in the world. I knew it would kill me. I opened my mouth to beg Jake to end my suffering, but no sound emerged. I had no voice left even to beg for my own death. Still, the siege continued, the images of horror flooding out of Jake and into me until it was a struggle to take the next breath.

Jake wrenched his hands from my head and I felt my body sink in a moment of pure relief. It was then that I saw the fire, towering and engulfing all in its path, and I realized suddenly that the air was thick with smoke. The chandelier trembled and then fell as parts of the ceiling gave way, plaster and tiny glass beads cascading onto the dining table. A few feet away the curtains went up in flames, scattering a shower of embers. I covered my head but felt some land on my hands. My body was still throbbing and shuddering from the impact of the horrific memories; my lungs were filled with smoke, my eyes stung, and my head was reeling. I could feel myself slipping from consciousness. I struggled against it, but I was losing the battle. All I could see was Jake's face framed by a circle of fire.

Then, the far wall was torn apart as if from an explosion. For a moment I could see the deserted street beyond, before a dazzling brightness filled the room. Jake staggered backward, shielding his eyes. Gabriel emerged from the rubble, wings outstretched and sword blazing like a pillar of white light in his hands. His hair streamed behind him like ribbons of gold. Xavier and Ivy came next, and both rushed to my side. Xavier, his face streaked with tears, went to gather me in his arms, but Ivy restrained him.

"Don't move her," she said. "Her injuries are too great. We will have to start the healing process here."

Xavier took my face in his hands.

"Beth?" I felt his lips close to my cheek. "Can you hear me?"

"She can't answer," Ivy's sweet voice said, and I felt her cool fingers on my forehead. I lay convulsing on the floor as her healing energy flowed through me.

"What's happening to her?" Xavier cried as my body shook

and lurched. I felt my eyes roll back in my head, and my mouth opened in a silent scream. "You're hurting her!"

"I'm draining her of the memories," said Ivy. "They'll kill her if I don't."

Xavier was so close I could hear his heart pounding. I fastened on to the sound, believing it was the only thing that could keep me alive.

"It's going to be okay" he repeated gently. "It's over now. We're here. No one can hurt you. Stay with us, Beth. Just listen to my voice."

I struggled to sit up and saw my brother emerge through a wall of flame. Light was rolling off him in waves, and it almost hurt to look at him, he was so bright and beautiful. He strode through the fire and stood face to face with Jake Thorn, and for the first time I saw a look of fear cross Jake's face. He quickly composed himself and curled his lip into its familiar smirk.

"Come out to play, I see," he said. "Just like old times."

"I've come to put an end to your games," replied Gabriel darkly.

He squared his shoulders and a howling wind blew up, rattling the glass in the windowpanes and casting the portraits from the walls. Cracks of lightning seared across the crimson sky, as if the heavens themselves were in revolt. In the midst of it all stood Gabriel, his powerful body rippling and glowing like a column of gold. The sword glowed white hot and hummed in his hand like a living entity. Jake Thorn staggered at the sight of it. When Gabriel spoke, his voice rolled out like thunder.

"I am going to give you one chance and one chance only," he said. "You may still repent for your sins. You may still turn away from Lucifer and renounce his works."

Jake spit at Gabriel's feet. "It's a bit late for that, wouldn't you say? Generous of you to offer, though."

"It is never too late," my brother replied. "There is always hope."

"The only thing I hope for is to see your power destroyed," hissed Jake.

Gabriel's face hardened and any trace of pity vanished from his voice. "Then be gone," he commanded. "You have no place here. Return to Hell into which you were first exiled."

He raised his sword, and the flames reared like living creatures to engulf Jake. They lurched over his head like vultures about to sweep on their prey—then suddenly froze. Something was holding them back—Jake's own power seemed to be protecting him from harm. And so they stood, angel and demon locked in a silent battle of wills, the blazing sword caught between them, marking the division between the two worlds. Gabriel's eyes flashed with the wrath of Heaven and Jake's burned with the bloodlust of Hell. Through the haze of pain gripping my mind and body, I felt a cold and terrible fear. What if Gabriel failed to defeat Jake? What would become of us then? I became aware of my fingers wrapped around Xavier's—his hands were cooling my seared skin. As he held me, I noticed that a strange light seemed to glow at the places where our fingers entwined. Soon it was enveloping us. It extended just far enough to cover both our bodies. I noticed that if I squeezed Xavier's hand a little tighter and drew him a little closer, the light seemed to respond and spread farther out around us like a protective shield. But what was it? What did it mean? Xavier hadn't even noticed—he was too focused on trying to still my quivering body—but Ivy had. She leaned down and whispered in my ear.

"It's your gift, Bethany. Use it."

"I don't understand," I croaked. "Can't you tell me how?"

"You have the most powerful gift of all—you know what to do with it."

My mind didn't understand Ivy's message, but somehow my body knew what to do. I summoned the last shreds of energy left inside me; pushed aside the pain that threatened to drag me under and lifted my head toward Xavier. As our lips met, every negative thought was driven from my head until all I could see was him. Jake Thorn leapt back as the light exploded in dazzling beams, streaming from our entwined bodies and flooding the room. Jake screamed and threw his arms around his body as if trying to protect himself, but the light engulfed him like tendrils of white fire. He thrashed and writhed for a moment, before giving himself up and allowing the ribbons to lick their way along his torso and wrap themselves like tentacles around him.

"What is that?" Xavier cried as he shielded his eyes against the blinding blaze. Ivy and Gabriel who were standing calmly as the light washed over them, turned to him.

"You of all people should know," said Ivy. "It's love."

Xavier and I held each other tightly as the room shook, and the light burned a gaping hole through the floor.

It was into this abyss that Jake Thorn disappeared. He met my gaze as he fell. He was tortured but still smiling.

32

Aftermath

IN the weeks that followed, my brother and sister did their best to tidy up the confusion that Jake had left behind. They visited the families affected by the crimes he'd perpetrated and spent a lot of time trying to rebuild trust in Venus Cove.

Ivy took care of Molly and the others who'd fallen under Jake's spell. The dark spirits possessing their bodies had been sucked back to Hell along with the one who had raised them. My sister wiped the memory of Jake's activities from their minds, careful not to touch any other unrelated recollections. It was like erasing words from a storybook—you had to select them very carefully or you might get rid of something important. When she was done, they remembered the newcomer Jake Thorn, but no one recalled having any association with him. A message was sent to the school administration that Jake had been withdrawn from Bryce Hamilton on the wishes of his father and he would be returning to boarding school in England. It was the subject of gossip for a day or two before the students moved on to more immediate concerns.

"Whatever happened to that hot British guy?" Molly asked

me two weeks after her rescue. She was sitting on the end of my bed, filing her nails. "What was his name . . . Jack, James?"

"Jake," I said. "And he left to go back to England."

"Shame," Molly commented. "I liked his tattoos. Do you think I should get one? I was thinking one that says, 'leirbag.'"

"You want a tattoo of Gabriel's name backward?"

"Damn, is it that obvious? I'll have to think of something else."

"Gabriel doesn't like tattoos," I said. "He says the human body is not a billboard."

"Thanks, Bethie," Molly said gratefully. "Lucky I have you around to stop me from making bad decisions."

I found it hard to talk to Molly the way I used to. Something had changed within me. I was the only member of my family who hadn't recovered from the conflict with Jake. In fact, weeks after the fire, I still hadn't left the house. At first it was because my wings, which were badly burned, needed time to heal properly. After that it was simply because I lacked the courage. I was happy to be a ghost. After all my previous thirst for human experiences, I now wanted nothing more than the haven of home. I couldn't think of Jake without tears springing to my eyes. I tried not to let the others see, but when I was alone, my self-control failed and I cried openly—not only for the pain he caused but also for what he might have been if he'd only allowed me to help him. I didn't hate him. Hatred was a powerful emotion, and I felt too drained for that. I found myself thinking of Jake as one of the saddest creatures of the universe. He had come to willfully blacken our lives, but he had achieved nothing really. Nevertheless, I tried not to think about what might have happened if Gabriel hadn't stormed my prison. But the thought kept creeping into my mind and driving me back to the safety of my bedroom.

I sometimes watched the world go by through my window. The spring drifted into summer, and I felt the days lengthening. I noticed the sunshine arrived earlier and lasted longer. I watched some sparrows build their nests in the eaves of the house. In the distance I could see waves lapping lazily at the shore.

Xavier's visit was the only part of the day I looked forward to. Of course Ivy and Gabriel were a great comfort, but they always seemed slightly detached, still strongly connected to our old home. In my mind, Xavier was an embodiment of earth—rock solid, stable, and secure. I had worried that his experience with Jake Thorn might change him in some way, but his reaction to everything that happened was to have no reaction at all. He threw himself back into the task of looking after me and seemed to have accepted the supernatural world without question.

"Maybe I don't want answers," he said when I quizzed him about it one afternoon. "I've seen enough to believe it."

"But aren't you curious?"

"It's like you said." He sat down beside me and tucked a lock of hair behind my ear. "There are some things beyond human comprehension. I know that there's a Heaven and a Hell, and I've seen what can come out of both. For now that's all I need to know. Questions would serve no purpose right now."

I smiled. "When did you become such a wise old soul?"

He shrugged. "Well, I have been hanging out with a crew that's been around since creation. You'd hope I'd get some perspective, having an angel as my other half."

"You'd call me your other half?" I asked dreamily, tracing my finger along the leather cord at his throat.

"Of course," he said. "When I'm not with you, I feel like I'm wearing a pair of glasses that turns the world gray."

"And when you are with me?" I asked softly.

"Everything's in technicolor."

Xavier's final exams loomed, and yet he still came every day, always attentive, always studying my face for signs of improvement. He always brought with him some small offering: an article from the newspaper, a book from the library, an entertaining story to tell, or cookies he'd baked himself. Self-pity wasn't an option when he was around. If there were ever moments in our past when I'd doubted his love, I didn't doubt it now.

"Should we try going for a walk today?" he asked. "Down to the beach? You can bring Phantom if you like."

I was tempted for a moment, then the thought of the outside world overwhelmed me, and I pulled my blanket up under my chin.

"That's okay." Xavier didn't press the matter. "Maybe tomorrow. How about we stay in and cook dinner together tonight?"

I nodded mutely, snuggled closer to him, and looked up into his perfect face with its amused half-smile and lock of nutmeg hair falling across his forehead. It was all so wonderfully familiar.

"Your patience is saintlike," I said. "I think we'll have to apply to have you canonized."

He laughed and took my hand, pleased to see in me a flicker of my former self. I followed him downstairs in my pajamas, listening to him talk about his recipe ideas. His voice was so soothing, like a cool balm easing my anxious mind. I knew he would stay with me and talk to me until I fell asleep. Every word he spoke tugged me gently back to life.

But even Xavier's presence couldn't protect me from the nightmares. Every night it was the same, and I would wake drenched in a cold sweat. I'd know immediately that I'd been dreaming. I'd know even as it was playing out in my head. I'd been having the same dream for weeks now, but it still managed to terrify me and I woke with my heart in my throat and my hands curled into fists.

In the dream I was in Heaven again, having left earth behind me for good. The deep sadness I felt was so real that when I woke it felt as if I had a bullet in my chest. Heaven's splendor left me cold, and I begged Our Father for more time on earth. I pleaded my case vehemently and wept bitter tears, but my pleas fell on deaf ears. In despair I saw the gates close behind me, and I knew there was no escape. My chance had come and I let it pass.

Although I was home I felt like a stranger. It wasn't the return itself that caused me so much pain; it was the thought of what I'd left behind. The thought of never touching Xavier, of never seeing his face again, tore at me like talons. In the dream I'd lost him. His features were blurred when

I tried to evoke them from memory. What stung the most was that I didn't even get the chance to say good-bye.

The vastness of eternity lay before me, and all I wanted was mortality. But there was nothing I could do. I couldn't alter the immutable laws of life and death, Heaven and earth. I couldn't even hope, for there was nothing to hope for. My brothers and sisters rallied around to offer words of comfort, but I was inconsolable. Without him, nothing in my world made sense.

Despite the distress the dream caused me, I didn't care how often I was visited by it, so long as I could wake and know that soon he would come. The waking was all that mattered. Waking to feel the warmth of the sun streaming through the French doors, my faithful Phantom sleeping at my feet, and the gulls circling above a cerulean sea. The future could wait. We had endured a great trial together, he and I, and survived it. We had emerged scarred but stronger. I couldn't believe the Heaven I knew could be so cruel as to part us. I didn't know what the future held, but I knew that we would face it together.

I'D been an insomniac for weeks now. I sat up in bed and watched the slivers of moonlight drifting across the floor. I'd given up on sleep—every time I closed my eyes, I thought I could feel a hand brushing across my face or sense a dark shape slipping through my doorway. One night I even looked out my window and thought I could see Jake Thorn's face in the clouds.

I climbed out of bed and opened the balcony doors. A

chilly wind swept through the room, and I saw that black clouds were hanging low in the sky. A storm was coming. It made me wish Xavier was there—I imagined him wrapping his arms around my shoulders and pressing his warm body against mine. I'd feel his lips against my ear, and he'd tell me that everything would be okay and that I'd always be safe. But Xavier wasn't there, and it was just me, standing alone and feeling the first droplets of rain splatter onto my face. I knew I'd see Xavier in the morning when he came to drive me to school—but morning seemed so far away, and the idea of sitting and waiting in the dark made me feel sick. I leaned against the iron railing of the balcony and sucked in the crisp air. I was wearing nothing but my flimsy cotton nightie, and it billowed around me as the wind tried to knock me off my feet. I could see the sea in the distance; it reminded me of a black sleeping animal. The rippling waves rose and fell almost as if it were breathing. As the howling wind rushed at me, a strange thought entered my head. It was almost as if the wind were trying to lift me up, to make me airborne. I checked the clock radio on my bedside table; it was after midnight, so the whole neighborhood would be asleep. It seemed for a moment as though the whole world belonged to me, and before I knew what was happening, I had lifted myself up and was balancing on the edge of the railing. I stretched my arms above my head. The air was refreshingly cool. I caught a raindrop on my tongue and laughed aloud at how relaxed I suddenly felt. A flash of lightning lit up the horizon where the sky and sea seemed to meet. An inexplicable sense of adventure took hold of me, and I jumped.

For a moment I wondered if I was falling before realizing that something was holding me up. My wings had sliced through the fine material of my nightgown and were gently beating the air. I let them lift me higher and swung my legs like an excited child. Within moments the rooftops were below me, and I was dipping and swooping through the night sky. By now peals of thunder were making the earth tremble, and cracks of lightning illuminated the darkness, but I wasn't afraid. I knew exactly where I wanted to go. I knew the route to Xavier's house by heart. It was surreal flying above the sleeping town—I passed over Bryce Hamilton and over the familiar streets around it. It felt as though I was soaring above a ghost town. But the knowledge at the back of my mind that I could be seen at any time was exhilarating. I didn't even bother trying to hide behind the rain-laden clouds.

Soon I was standing on the soft lawn of Xavier's house. I crept around to the back of the house where Xavier's bedroom was. His window was open to let in the night breeze, and his bedside lamp was still on. Xavier was lying with his chemistry book open across his chest. Somehow sleep made him look much younger. He was still wearing his faded sweatpants and a loose white T-shirt. One arm rested behind his head, and the other had fallen by his side. His lips were slightly parted, and I watched the gentle rise and fall of his chest. His face was peaceful, as though he didn't have a single care in the world.

I retracted my wings and silently climbed inside. I tiptoed closer to the bed and reached out to lift the book from his chest. Xavier stirred but didn't wake up. I stood at the end of his bed, watching as he slept, and suddenly felt closer to Our Creator than I ever had in the Kingdom. There in front of me was his greatest creation of all. Angels may have been created as watch guards, but I felt like I could sense in Xavier a great power—a power to change the world. He could do whatever he wanted, be whoever he wanted. Suddenly I realized what I wanted most in the all the world—it was for him to be happy—with or without me. So I got down on my knees, bowed my head, and prayed to God—asking Him to bless Xavier and keep him safe from harm. I prayed for his life to be long and prosperous. I prayed for all his dreams to come true. I prayed that I would always be able to connect with him in some small way—even if I was no longer on earth.

Before leaving, I took a final look around his room. I took in the L.A. Lakers flag pinned to the wall, read the inscriptions on the trophies that lined the shelves. I ran my fingers over the objects scattered on his desk. A carved wooden box drew my attention. It looked out of place amid the boyish belongings. I pulled it forward and slowly opened the lid. Inside, the box was lined with red satin. In the center lay a single white feather. I recognized it immediately as the one Xavier had found in his car after our first date. I knew he would keep it forever.

Epilogue

THREE months later things had settled down and were more or less back to normal. Ivy, Gabriel, and I had worked to heal the town and the students at Bryce Hamilton so that the terrible afflictions they had experienced or witnessed were reduced to nothing more than hazy, fragmented images or words that were unable to be linked together in any kind of logical sequence. Xavier was the only one granted full access to the memories. He didn't bring them up, but I knew he hadn't forgotten—would never forget. But Xavier was strong; he had dealt with enormous pain and grief in his young life-time, and we knew he wouldn't buckle under the extra burden.

As the weeks passed, we managed to fall back into our familiar routine, and I'd even made progress with getting back into Bernie's good graces.

"On a scale of one to ten, how close am I to being totally forgiven?" I asked Xavier as we walked to school in the morning sunshine.

"Ten," Xavier said. "I know my mom's tough, but how long do you expect her to hold a grudge? It's all in the past now."

"I hope so."

Xavier reached across and took my hand. "There's nothing to be afraid of anymore."

"Except for the occasional demon," I teased. "But don't let that put a damper on things."

"No way," Xavier said. "They were crashing *our* party."

"Do you ever worry that they might show up again and everything will fall apart?"

"No, because I think between the two of us, we'll always manage to put things back together."

"You always know just what to say." I smiled. "Do you rehearse those lines at home?"

"It's all part of my charm," Xavier winked.

"Bethie!" Molly ran to catch up with us as we reached the gates of the school. "What do you think of my new look?" She twirled around, and I saw that she had undergone a complete transformation. She had dropped the length of her skirt to below the knee, buttoned her blouse up to her chin, and fastened her tie neatly. Her hair was pulled back in a severe braid, and she had discarded all of her jewelry. She was even wearing the regulation school socks.

"You look like you're ready for the convent," Xavier said.

"Good!" Molly seemed pleased. "I'm trying to look mature and responsible."

"Oh, Molly," I sighed. "This wouldn't have anything to do with Gabriel, would it?"

"Well, duh," Molly said. "Why else would I walk around looking like such a loser?"

"Uh-huh." Xavier nodded. "High marks for maturity right there."

"Don't you think it's better to just be yourself?" I asked.

"Her true self might scare him," Xavier remarked.

"Oh, shut up." I slapped his arm lightly. "All I'm saying, Molly, is that Gabriel has to like you for who you are. . . ."

"I guess," Molly hedged. "But I'm happy to change; I can be whoever he wants me to be."

"He wants you to be you."

"I don't," Xavier began. "I want you to be . . ." He broke off with a laugh as I elbowed him.

"Could you at least try and be helpful."

"Okay, okay," Xavier said. "Look, girls that are fake or try too hard are a major turnoff. You need to chill and quit chasing him around."

"But don't I need to show him that I'm interested?" Molly asked.

"I think he knows." Xavier rolled his eyes. "Now you have to wait for him to come to you. In fact, why don't you try dating another guy . . . ?"

"Why would I do that?"

"See if Gabriel gets jealous. The way he reacts will tell you everything you need to know."

"Thanks, you're the best!" Molly beamed at him. She yanked her hair loose, tore open her buttons, and ran off, probably in search of some poor boy to use as her prop in the master plan to win Gabriel's heart.

"We really shouldn't encourage her," I said.

"You never know," Xavier replied. "She might be Gabriel's type after all."

"Gabriel doesn't have a type." I laughed. "He's already in a committed relationship."

"Humans can be strangely tempting."

"Tell me about it," I said, standing on my tiptoes to affectionately nibble his earlobe.

"I'm afraid that's inappropriate behavior for the schoolyard," Xavier teased. "I know my charm is hard to resist, but please try and control yourself."

WE parted in the halls of Bryce Hamilton. As I watched him walk away, I felt a strange sense of security that I hadn't experienced in a long time, and for moment I truly believed that the worst was over and behind us.

But I was wrong. I should have known it wasn't over, couldn't be over quite so easily. No sooner was Xavier out of sight than a little cylinder of paper fell from the top of my locker. As I unrolled it, I knew I'd see black calligraphy crawling across it like a spider. Dread settled around me like a fog as the words burned into my brain:

The Lake of Fire awaits my lady

ᴀ CKNOWLEDGMENTS

The Halo series is a project in which I have invested much emotion and energy. But it couldn't have been done without the contribution of the following people:

My agent, Jill Grinberg, for being so enthusiastic and totally believing in the story.

My mother, for her support as well as her ruthless honesty.

Jean Feiwel, Liz Szabla, and the team at Feiwel and Friends, for devoting so much time and energy to this project.

Lisa Berryman, for having mentored me since age thirteen.

My inspirational principal, Dr. David Warner, for his understanding of young people and their dreams.

Special thanks must go to Matthew DeFina (Moo-Moo), for his invaluable insight into the male psyche, for his considered answers to my endless questions, and for making me smile when things got too hard.

Thank you for reading

this **FEIWEL AND FRIENDS** book.

the friends who made

HALO

possible are:

JEAN FEIWEL, *publisher*

LIZ SZABLA, *editor-in-chief*

RICH DEAS, *creative director*

ELIZABETH FITHIAN, *marketing director*

HOLLY WEST, *assistant to the publisher*

DAVE BARRETT, *managing editor*

NICOLE LIEBOWITZ MOULAISON, *production manager*

ALLISON REMCHECK, *editorial assistant*

KSENIA WINNICKI, *marketing assistant*

FIND OUT MORE ABOUT OUR AUTHORS AND ARTISTS
AND OUR FUTURE PUBLISHING AT

WWW.FEIWELANDFRIENDS.COM.

OUR BOOKS ARE FRIENDS FOR LIFE